Must Love Wieners

Must Love Wieners

Casey Griffin

St. Martin's Paperbacks

This is a work of fiction. All of the characters, organizations, and events portrayed in this novel are either products of the author's imagination or are used fictitiously.

MUST LOVE WIENERS

For information address St. Martin's Press, 175 Fifth Avenue, New York, NY 10010.

ISBN: 978-1-250-08467-5

Our books may be purchased in bulk for promotional, educational, or business use. Please contact your local bookseller or the Macmillan Corporate and Premium Sales Department at 1-800-221-7945, ext. 5442, or by e-mail at MacmillanSpecialMarkets@macmillan.com.

Printed in the United States of America

St. Martin's Paperbacks edition / August 2016

St. Martin's Paperbacks are published by St. Martin's Press, 175 Fifth Avenue, New York, NY 10010.

10 9 8 7 6 5 4 3 2 1

Acknowledgments

This wiener tale all started because my agent, Pooja Menon, worked like a dog to find my writing a home and because my hilarious editor, Rose Hilliard, saw something in me and decided to take a chance. Rose, thanks for throwing this dog a bone. This book wouldn't be possible without both of them, their guidance, support, and sometimes their emergency therapy sessions. Of course, I can't forget all the staff at St. Martin's Press who worked so hard to help get my wiener up . . . err, and running.

A special thanks to Rodney Swift and Gail Onnis for sharing their extensive knowledge and expertise. Sorry for dogging you with so many questions. Then there are my fabulous critique partners, Claire Merle and Debbie Callaghan, and my family and friends who have encouraged me for so many years.

And last, but definitely not least, is a shout-out to you the reader—yes, you—for checking out my wiener. With so much support for this book, I feel like one lucky dog.

Dog Day

A yellow cab skidded to a stop in front of an old Victorian house facing the park, and the driver's side door flew open to reveal a pair of long, bare legs ending in red stiletto cowboy boots. Piper stepped out, tugging her baggy top down over her jean skirt, and circled around to the passenger side. As she reached in for the pizza boxes, her hand fell on the empty breadstick bag.

She glared at her passenger, Colin, and by the look on his face it was obvious he knew what came next; he was in crap. Piper continued to scowl at him, at that pitiful, remorseful expression, and the anger fizzled out of her.

Each time she gazed into those big brown eyes, she felt nothing but love for him, as strong as the day they'd first met. And when he leaned forward to kiss her cheek, she knew he loved her too, even if he couldn't say it.

"Bad dog." She wiped the Parmesan slobber off her face. "Those breadsticks were for the customer."

Confused by the reprimand paired with a smile, the black dachshund tilted his head, ears flopping.

Piper tried a moment longer to keep up the pretense, but she relented with a sigh. “Oh, I can’t stay mad at you.” She gave him a scratch behind the ears.

He responded by licking her hand, as if to say, *Yeah, I know I’m pretty amazing.*

“Now go hide.” She pointed to the floor. “My boss would kill me if he knew you were in here.”

Colin jumped down from the seat and parked his butt on the floor mat, his tail slapping the plastic as it wagged.

“Good boy.”

Grabbing the two medium pizzas, sans breadsticks, she headed for the door, overly aware of how cool and soggy the boxes felt in her hands. She shouldn’t have picked up that extra customer in the cab. They only wanted to go eight miles, but it took her completely out of the way to pick up Colin from home and then deliver the pizzas. Plus they didn’t even tip.

She climbed the cement stairs to the bright red door. It was fixed up in the classic San Francisco Painted Ladies style. It wasn’t as nice as some she’d seen while delivering pizzas around the city—and she’d seen a lot. The paint was peeling from the siding and the windowpanes had cracked, but hell, it was better than anything she could dream of affording.

She considered what it would take to save the down payment to buy a house like that before she turned sixty. A fourth job, that’s for sure. And on top of graduating from USF, studying for her big exam, and volunteering at the Dachshund Rescue Center? Yup, no problem! Who needed a life? Or sleep for that matter? She could do it. She’d be fine. Fine, fine, fine. But for now, the apartment she shared with Colin and her unwelcome six-legged roommates would have to do.

Pushing the doorbell set in the orange trim, she prayed

for college kids. College kids never complained; they'd eat anything.

But the middle-aged man who opened the door looked like he'd enjoyed a few pizzas in his lifetime.

She slapped on a giant grin. "Hello," she said tooth-achingly sweet.

"You're late."

"I know. I'm so sorry. Traffic was crazy."

He peeked over her shoulder at the taxi parked near the bottom of his steps, then glanced both ways down the street. Seeing no other cars, he squinted an eye at her. "You a pizza delivery girl, or a cabbie?"

"Right now, I'm a delivery girl." As proof, she tapped the Tony's Pizza logo embroidered on her shirt.

His eyes drifted down to her bare legs. With the oversized shirt, it almost looked like she was wearing nothing underneath. Well, she practically wasn't, but he didn't need to know that.

Piper's face warmed despite the lack of clothing. "Sure hot out today," she said by way of an explanation. He didn't reply, so she held out a palm. "That will be twenty-six eighty, please."

He counted the money out to the penny and exchanged it for the pizza. "Where are the breadsticks? There are supposed to be breadsticks."

"Yeah, they must have forgotten them at the restaurant." She didn't think he'd appreciate the real story. "Don't worry. I took the cost off your bill already."

She started to back away from the door and down the front steps, conscious that she was running late for her next gig. There would be some speeding involved to make it in time. But she could handle it. It was fine.

"Hey, this pizza's cold!" he yelled after her.

Biting her lip, she waved. "Don't worry about the tip."

"Tip? Tip–"

She leapt behind the wheel of the cab and shut the door, which cut the rest of his feedback off. Throwing her seat belt on, she turned to Colin. "Hold on."

She dropped her foot and gunned it all the way to the end of the street. Letting her cabbie skills take over, she raced across San Francisco, taking a shortcut through Chinatown to Montgomery Street.

Once Piper reached the Financial District, she glanced at her GPS for the address. A block later, the building came into view and she swerved into the taxi lane to park. Pulling out her phone, she glanced at the text message from the telegram agency. Colin hopped onto the center console, planting his front paws on her thigh while she read the details of the job.

"Looks like I'm headed to the top floor." Even when she leaned forward to glance up through the windshield, she still couldn't see the top of the building. She whistled. "Must be one important guy."

Colin licked her ear to remind her that he was the only important guy around.

Snapping her fingers, she pointed to the floor. He resumed his hiding spot but whined to let her know he wasn't happy about it.

"Good boy. I'll only be five minutes, and then we'll head over to the center to play with your friend, okay?"

He woofed, *Hurry up.*

Leaving the engine in idle, she detached the spare key and cranked the AC. She gripped Tony's oversized shirt and peeled it off to reveal a tight plaid top, red tassels dangling oh, so tastefully from the plunging neckline. Gathering what little dignity she could, she took a deep breath and climbed out of the taxi.

Piper adjusted the scraps of cloth her boss called a costume and popped the trunk. Bright balloons unfolded from the cramped space, floating up in front of her. She grabbed the strings before they could sail away. Each balloon had a different saying. "Be mine." "Love." Some had a picture of a heart.

Picking up a red cowboy hat, she slipped it over the chestnut waves of hair curling down her back and grabbed the box of Swiss chocolates. For the final touch, in case it wasn't demeaning enough, she pulled out a toy horse head glued to the end of a wooden pole. With one more glance up at the sky-rise, she headed for the doors.

"Hey!" someone shouted behind her. "You can't park here."

Recognizing the voice, she rolled her eyes before turning around.

"Hollo, Dom."

The short, balding taxi driver wore a black leather jacket despite the humidity. He always gave her a hard time—probably because she'd scooped one too many customers from him over the years. But today she didn't have the patience.

"What do you want?"

"Piper. I should have guessed." He leered at her outfit, eyes pausing on the red tassels. "Finally gave in to your urges and took up prostitution, I see. How much you charging?" he asked, playing with the gold chain around his neck.

"More than you could ever afford." She tipped her cowboy hat in farewell and turned to leave.

"Hey, I'm serious; this is a taxi lane. Not your personal parking spot."

"It'll only be a minute. I'm grabbing the customer from inside. The meter's running; I swear."

"Yeah, I bet."

Ignoring him, she spun on her stiletto heel and strolled through the circulating doors. Her boots clicked on the marble floors as she walked up to the reception desk. The female security guard's eyes slid over Piper's cowgirl costume, pausing on her midriff—which wasn't so mid as it was high, from hip all the way up to where her plaid shirt knotted under her boobs.

Piper pretended not to notice. "Hi. I'm here with Sam's Old World Singing Telegrams."

"You don't say?" The woman raised an eyebrow. "Flaunt it if you've got it, I suppose. I used to have a figure like that. Now I got four kids." She shook her head wistfully. "And who's the lucky person?"

"Name is Aiden Caldwell. Some investment firm on the top floor."

Slapping a book on the counter in front of Piper, she handed her a pen. "Sign here. And here. And I'll need a government-issued ID." She peered over the desk at the cutoff skirt that barely covered Piper's butt. "If you have any pockets to put it in, that is."

Reaching into her bra, Piper pulled out her driver's license. "Mother Nature's pocket."

The guard exchanged it for a temporary pass. "You can pick it up again on the way out."

"Thanks."

Scanning though the security gates, Piper slipped into an elevator. The suits shuffled to let her in, ducking to avoid the helium balloons. She tried to ignore the fact that she looked like a stripper at a funeral, but when the doors shut that was impossible; they were mirrored. It was hard to deny the humiliation when it was staring her in the face.

She tipped her hat low to block the sight and imagined that she was a real professional, dressed in a blazer and pencil skirt. Dressed in something meant for luncheons and quarterly meetings, not for swinging around a pole, stuffing dollar bills into her bra. But she reminded herself why she was doing this. All the shitty jobs would be worth it in the end. Everything would be fine. And she would have accomplished it all on her own.

Leaning over, she pressed the button for the fortieth floor, choking on the cloud of Old Spice cologne from the man next to her. His eyes followed the bounce of her cleavage as she stood back up. She wanted to tell him to take a picture, but instead she gave him a wink with her honey brown eye.

"Howdy."

He grunted in disapproval. Frowning, he turned away, studiously ignoring the reflection in the doors. She bit her lip to hide a smirk.

Floor by floor, the elevator thinned out. Old Spice continued the ride with her to the top, fixing his sad combover in the reflection. When the doors opened for the last time, he waved the balloons away and stepped out. Piper followed him into a modern foyer. She often delivered telegrams to offices, but never one this nice.

Wrangling her balloons, she crossed the high-gloss tile to the glass desk in the middle of the reception room. A girl a few years younger than Piper's twenty-six sat behind it, poised like a model for spray tan products.

"Hi there," Piper said.

The receptionist's eyes scraped over Piper's costume. She held up a finger while speaking into her Bluetooth. "I'm sorry. He's not available at the moment. He's in a meeting. Uh-huh."

Piper's gaze flitted around the room, taking in the expensive paintings and the bouquet of hydrangeas bulging from a giant crystal vase that probably weighed a ton—and cost as much.

"Okay. I'll tell him. Thank you." She ended the call and smiled; well, maybe it was supposed to be a smile, but it looked more like a sneer. "Hello," she said to Piper, although she was staring at the horse. "Can I help you with something?"

"I'm here with Sam's Old World Singing Telegrams."

"A singing telegram? For who?"

"It's for an Aiden. Aiden Caldwell?"

"Aiden?" She practically choked. As though with new eyes, she took in the sight of Piper again and smiled. But Piper didn't get the impression she wanted to be friends. "This should be interesting."

"Interesting? Why?"

"Go on through." She flicked her orange hand toward the glass doors to the side of the desk, bracelets jangling. "Third room on your left. Just head right in."

"Sure. Thanks."

The girl pushed a button behind the desk and the doors unlocked, allowing Piper access to the offices. She followed the directions, balloons trailing behind her, until she stood in front of a sign that said: *Boardroom One*. She reached out and gripped the door handle, but then she hesitated.

"Come on, Pipe," she whispered to herself. A few more weeks of tuition fees to pay off and she could quit the damn job.

The bigger the act, the better the tips always were, so she reached into her bra again and pulled out her phone. Cuing up the cheesy Western-themed music, she hit *play* and burst through the door. A single guitar, a warbling harmonica, and the rhythmic clip-pity-clop of horse hooves blasted through her phone speakers.

Shoving the horse's wooden pole between her legs, she yelled, "Yee-haw!" and skipped into the room, tassels swaying, heels clicking.

The lights were dimmed, the curtains closed. Unable to see where she was going, her foot caught on something. It sent her stumbling forward. She reached out to catch her fall. The horse clattered to the floor. Her knees took the landing hard, but her hand fell on something soft. When the lights flicked on, she saw it lay nestled in a man's lap.

Gasping, Piper fell back and stared up at the man. He held a dripping coffee cup, a brown stain spreading across his expensive white shirt and tie. And then she saw his face.

Of course he was gorgeous. He had to be gorgeous. That was so damned typical.

"I–I'm so sorry," she said.

"What the hell is this?" She turned to the angry voice. Old Spice.

Oh God. She hoped he wasn't the one she was supposed to sing to—if they didn't call Security to kick her out first. Delivering a telegram to a crotchety old guy like him? There was nothing worse.

She swallowed hard and struggled to untangle her boot from a cord that snaked across the boardroom floor. "I'm looking for Aiden Caldwell?"

When she glanced up, the hottie with the coffee-stained shirt was holding out his hand to help her up. A shadow of a smirk danced across his perfect lips. "I'm Aiden."

Correction: that was worse.

He wasn't the wrinkly, old businessman Piper had imagined. But he wasn't simply cookie-cutter young and attractive, either. He was the kind of hot you would join a gym class for just to work out in the row behind him. Five days a week! And Piper hated the gym. But by the fit of his suit she could tell he was a devoted member of one.

She hesitated. "You're Aiden Caldwell?"

He ran a hand through his ruffled bedhead hair that looked due to genetics rather than styling. His ears blazed a flaming pink, and he held a finger in front of his lips to try to hide an embarrassed grin. Suddenly, she wished it had been Old Spice she was sent there for.

"Yes," he said. "That would be me, unfortunately."

The music still clip-pity-clopped, and all the constipated-looking business types were staring at her from around a massive table. The presenter stood at the head of the room in front of pie charts and graphs, laser pointer frozen in his hand.

"I, uh, I've got a telegram for you." Piper tried to act peppy, like Sam paid her to be, but it was hard to rally after her most epic failure. The room filled with titters and chuckles. She kept her eyes on Aiden, waiting for some cue.

Old Spice huffed through his nose and gave Aiden an arched eyebrow. This seemed to sober Aiden up. Taking a seat, he gestured.

"Well. We might as well get this over with."

"Right," she said.

After a deep breath, Piper cleared her throat. With a country-western twang, she began to sing, looking at everyone in the room except for the intended subject.

"This ditty's for Aiden;
It comes from a fair maiden,
Who sent me to tell this to you:
Yer funny and sweet,
You swept me off my feet,
This I am tellin' you true.
Yer eyes they do glimmer,
Makes my heart start to simmer,
Every time that I see yer face.
My smile grows big as the ocean,
Sets my heart into motion.
It takes me to a higher place.
So you've got me down kneelin',
Beggin' that you're feelin'
What I know is true in my soul.
So if we're meant to be together,

Like cowgirls and leather,
You'll give a call to Nicole."

By the time Piper finished, the blood had drained from Aiden's face and he was no longer trying to hide a smile—although everyone around him certainly was. He didn't appear impressed with receiving the love note, any more than Piper liked giving it.

His clean-shaven jaw clenched. She had a fleeting moment of pity for poor Nicole, who would probably never hear from him again. But then, it was Nicole's fault Piper was there embarrassing herself. So really, she didn't feel too bad.

"That was very entertaining. Thank you . . . ," Aiden trailed off, glancing at her left boob where a gold star badge held a false name, "Amber."

Old Spice snorted next to him. " 'Entertaining' is not the word I would use. This"—he waved a derisive hand at Piper—"is not appropriate for the workplace."

Piper's own lip curled in response to Old Spice's sneer.

"No. You're right," Aiden said. "I'll have a talk with the admin assistant. This is an animal-free environment, after all. It's not appropriate to have horses in the building."

The tension in the room evaporated, and everyone relaxed in their ergonomic seats, laughing.

Piper was used to the laughing. People got a kick out of this sort of thing. But this time, it felt different. This time, it felt like it was at her expense. Like she had any choice. This was her job, after all. Not everyone could work for a Fortune 500 company.

She wondered if they would still laugh at her if they knew why she was doing this, that it wasn't her lifelong dream to be a slutty singing-telegram girl. She wanted to be a veterinarian. And she was working damned hard for it too.

But it didn't matter what they thought. She knew why she was doing this, and nothing else mattered. Who were these people to her, anyway? Who was this Aiden Caldwell? You know, besides an Armani ad come to life.

Nobody. That was who.

Shoving the balloons and box of chocolates at him, she swiped her phone off the table, wheeled her horse around, and galloped out of the room. She could hear Aiden call her fake name, but she kept her eyes forward and her head up until she was in the elevator.

When she saw him round the corner, she punched the button for the ground floor and tapped the *close doors* button repeatedly until his face disappeared. It wasn't until the elevator was descending and she stared at her pathetic reflection that she noticed the company logo stenciled on the mirrored doors for the first time.

It said: *Caldwell and Son Investments.*

Piper buried her face against the stuffed horse head and groaned. Aiden must have been the *and Son*. And she practically just gave him an over-the-pants hand job.

So much for not being a prostitute.

And he didn't even tip.

The Fur Flies

Piper half-ran, half-limped all the way back to her taxi where Colin greeted her. Letting him comfort her with kisses, she leaned back in the seat to find her breath. And her dignity.

She rubbed her throbbing knee and stared out of the windshield where sporadic raindrops began to spatter. That was one of the worst singing-telegram experiences yet. Maybe not as bad as the time some frat boy mistook her for a stripper, but this time left her feeling more humiliated than usual. And that was really saying something.

The cab's back door opened and a customer slid in, rocking the vehicle.

Piper cradled Colin close to hide him from sight. "I'm not in service right now," she said over her shoulder. "Sorry."

"You're a taxi driver too?"

She glanced in the rearview mirror to find a pair of dark, minty green eyes smiling in the reflection.

"You're a woman of many talents."

She spun around. "Mr. Caldwell."

"Aiden's just fine."

He looked strange in her cab. Like someone that successful and poised didn't fit in her awkward world. People like him didn't stare at her as if, well, as if they were seeing her, Piper, and not giving directions to a cabbie, or paying a pizza delivery girl, or eyeing up a telegram singer.

He appeared professional and collected in his designer suit and stylish narrow tie—even with the coffee stain—but in a way that she thought they might look even better coming off. Like when you're tempted to step on the grass that says: *Keep off* or to scream in a library. Aiden's composure certainly reminded her of an orderly, self-possessed librarian. A hot one that you wanted to dishevel behind the stacks.

Her eyes unconsciously drifted down to his lap where she'd had her hand not fifteen minutes earlier. The memory jarred her like a bucket of cold ice over her crotch.

"I'm sorry," she said. "You'll have to find another taxi."

"I wanted to apologize, Amber. I didn't exactly make that easy on you."

"The name's Piper. And don't worry about it. I'm used to it."

"No, really. That took a lot of courage. Especially after how things started."

Piper winced. She laid her forehead against the steering wheel, wishing an out-of-control streetcar would derail and plow into her in the next three seconds.

Three . . . two . . . one . . .

But he continued on. "I thought the whole thing was hilarious. But I have to maintain a certain professional attitude in the workplace. I don't like mixing business with pleasure. You understand."

"Then you should probably tell that to Nicole."

"Who?"

Piper snorted. Just your typical privileged playboy.

Probably had so many conquests every week that he couldn't remember their names by Monday morning. She knew his type. And he wasn't hers.

Sure, he was rich, but in Piper's opinion that was more of a con than a pro. Money created a different sort of man, and she wanted no part of it; otherwise she'd be living in Washington with her family rather than living paycheck to paycheck on her own in San Francisco.

She heard Aiden sniff in the backseat. "Does it smell like pizza in here to you?"

"Sorry about your shirt, by the way," she said to change the subject.

As if he'd forgotten about it, he ran a hand over the dried stain. "No problem. I have two dozen of them that look exactly the same at home. I won't miss it." A teasing smile tugged at the corner of his mouth. "But I thought you'd be more sorry about falling into my lap."

"Oh, I wasn't sorry about that." Which was a complete lie. "But I forgot to tell you that I charge extra for lap dances."

He was being friendly enough, even flirting a little. Okay, so was she. Shamelessly. But Colin was struggling in her arms to greet the newcomer, she wanted to put some clothes on, and as cute as Aiden was, she planned on blocking the whole experience from her memory. It's not like he'd be interested in her, anyway. Or if he was, she would just be another girl whose name he couldn't remember.

"Look. I have to go," she said. "I'm on the clock."

"Well, if that's the case, I'll take a ride." Laying his briefcase down next to him, he loosened his tie and relaxed into the leather seat. She could see a cocky grin spread across his lips in the rearview mirror, daring her to refuse a customer.

The clock on the dash informed her she was already late. Her volunteer shift at the Dachshund Rescue Center started soon and she still had to get the taxi back to the depot.

"I'm sorry. I don't have time."

"Please? You can't say no to this face." He batted his eyelashes. "I've been told that my eyes glimmer."

She couldn't help but laugh. "I thought you were in the middle of a big meeting."

"It got kind of boring once you left."

"I do know how to liven things up, don't I?" she replied coolly, but felt her cheeks flush at the memory. Glancing in the rearview, she saw his eyes crinkle, as though he was remembering it too, but not in the same negative way. Her skin burned hotter.

Annoyed at being left out of the conversation, Colin barked.

"Is that a dog?"

Piper sighed and let the creature wiggle free from her arms. Colin leapt onto the center console to investigate this new man in his cab. He was protective of Piper. Her little hero. In fact, she often imagined he looked like Batman. His short black fur and touch of light brown around his snout formed the same shape as the Caped Crusader's mask.

Aiden reached out to let the dog smell him. "Hello, boy. What's your name?"

"Colin," Piper said.

"Unusual name for a dog."

"Colin is an unusual dog."

As though in agreement, Colin barked.

Aiden laughed and scratched him behind the ears. "Actually, I just became a proud owner of a dachshund."

"Well, you made a good choice. It's a great breed."

She watched him make friends with her dog, which gave Aiden major bonus points—not that he needed them with that smile, and those eyes, and damn, he really did look good in that suit. "Maybe I'm headed your way," she conceded. "Where did you want to go?"

"Inner Mission area," he said. "Please."

She checked the clock again, not sure how she always managed to take on too much. It would be fine, she told herself. Just fine. Besides, that was near the rescue center. She could drop Colin off before heading for the taxi depot. That way, she wouldn't need to smuggle him out of the taxi in her backpack before someone saw. Plus having a pleasant view in her mirror for the trip didn't hurt.

"I think I can manage that. Colin, down, boy." She pointed to the passenger side mat.

With a whine of protest, the doxie hopped down.

Throwing the car into drive, Piper shoulder checked and stepped on the gas. Leather and gold flashed in front of the hood as someone leapt ahead of the taxi. She slammed on the brakes. Everyone lurched forward in the cab.

"Oh, crap," she mumbled.

"What is it?" Aiden asked.

"Trouble." She glared out the windshield where Dominic crooked a finger at her. "I'll just be a second."

Nudging the car forward, she tucked it back next to the curb and out of traffic. Dominic crossed his arms to wait while she crawled out. His pompous expression spiked her annoyance level.

Piper threw the door open, shivering as the rain hit her bare skin. "Do you have a death wish, Dom? Can't you see I'm working here?"

He pointed to her outfit. "You certainly look like a working girl to me."

"Ha-ha. You're hilarious."

The rear cab door opened and Aiden stepped out onto the sidewalk. He glanced between Dominic and Piper. "Is everything okay?"

"None of your business, pal." Dominic jabbed a finger at Aiden before turning back to Piper. "You shoulda moved your cab, sweetheart."

"Keep your panties on, Dom. I'm moving it. See? I have my customer now. We're leaving."

"Yeah, see, I don't think you were here for a customer. You know, I started to think–"

"And I'm sure it hurt." Her left boob vibrated, startling her. Reaching into her bra, she pulled out her phone. The rain was picking up, so she stepped onto the sidewalk and under the building's awning before checking it.

It was a text from her boss at Tony's Pizza.

Got another complaint from a customer. He said you were late, the pizza was cold, and the breadsticks were missing. I warned you, Piper. You're fired.

"Dammit."

Bringing up a foot, she banged her heel on the pavement in frustration. *Snap.* Her heel broke. She stumbled back, arms pinwheeling as she tried to regain balance.

Aiden lunged forward, catching her before she could fall. His hands rubbed hot on her bare stomach, and she took a moment longer than she needed to step away.

"Thanks."

He gave her an apologetic look. "Bad day?"

"You have no idea."

But that expression on his face and the way his hands lingered on her made it a teensy bit better. Like chocolate-covered Brussels sprouts.

Bending down, she picked up the broken heel and pouted at it. The cowgirl would have to take some time off until she could afford new boots. Sam was a tightwad and didn't like to spend money on decent costumes. The cheap crap he did provide he made his employees rent at a premium, so Piper liked to buy her own.

"Like I was saying." Dominic wedged himself between Piper and Aiden. "See, I think you've been moonlighting."

"So?" Piper threw her hands up. "What are you going to do about it?"

"That's not illegal," Aiden said. "The California legislation is clear. She's perfectly within her rights to work more than one job. What infringes on her rights, however, is harassment in the workplace." He took a step toward Dominic, but that single step held a lot of power. "So I suggest you leave this young woman alone and let her get back to her job."

Dominic balked. Piper wished she'd worn her cheerleading costume that day. She wanted to shake her pom-poms and cheer, "Go-o-o, Aiden!"

"Her job?" Dominic turned back to Piper. "And which one is that? Because the boss doesn't have a problem with you working more than one job. He has a problem with you working all of them at the exact same time."

"The boss? You told Dave?"

Aiden raised his hands and backed off. "Sorry," he said to her. "I can't help you there."

She cringed. "Bad timing. I couldn't get anyone to cover the shifts." Well, she supposed she might have if she'd asked for help for once. But she didn't need help. She would have been fine if it hadn't been for Dominic. Just fine, fine, fine.

Dominic shrugged. "I may have mentioned to Dave that I saw you here." He placed a hand over his heart, his expression the epitome of angelic innocence. "I was concerned, is all. After seeing you dressed like this, I was worried this was our new uniform." Laughing, he fiddled with the tassels dangling beneath her boobs.

She slapped his hand away. "What did Dave say?"

"Is that a dog?" Dominic asked.

"What?" Piper followed his stare to the open back door of her cab.

Colin dropped down from the seat and scampered across the sidewalk to join them under the awning. He sat down next to Piper's cowboy boots and stared up at her. Barrel chest protruding, he wagged his tail like he was such a good boy for behaving. His expression said, *Do I get a treat now?*

Dominic gaped at her like she'd lost her marbles. "You can't keep your pet in the taxis."

"He's not a pet. He's a copilot," she said. When Dom didn't look convinced, she tried again. "Seeing Eye dog?"

Colin gave an angry bark at Dominic, deep and intimidating for such a small thing. Duh-na-nuh-nuh-nuh-nuh-nuh-nuh, Batman!

"Sic 'em, Colin," she said, half-hoping he'd understand.

Dominic took a step back. Instead of Colin attacking, his tongue lolled out of his mouth, dripping slobber on his paw. He didn't make the best guard dog, since he didn't know any commands beyond your basic roll over and sit. And it wasn't like he could roll someone over to death. His head swiveled between the two of them, flinging dribble onto Dominic's shoe. That will show him, she thought.

Aiden's focus bounced between Piper and Dominic but mostly remained on the latter, mouth in a hard line, cool eyes watching, waiting, maybe for him to step out of line. But Piper was grateful he kept to the sidelines. She didn't need any guy stepping in on her behalf, far less one she barely knew. She was a big girl and she could handle a lowlife like Dominic on her own.

"It doesn't matter, anyway," Dominic said. "It can't be any worse for you. Dave said he wants the cab back to the depot. Now. And, oh yeah, he said something else." Dominic tapped his chin as though thinking, enjoying every minute of it. "He said something about wanting to see you in his office. If I were you, I'd wear that outfit. You might have a better chance of keeping your job."

Piper glared at the little weasel. "You think you're so goddamned clever, don't you?"

He scowled and opened his mouth to speak, but something brought him up short. He chuckled to himself.

"What's so funny?"

"Oh, nothing. Nothing." His snickering went on a little longer, drawing out his pleasure in her demise. "By the way, did you need a ride to the depot? I'm on my way there right now. I wouldn't want to miss the show."

She placed a hand on her hip. "I think I've spent enough quality time with you this afternoon. I've got my own cab, thank you very much."

"Oh, you mean that one?" Dominic pointed a meaty finger toward the street. To the empty taxi lane.

Piper's cab burned rubber as it whipped into traffic. It took off down Montgomery Street, smoke coming from the tires.

"Hey!" Piper yelled.

She hobbled away from the building and out onto the street with her one good boot. Winding her arm up, she threw the broken boot heel at the cab. It clattered into the middle of the street where a delivery truck ran it over. The taxi squealed around the next corner, the back door swinging closed, and it disappeared.

Slipping off her red cowboy hat, she stared after the taxi in disbelief, oblivious to the traffic honking behind her. Rain soaked through her skimpy costume in seconds. That couldn't have happened, she told herself. Right under their noses, thirty feet away. The thief only took it for a spin around the block, right? He'd bring it back. It would be fine. Just fine, fine, fine. Right?

But it didn't come back. It was so *not* fine.

"Did that just happen?" she asked no one in particular.

The weight of the whole day crashed down on her, and she sank to her knees on the wet pavement. Where was that streetcar when she needed it?

"My cab."

"My briefcase," Aiden said.

Colin peed on the tire of Dominic's taxi. *My treat?*

Dominic crouched down to leer in Piper's face. "Your job."

Head over Heel

Piper wrung the water out of her cowgirl costume in the tiny Dachshund Rescue Center bathroom. Her hair still dripped from the rain, but at least she was wearing her friend's warm yoga pants and a one hundred percent tassel-free sweatshirt. Tying back her hair, she completed her de-slutting transformation and sighed.

The walk to the center had been a long one, especially after giving a statement to the cops and calling her boss at the taxi company so he could fire her—she didn't see the point in showing up in person since she had no taxi to return, or a change of clothes, for that matter. And no matter what Dominic said, she didn't think the cowgirl costume would have saved her job.

To top it all off, when she'd said good-bye to Aiden Caldwell he'd given her a handshake. A *handshake*. Not that she expected something else, or anything . . . or wanted anything for that matter. Because that would have been silly. They'd just met. And he was totally not her type. But a handshake? Ouch. Maybe *she* wasn't *his* type. Double ouch. Then again, it didn't matter because she didn't care. Right?

Before she could replay the scene in her head yet again, she stepped out of the bathroom and into the reception room. "That feels much better," she said.

Her friend Addison sat on the back counter feeding the goldfish, since she was too short to reach from the floor. Sprinkling food over the water, she assessed Piper's new look.

"Looks good. Maybe people won't throw coins at you now like you're turning tricks."

"One guy. It was one guy on the walk here." Piper leaned against the counter and watched the fish dart around the rectangular tank gobbling up the bits of food. "The ladies are hungry today."

Since they were veiltail goldfish, Piper thought they looked like elegant ladies with their orange and white chiffon ball gowns floating behind them. The image fit since they belonged to the older Englishwoman, Marilyn, who managed the rescue center. She was rather stately herself. Or perhaps her posh accent gave that impression. That and the fact that the only other English people Piper knew were the stereotypes found in movies.

Zoe strolled out of the little kitchen carrying a jug sloshing with water. When she noticed Piper had changed, she gave her a wink. "Lookin' good, Pipe."

"Thanks for coming in to cover for me while I talked to the cops," Piper said. "And, more important, thanks for bringing the clothes. I didn't feel like cleaning out dog enclosures in my soaking wet telegram costume."

"No problem," Zoe said, watering the peace lily on the desk. "That's the nice thing about running your own business. When you want a day off, you get to tell the boss to shove it."

Piper picked up the tiny pieces of her cowgirl costume

from the bathroom floor. Since they were at the center, Colin thought it was time to play and started chewing on the tassels, yanking the shirt from her grip in a game of tug-of-war.

"Colin, no." She swiped the costume out of his reach and balled it up. "Out of all the jobs I lost today, why did I have to keep the one with the worst uniform?"

"That's true," Zoe said. "But I'm sure it was exactly what that hot businessman wanted to see you in. Not a greasy pizza delivery uniform."

"Yeah, well, it doesn't matter what Aiden Caldwell wants." Piper chucked the leather and tassels into a plastic bag to take home. "Because I won't be seeing him again." Not that she had a choice in the matter. Not that she cared, she added to herself.

Addison slid off the counter. "So that was it? You guys talked to the cops and left? You didn't exchange numbers with this guy?"

"What for? I sexually assaulted and embarrassed him in front of his employees, I lost not one, but two, jobs, proving myself to be a complete and utter flake, and he watched me lose the car. A whole car. Not to mention his briefcase. All the while, dressed like a Western porn star. Why would that man ever want to see me again?"

Zoe stopped watering the ficus and stared at her like "duh." "Because you were dressed like a Western porn star?"

"It's only sexual assault if he didn't want it," Addison said with a devilish grin. "I mean, he did follow you out of the office to talk to you. Maybe because he liked you."

"Maybe because he wanted more." Zoe leaned on the desk, eager for gossip as always. "Was it any good? I mean, did you get a good feel?" She made suggestive squeezing motions with her hands.

Piper swiped away Zoe's rude gesture, giggling. "You

two are unbelievable. Besides, the man is, I dunno, too rich, too privileged. What would I ever have in common with him?"

She thought about her brother, Ethan, and how little she had in common with him ever since he'd "made something of himself"—more like made an *ass* of himself, she thought. For all she knew Aiden was just like him, with his designer suits and handshakes. Hell, Aiden probably drove a BMW like Ethan.

Addison shook her finger. "You sound like Elizabeth Bennet."

Piper's forehead wrinkled. "Who?"

"You know, from *Pride and Prejudice*. Through the whole movie, she refuses to see how perfect Mr. Darcy is for her because she's too proud." Addison tapped her chin, thinking. "Or is she prejudiced?"

"Proud? What the heck do I have to be proud of?" Piper opened one of the cupboards and grabbed a few dog brushes. She tossed one each to Addison and Zoe. "Today wasn't exactly my shining moment, you know."

Not hearing a word she said, Addison clapped her hands and exhaled dreamily, already planning their wedding in her head. "He's your Mr. Darcy."

Rolling her eyes, Piper yanked open the door to the back room. The chorus of hellos was overwhelming. At least, it sounded like "Hello" to Piper since all the dogs perked up and pressed their wet noses to their kennel doors, tails wagging.

Most of their four-legged friends were, of course, dachshunds. Marilyn, the manager, was passionate about taking in stray and sick doxies. But any dog lover knows that you can't pick just one breed. It would be like saying you only liked caramel salted milk chocolate or dark chocolate cherry truffles. Sure, you had your favorite. But chocolate was chocolate. There was something to appreciate about every different kind.

Colin strode down the long passageway lined with enclosures, strutting ahead of the three volunteers like they were his entourage. The enclosures were stacked two high, large enough for your average dog to walk around in, but for the bigger breeds there were more sizable pens in the back. The corridor ended at a T-intersection. More kennels lined the way to the outdoor courtyard on one end, and on the other was the makeshift examining room.

It was nowhere near as well equipped as a vet's office, but the metal table did the trick when a dog needed an inspection. For anything serious—broken bones, kennel cough, heart issues—they took the dog to a real vet. Who charged real money. Heck, one time they paid for Picasso, a doxie with intervertebral disk disease, to have surgery. Marilyn took him home for months of rehabilitation. Needless to say, he was living with her permanently now, since she couldn't part ways once he had healed.

That was why the center was one of the poorest in town. Marilyn and her volunteers elected to treat more of the "hopeless" cases, where other shelters decided to euthanize. They would pull dogs off the euthanasia list and do their best to nurse the little fur balls back to health. At the Dachshund Rescue Center, the dreaded *E* word was reserved for the absolute last resort, if the dog was terminally ill and suffering. The volunteers stockpiled tissues for those days.

Piper clenched the brush in her hand until the handle cracked. She turned her back on the door. She knew it would be part of her job one day as a veterinarian, but that was why it was so important to become a vet, to educate people, to give a voice to the animals, so that they could live long, happy lives in the best health possible.

She made her way to the end of the hall. When a long-haired red dachshund came into view, Colin shot across the room to the kennel door like a black torpedo, toenails skittering along the cement floor. He began pawing at the door and Piper laughed.

Reaching down, she unlatched the enclosure. "Hi, Sophie."

She barely got it open before the two doxies were all over each other, gnawing on ears and necks.

"Come on, you two. It's been twenty-four hours and you act like you haven't seen each other in a month."

"It's lov-v-ve." Addison drew out the word like it was a warm gooey thing. "It's like when you meet a guy and no matter how often you see each other, or text, or phone, you can't wait to see him again."

"That's not love," Zoe said. "That's infatuation. And the best way to get over him is to get under him."

"Zoe," Addison chided her.

"It's true." She shrugged. "Get it over with and move on. I'm a busy woman. I don't like to waste my time."

Piper saw Addison's bangs shift as she blew out a breath, but she didn't bother arguing with Zoe's logic. Addison's idealistic views on romance were practically Disney trademarked, so she and Zoe rarely agreed on the subject of relationships. Or Zoe's lack thereof. The most intimate relationship she had was with her vibrators. And since she sold tasteful sex toys with her side business, Pure Pleasure Parties, she had plenty to choose from.

Piper thought Addison was right, though. The doxies were crazy in love—even if they couldn't consummate the relationship since they were both fixed. She wasn't sure she'd be able to stand it, but she supposed they had a deeper connection. A spiritual one.

Trying to separate the two, Piper began to brush Sophie while Colin chomped on the handle like a chew toy.

Zoe watched on, laughing, but she had her own hands full with a horny German shepherd who wanted to hump her leg more than he wanted grooming.

"Whoa, Toby. Heel," she said. "You're a little hairy for my taste." But Toby couldn't hear her over his lust. Out of the three girls, he preferred Zoe with her long, lean legs, since there was so much more to hump.

Addison opened the kennel of a chocolate dachshund and scooped him out. His short, dappled fur was patchy and missing on his hips, shoulders, and elbows, the skin dry and cracked.

"What happened to you?" she asked him.

"That one came in last week," Zoe told her. "Marilyn said the last owner kept him in the garage. Nowhere to sleep but the cement floor."

"Poor thing. Don't worry. You've got a comfy bed here." Addison held him in her lap and combed his fur, careful of the calloused spots. "So, Pipe. What are you going to do now that you've lost two of your jobs?"

"I don't know. They were both great because they were flexible. Plus there were the tips. You know, when I wasn't late. But I'm sure I'll find something"—she frowned—"before my landlord kicks me out, and the bank repossesses my car because I default on my loan, and the university kicks me out of the veterinary program. . . ."

She tossed the brush aside and watched Sophie and Colin fight over it. "School ends in a couple of weeks. I could have had a job as a veterinarian by the end of the summer. I only needed to stick it out a little longer."

"I'd hire you at my dog spa if I could afford the extra help," Addison said, "but as it is, I'm still getting my feet under me."

"That's okay. I'm sure something will come up." She took a deep breath, her shoulders kicking back, chin rising automatically. "I'll be fine," she told them. "Just fine."

Zoe shook Toby off her leg again. "Well, when you can't pay rent and get kicked out of your apartment, you can come stay with me."

"Gee, thanks."

The bell above the reception door jingled, and the light tinkle carried into the back, announcing a customer.

All around, the dogs danced in their enclosures, barking, *Who's there? Who's there?*

Piper gave up trying to wrestle the brush away from the doxies and stood up. "I'll see who's at the front."

Zoe dislodged her leg from Toby's enthusiastic grip. "We'll start getting some of these guys outside for playtime."

"Coming!" Piper called out.

When she reached the entry to the reception room, she peered through the window set into the door. Then she spotted the person waiting at the counter. Gasping, she ducked down and out of sight.

Addison returned to let more dogs out of their kennels and spotted her cowering. "What's wrong?" she called.

"It's him," Piper hissed.

"Him who?"

"The him I gave an accidental lap dance to."

"Really?" Addison's eyes widened. She skipped over to peek through the window. "Oo-o-oh, he's cute."

"What are you looking at?" Zoe called from the other end of the kennels.

"Aiden Caldwell," Addison stage-whispered over the barking. "Come check him out."

Zoe was a whole foot taller than Addison, and when Piper joined the two of them in the Aiden oglefest she had to peek over Addison's blond locks. They shuffled until all three of them had their noses pressed to the glass to get a better look, their breath steaming up the view—not that it wasn't already steamy enough.

While he waited, Aiden perused the message board cluttered with missing dog flyers, trying to pat down his windblown hair. Piper noticed he'd exchanged his stained shirt for a clean one since she last saw him.

"That is not how I imagined him," Zoe said. "He's not just hot. He's like cook the panties right off a girl hot."

"No," Addison breathed. "He's like Henry Cavill meets Chris Evans hot."

"Who?" Zoe asked.

"Superman and Captain America." She shrugged. "There was a superhero movie marathon on TV last weekend."

"He's like I wanna make babies with him just to see what they would look like hot."

"Oh, your babies would look amazing," Addison said. "With your Japanese background and that guy's jawline, it would be like winning the genetic lottery."

Piper's mouth popped open. "This coming from the girl who would rather commit to her vibrator for the rest of her life than a man?"

Zoe gestured to the front. "For him, I'd reconsider my silicone matrimonial plans."

"I know." Piper groaned, banging her head on the doorframe. "Which makes the whole thing all the more embarrassing."

"Piper, listen to me." Addison gripped her by the shoulders. "He's obviously here to see you."

"But how? I never told him I volunteered here. More important, after everything that happened, why?"

"It couldn't have been that bad, because the guy has somehow tracked you down and came here despite everything that went wrong. So get over it and get out there."

"You're right. He's just a guy," she said to psych herself up. "A totally average guy who maybe, quite possibly, might be into me."

Zoe caressed the glass with a manicured nail. "Yeah.

A mega-hot, superrich, I'd give up coffee for the rest of my life to have one night with him guy."

"Not helping, Zoe."

Aiden dinged the bell on the counter to get service. At the thought of facing him again, the events of her afternoon flashed through Piper's mind. The lap dance, the taxi, the handshake.

"I can't do it," she said. "Come on, Addison. You gotta go out there for me."

"Nope. It's your turn. Besides"—she started to back away, a playful smile on her lips—"I think I hear Sophie whining outside."

"No. Don't leave me." Piper reached for Addison, but she twirled away. Piper wheeled on her other friend. "Zoe. Look. You already admitted it. He could be the one for you. That could be your future husband out there."

Zoe narrowed her eyes. "Pony up, cowgirl." She gave her a wink before slipping out back.

Piper hesitated at the door a moment longer, remembering how he'd turned all professional executive on her in front of the cops. How he shook her hand like they were concluding a business meeting. She'd figured that was that.

So . . . what was he doing at the center?

Light footsteps tapped up the corridor behind her. She thought maybe one of the girls had come back to rescue her from reliving the humiliation. Relieved, she turned around, arms open wide to hug her savior. But all she saw was fur, teeth, and paws coming at her like a tsunami.

It hit her hard. She screamed as she was bowled over, her back smacking the door. It swung open under the weight of her and the attacker, and she fell on her butt, whacking her elbow.

With a grunt, she sprawled out across the reception floor, staring up at the water-stained ceiling tiles. At first she thought her body shook from fright. It took her a moment before she realized what the gyration really was.

Toby was humping her leg, going to town like she was a Siberian husky show dog. Right in front of Aiden.

Pooch Proposal

"Toby, no!" Piper yelled. "Get off. Stop."

She squirmed away, trying to push the lecherous dog off her thigh with her other foot. But the canine had been deprived for a while, and the movement only encouraged him.

Aiden circled around the desk, chuckling. "Whoa, boy. I think that's enough action for you." Grabbing him by the scruff, Aiden managed to pry the horny beast off Piper. "You should at least buy the lady dinner first."

Reaching down, he helped Piper up. While she brushed herself off, he held the German shepherd back. Her cheeks burned, but she forced herself to meet Aiden's eyes.

The second he saw her, he started. It was a good start, though. Like when you discover Bellinis are on special—and you're not the DD for the night.

"It's you," he said like he didn't believe it.

"It's me." Getting humped by a dog, she added to herself. She sure knew how to make an entrance.

And the humiliation marathon continued.

"I almost didn't recognize you." Aiden hesitated. "You know, in clothes."

He appeared as surprised to see her again as she felt. But maybe Addison was right. Why else would he be there other than to see her? Sure, it was kind of a stalkery move on his part, but maybe she had nothing to be embarrassed about. It didn't stop him from tracking her down somehow.

Letting the idea fill her with confidence, she tried to get her flirt on. "Mr. Caldwell. What a nice surprise. You wouldn't be following me now, would you?" she said in her most sultry, sexified voice.

"Following you?" He blinked a couple of times. "No. No. I had no idea you worked here."

"Oh, right." And with those words, all the things that had happened that day were equally as terrible. She would have preferred the creepy stalker scenario.

"I should have guessed we'd run into each other eventually, though," he joked. "You appear to work different jobs all over the city."

Feeling a little thrown, she tried to shake off her disappointment. This was a good thing, she told herself. It meant she wouldn't have to turn him down if he asked her out. Which she totally would have, of course, since she didn't have time for a relationship. "Yeah, I, uh . . . I volunteer here a few times a week."

She shooed the German shepherd into the back. Shoving the door open, she bumped into Addison and Zoe, who were listening in. She waved them away before closing the door again.

"So, what are you doing here, then?" she blurted. "I mean, is there something I can help you with?"

"Yes. I came in here a few weeks ago to see the manager, Marilyn, and well . . ." A boyish giddy look crossed his face. "I fell in love."

Piper felt her shoulders slump. Yes. Stalker would have been better. "In love?"

"With a dachshund."

"Oh, of course. A dachshund." She laughed a little too loud. "They'll do that to you. Irresistible, aren't they?"

"I received a call from your manager. Apparently, my application for adoption was approved. She said it would be all right if I came to pick her up today."

She recalled him mentioning his new doxie that afternoon in her taxi. "Oh, that's great. Let me check the books."

Walking over to the desk, she whipped out the communication binder. Her finger slid down the page as she scanned the adoptions in progress and found *Aiden Caldwell*. She read the name of the adoptee and frowned. "Sophie."

"That's her." When she was still frowning, he asked, "Is something wrong?"

"Wrong? No. It's just . . . ," she trailed off, thinking about how Colin and Sophie had grown up together. Colin arrived at the center a few months back, and Piper instantly fell in love. But the came Sophie. They were picked up off the streets separately. Sophie ended up at the pound and then at the rescue center. A scan of her ear tattoo revealed that she'd come from the same household as Colin—one that didn't want them back.

If Piper had known they were bonded at the time, she wouldn't have separated the two lovebirds, err, dogs, but she couldn't very well give Colin up once she'd adopted him. Neither could she adopt Sophie after the fact. It was bad enough that she was breaking her tenant agreement by bringing one dog home. She wasn't sure she could smuggle in two.

Since Sophie had arrived, Piper had been hoping to try to adopt both of them. That is, once she graduated, got hired as a vet, made some money, and could afford a bigger place where she didn't have to hide the fact that she had pets. Okay, so it had been a long shot, but now it was an impossible one.

She forced a smile. At least Sophie would have a good life with Aiden. A charmed one, really. "Oh, it's nothing," Piper told Aiden. "Follow me."

Piper led him into the back, past the kennels, and through to the fenced-in yard. Even though it was a small lot with a tall, rickety wooden fence, the grass turning brown and sad in some areas, at least the space allowed the dogs to play and stretch their legs. The girls were already outside, playing with some of dogs. When Addison noticed Aiden, she dropped the ball in her hands. The dogs dove for it, fighting like a bunch of bridesmaids over a bouquet tossed at a wedding.

"Hi," she said.

"Hello," Aiden replied.

Cool Zoe gave an aloof wave, but Piper knew she was eyeing him up beneath her sunglasses. Zoe's lips pursed in approval.

Piper pointed to Sophie, who was gnawing on Colin's ears and dragging him across the patchy, half-dead grass. "That's her."

Chuckling, Aiden bent down, and both Colin and Sophie scampered over to him. Sophie stood on her hind legs and laid her dusty front paws on his suit pants. He didn't seem to notice.

"Hey, girl. Are you ready to go home?"

"She must remember you from the last time you were here," Piper said, seeing the lovesickness in Sophie's eyes.

As Piper watched him kneel down on the grass in pants that had probably cost more than her entire tuition for that semester, hell, the whole year, Aiden almost looked like a normal, down-to-earth guy. Not the formal businessman who'd shaken her hand a couple of hours before. She'd always believed the way a man acted around dogs said a lot about him as a person. And Aiden was a natural.

"Well, grab your new best friend," Piper told him. "I have some forms for you to fill out up front."

All four of them made their way back to the reception area—though it didn't take four people to sign the papers. Colin trotted behind Aiden, a possessive eye on Sophie. The two girls began to not-so-subtly find tasks to keep them within earshot. Addison started the highly important task of reorganizing the junk drawer, while Zoe rewatered all the plants until they were drowning.

Ignoring her audience, Piper gathered the approved paperwork for him to sign. He was just another applicant, after all. That was why he'd come. For Sophie. Not for her—not that she cared.

She laid the paper on the counter in front of him. "Sign here, please."

Placing Sophie down on the floor, Aiden picked up the pen to sign. "I'm sorry about your job today, by the way."

"Jobs, in the plural form. I also lost my pizza delivery job." She waved it off. "It was my fault."

"Oh, that reminds me." Reaching into his back pocket, he pulled out his wallet. "I never had a chance to give you your tip." He planted a hundred-dollar bill on the counter in front of her.

She gaped at Ben Franklin for a moment but then, very decidedly, slid it back toward Aiden. Who was this guy? Throwing around money like it was nothing? It reminded her of the time she went to dinner with her brother after her father's funeral, how he'd whipped out his largest bill from a Dunhill wallet—which she only knew about because he'd pointed out the brand—to tip the waitress at Applebee's. Applebee's, for God's sake, she'd thought at the time. The tip amounted to more than the bill. It was a nice thing to do for the waitress, but Piper knew it wasn't for her benefit. He'd practically waved it around in the air like a flag for all to see.

"I appreciate it," Piper said, "but I don't need your handouts. I'll be fine."

Aiden pushed it back toward her, amusement tweaking the corner of his mouth. "It's not a handout. It was an impressive performance."

She snorted but found herself smiling too. "And I definitely don't need your pity."

"I'm serious." He held his hands up. "You have a pretty voice. Did you write that song yourself?"

"Yes, I did. The agency pays more when you write the songs."

Aiden seemed to be loosening up a bit, the business facade fading. "So"—he planted his elbow on the counter and laid his hand on his fist—"you really think my eyes glimmer?"

Behind Piper, Addison sighed. "Yes."

Piper laughed but pushed the bill back toward him again. "I didn't even know you when I wrote that."

Zoe set the water jug down with a bang and rounded the counter. "But now she does and yes, they do." She swiped the money off the counter, shoved it into Piper's back pocket, and patted her on the butt.

"Zoe," Piper said in a warning tone.

"And Piper thanks you for your contribution to her tuition fees," Zoe told Aiden, slinging an arm around her friend's shoulder. "She's putting herself through school, you know."

"Are you?"

"Thanks, Zoe," Piper said through a tight smile.

"No problem." With a cheeky smirk, she spun away to join Addison on her perch next to the ladies, who, strangely enough, also seemed to be enjoying the show from their tank.

Piper glared at the two girls who had given up pretending to work. She shifted her eyeballs to the back door in a desperate, silent plea for them to leave, but they managed to not notice.

"What are you studying?" Aiden asked Piper.

"I'm training to become a veterinarian."

"You must really love animals."

"I do."

He was still leaning on the counter, his glimmery eyes on her. They were back in full flirt mode, even though she wore sweats that left everything up to his imagination.

"So what do you plan to do now that you lost your jobs? How will you pay for tuition?"

"Well, I still have my singing-telegram job. And I'm a big girl. I'll think of something."

He tapped the counter with his knuckles, thinking for a moment. "Well," he began, "my company keeps me pretty busy during the week."

"I would imagine so."

"And I'd hate to think of Sophie cooped up in my place all day."

"I'm sure she'd hate that," she said, wondering what he was getting at. Or hoping, more like it, that it was a lead-up to asking her out. A doggy date of some sort, like a walk in the park. Not that she wanted a date with him, or anything. But Colin liked walks, as dogs tended to do. And then there was Sophie to consider. They'd both be devastated if they never saw each other again. So it was for the good of the dogs. Yes. She could do it for them, she supposed.

"So, I was wondering, you know, if you're free," he hedged, "if you would like to be my dog walker."

She blinked. "Your dog walker?" Of all the things she would have liked to be of his, she hadn't seen that one coming.

"I'd pay you well," he said. "And it would really help me out."

Addison piped up. "Yes. She says yes."

"I'll take it from here, Addy. Thank you," Piper said. "You too, Zoe."

Grinning, they waved good-bye and disappeared into the back. But they didn't get far. Both girls happened to find something important to do right next to the window. Piper snorted but pretended to ignore them.

"It's not a handout. I promise," Aiden told Piper. "Honestly, I need a dog walker. But if you're not able to do it? . . ." He let the question hang in the air.

As disappointed as she was by the turn of events—although what she'd hoped for she wasn't sure—she knew she didn't have a lot of options. She had bills to pay, not to mention her rent was due that day and she would be a few days late with it. How could she say no to a job that fell into her lap?

He rubbed the scruff of his five-o'clock shadow. "I guess I'll just have to find someone who loves dachshunds, is knowledgeable about animals, and needs a job. Do you know of anyone around here that would fit the bill?"

Oh, those glimmery, glimmery eyes. Piper wondered if that was why he was such a successful businessman. He simply glimmered people into making deals.

She rolled her eyes. "All right. I work the early shift for my practicum at the veterinary hospital, so I'm free most afternoons from two o'clock onward."

On weekdays, she started clinical practice at the veterinary hospital at 5:00 a.m. She could head to his place after that. Now that she did the math, she thought it might be nice to create her own schedule.

Aiden's dimple twitched. "Perfect."

She pointed at their two doxies cuddling in the patch

of sunlight streaming through the window. "I'd hate to split these two kids up, anyway."

"Right, do it for the children." Stealing a pen from the desk, he took a business card out of his pocket and jotted his telephone number on the back. "This is my personal number. Give me a call. We'll set up a meeting for this weekend." He scooped Sophie up, pointing her cute, quizzical face at Piper. "Because you wouldn't want to disappoint Sophie."

"All right, all right. I'll call." She could feel a giddiness infecting her face.

"Great. I'll see you this weekend."

He started to leave, but as soon as he neared the door Sophie struggled in his arms. Colin jumped at his feet, pawing his leg.

"They get this way every time," Piper said. She grabbed a handful of treats from the jar on the counter and gave them to Aiden. "Here, this might help."

"Thanks." He dropped them into his designer suit pocket.

She bent down to pick Colin up, thinking her life had done a complete 180 in a single day, so fast her head spun. Or maybe that was her nerves as Aiden paused in the doorway and reached out to her. But when her eyes drifted down, she was staring at his hand.

Confused, she reached out and shook it. Two handshakes in one day? More action than she'd had in months, she supposed—other than the vibrator Zoe gave her for her birthday.

With a brief nod, he turned and left. The door shut behind him, and she let Colin down. He skittered to the door, hopping from foot to foot. The two of them watched Aiden and Sophie jump into his black BMW—of course it was a BMW. At least it was black and not white like her brother's, she thought. He'd parked next to an old beater

Buick and she couldn't help but notice the contrast. It was a sign—a flashing neon one—that they were from two different worlds.

Colin stopped pacing and flopped down, contemplating what just happened. His expression appeared more lost and forlorn than usual. He glanced up at her. *Where's Sophie going?*

"Don't worry," Piper said. "I know how you feel. I think we'll have to go for a visit."

Her heart did a funny skip at the thought, but she ignored it and she slipped Aiden's card into her bra. It was the excitement of a new job, she told herself. Although when Sam had offered her a job singing telegrams she couldn't remember feeling this happy, nor did she try to imagine Sam naked. Not that she was thinking about Aiden naked. Oh, wait. . . . Now she was.

She shook her head to clear the daydream. She couldn't go there. A guy like Aiden? A girl in her position? It wasn't like they were rubbing elbows at upscale San Francisco soirees. He came from a different world, one she didn't want to be a part of.

She didn't want to waste the time daydreaming about Aiden. Okay, she knew perfectly well she would daydream about him—but not by choice. The handshake had alerted something inside of her, like a meerkat perking up, standing on its hind legs looking about. For what, she didn't know. Benjamin Franklin was burning a hole in her back pocket, and not in a good way.

While she peered out the window, she heard the two girls slip into the reception room and come up behind her.

"Well, you have one thing in common now," Zoe said. "You both own dachshunds."

"Yeah. We're a perfect match. On Sunday mornings, he can read *Forbes* while I read the classifieds."

"Oh!" Addison bounced on the balls of her feet. "It's

like *Pretty Woman*. He's Richard Gere and you're Julia Roberts."

"Are you calling me a prostitute?"

"It's so romantic. He's going to fall in love with you, and because he's rich he's going to save you from your poor, pathetic life. Just like in the movie."

"Gee, thanks," Piper said. "But I don't need saving. I'm a big girl. I can take care of myself, if you haven't noticed. I know where I want to go and I'm working hard for it."

"Just promise that you'll make *him* work for it, if you get my drift."

"Trust me. I'm not interested in Mr. Handshake." As she watched him pull out of the parking lot, she relented a little. "But if I were, that would be a tough promise to keep."

Barked into a Corner

Piper raced down her apartment stairs juggling her car keys, a sandwich, and a wriggling backpack. She patted the backpack. "Almost there. One day we'll live in a place where I won't have to hide you."

The backpack whined back testily.

Before heading out, she popped by the mailboxes in the small lobby and unlocked her cubby. She was riffling through the letters when her cell phone rang. Tucking it under her chin, she answered.

"Hello?"

"Hi, Piper."

She cringed. "Mom. Hi."

Piper cursed herself for not checking the caller ID. It wasn't like she didn't want to talk to her mother, but their conversations usually ended by her mother forcing Piper to talk to her brother by handing over the phone before she could say no.

"I haven't heard from you in a while." Her voice sounded

too cheerful, like forced casualness. "Thought I'd give you a call and see what's new."

"Why?" Piper blurted. "I mean, I'm good. Thanks for calling."

Her mom clicked her tongue. "Can't a mother just call to say hello?"

Not my mother, thought Piper. There was always an ulterior motive, and it usually had to do with her brother. Ever since her mom had moved to Washington to be closer to him six years earlier, she'd been on a mission to push them closer together, like they could be one big happy family again, as though nothing had happened.

"Yeah. I'm good. I've been busy. Only two more weeks of practicum left at the veterinary hospital. Then there's my licensing exam after graduation."

"That's good, that's good. . . . Actually, that's what I wanted to talk to you about."

Here we go, Piper thought.

"Have you checked the mail lately?"

"I'm checking it now." Piper sifted through the pile: junk mail, flyers, final notice, final notice. Their big, bold red letters screamed at her in capitals. Her neck and shoulder muscles tensed, but she couldn't do anything about them until payday—which would be the worst one ever with one paycheck instead of three.

She tucked the final notices to the back of the pile and saw why her mother had called. The next letter came from Washington. It was from Piper's brother—however, she couldn't help but notice the writing on the envelope looked suspiciously like her mother's.

Her eyes narrowed. "What is this, Mom?"

"Oh, you got it. Good. Well, with your graduation coming up, Ethan thought it would be nice to send you a present."

Piper waved the flimsy envelope. Something told her it

wasn't a bouquet of flowers. "Mom, this better not be what I think it is."

"You know, money is one of the most common gifts for a graduation present," she said. "And Ethan feels so bad about not being able to make it down for your graduation. The check was his idea."

Unless a roomful of people were watching, Ethan's generosity with his money rivaled Ebenezer Scrooge's, so she knew that wasn't true.

"I don't want it." She averted her eyes from the final notices burning her hand like cattle brands.

"But Ethan wants you to have it." Her mother's voice filled with hopeful desperation. Like if Piper accepted this one peace offering all would be well.

"Which is exactly why I don't want it," Piper argued.

Her mother tutted. "When are you going to put this grudge aside?"

"When I invent a time machine. Or you give me a new brother. Either one."

"But it was so long ago, Piper. It's been almost a decade."

"Nine years, Mom. It's been nine years since he died."

"And you don't think I miss your father too? But Ethan is your brother. He's family. What little you have left. And he's trying to make amends."

Too little too late, Piper thought. "And giving me money is going to fix what happened?"

"Look, Piper. We both know things haven't been easy for you financially. It didn't help that I moved up to Washington to be closer to your brother and left you to pay rent on your own."

"No. It's not your fault," Piper said. "Besides, the place is rent-controlled. I'm fine."

She didn't blame her for moving. San Francisco was expensive, and Ethan had helped their mom out with money ever since she moved closer to him. It made Piper happy to know she was doing okay, even though she missed her mom. But Piper had lived by herself for six years, since she was twenty. She'd come this far on her own. She wasn't about to pack it all in now because her brother wanted to buy her love.

"You could have moved with me, you know," her mom said. Piper could hear in her voice that she missed her too. "You still could. It would be nice having everyone together."

Not everyone, she thought. Her fist clenched until she realized that she was squishing her sandwich. She was tired of having the same conversation every time they spoke. She got it. Her mom wanted both of her kids to get along. But just because Piper had to love her brother since he was family, that didn't mean she had to like him.

Ignoring the notices in her hand and the rent that was past due, she took the unopened letter from Ethan and tore it in half.

"What was that noise?" her mom asked.

"My life is in San Francisco," Piper said. "I'm not moving. I'll be fine." Just fine, fine, fine, she thought, her shoulders drawing back a little.

"Well, I worry about you, is all." Something banged in the background. "Oh, your brother just arrived. Here, I'll hand you over." Her mother's voice grew faint as she passed the phone.

"Mom, I gotta go!" Piper yelled into the phone. "I love you. Bye!"

She ended the call before she could hear his voice. To make herself feel better, she tore the check up into minuscule pieces before throwing it away. When the last fluttering piece had settled to the bottom, she dared a glance at the final notices in her hand. Her mom would say she'd just cut off her nose to spite her face. But she didn't. She did it to spite Ethan. It was a stubborn pride that she'd inherited from her father.

"How are we going to pay the bills, Colin?" she asked her backpack.

Colin squirmed restlessly in her bag. She tossed her sandwich in the garbage along with the torn-up check—it's not like she had an appetite left, anyway—and headed to her poppy red VW Bug in the parking lot. Once inside the car, she freed Colin, who gave her an agitated sneeze.

"I know you hate the bag." She gave him a scratch behind the ears. "But we can't afford a new place that accepts pets."

His bushy tan eyebrows rose and she sighed in defeat.

Reaching into her backpack, she drew out Aiden Caldwell's business card. She hesitated, struggling to come up with another solution. One that was far less tricky.

It was an opportunity laced with potential complications and temptations. But when she considered the alternative, handing out résumés all over town, waiting days, if not weeks, for a call, then the interviews, the training. She'd already be kicked out of her apartment by the time she saw her first paycheck. Or worse, she and Colin would be forced to crawl up to Washington with their tails between their legs.

She grimaced. That wasn't an option. Unable to think of a better idea, she reached for her phone and texted Aiden before she could chicken out.

Hello, this is Piper, the telegram girl from the rescue center. I'm wondering if you still needed a dog walker.

She hit *send*. It felt weird to ask for a job this way. Especially after how they'd met the day before. She wondered if he only suggested it because he'd watched her lose two jobs. What if it was a handout? What if he just felt bad for her? She'd rather sleep in the rescue center than face his pity.

Her phone chimed with Aiden's response.

Absolutely. When would you be free to meet and have a chat?

A chat? She wondered what that meant in Aiden's world. Was it an interview type chat at his office or a casual coffee thing? Since it was for a dog-walking position, she chose neutral ground.

I'm free all day today or tomorrow afternoon. We can meet at the Presidio with the dogs.

Does two o'clock work for you?

Sure. I'll meet you in the Fifteenth Avenue gate parking lot.

See you then.

The exchange was professional and businesslike. No words wasted. Then why was Piper's heart beating so fast? It was nothing more than a job, she told herself. It wasn't like a date or anything.

She threw the phone in her bag and turned to Colin in the passenger seat. "Happy?"

His head tilted to one side in confusion.

"Sophie will be there."

At the mention of her name, his tail began to twitch back and forth. He stared out the windshield expectantly, as if saying, *You may chauffeur me now.*

Bowing, she threw it in drive and did his bidding.

Seeing a Man About a Dog

Piper drove her VW Bug across town while Colin stuck his head out of the passenger window. His flapping ears reminded her of little propellers. She imagined that if they caught the right wind they would balloon like a parasail and he'd go flying right out the car and down the boulevard.

The sun glaring through the windshield made her feel like an ant under a magnifying glass, so she followed his lead and rolled down her own window. Her long hair whipped around her face as they drove toward the north end of the city. While the vintage car was totally epic, it made a gruesome hot box in the warmer months since the air-conditioning had crapped out and she couldn't afford to fix it.

As they approached their destination, signs for the Presidio started popping up. She followed the signs onto the former military base and pulled into the parking lot where she told Aiden to meet her. Piper searched for a shady spot before parking; the vinyl seats had a tendency to heat up like molten lava and scorch her when she hopped back in. She killed the engine and climbed out.

It was a beautiful Saturday to be at the park. People were loading and unloading their dogs, kids, and picnic baskets from their cars. Those in bare feet hopped across the pavement and onto the grass like they were walking on hot coals.

Scanning the lot, she smoothed the wrinkles from her cotton tank and searched for Aiden. After all the time she spent Googling photos of him with Addison and Zoe, she was positive she would recognize him from any angle—and, as it turned out, he looked damned good from all of them.

Colin surveyed the scene from the passenger window. After a minute, his tail began whipping back and forth. His excited barks carried across the parking lot.

Piper followed his gaze and saw Aiden. Colin had spotted him before she did, or rather, he spotted Sophie rolling in the grass at Aiden's feet. Aiden was sitting on a bench, people-watching at the edge of the lot. While she could only see his profile, she recognized the stiff way he sat, back rigid. He wore a collared work shirt even though it was the weekend. His sports jacket sat folded on the bench next to him. At least he'd skipped the tie and rolled up his sleeves. The man knew how to let loose and party.

He was obviously a newbie to dog parks, or parks in general, or perhaps all things non–work related. He stuck out like a new pair of shoes on the first day of school. Or maybe a lost little puppy. And God knew how she liked to take those home.

Her palms grew moist. "This is a bad idea, Colin."

Colin spun in circles on his seat while she hesitated. Finally, he whined.

"Maybe we shouldn't go," she said to him, but she made no move to leave. Her gaze remained fixed on Aiden, kind of like when she worked at the veterinary hospital for practicum and she stared at the last donut in the box that the receptionist Terri had bought. Piper knew she shouldn't, but it looked so damned good. And Aiden was the chocolate-filled chocolate-covered chocolate donut. Mmmmmm, she thought as she continued to stare.

No, she told herself. Donuts were bad for her. And so was Aiden. Wiping her palms on her shorts, she opened her car door so she could get in and drive to the nearest McDonald's. Maybe she could fill out an application for burger construction artist or something. But Colin didn't care what she thought. The second the door cracked open, he slipped out between her legs.

"Colin, no."

She reached out to grab him by the collar, but his stubby legs moved in a blur as he scampered off in a direct line for Sophie. Racing over to the bench, Colin tackled his girlfriend. The two of them rolled across the grass in a writhing ball of torsos and ears. Aiden lunged toward them, thinking they were fighting, but he must have recognized Colin because he began to search the parking lot. He spotted Piper standing frozen by her VW and waved.

She was trapped.

"I'm going to kill you, Colin," she promised under her breath.

She waved back before grabbing Colin's leash and ball. At the last minute, she remembered her cell phone. She was on call for the veterinary hospital if any emergencies came in that day, so she had to stick close to the phone.

She didn't mind, since the hours were better than her previous clinical placement and she only had to work the occasional weekend shift. The reduced hours allowed her to take more telegram gigs, even when she was on call. However, one time she had to deliver a litter of kittens dressed as a sexy gladiator. Now she carried a spare change of clothes with her at all times. Her car was like a closet on wheels.

Heading across the parking lot to meet Aiden, she almost wished she'd worn something nicer, not a cotton tank and an old pair of sneakers. But she wasn't interviewing for a position at Caldwell and Son Investments, just as the son's dog walker. And she definitely looked the part. Plain old dog walker Piper.

"Hi." He stood up when she got closer. "I'm glad you could make it."

"Hey. Sorry we're late."

He gave her a brisk handshake. Again with the handshake, she thought. "That's okay. Traffic?"

"No. I'm infected with perpetual late-itis. The doctor says it's terminal."

"I'm sorry to hear that," Aiden said in mock seriousness. "Terrible diagnosis. My cousin had that."

"Oh, what happened to him?" she asked, clipping Colin's leash on.

"He said he'd meet me for lunch one day. I'm still waiting." He shook his head, his expression grim. "I don't like to talk about it much."

She laughed. "Come on. The dog park's this way. We can let them off their leashes there."

"Sure. Lead the way." He grabbed his jacket and folded it over an arm. "Come on, Sophie."

She stared at him from where she lounged on the mowed grass. He jiggled her leash, but she stayed put, resisting his tugs. Piper whistled through her teeth and called her.

Sophie heaved a sigh to say, *Oh, very well,* and jumped to her feet, deigning to join them.

Aiden laughed. "I guess she still doesn't know who's boss."

"Oh, if you wanted to be boss, you chose the wrong breed. You'll have to settle for administrative assistant."

"Or mailroom boy."

He followed her to the main trail, where they could walk side by side. The dogs stopped often to sniff out the new territory. It was busy, so they had to weave in and out of other people, giving Piper an excuse to watch the trail and keep her eyes averted from the temptation next to her. To forget about his glimmery eyes, and his adorable ruffled hair, and that one little dimple, not two, just one, and how could she have missed that before?

Not realizing she'd been staring at him, Piper tripped over a hump in the pavement and stumbled a few feet. After that, she kept her eyes straight ahead, reminding herself over and over again that this was an interview, not a date. Definitely, almost certainly, probably not. Right?

"So," Aiden eventually said, "I wanted to spend a little time together today to make sure . . ."

"That I'm not a crazy person?" she offered.

He chuckled and ran a hand through his scruffy hair. "Well, I wasn't going to put it quite that way. But yes. Before I hand over the keys to my home, it would be comforting to know you don't have any psychotic tendencies."

"Only when I don't have access to my daily dose of chocolate."

"Duly noted."

They reached a large area where wood chips littered the ground. Piper stopped to set Colin free and Aiden did the same for Sophie. The off-leash area spanned about an acre in size, surrounded by leafy green trees and plenty of benches where many of the owners were happy to sit and enjoy the shade.

"Here." Piper dug into her pocket and pulled out a gnarled tennis ball. "I thought our meeting could be both work and play."

She tossed it to him and he caught it. "Oh, good. But

just so you know, I'm not usually one to mix business with pleasure."

Piper knew he meant it as a joke. It was a tennis ball, after all, but the words struck her as familiar. He'd said the same thing the day before in her taxi. She recalled the straight-faced businessman at the office, the formal handshakes, and now he was wearing a suit in a park—with a pocket square, she couldn't help but notice.

Back when she'd helped her mother move to live near Ethan, they'd all gone to dinner together. He'd flashed his exclusive credit card, turning it in plain sight ten minutes before the bill came. Several times throughout the evening, he jingled his BMW keys with the big blue and white key chain in his hands when it was nowhere near. And while they were in the middle of dinner, he answered a call on his Bluetooth—still tucked in his ear—and began speaking loud enough so everyone could hear about his oh-so-important legal cases because he was such a big-time lawyer.

They were what he considered the badges of his new status, the things he thought made him better than where he came from—a farm in Oregon. It was a persona he wore, a mask of permanent fakeness, of empty gestures, leaving nothing but a hollow personality beneath it. Gone was the little boy she grew up with.

She appraised Aiden with a lingering look. "You know what they say, 'All work and no play . . .' "

"Hmm, nope. Don't think I ever heard that one," he teased. "What do they say will happen?"

"Oh, something about kidney stones or blindness."

"Well, in that case." He whistled. "Sophie."

Both dogs perked up. Aiden threw the ball in the air and caught it again, mesmerizing them. Hypnotized, they watched his arm draw back. The moment he released it, both Sophie and Colin took off like they were hot on the trail of a badger, their natural quarry.

Piper laughed, watching Colin fight Sophie for the toy like it was to the death. "Colin doesn't understand the words 'not your ball.' Every ball is Colin's ball. On the plus side, I've made lots of friends at dog parks because of it."

"And Colin some enemies?" Aiden asked.

"No way." Colin brought her the ball and she ruffled his fur in congratulations. "Look at this face. How can you hate this face?"

As she said this, Sophie tackled Colin and they went rolling. Sophie came back with wood chips stuck in her long red fur, and Aiden bent down to pick some of them out. "Well, these two seem to be the best of friends."

"Yeah, they love each other. They grew up together. After I adopted Colin, he still came back to the center with me to visit her."

"But you only adopted Colin?"

"Unfortunately, I couldn't take both home with me. I shouldn't have a dog at all. My landlord would kill me if he knew."

She tossed the ball back across the lot again. The dogs raced for it, wood chips flying up in their wake. Finding the shadiest bench, Piper took a seat and curled her legs up next to her. Aiden had to hitch his pant legs up a little to sit but tried to look casual, slinging an arm across the back of the bench.

Piper studied him out of the corner of her eye. If Aiden wore the same mask as her brother, he wore it so flawlessly, without having to flash his badges around, that Piper wondered if it was a mask at all.

But what did it matter? She came there for one reason—a job interview. Aiden was just her potential boss. However, when she recalled the final notices in her mailbox that morning she knew it wasn't *just* a job. It was her best shot at staying afloat.

She eyed her tank top and shorts wondering once again if she shouldn't have worn something different, maybe with a collar, or at least something that didn't show her bra straps. After all, dog walking wasn't to be taken lightly in San Francisco. It was a cutthroat job market. Not to mention the turf wars that occurred over dog-walking territory between the walkers. It was dog-eat-dog—no pun intended.

Aiden still looked relaxed and effortless in his suit next to her, playing with the dogs each time they returned with the ball. Nothing had changed between her and Aiden, but Piper grew tense. But he offered her the job in the first place, she reasoned, so surely she had nothing to worry about. Then again, if it were that easy why would he need to interview her? Straightening up on the bench, she crossed her legs. That was professional, right?

She cleared her throat. "So, what else can I tell you about myself to prove my sanity?" she asked.

"Maybe you can tell me about yourself. Your hobbies, your goals." He said it straight-faced like he was reading off a list of interview questions. "Your friend at the center said you're training to be a veterinarian. Tell me more about that."

"I'm in my fourth year, well, eighth if you count my undergrad. I have two more weeks of practicum left before I graduate."

The tennis ball fell at her feet and she paused to toss it again. When she leaned back, Aiden's dark green eyes were focused on her. Maybe it was a tactic, like one of the seven habits of highly effective communicators. Eye contact would be one, surely. But then why did his lingering gaze cause her cheeks to ignite?

"So you don't treat the dogs at the rescue center?"

"Oh no. Nothing like that," she said. "Not yet, anyway. I'd like to open my own veterinary clinic one day."

"That's ambitious."

She shrugged it off, feeling self-conscious. She knew it would be tough. It would mean remaining in her run-down apartment, working a lot of overtime, scrimping, saving, having more sleepless nights. But it would be fine. She knew she could do it. She *would* do it. And at the end of it all, she'd look back and say she did it all on her own.

Sophie won the battle this time, and she brought the ball to Aiden. He bent down to wrestle with her for a minute, but her grip was too strong. Eventually, he gave up fighting her, and she dropped the ball of her own free will. She sat on her haunches and waited for him to pick it up, staring at him like, *Come on. What are you waiting for?*

He chuckled before lobbing the ball across the expansive park. "Where do you want to work once you graduate?"

"Anywhere, really," Piper said. "But I want to be able to volunteer more time at the center. Right now we don't have the facilities or money to treat the serious cases that come in. Using an outside vet seriously drains our funds, which prevents us from taking more dogs off the euthanasia lists around the city."

"Really? That's terrible."

"Yeah. It is. Once I'm licensed, hopefully I can prevent some of that. We try to save as many dogs as we can and help find them good homes."

He nodded like he'd ticked off another question on his mental list. "So I'd like to go over some of the details of the job and what would be expected."

"All right." Piper didn't think she could sit up any straighter.

"The wage will be seventy dollars. You can come over—"

"Seventy dollars a day?" Piper interrupted.

"No. Seventy an hour."

"An hour?" she blurted. "Is that supposed to be a joke?"

He hesitated, blinking in surprise. "Is it not enough?"

"Enough?" Piper stared at him like he was the crazy one now. "It's too much." She wondered what would possess him to offer such a ridiculous wage. Who did he think she was, Cesar Millan?

Suddenly, she remembered stumbling into Aiden's office the day before wearing hardly anything and how he'd followed her down to the taxi afterward. Of course. He'd jumped to the same conclusions so many telegram customers had before.

Piper received this kind of treatment all the time, requests for "private parties" or "photo shoots." How did she not see it before? Probably because she'd never had a request for a dog walker. Plus there was something about Aiden Caldwell. She'd expected more class from the man.

He doesn't mix business with pleasure my ass, she thought.

She jumped to her feet and swiped Colin's leash off the bench. He scampered over with the ball, ready to play some more, but the moment he saw the expression on her face he dropped it. She clipped on his leash and turned back to Aiden.

"Look, Mr. Caldwell, I don't know what kind of girl you think I am, but clearly you have the wrong idea about me."

Aiden stared at her openmouthed as she spun on her heel and began to march right out of the park.

Never Mix Business with Wieners

Piper stomped back the way they'd come through the dog park—which was difficult to do on wood chips—burning with mortification. She should have seen it coming. A sexy CEO offering her a job the moment she needed it most? How desperate did he think she was? Piper, you idiot, she told herself. Of course it was too good to be true.

"Wait a minute!" Aiden called out to her.

She didn't turn back. She kept her eyes fixed straight ahead, weaving through the packed dog park. The crowd had grown since she last noticed. She'd been too busy ogling the man who wanted to proposition her for . . . well, who knew what.

When Aiden caught up to her, Sophie was in one arm, his coat in the other. "Hold on a second. Wait. You're mad because I'm offering you too much money?"

She spun to face him. "Seventy dollars an hour? What exactly are you expecting for that kind of wage? Another lap dance like yesterday?"

"I expect you to walk my dog." His voice rose with what

she guessed was insult. "It might be more than your average pay, but that's what it's worth to me."

"You can hire anyone else in this city for less than half that."

"I'm not asking anyone else," he said. "I'm asking you."

Piper gave him a hard stare, trying to figure out what game he was playing. She recalled her original fear, that he pitied her. And to her, that was worse than propositioning her. She narrowed her eyes. "I'm not a charity case, either."

He held his hands up in defense. "I never said you were."

"Fine," she relented. "But I earn my way. I work hard for my money." She said it like a warning.

"Then earn it. What will it take? Negotiate with me. I'm all ears." Aiden brought a hand up to where his tie should be, but he seemed surprised to find it missing, like he didn't often take a day off. His demeanor turned all business again, but this time he was giving her the power.

She felt her breathing even out as he waited for her counteroffer. "Well," she began. "I'll accept seventy dollars a day, but I'll be walking Sophie for two hours."

"An hour and a half," he countered.

"An hour and forty-five."

"Done."

"And I'll take her for regular grooming when I take Colin."

"All right, but I'll pay."

"The owner is a volunteer from the rescue center. I get a discount because she's my friend."

"And Sophie is my dog. I'll pay."

Piper frowned but wasn't sure how to argue that one. Sophie's head swung back and forth as they debated, pleased to be the center of all the attention.

"Anything else?" he asked.

"If you go out of town and you need a dog sitter, you

call me first and I'll work for a substantially lower rate." She thought Colin might like that.

"I thought you couldn't keep pets in your apartment."

"I'll hide her. What's one more?"

They had a brief staring contest while he considered all her demands. Finally, his dimple made an appearance. "You know, I've been running my business for a while, and this isn't how your average negotiations are supposed to go."

Her chin rose an inch. "Well, I'm not your average girl."

"So I've noticed." The tension broke and he stopped fighting the smile.

If Piper had a dimple, it would have been dimpling too. Okay, so he wasn't a creep who was propositioning her. And he didn't pity her. At least, she didn't think so. She felt ridiculous now. But what was she supposed to think? Who offered that kind of money for dog walking?

A small crowd had formed on one side of the open space, milling about and chatting. She spotted one of them carrying a large white sheet and assumed it was for a group picnic. When they went to spread it on the grass, two people each grabbed a corner and shook it out. Big red letters were painted across it: *SFAAC.*

Others in the group started picking up boards, holding them aloft for the whole park to see. *Stop the killing* and *Put an end to puppy mills.* A retriever mix trotted through the park with a sign strung around his neck: *I can't speak for myself. Please be my voice.*

"What is this?" Aiden asked.

A jolt of anxiety shot through Piper. "San Franciscans Against Animal Cruelty."

She wanted to duck and roll into the bushes before anyone from the group could recognize her. Most of them were pretty cool. She'd even protested with them in the past. It was one SFAAC member in particular whom she worried about running into. She'd never expected to see them there, or she would have suggested Aiden meet her somewhere else.

"A dog park seems like a strange place to protest," Aiden said. "They're preaching to the choir."

"I think that's the point." She watched flyers being handed out. "It looks like they're here to gain awareness and support from fellow animal lovers." She headed for the path, counting out her steps to make it look like she wasn't rushing. "Come on. It's about to get too noisy for an interview."

While Piper appreciated their cause, she hated to end the afternoon on such a sour note with Aiden. However, she felt relief as he clipped Sophie's leash back on and followed Piper to the edge of the clearing.

"So," she hedged. "Any hints of crazy yet? You know, besides accusing you of sexual harassment?"

"No red flags that I can see," he teased. "Yet."

"Tell that to my parole officer." He glanced at her in surprise, and she threw her hands up in the air. "Just kidding."

"You know," Aiden said. "I think it's generous of you to spend your spare time working with homeless dogs."

"Not really." Her cheeks warmed again and she turned away to hide it. "I love these guys, so it doesn't feel like work."

"I wish I had more time to do the same. There's the whole time is money factor, I guess."

Yet another thing he had in common with her brother, Piper thought.

She remembered her mother having to sell off farm equipment to pay the hospital bills and how quickly it all fell apart, especially after her father died. Even as her mother cried herself to sleep, she had to make plans for the funeral, for selling the farm, uprooting their whole lives. And where was Ethan? Sitting in on some large corporate merger in Washington. He caught a late flight the night before the funeral and left almost immediately after. Because *time is money.*

Piper fell silent, lost in thought, but when Aiden spoke again she realized so had he. "But there are some things money can't buy." The lightness had gone from his voice. "You know what I mean?"

He looked at her, like really looked at her, as though he wanted to know how she felt. And not just for part of the interview. It caught her off guard. For a moment, she wondered what a rich man like Aiden couldn't buy with all his money.

She considered the question with the same seriousness with which he asked. It was easy to say money didn't matter when you never had to worry about it.

"It's true," she said. "Money can't make you happy. But it can sure make you miserable when you don't have any."

"Are you miserable?"

She thought about her friends and the things that made her happy, and she realized none of those things cost her a penny. "No, finances are just stressful sometimes."

"Most people stress about money, no matter how much or how little they have."

Before she could answer, he clicked his tongue and stopped. "Money can, however, buy new shoes." He scraped his wingtips off on the cement path.

Piper pressed her lips together, trying not to laugh at the mess. "I should have warned you when I suggested we meet at the park. People are supposed to pick up after their dogs, but some don't. I like to call them dog-park *poop*etrators."

"I should have dressed more casually, but I didn't think the dog park had a dress code."

"Oh yes. The uniform is strictly enforced." She nodded

gravely. "Khakis and short-sleeved plaid shirts. Wrinkled, not pressed. And I wouldn't recommend flip-flops."

"I'll remember that for next time."

A middle-aged man approached to hand Aiden a flyer. She ducked her head and fell behind. She didn't think she recognized him, but she couldn't be sure. When she fell into step next to Aiden again, she saw that the glimmer was back in his eyes.

"So is that your dog-park uniform?" He eyed her tank top and jean shorts—a little appreciatively, she thought. "I was expecting something more Western-style."

"Very funny. I don't just do cowgirl, you know. I also have a cop uniform, a cheerleading outfit, and a construction worker."

"Wow, a couple more costumes and you could be a one-woman Village People."

"I don't do covers. Original material only, under the Piper Summers trademark. And those are just the popular outfits. I've got plenty more."

"You know, I wouldn't mind seeing them sometime," he said.

"I bet you wouldn't." She couldn't keep the suggestive waggle from her eyebrow. "I charge by the song."

A few minutes earlier, she'd become livid with him because she thought he had the wrong idea. Now that she knew that wasn't the case, the wrong idea felt a little right. She was glad they'd made it back to total Flirtville, population: two.

Her insides quivered like she'd swallowed butterflies. She hadn't experienced them since graduate school, so she knew they weren't merely any butterflies. They were rare ones, like morpho butterflies.

She wasn't imagining the chemistry between them. It was as obvious to her as a Western chorus frog singing for his mate or a male peacock shaking his tail feathers for a hen. She just wasn't sure that's what she wanted. Well, okay, she wanted it all right, but let's face it, she also wanted chocolate for breakfast, but that didn't mean it was good for you. Mmmmm, chocolate.

"Slut!" someone screamed.

Piper jumped and spun toward the voice, as did Aiden, as did the whole park. The protesters' chant broke off. A girl from within their ranks stepped forward. And her accusing finger was pointed straight at Piper.

"Whore!"

8 Dogfight

"Tramp!" the protester yelled.

Piper froze to the spot. All the eyes in the park followed the angry protester's pointing finger. The twentysomething girl was dressed in a green bohemian maxi-dress, her wild, curly hair snaking from her head like a furious Mother Nature incarnate. And Piper was her target.

But it wasn't Mother Nature. Just an old pain in the ass of Piper's. The one person she dreaded running into. "Oh, good," she muttered under her breath. "Laura."

"Liar!" Laura screamed again.

Not exactly the glowing recommendation one hopes for during an interview. Piper tugged Aiden's sleeve. "Let's go."

Colin stood his ground, ready to defend his lady's honor. Hoping to avoid a confrontation, Piper tugged on his leash and headed for the way out. But who was she kidding? There was always a confrontation.

For the last few years, Laura's hobby had been to harass Piper whenever possible—"stalk" was more like it.

And every time Laura confronted her in public, Piper tried to extract herself from the situation with her head high and her mouth clamped shut. But no matter how many times she tried to take the high road, she always found herself getting sucked in.

Aiden hurried to keep up with Piper. "Do you know that girl?"

She opened her mouth to answer, but Laura had caught up to them. "Hey." She gripped Piper's arm, her fingernails digging into her flesh. "I'm talking to you."

"Laura," Piper said. "So good to see you. It's been too long."

"How dare you show your face here," she growled at Piper.

Piper took a deep breath and tried to remain calm, knowing it would piss Laura off more. But Piper also knew that it wouldn't last long. Be cool, she told herself. Be cool.

"At a dog park? With my dog? Yeah, I'm pure evil."

"What, are you stalking me?" Laura eyed her up like she was Satan's spawn and Colin her hellhound—which, admittedly, he was at times.

Piper laughed incredulously. "*I'm* stalking *you*?"

"How many times do I have to tell you?" she spat. "You've already won. Why won't you just leave me alone?"

She loomed close enough that Piper could read her *I heart my dog* earrings, but she spoke loud enough for the entire park to hear. Everyone had stopped playing with their pets or reading their books to listen.

Getting the attention she wanted, Laura spun dramatically toward her captive audience. "You already lied and got me kicked out of the veterinary program. Are you trying to kick me out of my favorite park too?"

Piper's cool turned to lukewarm. Her fists clenched at her sides. "That is not what happened and you know it." Besides, that was *her* favorite park, and Laura knew it too.

"Are you denying that you got me expelled?"

"Your own actions got you expelled!" Okay, hot, boiling hot.

Colin and Sophie began to growl at Laura in support. *We got your back.*

Laura gasped in hurt shock, a hand on her chest. "Me? What did I do? Worked hard, did the best I could? I guess you just couldn't suppress your jealousy. You couldn't stand that I was at the head of the class and you couldn't even pass a pop quiz."

Piper rubbed her temples. She could have passed that pop quiz, but she'd forgotten to set her alarm that morning and missed it altogether. She snorted. "Head of the class? You couldn't have identified a flea if it bit you in the ass. You were only doing as well as you were because you were copying off your friends."

"That's the story you managed to convince our professor. I wonder how you did that?" Her eyes narrowed. "Well, I suppose lying is your specialty. Only for our professor you were lying on your back."

"I wasn't sleeping with the professor!" But no one heard her because Laura had turned to plead with the crowd, talking over her.

"I just want to move on with my life. She follows me everywhere I go. Someone please get her away from me. Call the cops."

Piper was steaming. Random people started getting to their feet uncertainly. A couple of her SFAAC friends took a few steps toward Laura and Piper, as though about to intervene.

Laura turned to Piper and beamed triumphantly, speaking low enough for only Piper and Aiden to hear. "You know, if it's in self-defense, I can't get in trouble for hitting you."

"I would have to attack you first," Piper said.

"Look around." She glanced back at the park. "All these people have witnessed that you're here to harass me. Who knows what you'll do when we cross paths again?"

Piper took a step forward, but Aiden spoke first. "Do it and she can press harassment charges. And lay another finger on her and I'll call the cops. That goes for the rest of you." He gave the advancing onlookers a threatening glance.

"This is a protest. We got a permit and everything. We're not doing anything wrong." Laura glared at Aiden. "But Piper here looks about ready to hit me. Are you going to hit me?" She tapped her own cheek, egging Piper on. "Come on. Do you want to punch me?"

"Don't tempt me." Piper's hands balled at her sides.

Aiden's warm hand clasped over hers. The touch was so unexpected, so gentle, that her fist relaxed in shock. His fingers interlaced with hers and he began to draw her away from the tense crowd.

All Piper could focus on was the sensation of his warm hand in hers, his own steady composure contrasting with her behavior, chastising her. She'd thrown a hissy fit like a five-year-old who hadn't learned how to play well with others, and here was the CEO of a Fortune 500 company who had probably never lost his cool in his life.

Who gave a shit about Laura, anyway? About what those people thought? About anything else but that hand in hers?

The park faded into the distance, the chanting, the yelling. She barely heard Laura call out to her back, "Maybe someone should expose you for what you really are, Piper! You hear me? Force you to confess how you cheated me out of a university education." Because Piper couldn't hear anything over all those morphos fluttering around inside her.

When she and Aiden had walked a little ways—she wasn't paying any attention to how far—his hand dropped away.

"I'm sorry," Aiden said. "I thought it was best to leave. There was no reasoning with her."

Piper nodded, not trusting her voice. Of course, he wasn't really holding her hand. He did it to get her out of the situation. Don't be stupid, Pipe, she told herself. She felt a pang of disappointment but quickly smothered it with annoyance. She didn't need him to interfere. She was doing just fine on her own.

She picked up her pace, marching ahead on the path so Aiden was forced to jog to catch up. With her shoulders pinned back and her chin raised high, she marched forward at a brisk clip.

A moment later, she felt Aiden's arm grab her firmly around the waist, stopping her in her tracks. Thrown off balance, she swung into him and found herself chest to chest with him. He held her, smiling down in surprise.

"What do you think you're doing?" she managed with a trembling voice.

"Uh, you were about to . . ." He glanced down at the ground, and when she did the same she saw that the *poop*etrators had struck again.

If she weren't so frustrated she would have laughed. But her heart was racing, with anger, with surprise, and, if she was honest, from Aiden's touch. How did she keep getting into such embarrassing situations? Ones that Aiden always seemed to be around for, to pull her out of.

"Are you okay?" he asked.

She knew he didn't mean physically. Piper turned away and began to straighten her disheveled tank top. It took a moment to find her voice, to pinpoint what feeling was plaguing her the most: embarrassment, anger, bitterness, or her pity for Laura the day the truth came out. Then of course there was the last three years of constantly having to watch her back.

"That was humiliating," she said.

All those people glaring at her like she was the one who did something wrong. Of course, they didn't know what had really happened. How could they? Laura was a little too convincing. She wouldn't have a future as a veterinarian, but she would make one hell of a soap star.

It occurred to Piper that Aiden didn't know what happened, either. She wondered what he must be thinking after witnessing that. She wouldn't have blamed him if he rescinded his offer of employment right there and then.

"I'm sorry about back there," she said. "It isn't like how she said it was."

"What was all that about?" Aiden jiggled Sophie's leash so she would follow him down the path, back through the park, back to the parking lot, to get away from Piper, no doubt.

Her heart gave a funny squeeze.

"I did get Laura kicked out of the veterinary program," she explained as they walked. "Only it wasn't because I was jealous. Far from it. It was because I caught her cheating. It was after class one day, and we'd all just handed in a final assignment for the semester. After I'd left the classroom, I realized my cell phone had fallen out of my pocket. When I got back to the room, I caught her rifling through the assignments while the teacher had stepped out. She was swapping her paper with mine."

"And her story about the professor?"

"I've barely had time to date, far less manage a highly unethical affair with one of my professors. That was just her way of trying to take the focus off her and to discredit me, not to mention the professor, who had his own doubts about her. After the investigation, it turned out she'd been cheating her way through the whole semester."

"I'm guessing that's not how she remembers it." Aiden thrust his chin back toward the off-leash park.

"Laura will believe what she wants to believe. In a way,

I feel kind of bad for her. I know how much she loves animals and wanted to work with them. But the program is tough. She never would have gotten very far. Besides, if I had to bring my sick pet to a veterinarian I wouldn't want one who didn't have the skill or knowledge to graduate on their own."

Aiden made some noncommittal noise in response. She wondered what he was thinking.

"She went to the media with her own version of the scandal, and it got completely out of hand. They ran the story without checking with the school first. Next thing you know, I'm crossing angry picket lines at school for weeks."

Aiden frowned. "That's not right."

"Once the newspaper heard of the real story, they printed a retraction."

"Did it help?"

"No. They buried it somewhere on page twenty-five. I guess the headline 'Newspaper Screws Up: Oops, Sorry' wasn't as catchy as 'Veterinary Violation: Student Wrongly Dismissed.' " She used sarcastic air quotes with her fingers. "Besides, the damage was done. Laura's slander campaign had reached enough of the campus that no one quite knew what to believe. They just knew to avoid me."

"That's terrible."

"It's been a lonely few years. Other students stayed clear of me. Not that I've had much time for friends, anyway." She shrugged it off. "But our professor got the worst of it. His reputation was damaged. The next week, he'd already been replaced. I think maybe he took a job at another university."

They walked in silence for a minute. Piper glanced at Aiden out of the corner of her eye. She wished she knew what was going through his mind. As good as she was at reading animals, Aiden remained a complete mystery to her.

"If you could go back?" he asked. "Would you make the same decision? Would you turn her in?"

Piper blew out a long breath. "Yeah. As terrible as it all turned out, I would have. Laura was wrong to do what she did."

And it was true. But deep down, Piper still wished it all could have gone so differently. That she could have avoided the public shame, the drama, the misplaced guilt. If only she hadn't left her cell phone behind, that her professor could have caught Laura in the act instead of her. But then again, maybe Laura would have gotten away with it. Maybe it would have been Piper forced to leave the program because she'd failed the assignment. No, as hard as it was, she'd done the right thing. She'd worked too hard to let someone like Laura take it all away from her.

"I thought once things died down, she'd move on with her life," Piper said. "But ever since, Laura has been harassing me any chance she gets. I was once a member of SFAAC. I used to fund-raise and protest with them on my free weekends. Then Laura weaseled her way in, spread her lies, turned certain members against me. It got toxic, so I left."

The steam that had built up inside of Piper from the argument condensed into tears, and without warning they filled her eyes and ran down her cheeks. She swiped at them with the back of her hand, but not before Aiden saw.

He reached into the sports jacket slung over his arm. Fishing out his pocket square, he handed it to her. If she hadn't been so grateful for it, she would have made up a new uniform rule about no handkerchiefs in a dog park—even a fashionable one.

"Thanks." She dabbed at the tears and tried to hand it back, but he waved it away. She tucked it into her own pocket. Maybe she'd keep it as a souvenir, a reminder of that not-a-date she once had with one of San Francisco's most eligible bachelors.

"Come on," he said. "Let's go back to my place."

The statement was so out of place, like a giraffe as a house pet, that she thought she misheard. "What?"

"I'll show you around and give you the codes to get in."

It took her a moment to comprehend what he was saying. "You mean, you still want me to work for you?" She couldn't keep the incredulity from seeping into her voice. "Even after all that?"

"No," he said. "It's *because* of all that."

Feeling tired, and confused, and emotionally drained, she stopped walking. "Come again?"

When he noticed she wasn't walking next to him, Aiden turned to face her. He drew close enough that she saw his eyes weren't just mint green; they also had a ring of brown around the pupil, making them appear larger, like all he wanted to see right then was her, to drink her in.

"I am confident that anyone as honest and ethical as you will take great care of Sophie."

When she didn't answer right away, he raised his eyebrows. "Will you be my dog walker?"

Piper stared into those eyes and felt herself get sucked right in. She wasn't sure she could say no even if she could afford to.

She nodded. "I will take great care of your wiener."

Underdog

Piper knew Aiden was rich, but she hadn't expected *this* rich. Sea Cliff rich.

She tailed his BMW back to his house, and the farther into the neighborhood they drove the more she became overly aware of her beater car. The imposing two- and three-story homes amplified the VW's rumbles and knocks as she followed him up the quiet, sloping streets of the cliffside neighborhood. She was relieved when Aiden pulled into the driveway of a Georgian-style mansion and she could kill the noisy engine.

She climbed out of the Bug and stared up at the grand whitewashed facade and rows of windows staring out beyond the cliffs. Her breath caught. She could sense Aiden approach and stand next to her, but she couldn't take her eyes off the magnificent structure.

"Nice little place you've got here," she told him.

"It's somewhere to hang my hat." He rapped on the hood of her car. "I see you didn't ride your horse today."

"No. I decided to go with something a little more modern."

"Modern?" he choked. "This thing's ancient."

"Hey. I prefer the term 'classic.' She's a 1979. I've had her since high school."

He opened his mouth, and immediately shut it—probably for the best. He settled on, "Come in. I'll show you around."

The interior of the mansion was no less impressive than the exterior, though considerably more contemporary. It was how she imagined an overpriced bachelor pad would look. Man-like, with clean lines, and grey. Lots of grey.

She slipped off her dog-park shoes at the front door, wary of the light grey welcome mat. After Aiden gave her the code to the alarm system, he took her around the house, showing her all the necessities: the washroom, where the dog food and toys were stored, the kitchen, where she could feel free to help herself to anything she needed.

Piper followed Aiden, listening to him, watching him in his own habitat. So far he'd always stuck out in her normal world, in her taxi, the rescue center, the dog park. Suddenly, she was the sore thumb in his world with her sweaty tank top and grass-stained socks on the hand-scraped hardwood floor. Of course, Colin padded from room to room like he owned the place.

They came to the living room view that overlooked the Golden Gate spanning the strait and, beyond that, the bay. It was a rare clear evening and the bridge stood out against the sparkling blue water and blushing spring sunset like two great vermillion ladders.

"Wow. Now that's a view," Piper said. "I can see why you bought this dump. Seems worth it now."

He chuckled at the joke but grew kind of quiet. "Actually, I didn't buy it. I inherited it when my father died. Along with Caldwell and Son Investments."

Piper's face went slack. "Oh God. I'm so sorry. I . . . I was just kidding about the dump thing."

"I know." He flashed her a wry look, his smile earnest, if a little sad. The magnificent view seemed to preoccupy him and he grew quiet. In the window's reflection Piper saw his expression had grown pensive.

She fidgeted uncomfortably next to him, thinking of a way to alter their conversation's collision course. They were fully enveloped in the famous awkward silence, something she was all too familiar with. Nobody ever knew what to say once they found out about her own father. For a moment, she considered sharing her own loss with Aiden, but she'd been enjoying their pleasant vibe, and she didn't want to derail it any more than she already had.

"Well, it's better than my view," she said. "My place looks out on an Indian restaurant."

"Sounds spectacular."

"Great samosas."

"You'll have to show me sometime."

Heat flashed across her face. With her embarrassment her eyes dropped to her feet, and she noticed the grass stains on her socks again. She wondered what she was doing flirting with him. This was all business. At least, she thought so. He'd only invited her back to show her around so she could do her job. But when she looked up again and caught him staring at her reflection, she hoped, for just a moment, that maybe it could be something. *Something more.*

Movement outside caught her attention and she shifted her focus to the stone patio below. Her gaze fell on a young woman lounging on one of the chairs. Bare legs kicked up on the cushions, she soaked in the spring sun, utterly relaxed in this mansion, in Aiden's world. Another Nicole, perhaps? But surely if this one hung out in his house when he wasn't around they knew each other well. Was she a girlfriend? Piper frowned, thinking samosas had sounded nice.

"Oh." Piper flinched away from the window, like it would be wrong to be seen. Like the naughty things she was thinking about Aiden were plastered all over her face. "I didn't know you had company."

"Company?"

Following her gaze, he spotted the woman too. Bringing up his fist, he tapped on the window. The woman started at the sound and tilted her beautiful face up. She gave a wave, her face breaking into a familiar smile. She sat up to slip on her pumps—no grass-stained socks for her—and disappeared from sight. Piper heard a door open somewhere in the house's depths, and a moment later the graceful brunette glided into the kitchen.

"Tamara," Aiden said. "This is Piper."

They shook hands and exchanged hellos.

"Tamara also works for me. She's my personal assistant."

Piper nodded, like this was all very interesting, but she couldn't help but notice a change in Aiden. His posture stiffened, he'd pulled down his shirtsleeves, and his expression turned distant, practiced. A professional stranger. Like he didn't want Tamara to catch him flirting with some grass-stained-sock-wearing dog walker. Maybe because his and Tamara's relationship was more personal than that of a boss and assistant. On top of that, Piper hadn't missed his words "also works for me," putting her in her place.

Right. It was just a job. That's why she was there in the first place. Absolutely nothing to feel disappointed about. And that little twinge in her chest? It must have been heartburn, that's all.

"I was showing Piper around the house," Aiden told Tamara. "She'll be walking Sophie while I'm at work."

"Oh, good," Tamara said. "Aiden works long hours. Too long," she chastised him teasingly.

"Well, at least Sophie will be taken care of."

"Yes. But who is going to take care of you?"

"Oh, you do a fine job of that." He smiled in an all too familiar way that made Piper take a mental note to pick up some antacids from the store.

She wanted to dislike the girl, not that she was jealous or anything. Samosas shamosas. But as Tamara squeezed his shoulder fondly Piper got a sincere vibe off the PA. She wasn't acting all beautiful and charming to rub it in Piper's face—it simply happened to be a side effect of absolute perfection. Self-consciously, Piper put one foot on top of the other, like that would help hide the grass stains.

An awkward silence settled over them—at least it felt awkward for her. Wanting nothing more than to get out of there, she said, "Well, I'd better go. It was nice to meet you, Tamara."

"You too." She flashed Piper a set of brilliant white teeth, but her left eye flickered like she had an involuntary twitch. The friendly curve to her mouth turned plastic, like it was melting off her face.

Piper pretended not to notice. Maybe it was a tic that Tamara was self-conscious about. Piper turned and headed for the entrance where she found Colin and Sophie curled up on the cool marble tiles together. She patted her leg and Colin trotted over.

Aiden picked up a sealed envelope from the table next to the door and handed it to her. "Here is the key."

She wanted to brush off the sudden seriousness that had settled over them like a warm-weather San Francisco fog, stifling and oppressive, to get back the Aiden from five minutes ago.

"The key to your place?" She took the envelope and

fanned herself with it, gasping like she couldn't catch her breath. "This is all moving so fast."

He'd been flirting with her at the park and ever since they got back to his place, so she expected an equally playful answer in return, but instead he said, "Well, Miss Summers. It's a pleasure doing business with you. If there are any problems, you have my cell phone number, or you can call my office. You may come over at any time you like Monday to Friday, but inform me of the approximate time. I will pay you every Friday unless you wish otherwise, and you can find the check on this table."

The abrupt change in his persona was so jarring that when he stuck his hand out to her she stared at it like he'd thrust a hedgehog at her. Finally, she reached out and shook it.

"Umm, thank you," she said.

He gave her hand a good, firm shake. And that was that.

Reaching around her, he opened the front door. In a daze, she stepped out onto the front porch, Colin following behind. Back in her sweltering car, sitting on molten lava, she turned to him. Maybe it was her imagination, but he seemed to be as mystified as she was.

"Well, that was certainly *something*."

Sick Pup

Aiden Caldwell had to be the most confusing, stupefying man that Piper had ever met. There was something between them. She was sure of it. It felt almost tangible. But then like a guillotine dropping, he would cut the emotion off like an unwanted head. And not just in front of Tamara, but in front of the cops after the taxi incident and when he left the center with Sophie.

Did she imagine it? Was she crazy? She didn't think so, but the only other witness she could consult with was Colin. At the next stoplight, she peered over at him in the passenger seat. He gazed back earnestly and gave a quiet whine—a sure sign of support if she ever saw one. Either that or he had to pee.

Since the moment she'd met the prosperous CEO the day before, her head had been so full of him and his wiener—and not the four-legged kind—that she hadn't been able to concentrate. But Piper had more important things to worry about than Mr. Handshake. Like her future.

And at that exact moment, her work phone rang, reminding her of just that.

She pulled over to answer it. It was an emergency call. A Lab retriever had an epileptic seizure while at home and the owners were bringing it in. Piper hung up and pulled back into traffic, heading straight for the hospital.

By the time she finished treating the tired pup and was on her way out the door again, there were two messages on her phone from the receptionist at Sam's Old World Singing Telegrams. She had a few last-minute bookings for telegram gigs.

Eager for the money and the distraction from Aideny thoughts, Piper dropped Colin off at home and picked up her costumes. Two of the events were parties downtown, and the last was a regular customer of hers. Telegram singers didn't usually have regulars, but Barney Miller wasn't what you would call regular.

She'd first met Barney at the post office. It was a long-term employee's retirement party and someone had ordered a singing telegram. It was fun, as telegrams go, but nothing special. Nothing out of the ordinary.

She hadn't noticed Barney then, but the next week Sam sent her back to the same post office. Lindsey said someone had specifically requested Piper. It was for a Mr. Barney Miller.

The telegram was for his birthday. However, no one at the post office could remember it being his birthday, and they could have sworn it was six months earlier, and who had ordered the telegram, anyway? But Barney acted surprised and Piper didn't think anything of it. Until she was called back for a third time. This time it was for someone else's birthday. But there was Barney, standing in the corner clapping along to her song.

The next week, she was sent to his house for a "Get well" telegram. He greeted her from his antique floral sofa, a pile of tissues scrunched up next to him. Piper couldn't help but notice he didn't sound sick and he didn't cough or sneeze once during her performance. She didn't want to dwell on what the tissues were for.

Each week she was hired to go to his place. Lindsey said the requests always came by e-mail, so there was no way to know if he sent them himself, which undoubtedly he had. But week after week Piper returned to sing "just thinking of you," "congratulations on your promotion," "good luck on your motorcycle exam"—but she doubted he could even ride a scooter—and "my deepest condolences." She was certain his grandmother had died three times already.

That evening, as she sang a farewell song for him in his Mission bungalow home, Barney's glassy eyes followed her movements with rapt attention. Piper held the sword high above her head, screaming Barney's Miller's name at the top of her lungs. Her pleated skirt sashayed around her thighs as she swung it around like a true highland warrior.

"Bravo! Bravo!" Barney called, and she dropped into a bow. "Can you sing it again?"

Piper pressed *stop* on her phone's music player, interrupting the haunting bagpipe that had wailed for background music. "You know I'm not supposed to. One performance. That's the rule."

Well, not really. That was *her* rule. Otherwise, Barney would keep her serenading him all evening.

"Please. One more time? I'm going to be gone for two weeks. I won't get to see you next week."

Piper sighed. She knew it wasn't a waste of time, because Barney always tipped better if she went two rounds. "All right. Just once more."

Picking up her broadsword, she cued up the Gaelic-themed music and pressed *play*. She returned to the middle of Barney's living room where he'd pushed the wingback chairs and antique coffee table aside for her visit. Clearing her throat, she joined the bagpipes.

"Oh, where has my Barney gone?
I been missing you, dear.
'Tis too long since I seen ye;
I'm wishing you were 'ere.
O'er yon hills I did seek ye,
Through brook and through field.
I looked up high and down low,
But not a thing did my search yield.
Oh, I fear you been slain.
Won't ye come back to me?
Lord deliver him safely,
My brave and gallant Barney."

He clapped and hooted from his usual spot on his French Provincial sofa. She gave another gracious bow. This time, when she bent over, she noticed a new addition to his décor. A large decorative mirror propped curiously against the wall behind her, at just the right angle to reflect her backside when she bent forward to bow—which he encouraged her to do every time she came over.

Shooting upright, she patted her short plaid skirt down, clenching her teeth against the swears and insults that rushed to her lips. At first she thought it strange how Barney requested that she perform in tartan, considering his trip wasn't to Scotland but to Pittsburgh. But now it made sense. Her plaid skirt was the shortest one she owned. He'd seen her wear it before.

Barney had always creeped her out in general, nothing specific, just a prickling along her skin like a spider crawling down her back. But the mirror crossed the line. He might have been steady income, but her self-respect was worth more than that.

She imagined him sending an e-mail to Lindsey earlier that day, requesting the Scottish theme after Googling some photos. The thought sent shivers down her spine. Goose bumps rose on her skin and she caught Barney staring at her bare thighs. Obviously he noticed too.

"What the hell is that?" She pointed at the mirror.

"What?" He licked his lips. "The mirror? Oh, I-I just bought that. Do you like it? It's rococo style. I saw it in the shop and adored the miniature carved scalloped shells on the outer trim. And the patina—"

"Why is it there?" she demanded.

He blanched at the fury in her voice. His cheeks that had been rosy during her performance drained of color. "You know how much I love antiques."

"No. I mean, why is it in that spot specifically?"

"I haven't decided where to put it," he mumbled. "Did you want me to move it?" He shifted on the couch but seemed reluctant to move the pillow that she noticed was placed across his lap.

"Like hell you didn't." Piper grabbed her phone and shoved it into her sporran. Plucking her coat off the chair, she wrapped it around her body and tied the belt in a knot. Make that a double knot. "You're a disgusting little weasel."

"Wait! Don't go. I haven't tipped you yet." Barney dug into his pants pocket, taking a moment too long to dig out a twenty-dollar bill. From the center of the couch he held it up for her. "You'll come back when I return from my vacation, right?"

"In your dreams, pal." She cringed as the mental image of him actually dreaming about her that night popped uninvited into her brain. Shaking it off, she beelined it for the front door.

"Wait. Wait! Here!" He reached back into his pocket again, this time pulling out more money. "Take it. Please."

She hesitated at the edge of the room, eyeing the wad of bills in his hand—they weren't small ones. She imagined her landlord waiting outside her apartment for her to come home, to ambush her, demanding rent for that month. Could she go home empty-handed? Aiden wasn't going to pay her until Friday. She could take the money from Barney and still storm out and never have to see the slimeball again.

Then the pillow slipped from his lap and fell to the floor, and she caught a glimpse of what hid beneath. She gagged. Forget that, she thought.

Choking on her own disgust, she whipped back around to the front door and "accidentally" knocked the rococo-style mirror with her sword as she passed it. A satisfying crack pierced the air as it hit the glass, then a musical chiming when the mirror shattered and the pieces fell to the hardwood floor.

"Whoops." She gasped innocently. "Did I just wreck the patina?" She wrenched open the door. "Don't call me again!" she yelled over her shoulder.

She slammed the door behind her and headed for her car. Reaching into her sporran, she pulled out her phone and texted Lindsey: *I'm finished at B.M.'s. Getting in my car now. You can call off the squad.*

Piper had worked out a system with Lindsey. She always texted before she went into Barney's and again after she escaped safely. That way, if Lindsey hadn't heard from her she knew to tell the cops they could find Piper tied up and gagged in Barney Miller's basement—she hoped not cut up into tiny pieces. She'd never thought he'd do it, of course, but for some reason the texts still made her feel better.

Barney had never laid a hand on her. His eyes, however, were another thing. The way they slithered up her body gave her the same gut reaction as if he'd reached out and grabbed a handful of boob. Over the last few years she'd dealt with all sorts of harassment. Catcalls, whistling, handsy drunks. But singing for Barney Miller was the only time she felt like she was doing something wrong. Something more obscene than singing telegrams.

The second she jumped in the Bug, she locked her car doors. While she fastened her seat belt, her phone dinged. It was Lindsey's response.

Safe for another week.

Safe forever, Piper replied. *I won't be going back there again. Don't book me with him. Will tell you about it on Monday.*

The good thing about the gig at Barney's was that it took her mind off Aiden for a few hours, but once she arrived back at home she was still wound up, now even more so. She decided to use it to her advantage, to get some study time in. However, between the colicky newborn in the unit below her and the horny newlyweds above her she knew there would be no concentrating.

Hoping for peace and quiet, she drove with Colin to the rescue center. She often studied there. Even the library could be noisy after school let out. And Starbucks was too expensive, considering her chai habit. She had just over three weeks left until her licensing exam. She'd worked too hard to let herself become distracted now. But even as she pulled into the center's parking lot and dug out the spare key Marilyn gave her for the building, her mind was still running over the events of that afternoon, trying to figure out exactly what it all meant.

There were moments when Aiden could be so approachable, a regular guy she could walk in the park or eat samosas with. But then he would pull a Jekyll-Hyde on her. It drove her crazy. And while she would have thought his smooth, hard-shelled CEO exterior would be a complete turnoff, all she could think about was how to crack that egg.

Once inside the center, she groped her way through the dark to the light switches behind the desk. The dogs were carrying on in the back, alerted by her presence. After she had a chance to say hello and they saw it was her and Colin, they settled down and resumed their normal conversations with one another.

Piper had grown so used to the barks, yips, and occasional growls. They were white noise to her, like the sound of crashing waves to a sailor or organ music to a minister. It felt like home.

Settling in for her normal study session, she put the kettle on for tea and opened the door to the back. Colin liked to come and go as he pleased, exploring and visiting the other dogs. Dropping her textbook down on the reception counter, she plopped herself into the chair and attempted to put Aiden out of her head. To fill it so full of fleas and molting, tapeworms and ingrown toenails, of rabies and lesions, that it would squeeze the thought of Aiden out like an unwanted tick burrowed deep in her brain.

But it wasn't long before she stared into space, imagining that adorable bedhead hair, the way his one dimple betrayed him when he tried not to smile, how affectionate he was with Sophie and Colin, and that rigid posture that she wanted to bend and contort in all sorts of positions in her bed—

There was a smash, the sound of glass shattering. Something banged on the counter in front of her. Her pencil case exploded, pens flying everywhere.

She held up an arm in front of her face to deflect the ballpoint shrapnel. Strands of her hair shifted in a breeze as something flew by her. A crash behind her, the sound of splashing water.

Piper screamed and whirled around. The chair went spinning across the room. Her heart throbbed in her chest, her legs shaking. She gripped the desk for support.

Colin was at her heels in an instant, shaking himself. In the back, the dogs were all losing it, startled by the commotion.

It took her darting eyes a few moments to see what was wrong. The large fish tank that sat behind the reception desk was completely drained. There was a gaping hole in the glass, cracks spreading from it like spiderwebs. She looked down at the floor. Her feet were soaking wet.

Out of the corner of her eye, she saw movement on the floor. Subtle flutterings and flip-floppings around her Walmart Special shoes. The ladies.

"Oh, my God."

Tiptoeing over the wriggling creatures, she ran to the dingy little kitchen and filled the first thing she could find with water: the coffeepot.

Scooping up the goldfish, she laid them inside. While she hadn't come across a chapter in her textbooks on emergency aquatic resuscitation, she didn't think it was possible to give them CPR. Although, that would give a whole new meaning to the term "fish-kiss."

"Please be okay," she said. "Please be okay."

After a few seconds, though a little lethargic the goldfish began waving their fins, propelling themselves around their new, considerably downsized home. Their eyes seemed to be bulgier than normal, their mouths popping open and closed as if they were scandalized.

"Don't worry," Piper told them. "That's better now, isn't it?"

They swished their fancy ball gowns indignantly as Piper set them on the counter. It was still possible that she would lose more than one to the toilet bowl by morning due to stress or injuries. She would have to keep a close eye on them.

Now that everyone was rescued and accounted for, she added a couple drops of water conditioner to the coffeepot and went to check on the frantic dogs in the back room. To soothe them, she offered some extra treats and spoke to them in a calm, comforting manner. However, she felt anything but, and she could have used a treat herself.

Once the dogs were more or less settled, she searched for the source of the damage. She found it in the fish tank between the sunken treasure and the pirate ship. It was a bundle with an elastic band wrapped around it.

Cautious of the broken glass, she plucked the bundle out of the wreckage. Surprised by the weight, she turned it over in her hands. It was a brick with a piece of paper wrapped around it.

Piper focused on the front entrance, at the gaping hole in the door window, at the glass scattered across the linoleum floor. The path of destruction continued to where it hit the desk. She'd been inches away from requiring her own first-aid treatment.

Carrying the hefty load to the counter, she slipped the rubber band off and removed the piece of paper. It was soaked through with tank water, but when she unfolded it the message read loud and clear.

Her own mouth popped open from the scandal of it.

It read: *Get out! Or I'll make you.*

11

Talk to the Paw

The police officer's boots crunched on the broken glass. He assessed the damage, this time from a new angle. Piper didn't know what was so tough to figure out. Brick fly through window; brick hit fish tank; tank go splash. Seemed simple enough to her.

She knew she wasn't irritated with him so much as the near head wound experience. Even now nerves shook her hands. But so far, Officer Tucker had proved himself less than empathetic or even mildly concerned. Maybe there were more important crimes to solve or wrongdoers to vanquish. He acted like this was the equivalent of hoodlums spray-painting a garbage can. Well, maybe it was. But it was *her* garbage can.

He took out his phone and typed a few words, probably searching for the nearest coffeehouse for a post-investigation latte. Consulting his notepad again, he wandered back to where she watched from the side.

"So you didn't see anyone when it happened? No one you could identify?"

"No. Like I said, I was busy studying." Or staring off into space imagining Aiden without a suit.

"And you said you arrived at approximately nine thirty p.m.?"

"That's correct."

"And did you see anyone when you arrived? Anyone loitering around the building? Maybe a car you noticed parked in the lot or on the street nearby watching the place?"

"No. Not that I can remember." Piper's skin crawled at the thought of being watched, and she thought of her altercation with Barney Miller a few hours earlier. Of course, she'd mentioned his name first, but she'd never actually seen the culprit.

She could hear Marilyn in the back, soothing the dogs in that "keep calm and carry on" way of hers. Piper had called her right after she got off the phone with the police. The dedicated manager came right away, concerned for her guests, as she called them. She liked to think that they were only staying for a short time before someone came to adopt them.

The bell above the entrance door dinged as someone entered. Piper was trying to read Officer Tucker's notepad upside down. She figured it was the other cop, so she didn't turn around until Officer Tucker said, "Sorry, sir. You can't be in here."

Piper had been anxiously awaiting the crack CSI team to arrive and bag the evidence, unveil invisible footprints, search for microscopic clues, so when she spun around his face was the last she expected to see.

"Aiden?"

"You know this man?" Officer Tucker asked.

"It's all right," Marilyn said, coming in from the back, She was dragging a piece of cardboard to the front with her. "He's the owner."

"The owner," Piper repeated. "The owner of what?"

"The property, dear. What else? Here, Piper, could you help me with this?" Marilyn handed her the cardboard. "We can use it to board up the window once the officers are all finished here."

Piper took the board numbly. "You own this property?" She almost sounded indignant, like they were possibly lying to her.

"Thank you for coming, Mr. Caldwell." Marilyn shook his hand. "But you didn't need to concern yourself at an hour like this."

"Oh, it's no problem at all. I just thought I'd come by and take a look."

"Well, how about I make us all a pot of coffee?" Marilyn hurried off to the kitchen.

Once she left, Aiden turned right back to Piper, his expression full of concern and surprise. "I didn't know you would be here."

"Sir," Officer Tucker interrupted. "May I have your full name for the record, please?"

Both Piper and Aiden spoke at the same time. "Aiden Caldwell."

"I was studying." Piper still stared at him like he'd claimed to be the king of England. "You're the new property owner?"

The officer cleared his throat to get attention. "I'd like to ask you a few questions too, Mr. Caldwell. If you have some time."

"Yes, certainly," Aiden replied without looking away from Piper. "That's why I came to the center in the first place," he told her. "My company recently bought this land. A few weeks ago, I came to renew the lease and discuss some future business with Marilyn. That's when I met Sophie."

Officer Tucker's pen hovered readily over his notepad. "And who's Sophie?"

"My dog," Aiden told him, and then to Piper, "Were you hurt?"

"No. I'm fine."

"That's good."

"Do you two need a minute?" the officer asked, although it didn't sound like he was offering so much as making a point.

Aiden didn't seem to notice. "If I'd known you were here, I would have come sooner."

"Oh, but the ladies were hurt," Piper said.

"And who are these ladies?" Officer Tucker asked. "Do they require medical attention?"

"Why are the ladies in the coffeepot?" Marilyn called from the kitchen.

The officer's forehead creased. "The ladies are in the coffeepot?"

"The fish tank broke!" Piper called back. "They're our goldfish," she explained to the officer.

"Tea then?" Marilyn sang back.

"Yes, thank you," Aiden replied.

"Excuse me," Officer Tucker snapped. "May we continue, please?"

Piper had answered the cop's questions three times over Aiden's sudden appearance was a lot more interesting at that moment, but Officer Tucker's tone of voice sobered the CEO up.

"Yes, of course," Aiden said. "Go ahead."

"Do either of you know of anyone who would possibly have a vendetta against the rescue center? Anyone with a grudge? Disgruntled employees?"

Marilyn shuffled out of the small kitchen with a tray of four mismatched mugs. "A grudge? Oh, dear. Do you think this was a personal attack?"

"Well, I can't say conclusively, but considering the note attached to the brick, I would speculate so."

"Well, there are the neighbors," she said. "They've been complaining about the noise for some time."

"The noise?"

"Yes. We only have a small courtyard in the back and dachshunds can be noisy for such a small dog, on account of their large lungs, you see. That's where they get that barrel chest from." She stuck out her own chest, mimicking it. "There are a lot of residential buildings surrounding us and my little guests can make quite the racket during playtime."

"Any neighbors in particular?"

"I don't have any names specifically. A whole group of them, I suppose. They petitioned for the city to do something about it on several occasions. We would build a sound-reducing fence, but they're rather expensive."

As Piper thought about potential suspects, she recalled her run-in with Laura earlier that day. "There's someone else. A local animal rights activist that belongs to a group called SFAAC."

"Why would an activist have a problem with a dog shelter?"

"It's a personal issue. I had a confrontation with her during a rally in the Presidio today." She relayed the events of that afternoon, remembering Laura's parting words to her.

"She threatened you?" he asked. "Did you report this to the police?"

"No. I didn't really think anything of it. She's made plenty of personal threats against me over the last few years. Just figured she was full of crap. I've lodged previous complaints about her with the police."

"Oh, I see." The officer made another note. "Do you have a restraining order against this person?"

"No." She scowled. "Not yet, anyway."

Marilyn frowned, watching the pen scribble across the

page. “Do you think she should take out a restraining order against this girl? I mean, if she’s a possible suspect. Maybe it could be a way to prevent further harassment.”

“I can’t say for sure, ma’am. Unless you know for certain it was her. Don’t worry, I will let you know if you need to take further action,” he assured her.

She didn’t look assured, so Piper reached out and squeezed her shoulder. Marilyn mumbled something about sugar and disappeared back into the kitchen.

He jotted a few more notes down. “Mr. Caldwell, do you have anything to add?”

“Well, the company is always receiving threats. It wouldn’t be the first time my property has been vandalized simply due to the association with my company.”

“And what company is that?”

“Caldwell and Son Investments.”

Another note. “Can you think of any reason why someone would target this property specifically?”

“Well, the recent property sale would have been pubic record, but . . .” He hesitated, turning to Piper. “The briefcase.”

“The one in my taxi?” Piper asked.

“You drive a taxi?” Officer Tucker asked.

“I did. Before it was stolen.”

“With my briefcase inside,” Aiden added. “Which contained the recently signed documents for the property transfer.”

Piper frowned, thinking back to the day before—although it seemed much longer. “You think that whoever stole my cab might have done this?”

“Or,” he said, “maybe it wasn’t a coincidence that your cab was stolen with my briefcase.”

Piper wondered if he might be right. Sure, she’d been pushing her luck that day with all three jobs, but she still found it hard to believe she was unlucky enough to have her cab stolen too. Maybe it was his bad luck and not hers.

"But that still doesn't explain why the car thief would want us to get out of the neighborhood," she said.

"Was a report filed for this incident?" the cop asked, breaking her train of thought.

"Yes," Piper said. "Just yesterday afternoon."

He made another note on his pad while Piper and Aiden shared a worried glance. Finally, he clicked his pen closed and tucked the notepad away.

"Okay, well, I think that will be all for now. I'll contact you if I need anything further."

Marilyn reappeared from the kitchen and took his cup. "Do you think my guests will be safe, Officer? Should we be worried about another attack?"

"For now, let's hope this is an isolated incident. It doesn't appear as though there was malicious intent. We'll chalk this one up to mischief, for the time being."

"Tell that to the brick that nearly rearranged my face," Piper said, a little insulted.

"I understand," he said, "but at that time the center had been closed for the day. There was no way to know anyone was inside, except for the dogs, and they're kept in the back. In my experience, this type of vandalism is just a warning. No harm meant."

Piper scowled at the officer, thinking about the poor ladies, but he didn't seem to care about them.

Marilyn saw the argument on her face and swooped in. "Well, thank you for coming, Officer. I'll walk you out."

Piper's glare session was interrupted when Aiden reached out to her. This time, it wasn't for a handshake. He laid a hand on her shoulder, warm and comforting. For the millionth time that day, she remembered what his hand had felt like in hers. Her palm twitched with the desire to feel it again.

"Are you sure you're all right? You seem rattled."

"Yeah. I'm okay. Thanks."

While she was still shocked to see him there, his presence calmed her. His confidence, his I'm-the-boss demeanor, all the things that had annoyed her earlier that day when she left his house. She must have been more rattled than she realized, because with his hand lingering she felt drawn to him, to lean against him for a second. But what was she? Some helpless damsel in distress? Shaking off the longing, she gave him her best "keep calm and carry on" smile.

"I'm fine," she said again. "Just fine, fine, fine."

Marilyn returned, and Aiden's hand dropped to his side.

"What a business, all this," she said. "Who would want to attack a dog shelter?"

"Scum," Piper said. "Don't worry. I'm sure they'll catch the guy." Not that she had all that much confidence in Officer Tucker. She said it more to reassure the woman, since Piper could already see that Marilyn would be up worrying half the night. Much like she would be.

"Perhaps I should cancel my vacation," Marilyn said.

"What? No. Don't be silly. You've been looking forward to this trip for months."

"I was planning on going on a Caribbean cruise this week with my sister and her kids," she told Aiden. "But I don't think it's such a good idea at a time like this."

Piper interrupted her. "You're going. And you'll have a great time. I'll take care of things here. I'll be fine."

"I'm sure you will, dear, but—"

"But nothing. Trust me. Go." Piper knew she could handle it. Along with clinical shifts at the vet hospital, her telegram job, studying for her licensing exam, dealing with the cops, and graduation, oh, and don't forget her new job with the world's most distracting boss . . . She wasn't taking on too much. Nope, not at all.

"I'll be fine," she said again, just to hear herself say it.

Marilyn clicked her tongue and walked over to the desk, fishing around in the junk drawer. After a moment, she plucked a roll of duct tape from its mysterious depths. "Maybe you're right. Even if I stayed, I'm not sure what good an old woman like me would do fretting about the place."

Piper made a show of rolling her eyes for Marilyn. She always referred to herself as an "old woman," but she was barely in her sixties. Hell, she could have passed for early fifties. And Piper had a feeling she knew it too.

Marilyn handed the roll to Piper. "Well, Mr. Caldwell, it was nice of you to come. Is it customary to check on your properties yourself if something happens?"

"Not usually. I wanted to come in person to make sure everything was okay. As you well know, I have a *vested interest* in this particular property."

Marilyn inclined her head and gave a knowing smile—or was it Piper's imagination? "Of course."

Piper's shoulder still felt warm where Aiden's palm had rested, but now he avoided her questioning look. She hoped that she was his "vested interest," but the exchange that passed between him and Marilyn was a strange one. It spoke of confidentiality, like there was a loop, and Piper was out of it. Loopless.

"Well, we appreciate your concern," Marilyn said. "Piper, would you mind helping me finish up here and settle the guests before heading home?"

"Sure, no problem."

Grabbing a chair from the corner of the room, Piper dragged it in front of the broken pane and stepped up. She reached down for the cardboard resting against the wall, but Aiden got to it first. He traded her for the duct tape in her hand.

"I'd like to stay behind and help, if you don't mind."

Piper opened her mouth to say she didn't need any help, but Marilyn answered before she could.

"Oh, certainly," she said. "Thank you. Well, if you've got a handle on things here, I'll check on the guests and grab a broom for all this glass."

The woman mumbled to herself as she headed into the back. The door closed behind her, and a silence fell over Aiden and Piper. She held the cardboard while he ripped off pieces of tape to secure it in place.

After a couple of minutes spent gnawing at her lip, she asked, "Why didn't you tell me you owned the property?"

He used his teeth to tear off another piece. "I suppose I just didn't think of it. I was being honest when I said that I like to keep my business life and my personal life separate. I know it's a bit old-school, but isn't that the golden rule? Don't mix business with pleasure?"

Piper frowned. "Right." She was dying to ask why he'd really come. What was his vested interest? He and Marilyn had done everything but tap the sides of their noses to hint at their little secret, but Piper supposed it was none of her business. No loop for her.

Aiden pressed the last piece of tape in place. Piper went to jump off the chair, but he reached up and put his hands around her waist. He helped her down, his arms and torso flexing beneath his shirt with what, she imagined, was thanks to a well-established gym regimen. Gym hater or not, she *needed* to join that gym. Just to look, of course. There was no harm in that, right?

When she was firmly back on the floor, he hesitated before pulling away, like he wanted to say something. That afternoon, he'd made it clear that she was just another employee. But the way his eyes softened, his hands still gripping her waist, made her doubt that.

"So, is this business?" she asked. "Or pleasure?"

The door to the back swung open, and Aiden's hands dropped to his sides.

"All right then," Marilyn sang out as she rounded the desk. "It seems the little ones have settled down already. I'll quickly sweep up. I don't think we can do any more here tonight. Might as well go home and get a good night's sleep."

"Oh, well, that's a relief," Aiden said, a little jumpy. "It was a pleasure, seeing you again, Marilyn." He shook her hand and turned to do the same to Piper.

Beating him to it, she stuck out her hand. He only paused a second before taking it, but long enough that Piper knew it caught him off guard. She shook his hand firmly, no-nonsense. Just business. They wouldn't want to confuse that thick sexual tension for pleasure, or anything.

"Thank you for coming, Mr. Caldwell," Piper said. "Good night."

Turning on her heel, she grabbed her backpack, whistled for Colin, and headed for her Volkswagen.

12

Teach an Old Dog New Tricks

Piper kicked off her military boots in Aiden's front entry and sighed like she'd just fought the battle of her life. Well, it certainly felt like she had.

A group of off-duty military boys had hired her to welcome their friend home from active service. Apparently, they thought it would be a good idea to engage her in a bit of friendly hand-to-butt combat. Good thing she had her pistols locked and loaded—with water, that is. The effect was like a cold shower and kept the troops at bay long enough for her to finish her song and make a hasty retreat. Between a waiting room of never-ending patients at the veterinary hospital that morning and the telegram, she was ready for a little fresh air in the park.

Reaching into her holsters, she pulled the guns out and laid them down on the entrance table. That's when she noticed the small box of imported chocolates. The little tag on them said: *Piper.*

She gasped and did a little happy dance in the foyer. Best tip ever! She wondered if he'd ever left anything like that for Tamara. The thought made her scowl at herself. She wasn't sure where that had come from, but she shoved it away. The tag said: *Piper.* The fact that at some point that day he'd been thinking about her when she wasn't around made her grin wickedly—in a totally professional, noninterested manner. She slid the box into her bag. Her day was looking up.

"Sophie!" she called out.

A light padding of paws on the hardwood announced her approach down the hall. Colin and Sophie gave their usual kisses hello. When they were finished, they both turned to Piper expectantly as if to say, *Okay, we're ready to be entertained now. Dance, monkey. Dance.*

"I need to change first; then we'll go to the park," she said.

She turned to head for the washroom and immediately got a faceful of silk tie. She yelped in surprise and jumped back. It was Aiden. Leaning against the wall, she laid a hand over her pounding chest, which was covered with nothing more than a camo sports bra.

"Sorry," Aiden said. "I didn't mean to scare you."

She heaved a sigh. "I'll forgive you, since you live here and all. I just didn't know you'd be at home."

"I had some extra time between meetings this afternoon and thought I'd run home for a late lunch." He seemed a bit edgy, like he had at the center the night before, like he was afraid of being caught. Again, his attractive assistant, Tamara, popped into her head, and she wondered if that could be why.

"But now that we're both here, maybe I'll join you for your walk. If you don't mind."

"You're the boss," she said.

"But I should have made it clear before. There's a strict no guns policy in my house." He pointed at the fluorescent pink water pistols.

She laughed. "I just finished a telegram job. I was about to change."

"Oh, please. Don't change on my account. In fact, I would feel much safer being escorted by a soldier."

"I don't think you need protection from all the poodles."

"No, but there's something about a girl in uniform." His edge had smoothed right out. A little too smooth, she thought as his eyes roamed over her tight midriff.

She could feel her face turning the same shade as her water pistols. "If it's all the same to you, I think I'll go change."

"Yes, ma'am." He saluted her. "We can take my vehicle."

She gasped in offense. "You don't want to ride in the classic?"

"Classic?" He laughed. "I'll show you a classic."

"All right. All right. We'll take yours then."

Piper stepped into the bathroom to change out of her fatigues and into her civvies. She was glad she brought something more flattering to wear that day. The breezy bohemian tunic and tight yoga shorts would keep her cool in the hot sun, but they were cute enough to show off her assets. Not that she cared what Aiden thought, or anything. Nope, not at all. But as Zoe would say, it would show the boy what he was missing out on.

She stepped back into the hall and noticed that Aiden had also made a wardrobe change. He'd swapped his usual business attire for a plaid shirt, cargo shorts, and tennis shoes. The ensemble was clearly new.

"I see you took my advice about the uniform," she said.

He gave a self-conscious tug on his shirt. "I haven't had a chance to put the wrinkles in yet."

"Looks good." She tried not to notice his toned arms peeking beneath his short sleeves as she headed for the foyer.

"Actually, we'll head out through the garage." He nodded toward a door in the hall. But when he opened it and flicked on the light, she thought "garage" was a bit of an understatement. It was more like an airplane hangar.

Her eyes widened. She took in the line of cars that could have been a museum for the evolution of the automobile. "You know, some people collect stamps or postcards."

"Well, I prefer e-mail, and I've been too busy to travel much except for business."

"So cars, then." She nodded. "Naturally."

She suddenly recalled the last time her mom tricked her into talking to her brother. He'd boasted about the classic car he'd been eyeing and she imagined he dreamed of having a garage just like Aiden's one day. The collection before her became a little less impressive.

"I only own these five. Well, eight if you count the ones I keep at the cabin."

Only eight. Meanwhile, she could barely keep the one running. Was he deliberately showing off with his nonchalance, or did he really not notice? And something told her the word "cabin" didn't quite cut it, either.

Sophie and Colin hopped down the wooden steps. Toenails clicking on the treated cement floor, they disappeared between the cars to explore. Piper followed them to take a closer look. She strolled by the first one.

"Jaguar Roadster," she said. "Nineteen-fifty . . ." She turned to him.

"Five. E-Type," he said. "Good guess."

"Good car." She pointed to the next one, painted a sparkling copper. "Nineteen-seventies Porsche."

His eyebrows shot up, clearly impressed. "Nineteen-seventy-six, nine-eleven turbo. You're not bad at this."

"I told you I like classics. I just can't afford a real one. My dad used to own a 1968 Shelby. He preferred domestic."

"He has good taste. I prefer imports myself."

"I noticed." Three more cars sparkled at the other end,

one of which was a Ferrari from the seventies. The next space held his BMW, which she assumed he drove as an everyday car. If every day you were stinking, filthy rich and didn't mind if people knew it. What was wrong with a good ol' reliable Ford Escort? Or maybe a Hyundai Accent, if he liked imports?

"So which one are we taking?"

He nodded to the last in line, a silver convertible with a red leather interior. "The Aston Martin DB five. Nineteen-sixty-three." He grinned at her like a ten-year-old showing off his shiny new bicycle. "Left-hand drive. Only nineteen of these were ever made."

"Oh, if we must." She managed to feign indifference for a whole two seconds before her expression cracked and her grin matched his. Okay, so it was a bit better than an Accent.

Aiden whistled for Sophie, who click-clacked her way across the cement floor to him. He folded an old blanket and laid it across the backseat. Plucking her up, he set her on top of it, followed by Colin.

Piper cringed at the sight of their tiny feet padding all over the blanket, their nails digging in. "Will the blanket be enough to protect the leather?"

"Oh sure. Besides, things are meant to be used. They're more fun to play with than to put behind glass and stare at. Or why bother owning them?" He slipped around to her side of the car and popped the door open for her. "My lady," he said in a mock serious tone.

She slid into the passenger seat and tucked her legs in while he shut the door. Crawling behind the wheel, he turned the key. The engine purred to life. His foot nudged the accelerator, pumping it a few times. The room swelled with the rich growl, and his smile widened.

Piper watched him, sitting in his casual clothes, relaxed and enjoying his man toy. She couldn't imagine herself fitting into a life like his, into the same world. What did a guy like Aiden know about hardships—besides the loss of his father, she amended.

Everything had been handed to Aiden: his money, his house, his company. How could he relate to her, to appreciate the things she'd accomplished? No matter how small they might seem to him, they were big to her. Monstrous even. He'd said he owned eight cars like he was referring to pairs of socks.

No, someone like Tamara seemed better suited for him. Polite, well mannered, sophisticated, and clearly comfortable when surrounded by all that luxury. But as Aiden slipped on his sunglasses and flashed her a grin, she thought she could at least sit back and enjoy the view.

He tapped the button to raise the garage door and backed the car out. They wound down the sloping streets of Sea Cliff toward the Presidio, the wind whipping past them. Piper released her hair from its messy bun and shook out her locks.

Tilting her face to the sun, she put on her sunglasses and soaked up the view. It felt good to have the wind blow through her hair. No air-conditioning necessary. Sophie and Colin seemed to be enjoying it as well. They sat on the bench seat, their noses stuck over the sides of the car, sniffing the air.

"So this is a classic, huh?"

Aiden seemed pleased by her reaction. "Told you."

"So I would have thought a big shot like you would be too busy to come home for lunch."

He shifted uncomfortably in his seat. "Well, I managed to sneak away. But don't tell on me. My boss is a real slave driver." He rolled his eyes.

"Tell me about it. Mine is exactly the same. He actually makes me show up for work at some point, and he leaves me chocolate."

"What an asshole."

"I know, right?" she said. "Thanks, by the way."

"Just trying to keep your psychotic tendencies at bay. I have to be careful, with you bringing guns into my house."

"A girl has to protect herself," she said. "It's a dangerous city. My taxi was stolen the other day, you know. Right from under my nose."

"I know how you feel, but I have my guard dog to protect me now." He rolled to a stop at a red light and glanced over his shoulder. "Isn't that right, Sophie?"

In response, she leaned on the back of his seat and gave his ear a sloppy kiss.

"That's some killer you got there." Piper laughed. "So was this your dad's car? Or is restoring classics an interest of your own?"

"It started as my hobby, but we worked on it together. We rebuilt the engine years ago."

"You rebuilt an engine?" she said in disbelief.

"Hey, you don't have to say it like that. I'm not just a pretty face, you know. I've got depth."

"Depth?"

"Yeah," he said, going for complete seriousness. "I'm like the ocean."

"An ocean that rebuilds engines."

"Yes. Here, I'll prove it."

Reaching over, he grabbed Piper's hand and placed it on the stick shift. He covered it with his own. She inhaled as her nerve endings went into overdrive, delighting in the warmth of his palm, the gentle sweep of his fingers, the unexpected intimacy of the touch.

The light turned green and he took off. He shifted from first to second. When he tried to take it into third, he had to jiggle it a little to get it home.

"Did you feel that?" he asked.

Oh, she certainly felt something.

"After we rebuilt the engine, we took it for a spin and it was jumping out of gear, so I had to replace the cogs in the gearbox. It was my first attempt and I ended up misaligning them." His smiled faded as he turned the next corner. "That was right before my father passed away. I've never gotten around to fixing it."

"Well, it's still pretty amazing," she said. "Very James Bond. It's almost as nice as mine."

"Almost," he agreed. She noticed that he still had his hand clasped around hers over the shifter, cupping it as he moved it into fourth, and she wasn't in a rush to remove it.

"So did you buy all the other cars yourself?"

"All handpicked. My dad wasn't a car collector," he said. "That was all my addiction. After he passed, he left me the house, but everything in it is mine. I had to make it my own, you know? Otherwise, I would have felt like I was living with his ghost."

She remembered when her mom had to sell their farm after Piper's dad died. Piper would have done anything to stay there. Not just because she loved the animals, but because everything reminded her of him. It kept him with her. From the feel of the horse brush in her hand right down to the smell of the fresh hay she used to help him stack. Even now, years later, over the scent of brine wafting in from the bay and the fumes from the old engine chugging away she could smell it. For just a moment, it brought her back to him.

She wondered if her brother had come around to help out, would they have been able to keep the farm? But she didn't like to go down that path. What was done was done. Ethan had his own life to live and decisions to make. She knew he wasn't to blame. Her father still would have died, either way, and they probably still would have lost the farm. But at the time, Ethan couldn't have known that. It was his apathy that she resented, his reluctance to take action to help his family.

"You don't think keeping some of his stuff would have made you feel close to him?" she asked Aiden. "Like a part of him was still here?"

"Not for me," he said. "I don't think things make the person. Everything I need in order to feel close to him is up here." He tapped the side of his head. "He taught me everything I know. He was a good businessman. Very old-school, so some of my business ideals might seem a bit archaic because of it, but he was successful, so he must have been doing something right. And now everything I don't know I fake."

She narrowed her eyes playfully. "I knew you were a fraud."

"Yup. I learned that from him too. Confidence was important when I took over as CEO of the company."

"How long ago was that?"

"Five years. When I was twenty-five. Everyone looked at me like I was some dumb privileged kid who didn't know what was going on."

"And did you?"

"Hell, no. But you know what they say. Nothing in life worth having comes easy. For years I worked twelve-hour days, seven days a week, until I got good at the job." He said it with a weary acceptance, making Piper rethink her earlier assumption that he didn't have to work hard for anything.

It's not like she knew any other rich people personally, other than her brother. Could she have been drawing parallels that weren't really there? Now that she thought about it, Ethan was more about showmanship than taking pride in his work and wouldn't ever work on his own car. He'd drive it to the nearest shop and toss the keys to the mechanic like he was Mario Andretti.

"So that's what you did to change everyone's mind? Worked your tail off for it?"

"That, and in the meantime, when it comes to confidence, you fake it till you make it. He always said that. My dad." He had a wistful expression on his face, that one cheek dimpling. "That, and if you're ever feeling caught off guard or have lost control over a situation you can't go wrong with a good, firm handshake. It's like a reflex now. A nervous twitch."

"So I've noticed." She bit her lip as he glanced her way, but if he noticed she was teasing he didn't say anything.

So what did that mean? That she caught him off guard? That she made him feel out of control? The idea sent a giddy wave through her. At the next intersection, she had the urge to take off her seat belt and climb over to his side of the car, to straddle him and kiss him already. It was just a kiss, after all. Not like she was marrying the guy.

But instead, she took the opportunity to pull her hand away and play with the dogs in the back. She reminded herself of all the reasons she'd been reluctant to go down that path—although the specific reasons weren't coming to her at the moment. *You're his dog walker*, Piper told herself. *This is just business.*

And she hoped that one day soon she'd believe that.

"So, did it work?" she asked him. "The faking it?"

"I'm still learning every day. But I have a lot of good, experienced people around me to draw from. Like Larry Williams, my Chief Operations Officer, my right-hand man. He's been with the company from the start. I couldn't have made it without him." He glanced over at her. "You would have seen him in the meeting the day we met."

"Oh, I've pretty much erased that afternoon from my

memory. I don't even recall which meeting you're talking about."

"Not at all? So when did we officially meet then?"

She thought for a moment. "I guess it was later that day at the center."

He peered over his sunglasses at her, cheek dimpling. "Is that before or after you were molested by a German shepherd?"

"Scratch that. I've forgotten that entire day."

"Oh, but that was a good day," he said. "I liked that day."

"Why? Because you enjoyed my suffering? Is that how you get Aiden Caldwell's attention? By falling flat on your face and making a complete ass of yourself?" Her cheeks started to burn, so she tilted her head away to stare out the passenger side.

"Hey." When she didn't look over, he shook her shoulder playfully, trying to get her attention. "Oh, come on." He laughed. "It was funny."

She groaned. "I was humiliated."

"You were memorable." And by the way he said it, she knew it was a compliment.

Piper was memorable.

There were worse things. She supposed that's what made him follow her out of his building in the first place and what made him ask her to be his dog walker. Maybe that's even what kept him walking in the park with her until his late lunch "hour" turned into two, then three, until she had to drag herself away because she was going to be late for a telegram gig. And maybe that's what made him available for lunch the next day. And the next.

And the next.

And the next.

Dog Dilemma

Knock, knock, knock.

Piper peeked out the peephole in her apartment door and leapt back, thankful for her sock feet that muffled her stumbling footsteps. It was her landlord, Steve. And man, was she not ready to see him. Or rather, her bank account wasn't ready. She'd used her most recent paycheck to handle the pesky little matter of her past due utility bills.

Colin trotted in from her bedroom to see who was at the door. Thankfully, the one—and only—trick she'd ever taught him was how not to bark when someone came to the door. Otherwise, she wouldn't have been able to keep him a secret for so long. She crept away from the door, afraid that Steve might see her shadow pass underneath, or hear her pounding heart, or smell the lack of money on her.

The clock on the microwave said she was already running late to open the center with Addison and Zoe. They'd be waiting for her. She gave it two minutes before very carefully, very quietly, tiptoeing back to the peephole. Steve hadn't left, and it didn't look like he had plans to do so anytime soon. He unfolded a lawn chair, setting it up to face her door. She watched him sit down, cross his legs, and unfold a newspaper.

It was a standoff. She could be stuck there for hours. Steve would probably wait her out. Didn't he have anything better to do?

She still didn't have the money for rent that month. Aiden was going to pay her on Friday, but it was only Saturday. It would be two weeks late by then. If only she could avoid Steve until she had it. Then she could hand over the check like, "Whoops! Must have slipped my mind." He couldn't evict her if he couldn't find her. Right . . . ?

Grabbing her backpack from the sofa, she coaxed Colin in by throwing a treat in the bottom. Once he was inside, she zipped it up and slipped it on her back. She picked up her shoes from beside the door and carried them over to the window that had a fire escape access. Slipping them on, she prepared to climb out. Piper drew the curtains aside and reached for the window latch, but her hand froze. Instead of her usual glorious view of the Indian restaurant across the street, her sight line was obscured by a message.

Lying whore!

The red spray paint dripped down the outside of the windowpanes. She gaped at it for a few seconds. It wasn't tough to figure out who-dun-it: Laura. Piper was impressed by how the activist managed to spell it from the outside so she could read it from the inside. Hell, she was surprised Laura could spell at all.

Knock, knock, knock.

This time the banging fell heavier and more insistent, rattling the lock. Jolted out of her shock, Piper unlocked the window and slid it high enough for her to sneak out. She would have to call to the cops at the rescue center, far away from her landlord. Maybe the brick incident had been Laura too. Maybe stalking just wasn't enough for her anymore. She had bullied Piper to leave SFAAC. Maybe she was trying to take the rescue center away from her too.

After creeping down the fire escape like a burglar, she whisked across the parking lot and over to her VW. Out of the corner of her eye she spied a bulky figure standing in front of the third-story stairwell window. Placing Colin inside the car, she started to move a little faster. The figure moved down a window, then another.

She turned the key; the engine slugged away, groaning with the effort. When the landlord-shaped figure burst out of the entrance doors waving his hands, the engine finally roared to life. Without glancing up, she threw it in drive and sped off. Because if she didn't see him, she couldn't very well acknowledge him. Right . . . ?

Piper raced across town to open the rescue center for the day. She pulled into the parking lot to find Addison and Zoe already waiting for her. They sipped their lattes, giving her a look that said they'd just been in the middle of talking about her. And by the devilish grins on their faces, she assumed Aiden was the hot topic of conversation.

Piper crawled out of her car and held the door open for Colin to hop down. He trotted across the small gravel lot to say hello to the girls. They were leaning against the building's whitewashed brick exterior. Piper had painted it herself after she showed up one day to find someone had spray-painted *Grade-A Slut* in large red letters. Of course, she suspected Laura—it wasn't exactly groundbreaking stuff. However, she did appreciate the acknowledgment that she was an A student. It was nice to get a little recognition from time to time. Currently the wall had a saucy graffitied scene involving both Minnie and Donald Duck that she didn't think Mickey would appreciate.

"I'm so sorry I'm late," Piper said. "I had a surprise message from Laura this morning spray-painted on my window."

"You're kidding," Addison said.

"Yeah. It's not a big deal, though." Piper wasn't about to tell them exactly how or why she found it. "I'll call the cops once we're inside."

"Well, you're not late." Zoe handed her a coffee. "So don't apologize."

Piper checked her phone. She was right on time. "Oh. Force of habit, I guess. Big shoes to fill this week."

Marilyn had flown out to Los Angeles, where her cruise ship embarked from, only after Piper managed to convince her that everything would be all right. Yes, she would be at the center every day. No, she promised it wouldn't be too much to handle with clinical practice, her jobs, and her final coming up. And no, she didn't think that "rotter," as she put it, would return to do more damage. At least, Piper hoped not. But she wasn't about to let Marilyn cancel her trip over some coward with a grudge.

"So-o-o-o?" Addison practically vibrated with curiosity. "How was your week? Did you see him?"

"Him who?" Piper feigned ignorance.

"Umm, that dreamboat you call an employer."

"Do people still say 'dreamboat'?" Zoe asked.

"Well, he is pretty dreamy."

Zoe conceded with an appreciative nod.

Piper took a sip of her coffee and pretended to think. She was acting all cool to torture her friends, but in reality she was bursting to gush about him.

"Oh, you're talking about Mr. Caldwell."

"Of course," Zoe said as they rounded the corner and onto the sidewalk. "How's the job going? Did you take his wiener out?"

Piper threw her a look. "It's good. He's"—she hesitated—"good."

"Just good?"

"Yeah. He always just so happened to be around at the

same time I was, so he walked the dogs with me every day this week."

"So was it just walks?" Addison asked. "Or were they like dates?"

"Well, there was flirting. Heavy flirting. But they were more like pseudodates. Or if they were dates, it was a covert operation and I wasn't in on the mission objective."

"I wonder why."

"Well, I know this is hard to believe, since I'm so amazing, but there's a small chance he might not be interested."

Addison gasped. "Blasphemy."

"I know, right?"

"He's interested all right," Zoe said. "A busy CEO wouldn't be coming home from work every day to walk his dog when he's already hired someone to do it for him. Sophie isn't the only wiener he's thinking about."

Piper snorted. "He's just so hot and cold. And then there's his personal assistant. I think there's a lot more than assisting going on there." She stopped on the front stoop to wait for Colin to mark his territory on the bench. "Besides, he makes up these excuses for coming home, like wanting to see me isn't a good enough reason. And don't forget the handshakes. Ugh," she groaned. "Those damned handshakes."

"Well, I doubt he was there for the fresh air and exercise," Addison said.

"Fresh meat is more like it," Zoe said.

"Oh, Zoe." Addison gave her a look. "He's not like that. I think it's romantic. He must be very busy at work and he's managed to find time to spend with her every day." She sighed. "It just goes to show you how much he cares."

"You're far too optimistic about men's intentions," Zoe said. "They're not all Disney princes, you know."

"And you're far too pessimistic. Maybe Aiden is Piper's prince."

Piper climbed the front stairs to the entrance. The soggy top step squeaked under her shoe. She took a mental note to pick up a few supplies from the hardware store to try to fix it. Pulling out the spare key, she unlocked the front door. She noticed she needed to add more duct tape to the cardboard covering the broken glass since it was starting to fall down.

"I'm confused," she said. "I thought Aiden was my rich pimp like in *Pretty Woman,* not a prince."

"Benefactor. Richard Gere isn't a pimp."

"Am I still a prostitute?" She laughed and held the door open for the others. Colin slipped in first. What a gentleman, she thought.

"All I'm saying is that I think he's into you. Just you wait. He'll ask you out soon enough."

"It doesn't matter, because I'm not even that interested." Piper flicked open the blinds, pretending she didn't see Addison and Zoe exchange exaggerated eye rolls.

When the morning sun filtered into the reception area, her mouth dropped open at the sight. She blinked against the light a few times as though the scene before her were just something in her eye. But it didn't go away.

Addison covered her mouth. "Oh, my God."

"Those assholes," Zoe said.

Books and papers were scattered everywhere; the picture frames had been torn off the wall and smashed on the floor; cupboards gaped open, their contents ransacked. It looked like a herd of buffalos recently migrated through the space. But that wasn't the worst of it. Scrawled across the wall in red spray paint were the words *Get Out!* And beneath that was an ominous deadline.

One week.

14

Bark and Enter

Piper froze at the sight of the senseless destruction in the reception area, at the red graffitied threat dripping down the walls. It hardly seemed real, like this wasn't the place that she spent most of her free time. They must have stumbled into the wrong building. Because who would want to do something like this to a rescue center? Her fists clenched as the name came to her. Laura.

Piper's ears tuned into the manic barking coming from the back of the building. The noise brought her crashing back to her senses. "The dogs."

The three girls rushed for the back. Skirting around the desk, they picked their way through the debris on the floor. Piper's heart jumped into her throat, sharp and constrictive, as though she'd swallowed a hummingbird.

"Be careful," Zoe told them. "Try not to touch anything until the cops get here."

Tripping over the upturned printer, Piper stumbled and fell against the door. The moment it swung open, she let out the breath she was holding. The dogs were all still safe in their homes, maybe a little more hyper than usual, but at least they were okay.

Nothing seemed out of place. The kennel doors were still secure, every guest accounted for. Upon seeing the volunteers, they barked and hopped around in their kennels, excited for playtime. Colin scooted around Piper's feet, unconcerned about the disaster in the reception room, and went to make his rounds.

"Thank God," Addison said behind her. "If they'd done anything to hurt them—"

Piper held up a hand. "I don't want to think about it," she said. "I'll go call the cops. Can you two stay with the dogs?"

"Sure thing," Zoe said. "They'll probably get a little agitated once they show up and start moving around the place."

Piper felt more than a little agitated herself at the moment. "Thanks."

While they waited for the police to arrive, the three of them tried to soothe the dogs. Piper took a few of them out to cuddle, although it was more for her nerves than theirs. The girls did what they could for their morning breakfast and grooming routines, but they thought it would be better if the guests stayed in their kennels while they dealt with the cops. Playtime and baths would have to wait.

When the squad cars finally pulled up front with their lights flashing, Piper met them out outside. It disappointed her to find the same officer as the last time climbing out of the cruiser. But while he was as heartfelt as he was about the brick, he didn't downplay this event. After one peek inside, he cued his radio to call for the "identification unit."

It was the same drill as the last time, although more involved considering the extent of the damage. Piper, Zoe, and Addison were separated and questioned. The identification unit showed up and photos were taken, things were measured, evidence was bagged.

After they determined that the point of entry had been the broken window in the reception door, the three volunteers were free to wait in the courtyard with a few of the more hyperactive dogs.

At lunchtime, they were still far behind in their usual Saturday duties. Zoe was attempting to shampoo two dogs at once, and Addison sat cross-legged on the grass, trying to give Smarties, a terrier mix, a pompadour.

Water dripped in streams from a collie Piper was hosing off when Officer Tucker stepped into the courtyard. Zoe lunged at the sopping pup with a towel, but she wasn't fast enough. The collie oscillated like an old washing machine, flinging water across the yard. Zoe threw the towel up to shield herself. The officer got the full force.

Officer Tucker swiped an arm across his face, soaking up the water with his sleeve. By the sneer curling his lip, Piper doubted he was a dog person. A satisfied snicker crept up her throat, and she turned to shut off the hose in an attempt to hide it.

"All right," he said, giving the collie a wide berth. "I think that will be all for now. Thank you for your cooperation, ladies. You're free to go back into the reception area."

"Wait a minute," Piper said. "So that's it? What happens now?"

"We'll check into that protester you mentioned and talk to some of your neighbors. See if anyone saw anything last night."

"That's if they weren't the ones who committed the crime to begin with," Piper muttered.

He pretended not to hear the comment. "Then we'll file the report. We'll be in touch if we learn anything."

"What good is filing a report going to do? You filed one

last week and now this happened. What's going to prevent this kind of thing from happening again? The message said 'one week.' What's next? A drive-by shooting?"

"It may be a scare tactic, but we'll be keeping a closer eye on the place. All we can do for now is take the evidence back to the lab and process it over the next few days. Hopefully it will tell us more."

Addison gave up on her pompadour and stood up, brushing her tights off. "Why can't you do your, you know, CSI thing and track him down, throw him in jail?"

"Yeah, did you find any fingerprints?" Piper asked.

"This isn't Hollywood," the officer said. "This is reality. I assume you have people coming and going all the time. There are probably hundreds of fingerprints in this building. And if the perp wore gloves, prints won't matter. Besides, they didn't need to break in. They just moved the cardboard covering the hole in the front door to unlock it."

Piper clenched her teeth wishing the window had been replaced—not that it would have slowed them down much.

"Unless you have more for us to go on," Officer Tucker continued, "camera footage, even the time that it occurred . . ." He shrugged. "For now, you'll have to be patient. These things take time."

Piper crossed her arms. "So what do we do in the meantime?" She knew most of her attitude was due to frustration over the situation, but his careless attitude wasn't helping.

Colin could sense Piper's anxiety, her anger rolling off her in waves to crash against Officer Tucker. The doxie sat by her heels, a low grumble reverberating in his chest. She reminded herself to start training him on those attack commands.

Officer Tucker removed his cap to scratch his head. "You should consider buying a security system for this place, or hiring a security guard company to monitor it." It sounded more like a reprimand than a suggestion.

"A security guard?" She snorted. "Isn't that what the police are for?" She felt so much safer knowing he was protecting the city.

Colin gave him a firm woof. Good thing Officer Tucker couldn't understand what Piper was sure was an expletive.

Zoe, who'd been leaning against the tall fence listening to the exchange, stepped in. "Thank you, Officer." Although her disappointed tone didn't exactly relay the gratitude and her icy stare could have cowed a grizzly bear protecting her cubs. "Let us know if there's anything else we can do to help."

Sidestepping the collie, he went back inside and headed for his squad car. Barrel chest jutting out, Colin plodded after him, escorting him from the premises.

Piper watched the man go, half-considering releasing horny Toby on him. "So I guess we're on our own."

"Looks like it," Zoe said.

Piper took a deep breath, her shoulders automatically kicking back, her chin rising. "It's fine. We'll be fine." It had become something of a mantra of hers lately. As though simply saying it out loud made it true. "Just fine, fine, fine," she muttered in case it hadn't worked the first time.

"Have you gotten ahold of Marilyn yet?" Addison asked.

"No. Her cell phone keeps going to voice mail. I can't remember what time the ship left port. She might already be gone."

"You could always call the cruise ship itself."

"I hear that's expensive. Besides, no one was hurt. I'll leave her a message, which she can listen to at the next port. I'll probably downplay most of this because I know how she worries. It will ruin her vacation. Even if she was here, I'm not sure there's anything more she'd be able to do."

Piper dreaded the conversation once Marilyn returned her call. She'd handed the keys over to Piper, and within a few hours under her care the place looked like an eighties rock band's hotel room. She knew it wasn't her fault, not really, but she didn't like the timing.

The three of them took a break from bath duties and headed up front. Now that it was time to tackle the mess, it seemed a lot worse than before. Piper didn't know where to begin. Colin nosed around the clutter on the floor, dismayed at the task before them.

She rolled her sleeves back and began by picking up the computer monitor lying facedown under the desk. There was a hole punched right in the middle of the screen, as though it had been hit by a bat.

"This isn't right," Piper said. "This just isn't right. We can't just wait around for something like this to happen again. We have to do something."

"Hey, I have an idea," Zoe said sarcastically. "Why don't we hire a security guard?"

Piper swiped a finger over the powder the identification unit used to dust for prints. She scowled when it didn't come off. Then she froze. "Wait a minute," she said. "Maybe Officer Sucker Tucker is on to something."

"About renting a security guard?"

"Not with the guard, but we really should have a security system."

"With what funds?" Zoe asked. "We can barely afford the dog food at the end of the month. Marilyn says we're stretched too tight as it is. I can't imagine the monthly fees for a system like that."

Piper chewed her lip, thinking. "It's not like I've got any spare cash to help." Hell, she didn't even have enough cash to pay the rent. "Maybe we can't afford it alone, but we can appeal to the community for donations."

"That's a good idea," Addison said. "What about Aiden?

He owns the place now. Maybe he'll help since it's his building."

Piper thought about asking him, but the very idea made her uncomfortable. Sure, he could afford it, but would that be overstepping her boundaries? Maybe that's the kind of thing Marilyn should discuss with him. Would he feel obligated to upgrade the place because he knew Piper? His don't mix business with pleasure rule suddenly came to mind. Maybe it made sense after all.

"No," she said finally. "We can do it on our own. We'll be fine. I'm sure people would help if they heard about what happened. San Francisco is like the dog capital of the world. There are more dog owners than parents in this city. We've done it before to afford medical treatments."

It was true they'd gotten by in the past through the generosity of their foster families, donations from dog lovers in the neighborhood, and bake sale profits, but this was going to take a lot more than a few peanut-butter chocolate-chip cookies.

"I wish we had the same PR connections as Passion for Puppies down the street," she said. "Their center does pretty well." Just then, Smarties wandered into the reception area from the back. His fur still hinted at the subtle swoop of the pompadour that Addison gave him.

Piper's eyes widened. "Oh."

"What is it?" Zoe asked.

Piper turned to the dog stylist. "Addison, when you opened your dog spa, weren't you interviewed for Channel Five News?"

Her eyes widened as she caught on to Piper's train of thought. "Yeah, by Holly Hart."

"Do you still have her number?"

"I do. That's genius." She dug her phone out of her purse and started speed texting.

"*The* Holly Hart?" Zoe asked. "That's perfect! Piper, put that computer back."

"On the floor?"

"Yes. We'll leave everything the way it is." She held up her hands like a frame, probably imagining how the scene would look on TV. She grinned, pleased with the shot. "A complete disaster."

Addison snapped her fingers. "Right. More of an impact on the viewers."

"Yes! And we'll get one of our sadder-looking dogs for the segment. It can make puppy-dog eyes at the camera in the background."

"I know! We'll use Charlie."

"Yes! He's perfectly pathetic."

Colin barked in agreement.

The girls had this wild look in their eyes. Piper couldn't tell if it spoke of genius or madness. Either way, they were on the same track. "You two are devious."

Zoe shrugged. "We like to think of ourselves as opportunists."

"We're just using what we've got to make the best of a bad situation," Addison said. "Trust us. Between Zoe's event-planning business and my dog styling, we understand marketing."

"Right," Zoe agreed. "We want to grab as many people's attention as we can. The more awareness, the more donations."

"Not to mention," Addison said, "someone might watch the news segment and they could remember seeing or hearing something to do with the break-in. Maybe they could give the cops a hot tip to help them solve the crime."

Piper was looking at the room with a glint in her eye. "Maybe we'll have extra funds left over to fix the place up a bit."

She thought of the rotten front step and the rickety fencing in the courtyard. Maybe it was an opportunity to turn things around for the center. To make it better than ever, or at least better than the junk pile it looked like at that moment.

Marilyn might have been the manager, but Piper loved the center as if it were her own. She couldn't bear to see the guests' home, *her* home, violated in that way—not while under her watch. Besides, if she couldn't handle this, then how would she ever own her own veterinary clinic one day? She could fix this. She *would* fix this. And it would be a nice welcome home surprise for Marilyn.

Addison's phone chimed and they huddled close as she checked it. She gave a sudden whoop. "Holly Hart is on her way! Don't worry, Pipe. You're going to do great."

Piper choked on her own air, coughing in surprise. "Me?"

"Of course you." Zoe grinned at her. "We did say that we're going for pathetic."

Piper tried to pull a face, but she only managed a grimace.

"Great impression of puppy-dog eyes," Zoe told her, not at all sympathetic to her sudden onset of chest pains. "Do it just like that when you're on TV."

Addison clapped her hands. "You're going to be our doggy delegate."

Piper looked to Colin, raising her hands. "A little support here?"

But he responded with an indifferent bark.

Piper sighed. "Why am I the one going on television again? You two are the advertising gurus. You're used to this kind of thing. I'll be nothing but nerves the entire time. I don't know what to say."

"Which is exactly what we need," Zoe said. "This is

about a crime. Something serious and scary. It's better if you're just yourself," she said, "not reasonable or confident at all."

"You sure know how to give a pep talk."

"Maybe you should call Aiden," Addison said.

At the mention of his name, Piper's cheeks reddened, like the fact that she'd been thinking about him was written all over her face. But it didn't take a psychic to figure that out, since he was on her mind more often than not lately.

Aiden would need to know for insurance purposes. She wondered if she should make the call or if she could wait until they got the place back in shape and maybe raised a little money so she could propose improvements. It felt like she was always getting into compromising situations around him. This could be her way to say, "See? I can fix my messes all by myself. I can handle a business just like you."

She bit her lip. "No, I haven't called Aiden yet."

"Called Aiden about what?" Aiden said. His voice in the room made all three of them jump. They turned to find him strolling in through the front door.

So much for not needing his help, thought Piper.

15

Doggy Delegate

Standing in the entrance to the rescue center, Aiden surveyed what once resembled a reception room. Frown lines creased his forehead. "Been redecorating?"

"There was a break-in," Piper said.

"Why didn't you call me?"

"I was going to call you once we had it cleaned up. I guess I thought you'd be busy, you know, with businessy things," she said lamely. "I didn't want to bother you."

"It wouldn't have been a bother. I was already on my way here."

"You were?" Her heart did a funny flip in her chest. She hoped he came to see her, but the last time she thought that he'd come for a dog. Plus he owned the place. Business, not pleasure, she reminded herself.

"Yeah," he said. "I brought a present."

"A present?" Okay, so there was pleasure.

He propped the door open and disappeared outside. That's when she realized why Aiden had taken them all by surprise. A thin chain above the door swung back and forth, burdenless; the little brass bell itself was gone.

She searched the floor until she found it. It was smashed in, flattened like someone had stomped on it. Holding it up, she tried to make it ring. It gave a single pathetic *thunk* before the clapper clattered to the floor.

Piper recalled the day eight years earlier when its sweet ring had welcomed her into the center for the first time. She hadn't been looking for volunteer work. She was looking for a dog named Jack. Jack was a ten-year-old piebald dachshund. Her dachshund. Or rather, he had been before her mother gave him up.

Back when Piper had been busy taking her high school exams, her mom went on ahead to San Francisco to get things ready for their big move. She'd taken Jack with her. It turned out their apartment had a strict no-pets policy. And it wasn't like they could find a different one because they'd lucked out: their apartment was rent-controlled. Not wanting to upset Piper before graduation, her mother had secretly given Jack up at a local rescue center.

When Piper arrived a few weeks later to find Jack missing, she was furious. She'd practically grown up with Jack. Hadn't she lost enough as it was?

Once she'd learned which rescue center he'd been dumped at, Piper stormed in there and demanded her dog be returned. But the Englishwoman who ran the place said he'd already been adopted. Of course he had been. He was a great dog.

Piper had felt like she'd finally lost everything. It was just her and her mom left, a few pieces of furniture that fit the two-bedroom apartment, and Mr. Wiggles, her childhood teddy bear. But there was something about being around dachshunds that made that loss a little less painful. As though she still had some connection with Jack, with her old life, by reminiscing about him with the other "guests," as the Englishwoman referred to them. Piper could imagine that they remembered their time with him and could share those stories with her.

So she returned to see them, week after week. And soon it was no longer just about Jack. It was about the other doxies, about finding them good homes, like Marilyn had done for Piper's Jack, for so many other dogs over the last thirty years.

When Aiden returned, he was carrying a hefty box. Despite his well-used gym membership, he looked to be struggling with it. Piper placed the bell on the desk and hurried over to help him carry it into the kitchen. They slid it onto the vintage table and stepped back.

"What is it?" Piper asked.

"It's a new fish tank."

"Really?" She beamed up at him, surprised by his thoughtfulness. "That's so sweet."

"I'm glad to see the ladies are still alive." He tapped on the coffeepot.

The goldfish were gliding around their temporary home, bumping into one another in the cramped quarters.

"I'm sure they'll be happy to get out of there," Piper said.

Aiden stepped back out into the reception room. He assessed the damage, scowling as he read the message scrawled across the yellow wall. "One week until what?"

"That's what I'd like to know," she said.

"I guess I should have picked up a couple gallons of paint too on the way."

"The damage is mostly cosmetic. It won't take much to cover up the graffiti and get things back in order." She just hoped that in a week they wouldn't have to deal with it again. Or worse. The first warning flashed through her mind. *Get out! Or I'll make you.*

Aiden slipped off his sports jacket and rolled up his sleeves. "Well, where do I start, boss?"

She held up her hands to wave him off. “You don’t have to do that.”

“Piper.” Grabbing her gently by both wrists, he gave her a strange look. “I’m free to help. I don’t mind.”

“But we’re fine.”

He waved a hand at the sorry excuse for a reception area and raised his eyebrows at her. “You’re not *fine*.”

A chuckle tinted his voice, like she was a hippo claiming to be a cockatoo. It made her muscles tense with indignation, like it was an accusation of sorts. That he thought she couldn’t take care of herself, that she needed help.

“Hey, Pipe.” Zoe gestured out the front window. “Looks like the news crew is here. Are you ready for your television debut?”

“You called the news station?” Aiden asked.

“Why? Do you think it’s a bad idea?” she asked. It suddenly occurred to her that she should have asked his permission first, since it was his property.

“Not at all. I think it’s a great idea to create awareness. Dogs in danger? It’s easy to appeal to the public’s emotions when animals are involved.”

“See? I told you,” Zoe said. “Pathetic sells.”

Piper narrowed her eyes. “Are you talking about the dogs or me?”

“I think I’ll go help Addison fill the reporter in.” She winked and headed outside.

Piper twisted and untwisted a strand of hair around her finger. “I don’t know if I’m the best person to do this.” It might have been her idea in the first place, but she’d expected to be the brains behind the operation. Not the poster girl for it.

“You’ll do fine,” Aiden said.

He stepped closer to her, enough that she could smell his aftershave. She took a deep breath through her nose until her lungs were filled to capacity with Aidenness. It made her a little dizzy.

"What's important is that you're passionate about these dogs. That much is obvious. I've seen it myself, and it will come across to the viewers." He gripped both of her shoulders and gave them a squeeze.

She was nodding. Not because she agreed, but because her head was so full of the delicious scent of his aftershave and she was wondering if he'd just brushed his teeth, because the air was crisp with mint as he spoke, and would his mouth taste like spearmint too? And God, his hands were big. How good would they feel touching parts of her other than her shoulders?

Heels clicked up the front steps and through the entrance, jarring Piper from her Aiden-addled thoughts. In strolled *the* Holly Hart, stylish in a fitted pale pink blazer and black jeweled Manolo Blahniks, with her cameraman in tow. She clapped her hands as though to get the attention of a bustling newsroom. All it did was get a bark from Colin.

"Okay, let's get started," she said. "Who's doing the interview?"

Piper took a deep breath and stepped around the desk. "I am. I'm Piper Summers." Taking a page out of Aiden's book, she shook the reporter's hand—fake it till you make it. "Nice to meet you."

"Holly Hart. Channel Five News. That's not what you're wearing, is it?" Her nose wrinkled, as though Piper not only had bad fashion sense but smelled funny too. *Achoo!* Holly sneezed, not once, not twice, but three times.

Colin barked, *Bless you!*

Holly sniffed. "Damn allergies."

"You're allergic to dogs?"

Aiden huffed behind the counter. "Or just about anything with a heart."

Holly turned toward his voice. Noticing him for the first time, she gasped and shoved Piper aside. "Oh, Aiden Caldwell." She said his name like she was ordering a warm fudge brownie with gelato. "What a coincidence seeing you here."

"Miss Hart," Aiden replied in a clipped tone.

"Are you sure you don't want to do the interview?" she purred, slinking close to him. "I've been trying to *nail you* for a while."

Zoe raised her eyebrows at Piper, like "Who does this chick think she is?" But Piper was still licking her lips, thinking about mint, and belatedly wondering what was wrong with her outfit.

"No, this is all Miss Summers. I'll be taking the sidelines for this one. My PR people handle that kind of thing."

"I know." Holly pouted like a disappointed trout. "They've stopped answering my calls."

"Maybe it was due to the last piece you did on me," he said coolly.

She laid a hand over her heart. "Hey, I'm just doing my job. I'm the voice of the people now."

"Yeah, well, it was a little over the top."

"I was concerned for a poor workingman's rights," she said, undeterred.

"And so you chose a disgruntled ex-employee to represent those concerns?"

She shrugged, a coy smile threatening the corner of her mouth. "How was I supposed to know that source was lying?"

"You're a reporter." He crossed his arms over his chest. "It's your job to check your facts."

"Sounded plausible to me." She ran a familiar finger down his silk tie and he stiffened. As did Piper. "Besides, you weren't available for comment."

"And I'm still not." He took a step back. "I believe you're here on other business."

"All right, fine." She dropped the sexy veneer like a fluff piece at deadline. Her voice was now brusque and severe, like the harsh smell of nail polish. "Now do we have a dog we could use? Like a supersad dog. It would be better if he was missing an ear, or a leg, or an eye, or something. All three would be best." She looked delighted at the thought.

Zoe leaned over to Piper. "I told you so."

"Yeah, I'll go grab Charlie," Addison said, and slipped into the back.

"Hey, you!" Holly Hart barked at her cameraman. Snapping her fingers, she began to order him about, getting him to test the light so that it highlighted her best feature—which was clearly her sparkling personality.

She took out a mirror and checked her lipstick as he set up the shot. She wrinkled her nose at her reflection, then *Achoo! Achoo! Achoo!*

Gesundheit! Colin barked.

Aiden watched on with his arms crossed, eyes narrowed. Piper sidled closer to him.

"She seems"—she hesitated—"friendly. Do you know her well?"

"Just from the press room." Piper liked the way he said it: firmly enough to assure her he and Holly had no history. Like it was any of her business to know. Not that she cared, or anything, but she couldn't help the little "Woohoo!" that shot through her brain.

Addison returned with Charlie limping at her side. Holly Hart pulled a horrified face, which was obviously a good thing, because she said, "Perfect. Totally sad. Okay, can we get one more? A small one maybe that Piper can hold?"

"Colin!" Piper called out. "Come here."

Papers rustled behind the desk. Colin appeared, emerging from the rubbish like a packrat, and trotted to her side. Balancing on his hind legs, he pawed at her thigh.

At least one of us is ready, she thought as she picked him up. But it was for a good cause, she reminded herself. And it had been her idea, so she had no one to blame but herself.

"Okay," Holly said. "Let's get this over with."

The cameraman hoisted the camera onto his shoulder and Holly held her microphone at the ready. She cleared her throat, stared into the lens, and smiled like she was the most trustworthy, honorable person in San Francisco, everyone's confidante. In other words, a completely different person.

Zoe gave Piper an encouraging shove from behind and she stumbled into place next to Holly. Addison gave a thumbs-up. Charlie whined beside Piper. The one ear that hadn't been chewed off the poor pit bull in an underground dogfight lay nervously against his head.

"You'll do fine," she told him.

Achoo! Achoo! Achoo! Holly sneezed.

The cameraman counted down, using his fingers as a mark. "In three, two . . ." His finger counted "one," and a light turned red—as did Piper's face. Taking a deep breath, she tried to mimic Holly's expression, but it felt more plastic looking than sincere. She focused on why she wanted Holly Hart to come there in the first place, the anger, the injustice, and her determination to fix this mess before Marilyn got back. To prove that she could do this herself.

"Every dog has its day. But it's not today," Holly began in her authoritative reporter's tone. "I'm standing in a rescue center full of dogs just looking for love, but what they got last night was an act of hate when the center was vandalized. I'm here with avid volunteer and dog lover Piper Summers, who was first on the scene." She turned to her. "Tell us, Piper, what were your first thoughts when you saw this senseless destruction?"

Holly turned the microphone on her and Piper jumped like it was going to bite her. Not the most persuasive or motivating attitude. This was about the dogs, not her self-consciousness, she told herself. She took a deep breath, feeling her usual confidence fall into place. Her chin rose on its own, her back straightening.

"Well, my first thought was for the animals."

"Were any of them hurt?"

"Thankfully no, but they were pretty spooked. I'm more worried about what will happen next time."

"Next time? Do you think that this might happen again?" Holly appeared scandalized, but Piper knew Zoe and Addison had filled her in beforehand.

"This isn't the first incident. Just last week we had a brick thrown through our window."

"And now this." Holly shook her head sadly, as though to ask "What is the world coming to?" and "Who would do such a thing?"

"We don't know. We're hoping that someone out there has information about the attacks so we can catch this person before one of the dogs get hurt. But in the meantime, we'd like to raise enough money to install a security system for protection."

"Definitely a cause worthy of this community's attention." She turned back to the camera, speaking directly to the audience. "Without your help, Piper and the other volunteers have about a dog's chance of uncovering the perpetrator. If anyone has any information regarding this heinous canine caper, please call the local police. In the meantime, the rescue center will be accepting donations to help protect these poor pooches. If you'd like to help, please call the number below."

The cameraman zoomed in, honing in on the reporter's pretty face. "This is Holly Hart reporting from the San Francisco Dachshund Rescue Center."

The cameraman ended the segment by closing in on poor Charlie's face, the unwitting pawn in their plea for money. "And we're out," he said.

Holly's earnest, imploring expression transformed again. She snapped her fingers at the camera guy. "Hey, you," she said again, like it was his name. "Get some pans of the damage and some close-ups of the dogs in the back."

Addison rushed toward Piper and hugged her. "You did great, Pipe. People will want to help for sure."

"I hope so. Thanks a lot for coming, Holly."

"No problem. Thanks for the story. This city loves dogs. It'll help boost my ratings. But why do you need donations? What about your boyfriend?" She nodded toward Aiden, who was across the room tidying up behind the desk with Zoe. "Can't he help? He's got more money than he knows what to do with."

"He's not my boyfriend. He's my boss."

Holly snorted. "If my boss looked at me the way he looks at you, I'd take him right to Human Resources. Although if my boss looked more like Aiden Caldwell rather than a fat, balding alcoholic, I'd take him right on the newsroom floor."

Piper watched Aiden, wondering if she could be right. After a moment, she shook her head, knowing she could never do it. "It doesn't matter. I'm not asking him for the money. This is our problem, not his."

Addison bit her lip. "Maybe Holly's right, Pipe. I mean, I know you're Miss Independent and everything, but he is rich. And he does own this place. Besides, it's not really you that has to suffer through it. It's the dogs."

"Addy, I don't feel comfortable. Besides, we can do this. Let's see what kinds of donations come in after the story runs. We'll have this place in top shape before Marilyn gets back from her cruise."

They would. She would make sure of it. Marilyn left the center, the guests, in her hands. She didn't need anyone to take care of her. She would protect them if she had to spend the night in one of the enclosures herself on guard duty.

The cameraman, or Hey, You, finished in the back and began packing up the equipment. Holly handed him the microphone and watched him cart it all out to the van parked on the street like a pack mule.

"Well, suit yourself," she told Piper. "Let me know if there are any big developments in the story so I can do a follow-up." Her nose wrinkled and she sneezed again. "Ugh, dogs. It's all I can smell. I need a shower."

Colin grumbled as if affronted and Piper shushed him.

"Thanks again, Holly," Piper said.

"You can catch the show at five." She waved over her shoulder, walking away without a backward glance. "You did great, honey."

"Thanks." Piper took in the chaos one more time. "Let's get to it, I suppose."

Aiden pulled off his tie, preparing to dig in with the rest of them, but Piper put up a hand to stop him. "You've done enough already. We'll be fine," she told him.

"But I haven't done anything," he protested.

"We'll be fine. I'm sure you have better things to do." The finality in Piper's tone caught him up short and she suddenly felt guilty. She'd assumed he wanted to stay out of some sense of obligation, but the expression on his face was a bit like when she told Colin he had to stay at home while she left for Clinical. "Thank you for the offer, though."

"No, that's fine." He seemed to recover. "I actually have some work to do at the office."

"On a weekend?"

"No rest for the wicked." He grinned. Reaching into his pocket, he pulled out a slip of paper and handed it to Piper.

Aiden said a quick good-bye on his way out the door. Once he was gone, Piper unfolded the paper in her hand. It was a check. With far too many zeros. She gaped at it for a moment, wondering if she'd forgotten how to read. But no matter how many times she read it, the amount remained outrageous.

"What is it?" Addison asked.

Piper folded it again before they could see. "Nothing."

The words *One week* loomed over her from the wall, threatening who knew what. She agonized over the check in her hand. It might have been made out to the center, but it didn't feel like business. It felt like it was for her. Aiden owned the place. If he really wanted to do something, he could have paid for it through his company, not his own pocket.

But could she turn down a donation that would buy them the security system they needed? Piper went back and forth about it all afternoon. She was still undecided as she replanted the peace lily in an "I heart dachshunds" soup mug with a missing handle—one of the few left intact—when the phone rang.

"I'll get it." Addison searched around the desk for a moment. "If I can find it."

Following the sound, she discovered it in the garbage. She picked it up, but it was broken in two halves so she held the earpiece and mouthpiece to her face separately. "Dachshund Rescue Center."

She listened for a moment while a smile spread across her Fuchsia Flirt pink lips. Gasping, she covered the mouthpiece.

Piper put the peace lily down. "What is it?"

"Donations!" Addison jumped up and down. "Lots of them! We're going to be okay."

Puppy Love

Piper and Aiden were on the perfect date. It was another beautiful late spring day—or, dare she hope, early summer. The Golden Gate Bridge stretched in the distance, the view clear and picturesque from Baker Beach. Free of their leashes, Colin and Sophie pranced ahead. They patrolled the shoreline, chasing the foaming waves away as they slurped back into the bay, only to skitter to safety when they returned to lick at the doxies' paws.

Piper strolled next to Aiden, sand squidging between her toes. They tried to keep up with the dogs, but they had to avoid the crowd that came to enjoy the nice weather. The doxies, on the other hand, had a tendency to plough through picnics and Frisbee games.

While the dogs maneuvered skillfully through the soft sand, the humans had a somewhat harder time. Sometimes it would throw Aiden or Piper off balance, and every once in a while their knuckles would graze each other's. The next time it happened, Piper's hand twitched. Despite her better judgment, she was tempted to reach out and grab his, to interlace their fingers and just see what happened.

That's the kind of thing she'd normally do in that situation. Piper was bold. She took chances. Sometimes they worked out, and sometimes, well, sometimes they ended up requiring payday loans or laser tattoo removal to fix—never date an impulsive tattoo artist. But this situation was a little different. Aiden was a little different.

Yup, it was the perfect date. Only it wasn't a date. It was another pseudo-non-date.

He'd joined her for a walk every day the previous week. And here he was again Monday afternoon. She wasn't sure what he was paying her for if he could make time to come home, but she wasn't about to complain. About the money or the company.

But now that she thought about it, why the heck was he paying her? Or overpaying her, more like it. It wasn't like he didn't trust her with Sophie, and he certainly didn't need the exercise judging by his physique—which Piper was trying hard not to gawk at. Addison insisted it was because he liked her, but that would defy his golden rule: don't mix business with pleasure. So what was the deal?

She thought back to the check he gave her at the rescue center on the weekend, which she never ended up cashing. He'd intervened on her behalf a few times, tried to bail her out, like he thought money would fix anything. Just because he had extra cash to throw around didn't make it okay to do so. It was insulting. Anger flashed through her and her mouth opened before her brain could stop her.

"Why are you here?" She flinched as she heard the acidity in her tone.

His eyebrows shot up and he opened his mouth, either in surprise or because he was simply unable to find an answer.

"I mean," she amended. "It's just, I thought you were

the boss, and everything. Aren't you more effective when you're at work?"

"But as the boss, I kind of get to create my own schedule. Don't get me wrong; I make up for the lost hours. I stay late in the evenings."

"Oh?" So did that mean he rearranged his schedule, stayed behind so he could be with her? She suddenly regretted her hasty conclusion. She seemed to do that a lot with Aiden. Every time she thought she had him pegged, he'd surprise her. She wondered how many other wrong conclusions she'd drawn about him.

"I just meant that if you can come home from work to walk Sophie, do you really need me?"

"Oh yes." His eyes crinkled with a secret, only Piper didn't quite know what that secret was. "I really need you."

He needed her? Piper stared at him, trying to decipher that look, but he turned away before she could even begin. She cursed her tactlessness. She'd have to work on that brain-mouth filter of hers.

Sophie paused up ahead and gave them a look that said, *Hurry up. You're holding us up.*

Colin found a stick floating back and forth near the shore. Dropping the chew toy he brought with him from the house, he battled Sophie for it. Clearly the dogs had forgotten they were afraid of the waves.

"So you never told me," Piper said to Aiden. "Why did you decide to get a dog?"

He shoved his hands in his pockets, like he didn't know what to do with them when he didn't have a tie to straighten. "I suppose I've been lonely ever since my father died. It's a big house to live in all by yourself. It's nice to have female companionship." He chuckled. "Even if it is another species."

"Aiden Caldwell, lonely? I'm sure you have no problem finding female companionship," she teased, trying to sound casual about it. And it would have been convincing too, if not for the high-pitched tone of her voice. She tried to laugh it off, but it sounded more like a flamingo call to her ears.

Aiden bent down to grab the chew toy Colin had dropped and stuffed it in his pocket. "My business keeps me busy. Too busy to meet people sometimes. Most of my interactions are for business rather than pleasure. I'm a little rusty when it comes to females who require more enticement than the words *Do you want a treat?*"

Sophie's sensitive ears tuned in to the magic words and she barked in response. Forgetting about the stick, she splashed over to him and stared up with round, expectant eyes.

Aiden fished around inside his pocket. A moment later, he produced a treat for both dogs and made them sit before he handed the treats over. Sophie thanked him by choosing that moment to shake off her long hair like some canine *Baywatch* babe, flicking the salt water and wet sand all over him.

"I've kept treats with me ever since you taught me the trick," he said. "My housekeeper says she always has to check my pockets before taking my suits to the dry cleaners."

"Be careful," she warned. "You'll spoil her."

"How can I say no to a pretty face like that?"

She thought about what Aiden had said about female companionship. It was hard to believe that someone as successful and droolworthy as him could have such a lackluster dating life. Not for the first time, she wondered about Tamara, his personal assistant. If he didn't mix business with pleasure, then what was their deal? Suddenly, she remembered the reason they met.

"Wait a minute. But you had a date with Nicole."

"Nicole?" He frowned for a second before a look of

understanding lit his face. "Ah, yes. Nicole." He said her name like it was an annoying hairball that plugged his shower drain. After the telegram fiasco, Piper couldn't blame him.

"That was a blind date that a friend set me up on. A very bad one. My fault, really. I'm a little out of practice, to say the least. The evening sort of died a horrible death."

"Well, it seemed to haunt you, so it couldn't have been that bad."

"Yeah." He rubbed the back of his neck, which was growing pink from the mid-day sun. "I suppose I gave her the wrong impression."

"The wrong impression?"

"I guess she thought I was more interested than I was."

Piper nodded, wondering what "wrong impressions" she'd gotten from him so far. And, more important, which one was right. "So what gives a girl the wrong impression?" she asked, way too innocently. "Could it be when you conveniently find yourself at home every time your super-amazing, attractive, and humble dog walker turns up? Would that count as wrong impression material?"

He chuckled, low and throaty, glancing at his feet. He had a nice laugh. It made him seem younger—or rather his own age of thirty—as opposed to the serious businessman he was forced to become so early on.

"That would certainly give an impression," he said.

An *impression,* she noted. But not a *wrong* impression. Feeling braver, she shook her head teasingly. "Well, whatever will you do, Mr. Caldwell?"

"Oh, I'm kind of hoping something will just"—he hesitated, his mouth fighting a grin—"fall into my lap."

She couldn't help but smile as she remembered their first meeting. She bit her lip. Now that wasn't just a hint. That was like shouting into a megaphone.

Pretending to watch a group of giggling coeds take selfies on the beach, she examined Aiden. He was more relaxed today than she'd ever seen him. The invisible pole that usually held his tight posture in place had disappeared, and she hadn't seen him subconsciously reach for where his tie should be even once that day. She felt as though she was really getting to know him, the off-the-record him. The *Tonight Show* Aiden, as opposed to CNN.

He was still as polite and reserved as ever, though, the ever-present professional barrier erected between them. It was as if he wasn't even conscious of it, always turned on like some optimized administrative robot programmed in HR dos and don'ts. But his smiles were easy; his eyes had a flirtatious glint.

"How have the donations for the center been coming along?" Aiden asked.

"Really well. We already have enough money to buy a surveillance system."

"Have you managed to get ahold of Marilyn on the cruise ship?" he asked.

"No. I've left messages on her cell phone, but I'm not sure she's getting them. Have you?"

"I've tried calling the cruise line, but I'm not having any luck." He took a breath like he wanted to say something more. Piper hoped it was something along the lines of "I need you. Right here, right now" or "Your eyes are like two pieces of amber burning in the morning sunrise." Or something to that effect, but in the end, he looked away. "It's busy here today."

Whatever he wanted to say, she decided to let it go. If he wanted to tell her, he would. "It's too nice to be cooped up inside."

"I come here sometimes to run in the morning, but I'm not often free in the afternoons."

Again she wondered why he was free so often as of late.

It certainly gave her a strong *impression*. Her traitorous fingers twitched again, reaching for his.

He turned his back to the bridge to face Sea Cliff, the cluster of houses clinging to the imposing cliffs that vied for the best view in town. Shielding his eyes, he searched like he could spot his home from there.

"Must be nice to live so close to a beach," Piper said.

"It has its advantages."

"Like a convenient nudist beach?" She nodded in the direction of the bridge.

She'd come there before, hoping to glimpse a school of dolphins, something not unheard of from Baker Beach. She found out the hard way that if you wandered too far north you'd see more than a few dorsal fins poking out of the water.

She grinned. "It's like a free striptease."

"Yeah, but unlike yours, you don't get a thoughtful song at the end."

"Hey!" She threw him a sour look, but the smile ruined the effect.

"Why is it that the only people you see on nude beaches are never the ones you want to see naked?"

"Oh, so you have taken a peek, have you?"

He shrugged. "I might have jogged a little too far one time."

"So if not them, then who do you want to see naked?" She bit her lip. Again, it was the kind of thing she'd normally blurt out, but when the skin beneath his close shave turned too pink to be from the sun her own cheeks heated in response.

But the idea made her wonder, not for the first, or second, or the tenth time that day, what he might look like if they wandered farther north to join the nudists. Date or not, they *were* at a beach. Was it so unreasonable to hope that he'd go shirtless that day? Even though he was her boss? Even though he kept saying he didn't mix business with pleasure? Even though he might be having some kind of tryst with his personal assistant? Even though . . . nope. She didn't care. "Take it off!" she wanted to scream.

It seemed only fair, since he'd seen her in next to nothing on several occasions after her telegram jobs. But so far, she'd already coaxed him out of his suit and tie and into another pair of light khaki shorts and a light blue shirt. At this point, she would have settled for a button or two. Just a hint, to add a little detail to her daydreams. Chest hair? No chest hair? A couple of fine pecks to match that pair of toned biceps peeking out beneath his sleeves?

She didn't realize she was staring at the collar of his shirt until Aiden reached out and grabbed her arm. He steered her to the side so that she narrowly missed stomping on a sand castle, still under construction by two little kids. The motion sent her stumbling against him—and if she "accidentally" copped a feel of those firm pecks, it totally wasn't her fault.

"Whoa, Godzilla," he said. "Leave the city alone."

Skirting around the kids, she shook off the fog in her brain. There were far too many people around for her to continue riding that train of thought. Keep it breezy, she told herself. Totally blasé. Big on the aloof, less on the doof.

She wandered closer to the water's edge, letting the cool waves wash over her feet as she and Aiden followed the dogs exploring the shore. Aiden removed his sandals and waded in next to her.

"So why did you decide to become a veterinarian?" he asked her. "When your calling is so obviously professional telegram girl?"

She gave him a withering look but answered seriously. "Because I love animals. All animals. We just have a connection, you know. Sometimes I think I can understand what they're saying. Like they're talking to me."

"See, this would have been important to mention on the day I interviewed you. This was the crazy I was looking for."

She laughed. "I know I can't *actually* hear them. But it's like if you pay enough attention they all have their own little personalities. Like miniature people."

"Why dachshunds?" he asked. "What drew you to them and the center?"

"We had a dachshund while I was growing up. We had to give him up when my mom and I moved to San Francisco. I guess I started volunteering at the rescue center because it reminded me of home. And then came Colin."

"And you just couldn't say no."

"Well, I did at first. It's against my tenant agreement to have pets in my apartment." They'd caught up to the dogs and she bent down to smoosh Colin's adorable face. "But how could I say no to this pretty face?"

"You're not one for rules, are you?"

"What can I say?" She shrugged unapologetically. "I march to the beat of my own kazoo. At least I'm not afraid to do what I want to do and say what I want to say." But apparently not when it came to Aiden, she added to herself. "Life is short. I could get into a car accident tomorrow and die."

"In *your* car?" he said. "Yes."

She gave him a playful punch on the arm. "Don't you ever do anything against the rules, Mr. Caldwell? Something crazy or unexpected?"

"Are you kidding? Me?" He held a hand to his chest. "Look at me. I'm completely outside-the-box. I'm a cargo pants and plaid shirt kind of guy." He waved a Vanna White hand at his ensemble.

Piper took the opportunity to give him another ogle, top to bottom. "I'm sorry to tell you, but it's not so outside-the-box when it's exactly what I told you to wear on the first day."

"Yeah, well, last week I wore stripes. And who knows what will happen next week? It could be Hawaiian flowers."

"Hawaiian flowers?" Her eyes widened. "You rebel, you."

"Are you making fun of me?" he said in mock seriousness.

"Me? Never."

"Don't you know who I am?"

She pressed her lips together, trying not to smile. "A cargo pants kind of guy?"

His head swiveled to her. The look on his face was like the moment before a cat pounces on a mouse. Her muscles tensed and she held her breath. The corners of his mouth curled. And then he leapt.

Piper was ready. With a shriek, she dodged his reach, but he stood between her and dry land. All she could do was run through the shallows, the water and waves slowing her down. She could hear him splashing close on her heels, gaining on her.

Laughing, she twisted away, trying to double back, but now she was too deep. The cool bay water splashed up her shorts and soaked though. His arms encircled her, lifting her up and out of the water like a deep-sea marlin plucked from the ocean.

"Oh no you don't," he said, cradling her in both arms. "You need to be punished for that insubordination."

She giggled. "I would prefer suspension with pay."

He waded out a few paces, deeper into the cool water. While the sun shone hot, only the bravest of beachcombers had dared to take a dip.

Piper struggled in his arms. The water lapped at the butt of her shorts and back. She squealed, but he strode until he was waist deep. She felt him shudder at the temperature. He had her completely at his mercy. And despite the threat of a dunking, that turned her on a little.

"You wouldn't," she said.

"Wouldn't I?"

"You know, they say a sign of a good boss is a merciful boss."

"You can't show weakness in front of your employees. Sometimes you have to make an example out of them." He hesitated and narrowed his eyes at her. "Unless you have anything to say for yourself."

She tightened her grip around his neck, determined that if she was going down he was going down with her. She couldn't help but notice his own hold on her tightened, hands hot against her skin, her breasts squishing up against his firm chest.

"You'll get your doggy treats wet," she tried to reason with him. "What will your dry cleaner say?"

This was obviously not the answer he wanted. There was just enough time to gulp a breath of air before they both went under.

A second later, they shot up, shrieking and gasping at the chill. Goose bumps rising on her skin, she darted for the shore, Aiden following in her wake. By the time they reached shallow waters, their shrieks were replaced with laughter. Colin and Sophie joined in, unsure of what game they were all playing but still enthusiastic about it.

Piper expected the involuntary dip to be like a cold shower that would jolt her out of her increasing lust for her boss that afternoon, but it only made it worse. Her skin was hypersensitive, every sensation in her body amplified. The foam from the waves tickled the insides of her thighs, skin tingled, cold muscles clenched.

He tugged her back playfully toward his body, the same desire in his touch, a greedy craving to feel more of her.

His fingertips brushed her skin, his body leaned toward her, connecting at every chance. When his hips pushed against her, it certainly gave her a whole new impression, one that pressed against the small of her back—and it wasn't the dog toy in his pocket.

His green eyes drifted down to her lips. "Are you ready to go back to my place?" His voice, though shaking with the chill, was low and deep, laced with purpose.

"I'm ready."

More ready than he could ever know. It was like a fire had been lit inside her, low in her belly, hot and smoldering. It had burned off any lingering doubts about the CEO. They headed for shore, and he placed a hand on her lower back, almost urging her back to his place. And she hoped it was so he could stoke that fire with his wood.

17 Territorial

After the chill of their dip, Aiden and Piper reveled in the relief of the sun-warmed sand as they made their way back to Lobos Creek, which fed into the bay. Colin and Sophie followed at their heels, still excited by the human game that began by splashing in the water. Whatever it was, even the doxies could tell it wasn't over, like they could sense the same tension in the air that made Piper overly aware of Aiden. His nearness, his breathing, and once in a while she'd catch him gazing at the wet clothes that clung to her body—when she wasn't busy staring at his, of course.

Finally, they reached the low wooden stairs at the base of the cliffs that led to Aiden's house. She went ahead of him, and after the third time he hissed from the pain of stubbing his toe on the uneven steps she knew exactly what his eyes were focused on. The steep climb up the low sand-covered steps warmed them up, but when they burst through Aiden's double front doors and into the central-air-controlled interior, Piper gasped at the cool wall of air that hit her.

She wrapped her arms around herself and danced on the spot to keep warm. Colin and Sophie thought it was part of the game and danced with her. She briefly wondered how much body heat they would throw off if she picked them both up and cuddled them.

Her teeth chattered. "I'm still soaked."

"Would you like to borrow some clothes?" Aiden asked.

"A tie feels a bit formal right now."

"I do own clothes other than suits, you know!" he called back as he disappeared down the hall.

Aiden returned with a luxuriously puffy towel, large enough to encompass two people. He unfolded it and held it up for her. "Here, this might help."

Desperate for its warmth, she rushed toward him. He wrapped it around her, only once he had, his arms were around her too. It was like an accidental embrace. One of those things that just sort of happens, and neither of them saw it coming until they were there, so close, his arms still around her.

Aiden seemed to realize it at the same time. But neither of them went to move. Instead, Piper shifted a half step closer, so that her body rubbed against his. His hands began to trail over her back, drying her with the towel.

For the first time, she was confident of how he felt. After everything he'd said that day, maybe more the way he'd said it, how relaxed he'd become around her since they'd met, there was no doubt.

The heat of his hands warmed her skin through the linen, or maybe it was the nearness of his body, the way his hands began moving slower, pressing her body against the contours of his. It had grown so quiet in the foyer that she could hear the sound of her heartbeat in her short breaths.

Her arms were pinioned to her sides by the towel. If they hadn't been, she might have reached up and pulled him toward her, wrapped them around his neck. All she could do was tilt her face up and let him do the rest.

For a moment, she worried she might be left standing there, head cocked at a weird angle like a burrowing owl, waiting for a kiss that would never happen. A wrong impression. Her heart lurched a beat, and another. Then his half-lidded eyes closed and his head dipped down to hers.

And then the doorbell rang.

He pulled away and straightened up. "Tamara."

"No." She pointed at herself. "Piper."

He shook his head as though in a daze. "I mean, I made an appointment with Tamara for this afternoon."

He stepped away and the towel crumpled to the floor. Cool air hit Piper's skin, shocking her out of her lusty fog.

There was a very distinct transition when Aiden transformed into his professional alter ego. He reached up, Piper thought to maybe adjust his tie, but when he found it missing he dropped his hands and reached for the door handle. She sighed, realizing the moment was over. Whatever had been about to happen, well . . . wouldn't.

"Hi, Tamara."

The graceful brunette stepped across the threshold with a radiant smile for Aiden. Then her eyes landed on Piper and it looked more like she was baring her teeth. She eyed the state of their clothing, still dripping seawater onto the floor. "Is this a bad time?"

Yes, Piper thought. "Hi, Tamara. Nice to see you again."

"We had a bit of an accident at the beach today," Aiden said in explanation, as though sweeping the experience under the rug. "I'll just go change. I'll be right back."

He climbed the broad, curving staircase to the second floor. The moment he disappeared from sight, Tamara took a step toward Piper, until they were practically nose to nose. Or rather, nose to chin, since Tamara was taller.

"Aiden is a busy man. He doesn't have time for distractions," she said as she swept her eyes over Piper's disheveled clothing.

Piper jolted in surprise. A smile formed on her lips like it was some kind of strange joke, but Tamara wasn't laughing. Her serene face had transformed, like her porcelain skin had cracked to release some kind of creature festering beneath the smooth surface.

Was it just Piper's imagination? Creating competition where there wasn't any? Let's face it, Pipe, she told herself morosely. There was no competition there.

"You're taking him away from his work." Tamara's eyes widened so Piper could see the whites.

"Away from his work?" she scoffed. "Or you?"

Tamara hissed. Actually hissed, like a feral cat. Piper took an automatic step back, unsure if she'd take a swipe at her next. Her foot caught in the towel lying on the floor. She tried to right herself, but Tamara was bearing down on her, all eyes, and teeth, and hissing.

Feet wrapped up, Piper fell straight back. Out of instinct, she reached out and grabbed hold of the nearest thing—which happened to be Tamara.

Her hand clamped around neatly curled hair. Tamara screamed out. Together they dropped to the floor in a heap, landing in the puddle of water that had formed beneath Piper.

They scrambled, their slick limbs slipping on hardwood and over each other. Piper thrashed to get away, but Tamara's efforts were more hinder than help. And painful, Piper thought as she felt a vicious tug on her hair, followed by a scratch of nails down her leg. She screamed out.

Colin and Sophie were jumping, growling, barking all around them, unsure if it was a new game or if Piper needed help. She slipped again, falling hard on her butt. Tamara rolled on top of her, that wild look still in her eye, her hands reaching out toward her. To what? Strangle her? Claw her eyes out?

Piper pushed her away with both hands. Aiden's footsteps pounded down the steps.

"What's going on down here?" he asked. "I heard—"

Like a tableau from a play, both Piper and Tamara froze. Piper only then realized where her hands had landed. Right on Tamara's supple breasts—which were far too perky and firm for their size. Come on, Piper thought, like it wasn't enough that she was utterly perfect? Besides the psychotic mood swings.

Aiden laughed, and Piper glanced at him in surprise. How could he possibly think this was funny? But then she looked at Tamara. Her expression appeared so docile that she had to do a double take. Her pretty face flushed as though from embarrassment, not from the effort of practically trying to kill Piper. The porcelain had smoothed out, the monster tucked back inside.

Aiden reached down to help Tamara up. "You two ladies wouldn't be fighting over me, now would you?" he joked.

If he only knew, Piper thought. "Actually—"

"The floor was wet," Tamara interrupted. "Piper accidentally slipped and I tried to help her up."

She got to her feet and stumbled against him, her hand sliding down the front of his shirt—the buttons still gaping open near the top. Tamara locked eyes with Piper, her hand lingering possessively on her boss.

Piper gaped at her. "What are you talking about? You attacked me."

Aiden just laughed, completely oblivious. "Piper clumsy? Now why doesn't that surprise me?"

"What? I'm serious. You don't believe me?"

"Don't worry. I'm sure it was just an accident." He

reached down to help her up, but she brushed his hand away.

"I'm fine." She untangled herself from the towel and scrambled to her feet. Without looking at either of them, she moved to the door, patting the side of her leg. "Come on, Colin."

Aiden froze in surprise at her reaction, but he seemed to recover and held the door open for her. "Thank you for coming"—he hesitated—"Miss Summers."

Piper automatically reached out to shake his hand. He took it, but his grip was weak, with disappointment maybe. She waited until she stepped outside to roll her eyes, but whether it was at him or herself she wasn't sure.

Clenching her keys in her hand until it hurt, she fixed an *I don't give a shit* look on her face—fake it till you make it, right? The sopping clothes that clung to her body no longer felt cold. She didn't notice the chilly breeze blowing off the ocean or the rocks under her bare feet as she carried her shoes down the driveway, past Tamara's Prius, and to her car parked on the road. She didn't feel any of it. She felt numb.

Piper marched back to her car, determined that tomorrow would be different, that it would be just a job again, that she was done trying to figure out which Aiden was the real Aiden and if either of them liked her. It wasn't worth dealing with a crazy bitch like Tamara. Besides, she was fine on her own. Just fine, fine, fine. Better, in fact. She didn't need anyone. Especially a confusing man like him, however handsome he was, and thoughtful, and there was the loving dogs, and making her skin tingle just by being in the room. . . .

She heard the door open behind her, but she kept her eyes forward until Aiden's voice carried down to her.

"Pleasure!" he called out.

Against her will, her legs stopped moving. She glanced down at Colin, who seemed to shrug at her. No help there.

Unable to keep the annoyance off her face, she spun around. "Excuse me?"

"It's pleasure," Aiden repeated. "At the center, you asked me if this was business or pleasure."

He closed the distance between them. She knew the I-don't-give-a-shit look was still in place, but mostly because her face didn't know what expression to make.

Undeterred, he braved on. "It's pleasure," he said again. "That's . . . that's if you want it to be. For it to be more than business, I mean. And if you don't, I wouldn't want you to feel like you have to leave this job. I know you need it until you're done with school. And it's yours for as long as you like. I'll understand if it's just business for you."

He was babbling, speaking so haltingly, so hesitantly, the opposite of his usual well-spoken, confident self. Every word rang so earnest. So him. Not the world's version of Aiden, CNN Aiden, but hers. He wasn't hiding behind handshakes and ties.

He ran a hand through his hair until it stuck up, stiff with seawater. "It has been, right from the start. I saw you and thought, how can I say no to that pretty face?" He paused. "Sorry, that was a reference, from before. What we said at the beach? About our dogs?" He held up his hands. "Not that I thought you were like a dog." Running a hand over his face, he groaned. "God. That sounded a lot smoother in my head."

And it was then that she knew he wouldn't convert back, not now. She wouldn't let him. Tamara she could deal with later. She'd found her Aiden and she wasn't about to let him go.

"Well, Mr. Caldwell." Piper held out her hand in front of her like she was waiting to shake his.

Aiden stared down at it, deflating a little at the sight,

but he nodded and took her hand in his, anyway. He shook it once, but Piper didn't let go. Instead, she tugged him closer, until their bodies were as near as they were before, no towel to separate them. Before he could react, she stood on her toes and kissed him.

His mouth was warm and soft, and soon she forgot all about how cold she felt because all she could focus on were those lips, and his hot hands that slid up her bare arms to cup her face. The touch was sweet and hesitant until he pushed her wet, tangled locks back and pulled her in closer, kissing her deeper, pressing against her.

His body heat was much more effective than a pair of dachshunds. Soon it was more than shared heat that ran through her veins. It warmed her until she thought her clothing might dry from that kiss alone. When she finally pulled away, she half-expected to see steam rising from their clothes.

Piper grinned up at him. "It's definitely pleasure."

Aiden returned the look. She'd never seen him smile so big. "Trust me when I say, it's all mine."

18

The Dog and Bone

Piper and Aiden's relationship had been promoted from employment to dating status, and the new position came with a lot of perks. Piper stared across the restaurant table at Aiden, and she thought that the view from her new office had to be one of them.

He hadn't wasted any time booking a reservation at The Dog and Bone, San Francisco's latest in five-star dining for both two-legged and four-legged connoisseurs. It was booked up for weeks, but not, it seemed, if you were Aiden Caldwell.

The waitress sauntered over, carrying two steaks with a side of butternut squash and blueberries. A decadent meal fit for a king and his queen, which Colin and Sophie were. The waitress placed the dishes on the table, setting them in the depressions bored into the rich cherrywood so they wouldn't move around the table as the customers devoured their meals.

Sophie sniffed at the food uncertainly. She glanced

from the juicy slab of medium-rare to the waitress, wondering if she'd made a mistake.

What cruel joke is this? Sophie seemed to huff at her. *Why are you teasing me, evil servant?*

The idea of sitting at an actual table set with fine china clearly threw the doxie. Her dark eyes turned to Piper and Aiden, as if to ask permission to eat. Colin had no such reservations. He'd begun to gobble his New York strip loin before the plate was even on the table. Terrible manners for a date.

The waitress picked up a frosty bottle of beer. "Some specially brewed Hound Hooch for your friends?" she asked the humans.

"Is that safe?" Piper asked. "For dogs, I mean?"

"Don't worry. There's no alcohol. It's supposed to taste like liquefied chicken."

Piper wrinkled her nose. "I'll take your word for it."

"And for yourself?"

"I'll go for the red wine," she said. "Hold the chicken."

"I'll have the wine as well," Aiden said. "In fact, why don't you bring the bottle?"

The bottle? Piper worried about the cost of the fancy restaurant, not for the first time. She knew Aiden could afford it, but it still made her feel out of her depth.

The waitress finished serving them and headed for the Bow-wow Bar, where a row of wagging tails swished back and forth from holes in the backs of the stools. Like any good watering hole, it took all sorts to ensure a good party; the furry customers ranged from Chihuahuas to Great Danes. A blond English cocker mix near the end of the bar barked, and the bartender put his cloth down to refill her glass.

The pooches drank from their ergonomically designed wineglasses, tilted at the tops of the stems so the mouths of the glasses opened toward them. Next to Piper, Colin's snout pressed into his own wineglass to sample his hooch. Between his lapping and Sophie's eager meat chewing, they sounded like a couple of teenagers making out for the first time.

Piper turned to her own dish of baked salmon festooned with lemons and watercress in a display worthy of the Smithsonian. She was almost afraid to ruin the masterpiece. Digging in, she took her first bite, and her mouth exploded in a savory orgasm.

"Wow. The food is amazing."

Aiden made a noise of agreement. "I think Sophie and Colin would agree with you." Eyeing the room, he observed the oil paintings set in gilded picture frames and the dripping crystal chandelier casting a warm, romantic light on their table. "I didn't expect it to be so"—he searched for the word—"decadent. I've never heard of this restaurant."

"More and more restaurants in the city are starting to cater to dogs. The world of doggy couture is growing."

"Doggy couture?"

"Yeah, you know, designer fashions, gourmet restaurants, puppy mansions."

"Is that so? I wonder what kind of mortgage rates you could get for one of those."

Piper laughed. "Addison owns her own dog spa. Business is booming. I heard about this restaurant from her after she came to the grand opening. She was promoting her business by offering complimentary pawdicures."

"Well, I'm glad we came." By the way he stared at her over his filet mignon, she knew he didn't mean because of the menu.

"Me too."

Of course, the second Addison told Piper how high-class the joint was she dug through Zoe's closet to find something suitable. Her style fit the bill with her sleek sophistication. And since Zoe mostly planned weddings, up-and-coming designers would often send her free samples of their latest bridesmaid dress designs in hopes that she would recommend them to customers.

Piper caught Aiden eyeing her plunging neckline for the eighth time that night before they dropped back to his plate. The dress was a hit. While Zoe was a lot taller and leaner than her, the red asymmetrical number she borrowed managed to hug her curves just right—Lycra, she was convinced, had magical properties.

"So," Aiden said. "Did you grow up here in San Francisco?"

"No. I was raised in Oregon on an onion farm." She automatically smiled. It sounded like the start of a bad joke. Hell, most of her life felt like a bad joke.

"An onion farm?" His eyebrows shot up. "Do they grow a lot of onions in Oregon?"

"They do. In eastern Oregon mostly, around the Snake River Valley."

He took another sip of wine. She could tell by the comical look on his face that those bad jokes were running through his mind.

"So did you have a lot of animals on the farm?"

"We did. A horse, a few pigs, a couple of dogs, about a billion barn cats, oh, and some Araucana chickens. They're the breed that lays green eggs."

"Green eggs? So Dr. Seuss wasn't kidding?"

"Nope. We ate green eggs and ham for breakfast," she said. "We wouldn't have had so many animals, but every year or so I'd find a new friend. I would beg and beg, and eventually, I'd get my way."

"Why doesn't that surprise me?" He grinned.

"Old habits die hard." Although that wasn't entirely true. If she had her way, she'd already own a veterinarian clinic and she wouldn't need to beg, borrow, and steal her friends' clothes for a date. But she couldn't complain too much. She did get Aiden.

"I decided at a young age that I wanted to work with animals. Not just wanted to. *Had* to. It's part of me."

"So you left Oregon to come here for school?"

"Not exactly. My mom found a job here after I finished high school, so I moved here with her."

"So do you still live with her?"

"No. We lived together for about two years. After that, she moved to Washington to be near my brother, Ethan. He's a lawyer there."

"You have a brother?" He sounded surprised, like he should know this by now. They'd talked almost every day for two weeks, and the subject never came up. But it wasn't by accident.

Inevitably, Aiden asked, "And your dad? Where's he?"

"He died," she said.

Aiden put down his fork. "I'm sorry." And he looked it.

Guilt crept through her, like maybe she should have told him all this before. After all, he told her about his father when they'd first met. Then again, until Monday he'd just been her boss.

"Sometimes the farm seems like an entirely different life from this one."

As though Colin could understand her as well as she could understand him, he leaned over and gave her neck a steaky kiss. She patted his head and poured him some more Hound Hooch.

"I don't cook with onions much," she said, trying to sound upbeat. "Even now, when I chop them up I can't help but get a little teary."

He huffed through his nose, acknowledging the joke, but didn't laugh. This was a date. Their first date. She didn't want to drag it down.

"It was a long time ago." She tried to wave it away. "It's fine. I'm fine."

But he stared at her like he could see right through her bullshit. He wasn't going to let her off that easy. "It's not fine. It never is."

Her plastic smile melted. He knew. He'd been there. And by insisting it was fine, it would only cheapen what he went through.

"You're right," she said finally. "It wasn't a joke. Not really. For years after, I couldn't tell if it was the onions making me cry, or . . ." She shrugged. "Now I stick to shallots and leeks. The cousins of the onion. Far less emotional."

This time he did smile a little. "I didn't realize that food could be so emotional."

"Oh yes, you should see me at Halloween time. All those pumpkin craniotomies. Then to top it off they get their guts scraped out. I'm a basket case."

"I'll never look at a jack-o'-lantern the same way again." He picked up his fork and laughed to himself. "Actually, when I was a kid, I had my own food issues. After reading *Charlotte's Web*"—he ducked his head—"I became a vegetarian for two years."

She almost choked on her wine. "Really? That's adorable."

Blushing, he focused on cutting his steak, and when he'd finished that he decided the pieces needed to be smaller. The next time Aiden looked up, he took a sip of wine, and his gaze focused on Piper over the rim of his glass. His eyes flicked away from her for only a moment, but this time it wasn't her cleavage that distracted him. It was something behind her.

He cringed like his wine had turned sour in his mouth.

"What's wrong?" Piper shifted to look behind her, but he stopped her with a wave of his hand.

"Don't look. I don't want to draw attention to us."

"Why? What is it?"

"Trouble." He sighed, putting his fork down. "Holly Hart just walked in."

Who Let the Dogs Out?

Aiden's attention, which had been so absorbed by Piper the entire evening, shifted and focused on another woman. *The* Holly Hart. He glared across the restaurant over Piper's shoulder, his jaw clenched.

"Holly Hart?" Piper said. "Seriously? Why do you think she's here?" Piper had to fight the urge to spin around, curious whether Holly came with a dog or a man.

"I think she's on a date," he said. "I just don't want her to see us."

Piper frowned. "Why not?"

He hesitated, eyes darting from Holly to Piper. "You're right." Picking his fork back up, he dug into his meal. "You're right. Who cares if she sees us?"

Him, she thought. That's who. He cared. That much was obvious to Piper. She just didn't know why.

She reminded herself that the pushy reporter had stalked him in the past, fabricating stories about him and publishing them. But what story could she possibly concoct about seeing him at the restaurant, with Piper?

The largest leap Holly could make was the assumption they were on a date together. And while Piper still had a tough time believing it herself, would it be such a bad thing for that to get out? Was it so shocking or newsworthy?

She peeked down at her dress. Thanks to Zoe's fashion advice and Addison's hair and makeup skills, she knew she looked like a million bucks. That couldn't have been it. Maybe he wanted to avoid the harsh glare from Holly's shining personality.

Piper kept telling herself this, but for the rest of the meal Aiden seemed distracted. It wasn't anything he did on purpose; however, she couldn't help notice that he sat a little lower in his chair, the constant leg jiggling under the table, and was he eating faster, or was it just her?

"Is everything okay?" she asked.

"Of course," he said. "Why do you ask?"

"Oh, no reason," she said with forced lightness. "You seem a little . . . distracted."

He paused with the fork halfway to his mouth and he noticed his nearly empty plate and her half-eaten fish. He cringed sheepishly. "Sorry. I guess Holly gets me a little riled up." He ate a little slower after that, but he remained distracted no matter how hard Piper tried to snap him out of it.

By the time the waitress cleared away the dishes, Colin and Sophie had mopped up their side of the table with their tongues and started to work on the food stuck to their tiny dog bibs tied around their necks. A black bow tie topped Colin's for a formal touch, while a lace collar adorned Sophie's, along with a string of pearls around the neck.

"Would you like to see our doggy delights menu?" the waitress asked. "Our new items include bacon-flavored popcorn, turkey and banana biscotti, and beef carrot cupcake topped with cream cheese icing."

Piper's mouth started to water. "Is it gross that I think that sounds delicious?"

"Don't worry. We have people desserts too. I can go get the menu, if you like."

Piper thought, What the heck? It was already going to cost a fortune. She might as well have a good time.

"We'll just take the bill, please," Aiden cut in.

"Sure. I'll be right back." The server turned, almost tripping over a Pomeranian, and went back to the bar.

"Watching your girlish figure?" Piper asked, disappointed there would be no dessert.

"I know of a great gelato place near here." He gave her a tight smile. "I thought it would be nice to go for a walk."

With the *W* word, Sophie's ears perked up and Colin gave a short bark, initiating a ripple of responses from the furry patrons nearby.

Piper laughed. "Looks like the decision's been made."

Aiden's credit card appeared in his hand before the waitress returned. Piper reached for her own purse, but he gave her a withering look. "At least let me pay for our first official date." When she continued to fish out her wallet, he added, "Please?"

It wasn't like she could afford it, anyway, so she gave him a grateful smile. "Sure. Thank you. But I'll get the gelato."

"Sounds fair."

Probably not, she thought.

The moment the waitress handed Aiden's card back, he was out of his seat. He turned his back to the restaurant, or to Holly, she supposed, and dipped his head closer to the waitress.

"Do you happen to have a back way out?" he asked her in a hushed tone.

"Certainly," she said without missing a beat. "It's right

through there." She pointed to a hall at the back of the restaurant.

Piper wondered if this was a common request. She'd seen more than one celeb-type person with their furry friends in tow that night. The type of clientele that would come to a swanky place like The Dog and Bone might want to keep a low profile, avoid paparazzi. However, in this case, the paparazzo happened to be dining there.

Aiden and Piper clipped the leashes on to Colin and Sophie and headed past the relaxation area. Stuffed puppies lounged on oversized pillows, some twitching while they napped, dreaming of chasing rabbits. Ducking through the quiet hall, Aiden held the back door open for her. The cool night air rushed in, but before she stepped out Piper stopped.

"Oh. I forgot my purse." She handed over Colin's leash. "I'll be right out."

She returned to their table and found her purse dangling from the arm of her chair. Grabbing it, she turned to head back, but then she heard her name.

"Piper?"

She froze, cringing as she recognized Holly's voice. So much for sneaking out. Rolling her eyes, she turned around and waved.

Holly Hart sprang from her chair and sashayed across the room, sneezing repeatedly as she passed the Bow-wow Bar.

"Piper. So good to see you." She gave the air near Piper's cheeks a couple of kisses, like they were best friends meeting in Paris.

"Holly, I'm surprised to see you here with your dog allergies."

She leaned in, whispering conspiratorially. "It's a marketing ploy. My ratings jumped after that segment about your dog rescue center. It seems the way to this community's heart is through their mutts. I've gotta keep up appearances, you know?"

"Right. Yeah." Piper tried to keep a straight face. "That's why I do it."

"So." Holly smiled coyly like they were just two girls gossiping. "What are you doing here?" Her eyes darted around the room, undoubtedly searching for Aiden.

God knew, Piper could never afford to eat at a place like The Dog and Bone. Anyone could see that. But Aiden wanted to avoid Holly, so she didn't want to give him away. She pretended not to notice Holly's surprise, as though she rubbed elbows with the rich and famous on a daily basis. That her shoes were Jimmy Choos and not on clearance at Target.

"Just thought I'd pop in for a bite to eat."

"Only you?" Holly asked. "All alone? Not with one of your four-legged friends?"

"Colin's outside," she hedged.

"All by himself?"

She wasn't going to lie, but quite frankly, it was none of Holly's business. "No."

When it was clear she wasn't going to spill the beans, Holly gave up the pretense. "Don't worry. I won't get you into trouble. I'm off the clock now, anyway." She blew a seductive kiss to the man back at her table, who was still wearing his sunglasses inside, at night.

"I don't know what Aiden's so worried about," Holly continued. "It's not like his love life is the stuff of Channel Five News or anything. I'm a hard-hitting journalist now. I don't work for the *San Francisco Gate* anymore."

"You used to work for the *Gate*?" Piper asked.

"It's where I got my start. While I worked there, Aiden Caldwell was something of a fetish of mine."

Now that Piper could understand.

"He was one of the city's most eligible bachelors. Still

is. And boy, did that guy have taste." She shook her head wistfully.

Piper wasn't stupid. She knew that Holly was trying to get information out of her. She gnawed at her lip before plowing on, anyway—she couldn't walk away after a statement like that.

"Taste? You mean, in women?"

Holly widened her eyes. "We're talking the bluebloods of the financial kingdom, daughters of the most successful Fortune Five Hundreds. The upper-crusters. Ivy League, part-time model types. Made me grateful for my mega zoom lenses." She winked conspiratorially. "You know what I'm saying?"

"Right," she said, but she didn't want to think too hard about what that meant.

"He made my job real easy, you know? Always showing off his new trophies, making a real spectacle of it. But things got kind of quiet after his dad passed away." She shrugged and patted Piper on the shoulder. "Well, looks like he's back in the game."

The game?

"The bad boy of the Financial District is back."

Piper knew she should deny it or say something vague. Her silence was practically an admission that Aiden was hiding somewhere. But suddenly she didn't feel like covering for him anymore. She wondered why she was supposed to, why she had to slink out the back into a dark alley to avoid being seen.

If what Holly said was true, then it wasn't like he worried about keeping his private life a secret. He never did before. But then again, he'd been dating models and socialites, graduates from the country's top universities, not a singing-telegram girl. Not exactly a headliner for the *Gate*.

Or maybe it was. Only when she imagined it it wasn't her and Aiden caught in a glamorous, well-lit red carpet shot. It was one of those poorly timed photos, where a transition between facial expressions could also be construed as being drug addled or a having a mental breakdown.

Piper's headline would read: "Tycoon Aiden Caldwell: Who Let the Dogs Out?"

Maybe it wasn't about keeping his private life under wraps but Piper herself.

Deep in thought, Piper said good-bye to Holly and slipped out the back door. When Aiden saw her, his face lit up like the flash from a paparazzi camera. Distracted as she was, she couldn't help but smile in return.

It was all in her head, she told herself. A ploy constructed by Holly to stir things up. Besides, she had nothing to be ashamed about. She was as good as any Ivy-Leaguing, elbow-rubbing, champagne-drinking, hoity-toity model. Hell, better. She had street cred.

Part of her wanted to be frank and confront Aiden about it, to blurt it out and be done with it. Walking next to her down the dark, narrow alley, he reached out and took her hand in his. It felt so warm and wonderful. Suddenly, like a giant Araucana, she was too afraid to ask him about it. Because what if it was really true?

Don't be stupid, she chastised herself. If it was true, then he wasn't the guy for her and she was wasting her time. Pulling away, she turned to face him, but as though Colin could sense her annoyance, he began to growl next to her, loud and steady like a gas lawn mower.

"Colin, what's wrong, boy?"

He ignored her. Hackles raised, he stared at the end of the long alley like he suspected it of foul play. Piper followed his glower and noticed a dark car parked about halfway down. It could have been blue, black, green, anything really, since the alley was dim. The headlights were off, the engine idling, absolutely nothing out of the ordinary. Right? They might have been waiting for someone. Anyone.

Even her and Aiden.

The headlights flicked on and her skin began to crawl.

"Let's go around the other way," Piper told Aiden.

Colin resisted her tugs on his leash, like he was playing a game of chicken with the car and he was confident he could win. Her money was on the big metal thing, so she bent down to pick him up, smoothing his hackles down.

"Come on, Colin."

The dark car flicked on its high beams. Harsh LED lights filled her vision. She grunted, shielding her searing retinas against the light. She couldn't see a thing, but she heard the engine rev, high-pitched and whiney.

"Piper." There was an urgency to Aiden's voice, matching her own building unease.

She scooped Colin up into her arms and reached for Aiden's outstretched hand. Sophie was already in his other, pressed protectively to his chest.

The engine revved again. Tires skidded on loose gravel until they found purchase on pavement. The rubber chirped and the car sped toward them.

Blinking light spots from her vision, she stumbled as Aiden tugged her along. She was more grateful than ever for the Lycra dress, which allowed her to move freely. They were running, sprinting, gasping for air. There was no longer any doubt whom that car had been waiting for. She wanted to cry out for help, but she couldn't catch her breath.

Up ahead, the alley narrowed to single traffic where a Buick had parked alongside the rear of a building, next to a Dumpster. Their pursuer's headlights lit up the space. It sped closer. Both she and Aiden weren't going to make it around the Buick in time. They had to split up.

As Aiden and Piper approached the next building, she

noticed an alcove to a back entrance. She wrenched out of Aiden's grip and pushed him aside. He grunted, taken by surprise. His step faltered and he pitched to the side, careening into the alcove with Sophie in his grasp.

Holding Colin to her chest, she dove in the opposite direction and rolled on top of the Buick's wide hood. Aiden called out to her, but she couldn't see if he was safe, or anything for that matter, beyond the blinding lights. She couldn't see the car, not the color, the model, or the driver. The lights were coming straight at her. And her money was still on the car.

She crawled farther back on the hood, leaning against the window, and curled her body protectively around Colin. She hoped the car would avoid colliding with the solid Buick.

She was wrong.

The impact threw her forward, or maybe the Buick back. Metal crunched against metal; headlights flashed too close to her face. The impact threw her off the hood. She tumbled down between the side of the Buick and the brick wall of the building it was parked next to.

Her bare arms scraped down the rough bricks. She twisted her body so she didn't fall on Colin. Pain shot up her right side as she hit the ground, bits of gravel piercing her skin.

The Buick shifted next to her as her attacker scraped by in the narrow space and sped toward the other end of the alley and out to the main street. Claustrophobia kicked in, compressed as she was between the Buick and the wall. Like a Piper panino.

She felt dazed, scared, certain this was the end. Her eyes were still blinking with flashes of light. Engine sounds faded into the distance; then she heard someone's name being called over and over again above the ringing in her ears.

"Piper!"

Oh . . . it was hers, she thought belatedly.

"Piper, answer me. Can you hear me?"

Some part of Piper's rattled brain told her it was a good idea to answer back. And then she thought, Oh, good, I still have brains. They weren't splattered across the parking lot.

"Piper!" Aiden called again.

"I'm here." Her voice squeaked out as tiny as a mouse's, like she'd sucked the entire contents out of a Macy's parade balloon. She cleared her throat and tried again. "In here." Although she still hadn't pieced together where "here" was.

She blinked and took in the dark space, the Buick, and the brick wall. Oh yeah, she thought, the alley. From under the car, she watched Aiden's feet move to the other side. Footsteps shuffled as he searched for a way to get to her. The car hood banged as he squeezed between it and the garbage bin.

She glanced up and his face appeared in the narrow gap between the wall and the car. He squatted down and peered into her panino.

"Oh, thank God," he said, resting his forehead on the Buick's hood for a moment. "Are you hurt?"

Hell, yes, she thought. She became aware of Colin grunting and squirming beneath her, trying to free himself from her vice grip. Relaxing her arms, she flexed them and straightened her legs to see if they all worked. Her right side throbbed from her fall, but nothing else seemed to hurt too badly.

"I think I'm all right," she said, but groped her head just to make sure it was still attached.

"Can you squeeze out of there?"

"I'll try."

Rolling onto her stomach, Piper wormed her way to the front of the car, ignoring the sharp bits of gravel that scraped her arms and God knows what else that squished under her hands. Colin scuttled around, licking her face and shoving his snout in her ears and hair to assess for injuries.

"Not helping, Colin. Yes, I'm happy you're okay too."

Once she'd wiggled her way between the front tire and the brick wall, Aiden helped her to her feet. She didn't even have a moment to catch her breath before he crushed her against his chest.

She held on to him for physical support as much as emotional. Her legs were shaking, her hip and elbow throbbing, and her world still spun.

When she glanced back at what little space was left between the Buick and the wall that she'd been sandwiched between, Piper the juicy jam squished in the middle, she thought it was a miracle she escaped. And Colin had tried to warn her. He sensed something wrong, like he could smell the danger. It was that inexplicable instinct that animals had—they just had a way of knowing.

"Are you hurt?" Aiden asked, his eyes dark, his hands moving over her like he wasn't convinced she was safe in his arms yet.

Adrenaline-soaked as her body was, she wasn't ready to believe her senses. She took stock of her injuries, counting limbs and fingers to make sure they were all present and accounted for. To her surprise, she found very little wrong. Some missing skin on elbows, gravel imbedded in her palms. It was likely she'd discover new injuries for days to come as aches surprised her and the bruises blossomed. Oh, how there would be bruises. Zoe's dress, on the other hand, had seen better days. Piper's dry cleaner would have to be a magician to save it.

Colin circled her feet, sniffing at her ankles, coming up with his own diagnosis. After a moment, he sat back on his haunches and barked up at her anxiously.

She bent down to pick him up and cradled him in her arms, letting him give her kisses. "I'm not bad. But the night's still young." She said it jokingly, only she wished she were joking.

"I'm not letting you out of my sight for another second." Aiden pulled her back toward him, like he couldn't stand to not be touching her. "I wish they'd find that taxi already."

"The taxi?"

"Yeah, maybe there will be some clues as to who's doing this. This can't be a coincidence. It has to be related to the attacks on the center."

Piper realized that he'd been blaming himself all this time, for everything. That he thought it was because of his briefcase and the information contained in it. Meanwhile, the entire time, she figured it had something to do with her.

She didn't bother responding, since she couldn't be sure. The fact was, she did piss off a lot of people; at least she had recently. It could have been the person targeting the center or Laura, or Barney Miller, or even Tamara for that matter—although a catfight in Aiden's house was a lot different from vehicular homicide.

"Did you happen to see the plates on that car?"

"No." He pulled out his cell phone. "But I'll call the cops. Maybe they can track them down before they get too far."

"I should have them on speed dial by now," she said dryly.

He still hadn't let her go. For once, she didn't mind him looking after her. "Well, hopefully this will be over soon."

Piper hoped so too. Only she hoped it was because they caught the guy. Not because he got what he wanted.

20

Piece of Tail

The elevator dinged as it reached the top floor of Caldwell and Son Investments. Remembering how things went for her the last time she was there, Piper hesitated before getting off. She dreaded facing that snooty admin assistant. But Piper's assets were covered a great deal more than they were the last time. And besides, what did she have to feel out of place for? She'd been invited by the boss, after all.

Tightening the belt on her raincoat, she stepped into the foyer and strode right up to the reception desk. It might have been Piper's imagination, but the girl working the desk appeared more orange than the last time, as though she'd swapped her tangerine self-tanner for a lovely shade of marmalade. The girl recognized her, because she smiled, a little devilishly, Piper thought.

"Hello." She glanced around like she expected to see the horse head.

"Hi. I'm here to see Aiden Caldwell?"

"Are you here for another singing telegram?" Her face lit up, not unlike a big orange jack-o'-lantern.

"Not today. I'm just here to speak with your *boss*." Piper made sure to emphasize the word *boss*.

It had the effect she was looking for, because the girl's mouth tightened like a drawstring purse. Standing up, she tugged her pencil skirt down and smacked the release button on the secure doors. "This way, please. He's expecting you."

Piper pressed her lips together to hide a triumphant grin. She followed her through the glass doors and down the long corridor lined with offices. She was only limping a little that day, although she'd had to skip her high heels for her telegram gigs. But it could have been much worse.

It had been two days since the attempted hit-and-run and the cops had found no leads. Nor did they receive any tips about the rescue center vandalism like she'd hoped they would after her appearance on the news. Their "one week" was up that night, and they had nothing.

The receptionist led Piper down a hallway with walls that were top to bottom glass, including the door to each office that faced on to the corridor. She imagined the staff probably felt like the ladies did in their fish tank. However, each room was outfitted with blinds in case privacy was needed. The space was modern, the furniture included, reminding Piper of Aiden's home.

She saw Aiden long before he saw her. His office sat at the end of the hall, the space larger than the others, with a view of Montgomery Street down below. He was on the phone, pacing back and forth behind his desk, stroking his tie. It stirred something deep in Piper's belly. He looked so professional, so powerful, so in control. She wanted him to use some of that control on her.

The door was open, so orange girl tapped on the glass door to announce their presence. Aiden turned to see who it was, and his eyes fell on Piper. Her knees buckled.

"I'm sorry. I'll have to call you back." He hung up the phone. "Thank you, Veronica."

The moment she left, Aiden crossed the room and closed the door. Piper couldn't help but notice that he glanced out the glass wall to make sure no one saw before giving her a quick kiss on the cheek. Maybe he wasn't just afraid of Holly seeing them together, or Tamara, but anyone. Or perhaps it was his "I don't like mixing business with pleasure" motto.

"You made it." He moved around to the other side of his desk.

"Are you sure it's okay that I'm here?" she asked after the cool reception. "I mean, I could study at Starbucks or something."

"No. You have your exam soon and there are plenty of spare offices you can use. If the boss catches you, though, just say you're the new temp." He winked.

It was obviously easy for him in that setting. To be the boss, to be in control. It was a comfortable role for him. He had his safety blankets like his tie to readjust, his desk to hide behind, papers to reshuffle. Piper found it quite annoying. Naughty thoughts forced their way into her mind, making her want to break the rules, to toss those papers aside and create some chaos.

"Oh, I've already got a cover story," she said. "I can say I'm here for a singing telegram. I just finished a gig a few blocks from here. I haven't had a chance to change." She raised her backpack that contained her clothes and textbooks in explanation.

He stopped straightening the papers on his desk. "You're still wearing your costume?" He gave a fleeting look over her shoulder, out to the hallway. Since his office was located at the end, it could be seen by anyone who stepped out of their door and looked that way.

His eyes drifted back to her. He cleared his throat. “Which one is it?”

She batted her eyelashes. “You’ll just have to use your imagination.”

He perched himself on the edge of his desk, eyes darting back and forth from her coat to the hall. The temptation lit his face. Temptation of experiencing pleasure while in his place of business.

“Surely”—he hesitated—“you can give me just a peek.”

She followed his gaze down the hall. Seeing no one coming their way, she reached for the belt on her raincoat. Slowly, she untied it, running the length of the belt ends through her fingers until they dropped to her sides. Gripping the collar, she slid her hands down, keeping it closed, teasing him.

His eyes remained fixed on hers, flirtatious until she spread open the coat, revealing the costume beneath. The short skirt was striped red and white, exposing nearly every inch of her smooth legs. White stars speckled her collared vest, in Old Glory Blue. It hugged her waist and pressed her breasts up so that they bulged out the top of her sparkling gold bra underneath.

He remained very still, contemplative, like he stood in an art gallery appreciating a masterwork.

Closing the coat again, she tied the belt around her.

He snapped out of wherever he’d gone—which was certainly not at work. “Hey. I wasn’t finished.”

“That was more than a peek. That was like a gawk,” she said, “or a stare.”

“No, no.” He slid off his desk. “It was barely a glance. A glimpse at best.”

“Well, maybe you should have thought about that before you installed all these revealing windows.”

“I can take care of that.” Crossing the room, he brushed past her and hit a knob next to the light switch. There was the whirring sound of a motor as the blinds slid across the glass wall, completely obscuring the outside world. He locked the door and loosened his tie as he moved toward her.

Piper gasped. "But Mr. Caldwell," she teased. "This is completely inappropriate for the workplace. What would Larry Williams say?"

"I don't care what he would say," Aiden growled, his voice low and thick. "I'm feeling rather . . . patriotic at the moment." Bending down, he grazed his lips across hers.

"I can tell," she muttered. "I can feel your flag flying at full mast."

His eyebrow quirked up and his smirk was so delicious she wanted to bite his lip. "That's only half-mast. You'll know when it's full."

Her eyes widened, but she couldn't think of a comeback as his lips drifted down her neck, tickling her skin. Moving her hands up his chest, she groped the hard muscles beneath his shirt. She peeled off his jacket and dropped it to the floor in a rumpled heap.

Her hips were squirming to press closer even as she said, "But you're at work." She wanted to hear him acknowledge the pleasure, to throw away the business side for a moment and give in to it. To give in to her.

He pulled her collar aside to kiss the curve of her neck. "You're not trying to prevent me from expressing my love for my country, are you, Miss Summers?"

"No, sir," she breathed. "It's your constitutional right."

He backed her up until her butt hit the desk and leaned her back. "It's my duty."

"You're obligated, really." She reclined across his desk, dragging him down by his tie until he laid his mouth against hers.

"I don't think I'll get much studying done here," she said between kisses.

"No." He moved his kisses down her plunging neckline. "But I might get a little done myself."

"Oh, and what will you be studying?"

"Anatomy." He tugged at the top golden button on her vest until it popped open beneath the pressure of her breasts. "Particularly yours."

He slipped each button free until he could slide his palm across her bare stomach, exposing her golden bra. Pulling away, he took a moment to run his eyes over her body. When he bent to kiss her again, she reached out for his flagpole to discover it at full mast.

"Oh, glory," she breathed.

At her touch, he moaned against her mouth. Pleasure had clearly won.

Aiden's hand burned hot over her calf, her knee, and all the way up her leg. She squirmed on the desk. His fingers crept higher up the soft skin of her inner thigh. She gasped for air, unable to stand it. Her heart hammered, her head spun with anticipation, until she heard ringing in her ears. It wasn't until Aiden grunted in frustration that she realized he heard it too.

Reaching over to the phone on his desk, he pressed a button. "Veronica, I'm busy at the moment. Hold all my calls."

"Sorry, sir. Larry Williams would like to speak with you regarding the rezoning for–"

Aiden practically leapt over the desk to pick up the receiver. "Veronica, I have Miss Summers in the room. Please refrain from discussing business around other clients"—he hesitated—"err, people. . . . Yes. Fine. Tell him to wait for a minute and I can speak to him privately."

The moment he hung up the phone, he began tightening his tie again. Back to business. So hot and heavy one moment, but then to be ushered unceremoniously out of his office the next was jarring, to say the least. Piper slid off the desk and pulled her raincoat back on.

"I'm sorry," he said, picking up his jacket. "But this is important. We're on a tight schedule with this project."

"Of course, I understand." Which was a lie. She didn't, really. Aiden was the boss. He could have told Larry to come back. What was Aiden's receptionist about to say that he didn't want her to hear? Why was he being so secretive? It was taking his mixing business with pleasure thing a bit far.

"The bathroom is down the hall if you'd like to change," he said. "Ask Veronica to show you to a spare office after. Stay for as long as you like. Maybe we could do a late dinner tonight?" he asked, a kind of pleading hopefulness in his face.

Piper softened a little. She'd felt his flagpole rise and knew that he was as sorry as she was. "Yeah, sounds good."

There was a knock on the door. Piper fumbled to check that all her coat buttons were done up, hiding any evidence of the American flag beneath. Once she was all sorted, she gave Aiden a nod and he opened the door.

The Chief Operations Officer stepped into the office. She was finally able to put a name to the face—or smell. Old Spice.

"Come on in, Larry," Aiden said.

Piper gathered her backpack and swung it over her shoulder, eager to leave, but when the businessman noticed her he did a double take.

"Oh, I didn't realize you were already in the middle of a *meeting,*" he said. But the way he said *meeting* made Piper blush.

She formed the most innocent expression she could, like she and his boss hadn't just gotten to third base on his desk.

"Larry, you remember Miss Summers."

"How could I forget? Did you come to entertain us again with another little song?"

"No." She bristled but then reminded herself what she had on beneath her coat. "Aiden has offered to let me use a spare office to study."

"She's studying to be a veterinarian," Aiden explained.

Old Spice planted his briefcase on Aiden's desk. "Oh, that's right. You volunteer at that dog shelter, don't you? I heard about the vandalism. How very unfortunate."

He spoke to her like she was a ten-year-old with a ruined science fair project. She felt her chin rise in response. "We'll be fine."

"Piper went on the news to raise donations to help improve security on the building."

"Is that right? That was you?" He seemed to think for a second. "Yes, I think I might have seen that segment. How very . . . industrious of you. Well." He unlatched his briefcase, signaling it was time to move on to grown-up things now. "I hope it all works out for you."

He began laying out documents and blueprints on Aiden's desk, and she smirked as she imagined Old Spice reviewing important documents where her star-spangled butt had been only a few seconds before. If he knew, it would probably have knocked his argyle socks off.

Noticing the documents, Aiden reached over and slammed the briefcase shut, like this wasn't an investment company but the NSA, highly top secret. He reached over and gathered the loose pages, flipping them facedown.

"I'll show Miss Summers out before we begin." He gave Larry a pointed look before turning back to Piper.

"Piper, I'll speak to you later." He held the door open for her. Laying a hand on her lower back, he practically shoved her out of the room. He smiled at her, but it was strained. "And help yourself to coffee and snacks. Veronica will show you around."

"Right. Thanks."

Piper turned back to the reception room and the door shut firmly behind her. She flinched at the sound. At least it wasn't a handshake. But somehow, it felt worse.

What the hell was going on? She was tired of being in the dark. She wanted answers, but the kind of answers she needed she wasn't going to get from Caldwell and Son Investments.

Abandoning her plans to study, she headed back to the elevator and drove to the police station.

21

Hound Horror

Piper pulled into the rescue center's parking lot and killed her headlights—or, rather, her one headlight, since the other had burned out months before. Colin reclined in her purse like it was a chaise longue, so she had to dislodge him before fishing out her phone. There was a message from Aiden.

Hey. Long day at the office. Just wrapping up now. I came to see if you were still around, but Veronica said you'd left already. Are we still on for a late dinner?

She hesitated, her fingers hovering over the reply button. It was late. The clock on the dash said it was almost nine. She'd stopped by the police station to get an update from Officer Tucker in person. When she pestered him about the attempted hit-and-run, he said he was looking into Barney Miller and Laura from SFAAC. He also said that Aiden's PA, Tamara, had a solid alibi. Apparently, she was tied up at work in a meeting. Aiden still didn't know that Piper had listed Tamara as a possible suspect.

One week. The message rang through her head. She'd

reminded Officer Tucker that their time was up. He said the police would increase the patrol units to the area throughout the night. In other words, she was on her own again. She'd thought she'd been joking about spending the night sleeping at the center, but tonight that was exactly what she was prepared to do. Anything to keep her charges safe.

She'd wanted to get to the center a little earlier, but Lindsey from Sam's office had texted her that afternoon with two last-minute telegram bookings. Well, three, but one of them had been Barney Miller.

Supposedly he'd sprained his ankle and couldn't go on his vacation, which of course meant he needed a "Get well soon" telegram. She wondered if it was possible to sprain an ankle during a car chase in a dark alley. Obviously she turned that gig down.

As she hesitated with her phone in her hand, Colin grumbled from the passenger seat. She glanced at him out of the corner of her eye. She could swear there was a disapproving tilt to his head.

"What?" she asked. "I can't see Aiden tonight. I have to study."

But Colin's judgmental stare indicated that he wasn't convinced.

She sighed and flopped back in her seat. "You're a real ball-breaker," she told him.

If she was honest with herself, and Colin, she was still dwelling on her dinner date with Aiden. Dwelling on what Holly had said.

Sure, Piper had seen him every day that week for their usual dog walk, out in public, in broad daylight. But each time she saw him, it only reinforced her sneaking suspicion that Aiden didn't want to make their relationship public. Even when old Larry Williams showed up at Aiden's office that afternoon, he couldn't wait to get rid of her.

There was no handholding, no kissing, no touching of

any kind. That is, until they were alone. Then the touching began.

And boy, was there touching.

At the thought, Piper's mind drifted back to their little office rendezvous. Even hours later, the memory had her fidgeting in her seat.

"No. No. No." Piper banged on her steering wheel, trying to shake off the memory and startling Colin in the process. "I have to study," she told her doxie. "And if I'm not here, then who's going to make sure nothing happens to the center tonight? All that will have to wait. Aiden will have to wait."

She hit the reply button on her phone.

Sorry, she typed. *I can't. I'm studying at the center tonight.*

With difficulty, she forced her finger to hit *send.*

Besides, she'd just finished her telegram gigs. It wasn't like she'd dressed for dinner. In her peaked police cap, black booty shorts, and skintight spandex top, she was dressed for an undercover police sting op at a brothel.

Grabbing her textbook-laden backpack, she turned to Colin. "Shall we go say hello to the guests?"

Piper locked the VW Bug and made her way around to the front of the building, calf-high boots crunching on the gravel. She used her phone to light the path. The days were getting longer, but the sky was thick with clouds that evening, obliterating the day's last light. Already she could smell the rain coming. A drop or two fell on her bare shoulder as she climbed the front cement steps.

Reaching into her fake gun holster, she fished the center's keys out and unlocked the door. She swung it open and stepped into the reception room. She couldn't see a thing. The only light came from the glowing red exit sign above her and the fish tank buzzing on the far back counter.

The familiar scents and sounds welcomed her inside.

The guests were already going nuts in the back, barking and howling like maniacs. She wondered if they'd ever get used to her coming and going at strange hours. Once they saw it was just her and Colin, they'd settle down.

Piper dropped her backpack on the floor and held the door open to let Colin slip inside. He'd barely taken two steps past her before he froze to the linoleum. His long ears were perked, well, as high as the floppy things could go. She grinned. Her tough little guard dog, making sure the coast was clear.

But she couldn't hear anything but the dogs in the back. Not even out on the street. The traffic dwindled at this time of night, everyone having gone home for the day to eat or party in Mission. And that's when Piper realized it had been perfectly quiet since she stepped inside, no creak of the door, no cars out on the street. She'd made no sound coming in but for the key turning in the lock. Marilyn's bell had been torn down during the break-in.

Her breath caught in her chest. So if they weren't barking at her, she wondered, what were the dogs barking at?

A muffled noise came from the kitchen, a soft splashing like someone washing their hands in the sink. Colin heard it too, because he started growling next to her. It was a menacing sound, low and deep in his barrel chest, too quiet to be heard over the barking in the back. Although she couldn't see him clearly, his black fur blending into the darkness around them, she knew his hackles were bristling, because hers certainly were.

Maybe Marilyn had come home early from her trip. Or maybe it was Zoe or Addison. But neither of their cars were in the parking lot. And besides, she was the only one with a key—and absolutely no life on a Friday night.

Hand still gripping the doorknob, Piper froze with indecision. She was torn between running for help and heading in to investigate. She knew she should back out, go call the police, like any sane person would do. Although, she reasoned, if someone was there, at night, in the dark, it couldn't mean anything good. It could mean their criminal was back and the dogs were in danger.

Get out! Or I'll make you.

She wasn't going anywhere.

Soundlessly, she shut the door and waited for her eyes to adjust. Every scary axe-murder movie she'd ever seen conveniently rushed through her brain at that moment. Her heart thumped like there was a competitive paddleball game being played inside her chest. Suddenly remembering her costume, she reached for her belt and slid the police nightstick out of its holder. She weighed it in her hand like a baseball bat. Nice and heavy.

The costume originally came with a hollow plastic police stick, no more dangerous than a pool noodle. But after her first gig at a college party, she'd swapped it out for a hefty rolling pin that she painted black—just in case there were too many beers and not enough witnesses around.

She'd only used it once, but at least she knew it could break a finger or two.

There'd been no tip that night.

Something brushed against her leg. She bit her lip hard to keep from screaming as she looked down to find Colin at her heel. If only it weren't so damn dark, things wouldn't seem so scary.

From memory, she could visualize the light switches on the far wall behind the desk. Forcing her legs forward, she moved inch by inch, trying to soften her footfalls, to be stealthy, like she really was a cop about to bust the bad guy. Although she didn't think flashing her plastic badge pinned over her left boob would be very convincing with the fishnets.

By the time she crept across the linoleum floor and skirted around the desk, her breaths were coming in quiet, panicked gasps, as though the air were thinner there compared to the other side of the room. Like climbing Mount Everest. She just hoped there was nothing to see at the top.

With her back to the wall, she inched her way to the light switch by the kitchen. The nightstick shook in her hand, but she gripped it tighter. Before she could flick on the lights, a caustic scent wafted through the air, burning her nostrils. Wrinkling her nose, she flinched away.

Something dropped on the floor by her foot, making her jump. Her eyes darted down. A red plastic canister rested at her feet. It was then that she recognized the smell. Gasoline.

The sight was so unexpected that she frowned at it while her brain groped for an explanation. That is, until a match struck in the kitchen, piercingly bright, and illuminated a silhouette.

The scene hit her with nauseating horror that made her stomach shrivel up. She covered her mouth with a hand and yelled through her shaky fingers, "No! Don't do it."

The person spun around. It was a man, but that realization only came as an impression, as vague, shadowed features and a stalky figure. She strained to see through the dark, but dots of light blurred her vision from the quivering flame.

The match was burning low, dancing toward his fingers. Piper clenched the nightstick in her hand but was too afraid that if she attacked him the match would surely fall and ignite the gasoline.

Piper tried to steady her voice, to remain calm. "Please. I'll let you leave. Just don't do it."

He snorted, as if she could stop him. In response, he flicked the match aside with the carelessness of someone who'd just lit a cigarette. She screamed as it fell onto the floor, automatically lunging forward as though she could catch it. With a deep woofing sound like the bark of a breathy Neapolitan Mastiff, that tiny flicker of light set off an explosion.

The flash of light blinded her. A wave of heat hit her like an oven door opening—if Hell had ovens. The force of it threw her back against the counter, nearly knocking the fish tank onto the floor.

Everything happened at once. The heat, the light, the high-pitched fire alarm needling her eardrums, the bright white light blinking above the exit, telling her to get to safety. Colin was barking now too, although she could barely hear him. Overwhelmed, Piper tried to blink against the mid-day sun that had risen in the kitchen, just in time to see the man barreling toward her.

She automatically raised her weapon. As he plowed into her, she brought it down. It connected with a crack, and she was reminded of her Little League Softball days.

The man cried out at as they both went down in a twisted pile on the floor. Piper's hands flew out to catch her fall. The nightstick rolled away, out of reach.

The arsonist struggled to get to his feet, but she kicked the backs of his knees so they folded under him. He wasn't getting away that easily.

The fire was growing eerily brighter behind them, casting violent light and shadows on the reception room. With her too caught up in the struggle, Piper's only thought was of keeping him there. They wrestled behind the desk, arms swinging, legs flailing, as the arsonist desperately tried to escape. But Piper wasn't going to let that happen. If she could only just see his face, she could put a stop to all this.

Ashes and embers fluttered down on them. Piper hardly noticed as they landed on her and singed her bare skin. It was hot, even in the reception room. Soon she was soaked with sweat, and then water as the overhead sprinklers kicked in. Instead of it being a reprieve, it was no different from having a hot shower in a sauna.

She wasn't alone in her battle. Colin was doing his best to defend her by nipping the man with his sharp razor teeth. But dachshunds were bred for hunting badgers and this guy was definitely bigger than a badger.

The intruder wormed away. Piper clawed at his sodden clothes, gripped his coat, his arms, his hood, but she was tiring quickly. She was grunting, and swearing, and cursing him, but she could barely hear herself over the alarm.

He lurched for the back door, and Piper slipped on the linoleum. She lost her grip and he managed to wrench away from her. He reached up and grasped the door handle. When she pounced on him again, something jangled against her side. The handcuffs. Just what every good fake cop needs.

Reaching around, she gave them a good tug, ripping the belt loop they were hooked on. Slapping one cuff around his wrist, she clamped the other around the door handle.

The intruder tugged at his bonds while Piper groped under the desk for her rolling pin, but it was lost. She searched the desk for something weighty or sharp. Hopefully both. She grabbed the three-hole punch and turned in time to see a backhand swinging toward her face.

The blow landed on her cheek, throwing her back against the desk. As she went down, her head cracked on the edge. It wasn't like the cartoons; stars didn't flash before her eyes. It was a constellation. The Milky Way. Apparently, she needed to buy stronger handcuffs.

Piper tried to get to her feet, but he blocked her under the desk. His leg drew back and he kicked out at her. It connected square on her chest, knocking the wind from her lungs. Stunned, she crumpled to the floor.

He lurched toward the door. All Piper could do was watch. Watch and claw at her constrictive clothes, coughing and gasping for air, unable to manage anything more than tiny squirrel breaths.

The man tugged on the door handle, the broken handcuff still dangling from it, but he hesitated in the doorway. Over the steady pulsing alarm and the thunderous crackling coming from the kitchen, Piper could hear vicious snarling. Colin had a hold on the man's pant leg. Not ready to let him go, either, Colin jerked and yanked violently on the hem, thrashing his head about, ears flopping left and right.

"Colin, no!" Piper yelled, but it was barely a whisper, too quiet to hear over the commotion.

The arsonist wrenched back in a tug-of-war, trying to free his leg. He finally tore himself away, but Colin just sprang at him again. This time he must have caught the man's ankle in his jaws, because he screamed out and his knees buckled.

Snarling like a Rottweiler, the man wound up and gave a powerful shake of his leg. The fabric tore. Colin flew across the linoleum. There was a *thunk* as he hit something. A high-pitched yelp.

"Colin," Piper croaked.

She watched as the attacker slipped into the back, coat flapping behind him as he sprinted for the exit. Caught in the moment, Piper made for the door, but when she stood up she choked on the first few breaths. She felt dizzy. The back of her throat stung. It smelled and tasted like she'd just wrapped her lips around her VW's exhaust pipe and given it a thorough blow job.

Suddenly, she became aware of her surroundings. Of the thick, black smoke pouring from the kitchen door. It billowed up, like polluted water flowing upwards to curl along the ceiling tiles. There it pooled in a hot, toxic blanket that threatened to fall and smother her and Colin.

Through the kitchen door, she could see the room glow like daylight. The ignited gasoline flowed down the edges of the countertops, the tables, and the chairs, dripping onto the floor like molten lava. The reality of it slammed through her one-track mind.

It had only been maybe a minute since he'd dropped the match, but that minute allowed the fire to spread. That minute might have meant the deaths of all her beloved dogs locked away in their kennels.

22 Hot Dogs

Fire extinguisher. Fire extinguisher. Dammit, Piper thought, where the hell was it? The thing that you always hoped you'd never need, so you don't know where it is when you actually need it.

Wheeling around, Piper scanned the room, the walls, the exits. She had to duck her head to keep below the smoke. And there, by the entrance, fixed to the wall, was a small red fire extinguisher.

As she ran for it, Piper found Colin limping toward her, tail tucked between his legs.

"Oh, come on, boy," she said as she shooed him toward the door to the kennels. She couldn't worry about him at the moment. He'd be safe back there. For now.

When she opened the door, she noticed another full red gas can sitting on the corridor floor.

"That asshole," she said.

Once he was finished with the front reception area, he had planned on dousing the back of the building where the dogs were held captive in their kennels. Not that she would have expected any less, but the imagery it conjured made her wish she could get her hands on him again.

Shutting Colin safely in the back, Piper bolted across the room. She knew the building's system was rigged to alert the authorities, so she didn't have to waste precious time making the call herself. She just hoped she could keep the flames at bay until the fire department arrived.

When she reached the fire extinguisher, she grabbed the metal hammer and smashed the glass. The canister was heavier than she expected, or maybe she was weaker. As she wrenched it out of the casing, it dropped to the floor.

Half-carrying it, half-dragging it over to the kitchen, she gasped as she reached the threshold. It was as though she stood at the mouth of a dragon. Between coughs, she could barely catch her breath as the hot air pushed out at her. Her exposed skin prickled in the radiant heat. And she had a lot of exposed skin.

She squatted low to the floor where the air was clearer. The metal on her belt buckle burned against her stomach where it made contact. It was cooler below the thick cloud forming overhead, but it was creeping lower and lower by the second. The crackling was so loud, so constant, like a thousand hands crumpling plastic wrap.

Piper crept as close to the kitchen as she could stand until she could aim the extinguisher inside the dragon's mouth. Fingers shaking, she yanked the pin, aimed, and fired.

The nozzle kicked back in her hand. She gripped it tighter as the white powder shot out. However, the second the sprinkler water showered on it from the ceiling the chemical fell down in heavy clumps. Only the small drizzle of water wouldn't be enough to douse the flames, considering the amount of accelerant the arsonist had splashed around the room.

Cringing from the heat, she inched closer so the stream

would reach the worst of it. She swept the hose back and forth at the base of flames. They fought back like they were alive. And hungry.

The fire had grown fast, already consuming the cupboards, licking up toward the ceiling. Stray flares danced around the room, searching for new objects to alight. The round vintage table was engulfed, the chairs, the wall of greeting cards. Linoleum tiles curled in on themselves.

A stack of romance novels on the shelf next to her ignited spontaneously. The gust of fresh flames forced her to stumble back a foot. She noticed an imprint of her melted boot sole where it rested a second before.

The glass door on the microwave suddenly burst, the glass shattering. She screamed in surprise but held her ground. Tears streamed from her stinging eyes. She blinked past the pain and into the light, focusing on controlling the hose.

Piper hadn't even tackled the second set of cabinetry before the white mist spewing out of the extinguisher sputtered and died.

"Shit."

Staring at the job left before her, she shook the nozzle like it would come back to life. But it was no use. The canister felt considerably lighter and she knew it was empty. Frustrated, she threw it aside. It hit the floor with a hollow clank.

Piper took a step back, and then another. She had two choices; she could spend the next precious few minutes grabbing another extinguisher and battling the fire or give up and try to get some of the dogs out of their enclosures and to safety. Some. But not all.

In the end, that was her priority. At least she could save a few. It wasn't the building that made this home for her, after all. They could always build a new one.

Just as she gave up, a jet stream of white powder shot past her and into the kitchen.

Jumping out of the way, she spun around to see Aiden ducked low, advancing on the flames with a new extinguisher. For a mind-boggled second, she thought she was imagining the sight of him there. Or maybe she'd died and he was an angel sent to pluck her up and take her to Heaven.

Or, more realistically, Hell.

Just to be sure, she reached out to touch him. He was solid. But still her angel.

"Are you okay?" he yelled out over the alarm.

She didn't quite know the answer to that, so she said, "I'm going to get the dogs out." Her throat felt dry and scratchy as she spoke, and she began coughing uncontrollably.

"Okay, bring another extinguisher back!" he called over his shoulder.

Piper wrenched open the back door to a cacophony of barking, whining, howling, and a mixture of other noises all saying the same thing. *Danger! Danger!*

She could barely see a thing. Except for the few dim night-lights they kept on for the dogs and the flashing beacon above the exit sign, it was dark. Groping along the wall, she flicked on the lights.

"I'm coming!" she called.

Barreling into the back, Piper nearly tripped over Colin. He was standing on the other side of the door, anxiously dancing from paw to paw.

"Colin, get back," she said. When he didn't move, she repeated the command, her voice angrier than she'd ever sounded. There was no time.

As she pulled rank on him, his ears drooped even more than usual. Tail tucked between his legs, he scampered farther down the corridor.

The sprinklers were going off back there too, but the air was clearer and Piper could breathe easier—except for the throbbing pain in her chest the shape of a shoe print. Away from the flames, her panic lessened. She could think straight again.

Starting with the lower kennels, she opened them one by one. With deft fingers, she unlatched each of the doors and flicked them open. She didn't wait to see if the dogs were brave enough to come out as she hurried toward the spare fire extinguisher in the back.

By instinct, the dogs knew to run in the other direction, toward the door to the backyard. A tidal wave of wet fur rushed past her legs and ankles, nearly taking her out. Only Colin remained by her side until she came to the end of the long hall.

She waded through the jostling bodies and opened the fire door. They immediately flooded outside, filling the small courtyard, yipping and howling in agitation.

Colin hesitated in the doorway, looking up at her with those sad puppy eyes. *Why aren't you coming?*

"Get!" she yelled. "Go!"

With no time to waste, she prodded him out the door with her foot. Tail tucked, head lowered, he scampered outside with the others, a pathetic look of rejection on his narrow face. It broke Piper's heart, but she would worry about his sore feelings later. He was safe, and that was the important part. She shut the door so he wouldn't follow her back inside.

A new extinguisher rested in a bracket by the door. She swiped it off the wall, ready for the weight this time. Using her shaking legs, she hoisted it up and cradled it as she ran to the front.

Aiden had already run out of suppressant. He met her halfway down the corridor. His eyes were red from the smoke and round with stress. He'd lost his suit jacket, and his white button-down shirt clung soaking wet to his tense muscles. Using his sleeve, he wiped at the beads of sweat and water that rolled down his forehead and into his eyes.

She handed over the new extinguisher and automatically reached up to touch his cheek. It felt hot. “Are you okay?”

“I’ll be fine,” he said in a scratchy voice. “Get yourself out. I’ll see you outside.”

“I will. But I have to get the rest of them out,” she said. “I won’t be long. I promise. Don’t wait.” She didn’t want to have to worry about him too.

A disapproving frown screwed up his face, but he didn’t waste time lingering. He wheeled back to the kitchen, calling over his shoulder, “Don’t take too long!”

He was about to disappear into the ominous glow on the other side of the door, back to fight the fire, to put his life in danger. She felt the wind escape her lungs, sucked out like she’d been kicked in the chest again. Because it suddenly hit her, just how much it would hurt if anything were to happen to him. If he walked though those doors and didn’t come back.

“Aiden!” she called to his back. “Be careful.”

Halfway through the door, he paused and gave her a look that told her he understood everything she had just felt. It was only a brief look, but she hoped it was her own feelings being reflected back at her.

The door closed behind him and he was gone. She knew the fresh tears stinging her eyes weren’t from the smoke.

Wiping them away, she unlatched the first top enclosure. The little terrier shivered in the corner from fear, his wet fur plastered to his tiny body from the sprinklers. She reached in and drew him out. Over and over, she did the same for the rest, setting each one down on the floor. They immediately scampered off in the same direction as the others.

Finally, she freed the last of her furry friends and opened the door to the backyard again. Over the alarm sounding above her head, she could hear distant sirens wailing in the streets. They were growing closer by the second.

She grabbed the last extinguisher and made for the front. Bumping the door with her butt, she hissed as the metal burned the backs of her exposed legs.

Stumbling into the reception area was like falling into the pits of Hell. During her reprieve in the back, she'd forgotten about the heat, the unbearable, stifling heat. She half-expected to hear the devil himself fiddling away in the corner.

The layer of smoke building near the ceiling had shrunk, so she didn't have to duck. She glanced at the entrance. Aiden must have propped open the door on the way in. She could feel the exchange of air as the smoke filtered out into the cool night, bringing in fresh, sweet oxygen.

But the smoke had turned to a thick haze settling over the room like a fog. It illuminated red, blue, red, blue, flashing with the emergency vehicles' approach, until it was all she could see before her eyes. It was like some crappy rave that went fog-machine happy.

Red, blue, red, blue.

Lugging the fresh canister toward the general direction of the kitchen, Piper searched for a sign of Aiden, coughing, sputtering, groping her way through the haze and the water sprinkling down. Everything she touched was hot. Out of the corner of her eye, she saw the fish tank. The ladies hadn't made it.

In the brief microseconds between each strobe light flash, she could make out a silhouette against the front windows. Aiden. Dropping the canister, she went to him.

White chemical retardant and grey ash streaked his wet, sandy blond hair like he suddenly aged ten years in the last five minutes. By the exhausted expression on his face, it looked like he felt it too.

He never looked more un–put together. More un-Aiden. Suddenly, he wasn't the CEO, a privileged rich boy, or the usual tabloid suspect. He was just a man. A man she'd never wanted to kiss more than she did right then.

"It's pretty much out," he rasped, coughing from the effort.

He never got another word out, because Piper's mouth found his, in the dark and the fog, over and over again. And he seemed just as relieved to see her, because his arms automatically wrapped around her waist and pulled her close like he'd never let her go again.

Despite the emergency of the situation, the sirens, the lights, the firemen rushing in, nothing seemed as urgent in that moment as that kiss.

23

Smoky Wieners

Firefighters barreled through the smoke and into the reception area. Piper and Aiden were rushed out of the building. The moment they were outside it was like a veil had been lifted. The cool air and spattering rain smacked Piper's wet, half-naked body like a sack of ice cubes and she began to shiver.

With the clarity of the fresh San Francisco air came the blinding red and blue strobe lights, an overwhelming discord of noises, and the chaos spilling out into the street. Orders were shouted, sirens wailed, onlookers cried out, and over it all the dogs were barking wildly in the rear courtyard.

It was bewildering. An entirely different kind of fright than the one Piper just went through. She reached for Aiden's hand, but they were steered in opposite directions, toward different ambulances. He was sucked into the crowd of firemen, police, ambulance attendants, and lookee loos.

Strong hands reached out to Piper. They helped her onto

a stretcher, but it didn't feel like help. She pushed them away, struggling against their firm grips.

"I'm fine," she kept saying. "I'm fine."

Which was true—at least, she thought so—but she didn't sound like it. Her voice had the refinement and lilt of gravel under a boot. And as the adrenaline faded, new aches and pains began to introduce themselves in an all too intimate way.

For all she knew, she could have been missing both eyebrows, looked like Batman's Two-Face, and still had the arsonist's shoe implanted in the center of her chest. If the way she felt was any indication, it was a definite possibility.

Piper's body didn't yet understand that it was time to relax. That the fighting, the danger, was over. And all she could think about was getting to Aiden, to see that he, his eyebrows, and every bit of him was okay.

She glanced up. A female attendant hovered at the head of her stretcher. She helped slide Piper into the back of the ambulance. The embroidered badge on her uniform said: *Mollim.*

"Look," Piper said. "I'm fine. Really."

"We're just going to check you over to make sure," Mollim said. "Just relax. Everything is going to be okay."

A second attendant hoisted himself into the back and shoved a mask onto Piper's face. Oxygen hissed at her. Various other attachments followed, monitoring things like blood pressure, temperature, oxygen saturation.

The rapid treatment made her anxious, like maybe there was more wrong with her than she knew. Out of frightened instinct, she batted away their nursing, but a hand appeared and held hers down.

Now she knew what one of her own furry patients went through when she poked and prodded them during practicum. Scared, helpless, anxious. Any more and she thought she might start biting.

A warm cotton blanket was pulled from a toasty oven somewhere and laid on top of her. It didn't take long for the oxygen to clear her head a little, and she regained enough sense to relax and let the EMTs do their job.

Mollim, or Willow, as it turned out in the right-side-up, oxygen-rich world, leaned over Piper with a stethoscope. "This might be a bit chilly." She reached under the blanket and stuck the ice-cold instrument against Piper's chest. "Take a deep breath." She moved it to another spot. "And again. Good."

Piper kept breathing until Willow pulled away. "Clear to bases bilaterally, air entry adequate," she told her partner, who jotted it down on a clipboard.

After a million questions like "Do you feel short of breath?" and "Any difficulty breathing?" Willow finally backed off.

A police officer lingered off to the side. At a brisk nod from the attendant, she moved in with a whole new set of questions. She wanted to know about the arsonist, if Piper saw what he looked like, where he went once he left, if it was on foot or by car, approximately how long had it been?

Piper could tell her very little about what he looked like, but once the officer was satisfied with the answers she tilted her head to the radio clipped to her shoulder and called for the "canine unit."

"Someone will come find you shortly to ask more questions," the cop told her. "Don't go too far."

"Thank you." It wasn't like Piper had any plans. She turned back to Willow. "So, what's the prognosis? Am I going to live?"

"You seem to be in good shape, considering," she told Piper.

"I told you." She yanked off the oxygen mask.

"You're very lucky."

"My boyfriend fought the fire for longer than I did. He

probably inhaled more smoke." She was vaguely aware the *B* word had slipped out, but she blamed it on the oxygen deprivation.

"It's not smoke inhalation that's the worst of it," Willow said. "It's heat inhalation."

"Uh-huh." Piper was only half-listening. She craned her neck, trying to see out of the open ambulance doors and past the shifting bodies on the street. "Is he all right?"

"We can find out about your boyfriend in a second. It's you I'm worried about right now."

"But you said I'm fine. Am I free to go?"

"I didn't say you were fine. I said you were in pretty good shape, *considering*. It's always a good idea to get checked out at a hospital."

Piper thought about Colin and the distressed dogs cooped up in the tiny courtyard and what they must be going through at that moment. The sooner she could get to them, the better. These dogs came from troubled pasts to begin with; they had a hard enough time trusting and feeling safe. An event like this could lead to post-traumatic stress disorder. Not to mention, she had some apologizing to do for yelling at Colin.

Besides, she thought about the treatment in the emergency room, the diagnostics they would run. Each one meant more dollar signs, more decimal points. She knew firsthand how expensive medical care was, and she didn't want to watch her tuition money go down the drain just so a doctor could tell her she was just fine.

Nope. She'd had enough of hospitals for a lifetime.

"No. I'm fine, really. I feel great. Nothing a strong cup of coffee won't cure." She chuckled, but it only brought on a coughing fit that shook her body until her face turned a bright magenta. "And maybe a lozenge."

Willow frowned. "Well, you know my opinion, but I can't force you to come with us."

Relieved, Piper began unhooking herself from the monitoring equipment. "I'm fine, really. You were awesome. Thank you."

Sitting up, she swung her legs over the side of the stretcher. Her head spun with the motion. She thought it prudent not to mention that, or that her thoughts were still disorganized like she had just woken up after a graduation day bender.

Willow passed her a clipboard and pen. She pointed to an *X* marked at the bottom of a page that was too blurry and scratchy to read. Or maybe that was just Piper's eyeballs.

"You need to sign here. This is a release form to indicate that you're refusing further medical care."

Piper signed in the general area of the *X* and passed it back.

Willow riffled through some drawers and produced a package of lemon lozenges. "Watch for shortness of breath, dizziness, and labored breathing," she told Piper. "You'll cough. A lot. But if you start coughing up anything strange, get it checked out. If you have any doubt at all, please get yourself to an ER."

Piper popped a lozenge out and thanked her. She crawled out of the back, where the other attendant helped her down to the pavement. The night air blew up her short police shorts, and cool drops of rain fell on her shoulders. At least it had slowed to a mere sprinkling.

Piper shivered. She'd forgotten she was still in costume.

Willow leaned out the doors with a freshly warmed blanket. "And you might need this." Her mouth quirked up, but she made no comment about Piper's choice of firefighting gear.

Too tired to explain the costume, she took the blanket gratefully and wrapped it around herself. "Thanks, Mollim. I mean, Willow."

It was chaos outside. Police, firemen, news vans, squad cars, fire trucks. Beyond the police tape, the street spilled over with locals who had nothing better to do at almost ten at night but gawk at someone else's misfortune. And that was where she spotted Holly Hart and her cameraman, Hey, You, shoving their way to the front of the crowd.

Holly scanned the crime scene and spotted Piper right away. Not that it was hard to spot a drenched, half-naked girl covered in dog hair and soot. Holly waved her over, like Piper was the bouncer of a nightclub—the worst one ever—and Holly desperately wanted to skip the line.

Piper waved but had no intention of doing an interview that night. She would do enough talking to the investigators. Ignoring Holly's frantic shouts, she carried on, weaving through the officials, over fire hoses, and under police tape.

All around her, people moved with less urgency now. The danger had passed and it was about containment and finding out the who, what, where, when, and, most important why. Why would someone do this?

Was it someone helping Laura? But if that was the case, surely she wouldn't want to hurt the dogs. Or was it a disgruntled neighbor? Then again, maybe it had something to do with Aiden. The night she was nearly flattened in the alley came rushing back to her. They'd been targeting her, not Aiden. Was Piper to blame somehow?

Her already-spinning head was starting to feel heavy from all these thoughts. She had to squint against the sudden pain in her forehead to see through the flashing lights.

Finally, she spotted another ambulance. The doors were flung open. The EMTs were in the back fetching and organizing supplies. She scanned the area, her eyes darting over the chaos, but she couldn't see Aiden.

Maybe they'd taken him to the hospital. Maybe his

condition was worse since he'd been closer to the fire for longer. Anxious to find him, she half-jogged toward the vehicle. When she rounded another cop car and squeezed between two officers, she finally saw him.

The head of his stretcher was inclined, so he saw her immediately. He sat forward as she approached, pulling the mask away from his face to talk.

"Are you all right?" she asked.

"I'm fine." He reached out to take her hand. "How are you?"

"Safe and sound, despite sounding like an eighty-year-old that smokes two packs a day." She tried to laugh it off, but it sounded less cute and more true.

"No. No. It's sexy."

"Old bingo lady voices are sexy? I gotta tell you, I don't think I want to role-play that one."

He laughed. "You sound like a smoky hotel lounge singer."

"It could be the start of a whole new career for me. Forget that veterinarian nonsense."

"That's the spirit."

It felt good to be joking with him, acting lighthearted. But they pawed each other, holding hands, gripping arms, like they were each other's anchors. Like if they let go one of them might fall away.

"What are you even doing here?" she asked.

"I came to see you. To apologize for this afternoon at the office."

She shook her head. Her silly insecurities all seemed so unimportant now. "It's fine."

"I just wanted to make sure everything was okay."

"We're okay."

Piper watched a firefighter roll up a water hose. The metal nozzle smacked the glass door in passing and the pane shattered. She cringed.

"I'll call the insurance company tonight," Aiden said. "Get the ball rolling."

"That would be great, thanks." Piper shook her head. "There's so much damage."

"Don't worry. I've had a lot of dealings with insurance companies through my investment properties. They won't take long for a case like this."

"Yeah, sure. So we renovate and repair the damage. Then what? If we don't find this guy, he'll just keep coming at us."

She stared at the building, at the broken glass, at the smoke damage, and had a hard time imagining where they would begin. She wondered how Marilyn would have dealt with everything had she been there. Hell, if Marilyn was still in charge maybe none of it would have happened in the first place.

Maybe Piper could have done more to prevent it, something different. She remembered Aiden's check. If she had cashed it, she could have gotten a security system right away instead of having to wait for the donations to roll in. Would the fire have happened at all? She felt sick at the thought that her refusal to accept help might have caused this.

Aiden brought a hand up to her cheek and turned her worried gaze toward him. He gave her an even stare. "Everything will be all right."

"Wishful thinking."

He opened his mouth to speak but then grimaced, like whatever he wanted to say caused him pain. He seemed to think a moment longer before asking her, "Do you trust me?"

She looked him in the eye and considered all he'd done for her so far, how he'd been there. After knowing him for only a couple of weeks, the answer surprised her. "Yes. I do."

"Then everything will be okay."

As overwhelmed as she was, deep down she knew it would be. No one, and no dog, was hurt. Except, of course, for the goldfish. Her heart hurt when she thought about their tragic end, but at least all the dogs survived.

"Okay. You're right." She took a deep breath. "Now, if only the guests could put themselves to bed."

Aiden pushed the ambulance blanket aside and swung his legs over the stretcher. "Don't worry. I'll help you."

She opened her mouth to say she would be fine, but he seemed to read her mind. Reaching out, he held her face in both of his hands, his eyebrows drawing together to form a stern line. "Piper. I'm not going anywhere."

She bit her lip, battling her instincts to turn him down. If there was ever a time she should accept help, it was that night. "That would be great. Thanks." But she couldn't stop herself from adding, "I owe you one."

Aiden focused over her shoulder at someone approaching. She turned to find a man, maybe in his late fifties, headed their way with a determined walk. He was in plainclothes—a pair of dark jeans and a tucked collared shirt under a light rain jacket.

There was going to be a lot of questions to answer. Some that she didn't want to explore, moments she didn't want to relive. She wanted to block it all out. To go shower, stuff Colin with treats, crawl into bed, and snuggle with Mr. Wiggles, the stuffed bear she hadn't slept with since her father died. But something told her the night was far from over.

When the man got closer, he flashed a badge. "Inspector Samuels," he said. "Are you Piper Summers?"

"Yes, I am."

He tucked the badge away and replaced it with a notepad. "I hope you're feeling up to answering a few questions."

Did she have a choice?

"Are the dogs okay?" she asked.

"Yes. They're all still in the courtyard."

"Do you think I'll be able to move them back into their kennels tonight if we don't go into the front of the building?"

"Not possible, I'm afraid. Both myself and the fire inspector will need to do our independent investigations. It will be tomorrow at the earliest before it's handed back to the building owner, who is, I believe"—he flipped a couple pages back in his notepad—"a Mr. Aiden Caldwell."

"That's me," Aiden said.

"Oh." Inspector Samuels's bushy eyebrows twitched. "Well, that's convenient. And rather unfortunate for you."

"What happens when it's released to him?" Piper asked.

"Well, then it's the insurance company's call. They'll perform their own separate investigation. I suspect the damage is severe enough that health and safety will have to get involved. Then you're looking at claims adjusters, contractors—" He started to count on his fingers, but Piper interrupted.

"How long? I mean, I can't keep them cooped up out there forever."

"A few days at least."

"Right, the neighbors are going to love that." Not that she cared at the moment.

"Is there nowhere else they can go?" the inspector asked.

"Why do you think they're here?" Her shoulders slumped. "Need a pet dog?"

He chuckled. "No, I don't. I bring my job home enough as it is. Sorry."

"Yeah, me too." She shook her head. "I'll figure something out."

"You know, you're very lucky you got out of there alive, not to mention all the dogs."

"Luck had nothing to do with it," she said. "I had help." She glanced at Aiden, who squeezed her hand in return.

"About that," the inspector said. "I'd like to ask the two of you some questions about what happened tonight. I'd like to interview you both separately." He gestured to a quiet area on the sidewalk. "Piper, if I could start with you first."

With an exasperated look at Aiden, Piper followed until they were out of earshot. She took a deep breath. Becoming all too familiar with the drill, she explained what happened. It all went down in probably less than ten minutes. Yet as she retold it, there was so much information to relay that it could have happened over the course of an hour or two.

Yes, she saw the guy start the fire. No, she didn't see his face. She gave guesstimations about height and weight, but it had been dark, and it happened so fast. The only helpful thing she could recall that might identify him was that he'd have, she hoped, a large goose egg on his head and a nasty dachshund bite-mark anklet to match.

Piper watched the inspector scribble his notes onto his pad, serious and attentive. Two great bushy eyebrows with long strands of grey drew together or arched during her recounting, like a pair of thoughtful furry caterpillars crawling quizzically on his face. Already she had more confidence in Inspector Samuels than she did in Officer Sucker Tucker.

"So now that there's a detective involved, does that mean an actual investigation is under way? Or are you going to tell me to hire a security guard too?"

"I've been briefed on this case already. I think that whoever is targeting this property isn't going to stop."

"Yeah. I'm starting to get that message."

"Tonight, you interrupted him before he could finish his task. This could have been much worse."

Piper remembered the second canister of fuel and grimaced. She thought of the dogs trapped in their kennels as the place burned down around them. "And there might still be a next time."

He held up a hand. "Now, I'm not saying this to scare you. I'm trying to prepare you for the possibility."

"You mean the eventuality."

"We will do everything we can to find and stop whoever is doing this. But after tonight, it's obvious that he'll go to any lengths to get you out of this neighborhood, if that is his true motive. If we don't catch him sooner rather than later . . ." He didn't finish.

He didn't need to.

They could raise funds, rebuild, add new locks, buy a new security system, but at the end of the day this guy was going to keep coming.

Her blanket had lost all of its toasty oven warmth and the soggy cold sank in, deep, like it had seeped into her bones. She thought she would never feel warm again. "Then our only option is to give him what he wants."

"You don't need to worry about all of this tonight," Inspector Samuels said. "You've been through enough, and I realize you'll need to discuss this with the property owner and business manager. In the meantime, we'll be placing a patrol car outside to monitor the premises twenty-four hours a day for the next few days."

"Do you think this guy will try something again? So soon?"

"Arsonists have a habit of coming back to see the results of their work. It's common for them to even return while it's still burning."

Piper examined the crowd gathered outside the police tape, searching each face, wondering if the arsonist could be out there. Watching. Waiting to try something again. She shivered at the thought.

And to think, she'd been face-to-face with the slimeball, had been so close to seeing him. She might have been able to identify him, to put a stop to all this.

Suddenly, it occurred to her that while she didn't see his face, he might have seen hers. In a way, she'd been there to thwart him both times, to undo what he did. He could have seen her on the news after the break-in, asking for donations. Maybe that's why the car had tried to run her over in the alley during her date with Aiden. Maybe the guy wasn't after both of them. Just her.

The inspector said the arsonist likely wouldn't give up until he got what he wanted. What if this guy saw Piper as the one standing in his way?

Newshound

"Hi. Marilyn. It's Piper. I have some bad news. You remember that dog shelter you asked me to look after? It burned to the ground. Oh, and all those sweet, homeless puppies that were inside? Yeah, they're horribly traumatized. Hope you're having a great time on your cruise. Cheers!"

Piper realized she looked crazy pacing back and forth in front of the rescue center, talking to herself—well, to Colin. The cops who were parked across the street for surveillance on the building were glancing over at her. They probably thought she was nuts. Hell, she felt a little nuts. Maybe they'd already put in a call to Inspector Samuels to tell him she should be the lead suspect in the arson case.

She wanted to rehearse what to say to Marilyn's voice mail. To get it just right. Piper still hadn't been able to get ahold of her since she'd left for vacation. Boy, was she going to get a bad string of voice mails when she finally checked them.

Piper turned to Colin, who watched her from the front

steps. In Colin fashion, he sat just behind the bright yellow tape wrapped across the stair rails that said: *POLICE LINE DO NOT CROSS*. Rebel without a cause.

After taking him home from the center the night before, she had assessed him thoroughly, patting him down, manipulating his joints. Or at least, she'd tried to, but he seemed to have mistaken her face for a lollypop. It seemed he graciously forgave her for yelling at him during the fire. Either that, or it was his five-minute memory span at work.

After her assessment, she was relieved to discover that other than being a bit sulky—nothing a treat couldn't fix—he'd fared a lot better than she had. She had quite a bit more than a limp, but hell, at least she was alive.

The rest of the animals were fine—physically, anyway. Who knew how the traumatic event would affect them mentally long-term? But at least they were safe. She'd found temporary homes for most of the guests. A lot of the center's usual foster families stepped up to help them out, and she managed to find a few of the other no-kill centers that opened their doors until she could figure something else out. Addison was out delivering some of the guests now. Unfortunately, Zoe was working a wedding gig that weekend. She couldn't be at the center to help, but she sent her love and checked in frequently.

"So?" Piper asked Colin. "What do you think of my speech?"

He grumbled before laying his head down and covering his face with his paws.

"Yup. That's what I thought. It's perfect." Taking her phone out of her pocket, she searched for Marilyn's number and hit *dial*. She'd hoped—and dreaded—that she might actually pick up, but like usual it rang until it went to voice mail. The beep sounded, and suddenly, anything Piper could say about the fire in a few sentences sounded so inadequate.

Until they caught the asshole responsible for the attacks there was no telling how bad things would get. Piper had never felt so helpless, so powerless. It was the worst kind of feeling. However, being thousands of miles away, somewhere in the Caribbean, Marilyn would feel this even more. When Piper thought about what it would be like to get a message like that, unable to ask any questions, she decided that less information was better.

"Hi, Marilyn. This is Piper. Listen, I'm not sure when you're going to get this message. I've tried the cruise line a few times, but I can't seem to get ahold of you. Please call me as soon as you get this, no matter what time it is. Hope you're having a good vacation. Bye."

As she hung up, Aiden rounded the corner of the building. He smiled when he saw her. She stopped pacing and took a deep breath, her muscles unknotting themselves.

That morning, she'd dragged her butt out of bed after only a few hours of sleep, wondering how she would get everything done. But then she arrived at the center, and Aiden was already there. While she and Addison sorted out temporary homes for the guests, he dealt with the business end of things.

To say he'd been amazing was the biggest understatement of the century. Without him, the center might have burned down completely. There might not have been anything left to sort out. Hell, she might have died. But she thought it was best not to dwell on that particular anecdote for now.

"I just left Marilyn a voice mail," she said. "Did you want to leave a message? I could call her back."

He shook his head. "No thanks. I e-mailed her earlier."

"Really? Did she respond? What did you say?" She didn't like the idea of Marilyn hearing about the fire from anyone else. She'd left Piper in charge of the rescue center.

She wanted to be the one to answer for what had happened to it.

"Oh, nothing specific," he said. "I just had some things to discuss with her about the center."

"What things, exactly?" Piper asked, aiming for airily.

"Business things." By his pointed tone of voice, she knew he wanted to end it there.

Piper's eyebrows arched. "Business things?"

"Yes." He countered with an eyebrow of his own. "Marilyn's business and my business."

"As in, not *my* business?" Irritated at being shut out, yet again, Piper's jaw clenched. What was he keeping from her? Did Marilyn know what it was? "I guess I have no right to know what's happening to the center?"

Aiden groaned, like the last thing he wanted was an argument. "I know I sound like a broken record, but I was serious when I said that I don't like mixing business with pleasure."

She remembered his motto all too well. "And I'm what? Doing all this"—she waved a hand at the general destruction—"for pleasure?"

"I don't know," he said testily. "I guess that's your business."

"Fine. Then excuse me while I go help feed the dogs. Unless, of course, that's none of my business, either." Whistling for Colin, she turned to head for the back, but Aiden grabbed her arm.

"This is exactly why I don't like mixing the two."

She pulled her arm away, but he gripped both her shoulders and turned her to face him. "If it were something that you needed to know, I would tell you. But this is between Marilyn and me." He sighed. "I don't want business to come between us. I don't want you to be business at all." He reached up and cupped her face in both hands. "I want you to be one hundred percent pleasure. Let me deal with this."

"I don't like not knowing what's going on. Marilyn left the center in my care." And look what's already happened, she added in her head. She pushed away the thought. "I want to make sure everything turns out okay. I'm not used to people doing things for me that I should be doing."

"It's not *for* you. It's *with* you. You have your part to play, so does Marilyn, and so do I. We'll all work together. You're not alone in this. We're a team."

She sighed, realizing she was turning into a control freak like Zoe. The issue wasn't so much control as it was accepting help, admitting she needed it—which she totally didn't, by the way. It tasted of failure, of bitterness, in her mouth. She closed her eyes for a moment, regaining a bit of perspective and tried for an easier-going expression, maybe even a hint of a smile.

"Is that the spirited speech you give your office every Monday?"

Aiden's expression softened. "Something like that. Did it work?"

"Strangely enough, I suddenly feel like stapling things and sending interoffice memos."

His arms wrapped around her waist, pulling her tight to him, and he dipped his head in for a kiss. Something neither of them could get enough of that day, not after the fire the night before. After coming so close to—

"Mr. Caldwell!" a shrill voice called behind them.

Aiden whipped around to find Holly charging down the sidewalk, the cameraman in her Chanel wake. With a God-give-me-the-strength sigh, he stepped away from Piper. Hey, You fiddled with his equipment and Holly snapped her fingers at him impatiently.

"A little strange to be viewing your investment properties on a weekend, isn't it?" she asked Aiden. "Or was it something else you were hoping to view?" Her eyes widened and darted meaningfully to Piper.

"Holly, so nice to see you again." But Aiden's expression didn't relay that happy feeling. It was guarded as she waved the cameraman in close, signaling with a flick of her manicured finger to get a shot of the young CEO.

She held the microphone dramatically in front of her. "Holly Hart, here, on location at San Francisco's Dachshund Rescue Center to report on more bowwow woes. After last night's devastating fire, the volunteers are hard at work trying to make the best of their dog day. So, tell us, Mr. Caldwell, where do you fit into all of this?" Holly shoved the microphone into his face.

"I'm here to help Miss Summers deal with the aftermath of last night's fire."

Holly leapt into Piper's bubble, leaning aggressively toward her, on the trail of a hot story. "Rumor has it, you were inside the building when the fire started."

"Ah, yes. I came by to check on the dogs and caught the arsonist setting fire to the place."

"That must have been terrifying. What did you do?"

"Well, I tried to stop him, but it was too late and he got away."

"Those could have been some hot dogs. But you bravely put your life on the line and fought the fire to protect the dogs you so love." Her voice oozed drama. Piper thought she must have been good at her job at the *Gate*.

"Errr, well, I guess. I mean, I started to, but I never would have been able to do that and get the dogs to safety if Aiden hadn't showed up."

Holly spun to face Aiden. She grabbed his upper arm, and Piper could have sworn she squeezed his biceps. "That makes you quite the hero, Mr. Caldwell. Not only are you the most eligible bachelor in town, but a local hero."

"I believe Miss Summers is—"

Holly pulled the microphone away before he could finish. "So what will happen to the residents of the Dachshund Rescue Center now? Where will they go?" She turned the mic back on Aiden.

"The building will need extensive repairs, which will be reviewed later today. In the meantime, Miss Summers has sorted out temporary arrangements until the renovations are complete." He nodded to Piper, but Holly seemed reluctant to shift the focus away from her target.

"Mr. Caldwell, with your affiliation with the rescue center"—her eyes flicked to Piper, but so subtly she didn't think the camera caught it—"does Caldwell and Son Investments have any plans to offer the center aid?"

"Yes, the company plans to do whatever it can to assist the center. Discussions have already begun for future planning."

Future planning? Piper's gaze shot to him, but he studiously ignored her. Discussions? Piper's brain scrambled. Maybe that was what he e-mailed Marilyn about. Or was it a vague business term to avoid giving a real answer? Piper sure wanted some real answers.

"There you have it," Holly said. "The hound hater has struck again, but they haven't shut this doghouse down yet. Is this dogfight over, or is it just beginning? This is Holly Hart for Channel Five News."

Her veneer smile shone on her face like a plastic Barbie until Hey, You said, "And cut."

She spun on her heel to face Piper. "Thanks for the interview. Bad luck for the center, but these stories have really boosted my ratings. The whole man's best friend heart-wrenching angle has warmed the viewers up to me. Can you believe people rate me as insincere?"

Piper tried to keep a straight face. "Shocking."

"I know, right?" She rolled her eyes. "Well, let me know if there are any big breaks in the case. I'd like to finish off with a good heartwarming piece. Something uplifting."

"You and me both."

"I'm thinking something along the lines of cute puppies and old people or, better yet, babies. You know, happily ever after kind of crap."

"I'll be sure to work on that."

Holly turned and strutted back to the news van and snapped her fingers at the cameraman. Rolling his eyes, he muttered something under his breath before following her.

Piper turned back to Aiden, not quite ready to give up on their earlier conversation—not to mention, Holly's interview had raised a whole new set of questions—but as she opened her mouth to confront him a BMW pulled up in front of the building. Aiden's BMW. That would explain why he drove the Jaguar that day.

The driver's side door opened and Tamara crawled out. Piper groaned inwardly. When Aiden gave her a funny look, she realized her brain-mouth filter had malfunctioned again and her inward groan was an outward one.

Piper thought it was time that she addressed the Tamara issue. She sidled closer to Aiden while Tamara grabbed some documents from the back of the car.

"Why is she driving your BMW?"

"Her car needs to go in for service." He shrugged like he did that kind of thing all the time.

"I don't trust her."

"With the center?"

"No. With me. With anything. She's different around me than she is around you. That day at your house, she really did attack me."

He laughed, like Piper was being ridiculous, but kept his voice low. "This is Tamara we're talking about? She wouldn't hurt a fly."

"Not a fly. *Me,*" Piper said. "Aiden, I think she's jealous."

His forehand creased. "Jealous of what?"

"What do you think? Of our relationship. I think she might have feelings for you."

"I've worked with Tamara for three years. It's nothing more than business."

"But—"

"You know what I think?" He reached out for Piper and pulled her back in. "I think that Tamara's not the jealous one."

"What?" Her mouth dropped open. Was he not hearing her? Could he not see what Tamara was really like? But she supposed not. The first time they met, she never suspected Tamara was anything but sincere. Maybe she'd never showed Aiden that other side of her. And he'd known her a lot longer than he'd known Piper. How could she make him see?

"Look, Tamara's here to help. It's just business," he explained. "I have some things to deal with at the office."

"On the weekend?"

"Unfortunately, one of my deadlines unexpectedly moved up on me." He chuckled. She threw him a questioning look, but he waved a dismissive hand. "I won't bore you with the details."

"Business?" She felt her mouth twist with annoyance.

"Business. But don't worry." Planting a kiss on her cheek, he began backing away to his Jaguar in the parking lot. "You'll find out soon enough."

"But—" she began, but her cell phone rang, pulling her up short. Taking it out, she checked the display. It was the vet hospital, probably calling with an emergency.

Tamara joined her on the sidewalk with an armload of insurance papers and documents. The moment Aiden was out of sight, the PA hissed at Piper. It was going to be a long day. But Tamara wasn't even on the top of her to-worry-about list at the moment.

You'll find out soon enough.

Aiden's voice had been layered with something she couldn't name, his expression suppressed of emotion, like a secret pleasure. Whatever it was, obviously he wasn't going to tell her right then.

Were his company secrets something she could learn to live with? Maybe it really was none of her business. Maybe she didn't need to know, she told herself, answering her phone before it went to voice mail. But the way he'd said it, like it was some inside joke between the two of them that he forgot to tell her, she worried that maybe she did.

25 Dog Tired

Piper took one last look around the rescue center courtyard, making sure the few remaining dogs had everything they needed before she left for the day. It felt wrong to leave them, like it would be perfectly reasonable to curl up with them and sleep there for the night. But they were all safe in their temporary doghouses that Tamara had ordered from the pet store. They would be fine.

Fine. The word was beginning to lose its comfort. Like each time Piper thought the word or said it out loud, an invisible question mark popped up behind it.

She let Colin slip out through the gate and into the back alley. He sniffed around, searching for the ultimate place to mark his territory. Some days he acted choosy, like a connoisseur of pee spots. Others he just went crazy, like he owned the whole world. *It's mine. All mine!* he would declare maniacally as he swung his leg into the air.

Piper shut the gate behind her and closed the padlock, yanking on it to make sure it was secure before turning around. Someone was standing out there in the dark. Her body froze for a half second and her heart jumped into her throat. Had Tamara come back to corner her after dark? Did she not have enough opportunities to harass her that day? Or maybe it was worse. Maybe it was the arsonist.

She got ready to scream for help. Surely the cops stationed in front of the building would hear her. The person stepped out of the shadows and she quickly bit it back. It was just Aiden. She slumped against the fence in relief.

"Sorry, I didn't mean to scare you," he said. "Are you okay?"

"Yeah. I'm fine." She swallowed her heart back down into her chest. "I'm more worried about the dogs."

"They'll be okay. There's no call for rain over the next few days, and they've got everything they need. Besides, the police said they'll still be watching the building."

Piper nodded, knowing everything that could be done that day was done—and then some. Addison had been in and out all day delivering guests to their temporary lodgings. On top of running to the vet hospital twice for emergency weekend calls, Piper had organized it all while doing the rest of the chores. There was nothing more she could do. Except sleep. Possibly forever.

"Did you just get finished at the office?" she asked Aiden.

"Yeah."

"That's a long day."

"I bet yours was longer. I hope Tamara helped."

"She did." There was a definite "but" to Piper's tone of voice. *But* she insulted me every time we were alone. *But* she threatened to feed me my own hair. *But* she's bat shit crazy. However, Piper didn't want to get into that at the moment. Tamara did deal with the investigators and insurance in Aiden's absence. Although if Piper could take that responsibility on she would have, just so she didn't have to deal with Tamara all day. But Piper was just a volunteer. It was a job for the landowner.

"That's good. And I heard from the police today about the taxi."

"You did? Did they find it?" Answers. Finally. Piper didn't think she could fit any more questions or worries into her stuffed brain.

"Yes. Along with my briefcase. They think it was just a joyride, or else they were going to chop it for parts and decided not to. Whatever the reason, it seems it had nothing to do with the documents in my briefcase."

So no answers, then. Just the lack of them. She rubbed a hand over her face and groaned in frustration.

Grabbing her hand, Aiden dragged her away from the fence and into his embrace. His hands rubbed her back comfortingly. The rubbing slowed until it became caressing, exploring, groping. Her brain, exhausted from one of the longest days of her life, relinquished control, and her body responded to his touches like he was her puppet master.

In the back of her mind, questions jingled like loose change. She knew she should pull them out and see what they were. However, like when she searched the bottom of her purse, she knew loose change never paid the bills at the end of the month. Never amounted to much . . . until you added them up, of course.

But it had been a long day. Piper wasn't in any mental state to do the math, especially not as Aiden brought his mouth to hers. Questions? What questions?

He drew away. Even in the dark alley, she could see the desire in his half-lidded eyes. He grinned down at her. "You know what you need? Something to take your mind off things."

"You're totally right," she teased. "Maybe I'll go find

something." She pretended to pull away, but he yanked her back and pressed her up against the fence.

"I meant me." He bent down and brought his lips back to hers.

"Be careful," she said between kisses. "Holly might still be lurking around. She could catch us." She bit her lip. That was a question she hadn't even meant to ask. But there it was, just hanging out there. And now that the subject was broached, could she ignore it? Should she?

He paused along his trail of kisses down her neck. "And I'm supposed to care?"

"You mean you don't?" She tried to make it sound breezy, which was aided by the fact that she couldn't catch her breath at the moment.

He snorted and resumed his path. "Of course not."

She bit her lip, trying hard to ignore the little voice in the back of her head, that worry that had been rubbing her the wrong way ever since they'd gone to dinner earlier that week. But rubbing turned to blisters, and this one was about to pop.

"Are you sure you wouldn't want someone, I dunno, say more . . . model-like or Harvard material?"

Yeah, real breezy, she chastised herself. That blister didn't simply ooze out; it erupted.

The hand that had been sneaking up the hem of her shirt froze. He pulled back, and in the light glowing between the fence's wooden slats she could see him cock his head.

"Been doing your research?"

She shrugged like, "No big deal." It's not like it had been on her mind since Wednesday or anything. It's not like she had been unable to think of anything else, well, before the fire, that is. "Holly Hart might have let something slip at dinner the other night."

Aiden sighed and stepped back. Way to kill the mood,

Piper thought. Her brain was starting to find this coin particularly interesting, while her body threw a tantrum.

"Well," he began. "I'd like to say that Holly is full of it. But there's probably some truth to what she said."

Piper's heart clenched like it too was about to burst, like a miniexplosion in her chest. "There was?"

"It seems like a long time ago," he said, kicking at the gravel underfoot. "Before my father died, I guess I took advantage of the easy life I had. Let's just say, I overindulged."

"In . . . models?" she asked.

He laughed. "In the lifestyle in general. I didn't have a lot of responsibilities or care, but I possessed a large trust fund. I didn't need to be the serious, focused CEO I am now. But then I lost one of the most important people in my life and the weight of the world fell on my shoulders, and I guess I started to care. I began to realize what was important in life." He gave her a pointed look, like this was a message for her. Maybe even that he meant *she* was important.

"But what about at the restaurant the other night? It came across like you were embarrassed to be seen with me." He looked about ready to argue, but she continued before he could interrupt. "We ate in a far corner of the restaurant, we snuck out the back alley, and when you saw Holly you practically hid under the table. It was obvious that you didn't want us to be seen."

"I didn't."

Kaboom. There went her heart. "Oh, well, glad we cleared that up." She took a step back, feeling herself close off to him. She couldn't help it, what with her exploding heart and all.

"Piper, I wasn't embarrassed to be seen because I was with you. How could you think that?" He reached for her hand and squeezed it even as she tried to pull away. "I was embarrassed of my life, of exposing you to self-important snobs like Holly Hart, or making you a paparazzi target. I remember how nervous you were just to go on television last week. I wanted a normal night where the two of us could be . . . us, like when we go to the park." His thumb made nervous little circles on the back of her hand. "I wanted you to go on a date with me: Aiden. Not the CEO of Caldwell and Son Investments."

Now that she'd calculated that coin's worth, it turned out to be worthless. Nothing. It was barely a penny. No, it was a button. She took his answer in, struggling to maintain a straight face while what she really wanted to do was a relieved happy dance. Either that, or take a page from Colin's book and mark her territory. *He's mine, ladies. All mine!*

She recalled that night at the restaurant. You can take the journalist out of the tabloid, but you can't take the tabloid out of the journalist. Holly had been fishing for information, manipulating Piper's insecurities for dirt on Aiden. She'd known Holly had targeted him for years, and yet Piper let herself be played.

"Well," she began, reining in her sudden irritation with herself, "sometimes that's going to be your life. You can't escape it. And if I date you, I have to accept that." Which was the nicest way she could find to tell him he was being a complete idiot.

He gave her that lost puppy look. "*If* you date me?"

"*Now* that I'm dating you," she corrected. God, how those words made her heart dance in her chest. Oh, look. Not exploded at all.

His dimple made an appearance at her answer. "I wish I could make it up to you, take you on another date right now. But I suppose it's getting a little late." He eyed the sky. The sun had long since set. What light was left blushed along the skyline.

"But we could still pretend," Piper said hopefully. "That we had our date and you're walking me to my car." She pulled out her keys and started to stroll to the VW Bug waiting in the dark parking lot. Colin followed behind, marking things as he went.

"And how did it go?" Aiden asked, playing along. "You know, any initial feelings, ideas, impressions?"

"It went well. I had the chicken; you had the risotto. We shared some wine. I probably had too much, because I was nervous."

"And how was I? Was I charming? Funny?" He pulled a silly face, but his posture tensed, like he was waiting for honest feedback.

"Yeah. You made some good jokes. A couple times I laughed when it wasn't funny, but overall, very charming."

"Oh no. A pity laugh." He ran a hand through his already tousled hair. "Did I make up for it? Did I at least get a good-night kiss? Was it good enough to warrant another date?"

"I don't know. It hasn't happened yet." She slowed down as they approached her car and she fiddled with her keys. "I'm still waiting for one."

"I suppose it better be a good one to make up for that pity laugh." He rolled his shoulders, straightening his collar like he was preparing.

She laughed and pulled him in. He kissed her softly once, then again, his lips lingering against hers. A kiss worthy of a second date, sure. But after two weeks of seeing him almost every day, Piper was ready for more than second-date action; she craved a tenth-date kiss.

Dropping her keys, she reached up and gripped his collar, pulling his body closer. Aiden backed her up until her butt hit the trunk of her car, pressing, grinding against her until something firm pressed against her stomach and she knew it wasn't the dog treats in his pocket. And if it had been a dog treat, he must have switched to feeding Sophie extra-large bones. What would his dry cleaner have to say about that one?

Her body was back in control. Her brain wasn't just taking a break; it was gone. Away on vacation. His mouth found her earlobe and he tugged with his teeth. She felt a shiver run down her neck and right to her toes.

The little German car rocked on its wheels, squeaking with each nudge from Aiden's hips. Piper's groans added to the rhythm. His hand slid over her jeans and across her butt. He gripped her thigh and hiked her leg up until it wrapped around his hip in order to get his bone closer. She moaned, the sound echoing across the empty lot.

The fire the night before had done something to her. That sense of urgency, the adrenaline, still lingered in her veins, reminding her how precious life was, bringing her feelings for Aiden to the surface.

Now that the fire was out and the danger settled, all that remained, all that mattered, was the two of them. Being in his arms, feeling the touch of his hands, his mouth, the pressure of his body against hers, was a reassurance. Because life was too short.

His five-o'clock shadow rubbed against her collarbone, and she was certain she'd already died and gone to Heaven. Heaven's gates had opened up and, oh wow, she could see the light. And it was dazzling. And bright. Really, *really* bright.

Piper squinted, cringing away from it, and held up a hand in front of her face. Turns out, that wasn't the heavens smiling down upon her and Aiden. It was an LED flashlight pointed at their flushed faces.

"Is everything all right here?" a voice asked.

And those weren't angels in white. They were cops in blue.

"We heard sounds of a struggle," the other said.

Aiden jumped back, and Piper ran a hand over her clothes to make sure everything was where it should be. She tried to act natural, leaning on the car like what could they possibly be doing alone in a dark, quiet parking lot at night?

"N-n-no. No struggle, Officer," she stammered. The only thing she would struggle with that night was her libido. "We're fine."

Aiden cleared his throat, straightening his tie. "Thank you, Officers."

The flashlight lowered and Piper could see again. She didn't miss the look that the two cops exchanged. They didn't appear annoyed or like they were about to arrest Aiden and Piper, although it was a good thing they showed up sooner rather than later, because the things she'd wanted to do to him in her car would have been all sorts of indecent public exposure. They would have spent the night behind bars for sure. She could just imagine the headlines that Holly would come up with for that one.

"All right," the first cop said, an unspoken warning beneath the amusement in his voice. "You two have a good night."

"Thank you," Piper said, stifling a giggle as they turned away.

Aiden rested his head against hers, his own shoulders shaking with silent laughter. "So?" he said when he got it under control. "What do you think? Does that warrant another date?"

"I think that warrants the next hundred dates."

"Well, at least it didn't warrant a trip to jail," he said as though he'd read her earlier thoughts.

Laughing, she bent down to find her keys where she'd dropped them on the ground. She groped among the gravel in the dark, listening for the telltale jingle; then something sharp stabbed her finger. She hissed.

"Ouch!"

"What's wrong?"

"Something cut me."

Slipping his cell phone out of his pocket, Aiden turned the screen on and faced the light toward the ground. The gravel beneath their feet shone like it was littered with diamonds. It took a second for Piper's eyes to adjust to the light. She kicked a glittering piece and realized what they were seeing: broken glass.

Aiden raised the light to Piper's passenger window, which sported a gaping hole. But that wasn't all. Spray-painted in white across the entire side of her poppy red "classic" car was the word *Floozy.*

"Laura." She clenched her teeth. "Who even says 'floozy' anymore?"

"Maybe she got bored of the usual."

Reaching past Aiden, Piper wrenched open the door and saw more glass spread over the interior, the console, the floor, the seat. It felt surreal, like they'd gotten the wrong car. This couldn't possibly be hers. But it was.

"Can I see your phone?"

With a shaking hand, she reached back over her shoulder. Aiden passed his phone to her and she aimed the light around the cramped interior. She had a lot of crap in there, bits and pieces of telegram costumes, textbooks, evidence of her Starbucks obsession. But none of it had been touched. Her purse was still lying behind the driver's seat. Except . . . she checked her console again.

"Did she take anything?" Aiden asked.

"Yeah. I grabbed my mail on the way out of my apartment this morning. There was a letter—" She caught herself before she said any more. It had in fact been a notice from her cable company, saying if she didn't pay her bill they'd turn it off. "Err, yeah. Just junk mail."

His face turned grim. "It would have had your address on it."

"But Laura already knows where I live. She would have no reason to take my mail."

The phone's light cast deep shadows on both of them. It made Aiden's jaw seem sharper as it clenched. "Then obviously the arsonist's not done playing with us."

Piper froze in her search. She'd assumed it was Laura because of the less than original message. But what if it was worse? Maybe she wasn't the only one who stopped by.

She recalled Inspector Samuels's words from the night before. *He'll go to any lengths to get you out of this neighborhood.*

Swearing, she slammed the car door, watching the rest of her window disintegrate to the ground. She may have come face-to-face with the arsonist the night before. Had fought for her life and for her precious guests. But this was something different. This felt a little too close to home.

"It looks like it just got personal."

26

Hounded

The little ball of fur lolled sleepily in Piper's hand. She chuckled at the fur on his belly and around his chest. In order to stitch the little hamster up, she'd shaved the fur—butchered, more like it. Now he reminded her of A Flock of Seagulls.

She finished dabbing the last of the ointment over the stitched wound on Theodore Copenhagen II. "There we go, Teddy. That's much better now, isn't it?"

He turned his glazed hamster eyes on her, looking a little doped up. *You think this is bad? You should see the other guy.*

The other guy being a particularly playful Siamese who didn't know his own strength. "Now don't get into any more fights."

I can take him. Bring it on! He raised a tiny, clawed fist, but the effort sent him rolling onto his back, fat furry body sprawling out in Piper's palm.

She laughed. Dr. Fullerton, the primary vet at the veterinary hospital, was bent over her notebook on the stainless-steel table. She glanced up from her notes, looking over her glasses. "So? What's the prognosis?"

"Oh, he's still got some fight left in him."

"Good." She smiled, signing her name and closing his file. "Thanks for coming in today. I know it wasn't your normal scheduled shift."

"No problem." Sure, she had a million other things to worry about, but since she'd now completed the required clinical hours, it meant this was her last day.

"Could you bring our patient back to his owner?" Dr. Fullerton asked.

"Sure thing."

"I think it's break time." She glanced at the clock on the treatment room wall. It said 7:00 p.m. Slipping off her lab coat, she hung it over the back of a chair. "Your shift's just about done. I'll meet you in the back?"

"You bet."

Piper grabbed Teddy's painkillers from the cabinet and headed up to the reception area. "Watch out for Mr. Whiskers," she said to him.

There was only one person left in the waiting room. She was sitting with her back to Piper.

"Here's Teddy!" Piper called out.

The woman turned around at the sound of her voice. Piper saw her face and she backed up until she hit the wall.

"Laura."

Piper wondered if the SFAAC activist had come to taunt her some more. But then she saw the small cage on the seat next to her and realized she was Teddy's owner.

"What are you doing here?" Piper asked.

Laura's mouth had fallen open. It snapped shut and she scowled across the room. "For my injured pet, obviously." She took a step forward. "Now give him to me."

But Piper cradled the hamster protectively. Crazy scenarios ran through her mind. Considering everything that had happened recently, nothing was far-fetched. "Why did you choose this hospital?"

Laura folded her arms. "I live close by."

Piper's nostrils flared with anger. "Are you sure about that? Or did you use him as some sick excuse to come harass me at work?"

"I would never hurt my own pet!" Her eyes filled with rage. "I love animals."

"But you hate me more."

She twisted a wild curl of hair around her finger. "True."

Well, at least they agreed on one thing. Their mutual hatred.

"It was you, wasn't it?" Piper said. "You were behind the attacks on the center." She wasn't sure if that was true or why she thought Laura would simply confess, but she was tired of waiting around for the cops to figure it out. Or someone to get killed. One of the two. "You had something to do with it, didn't you?"

Laura snorted. "Are you serious? I was out of town. Besides, I'm an animal rights activist, stupid."

Piper wasn't sure if it was the truth. However, as much as Laura hated her, the motivation didn't make sense. And it couldn't possibly be that easy. But still, she didn't exactly deny her hatred for Piper. Who knew how far she was willing to go?

Laura held out a hand. "Now give me my hamster."

Piper looked at the sleeping lump in her hands. As much as she despised Laura, the crazy girl did love animals. It wasn't like Piper could refuse to hand back a beloved pet. Frowning, Piper crossed the room and turned the recovering patient over, along with his medication.

She watched the two of them leave, feeling no more closer to the truth than before. She tried to shake it off, storing the conversation away to tell the cops later.

Piper sighed. Teddy was her last official patient as a student. Now all that was left was her graduation commencement the next weekend and her licensing exam right after that. Eight years. It was so surreal. She never thought this day would come. And now it was here.

She wanted to high-five or fist-bump someone, but when she turned to the reception desk it seemed everyone had already cleared out for dinner. Well, that was certainly anticlimactic, she thought as she opened the door to the break room.

"Surprise!"

Piper jumped as the whole room erupted into happy cheers. She was passed around the room from hug to hug. Streamers and balloons clung to every chair and cabinet in the staff kitchen, and a giant banner draped across the wall said: *Congratulations.*

"What's all this?" she asked Dr. Fullerton.

"A thank-you, for all the hard work you've done here for the last several weeks." She yanked her in for a hug. "As far as I'm concerned, the second you have your license, you're hired."

Piper pulled away and stared at her in shock. "Really? Are you serious?"

"Absolutely. That's if you want the job."

She threw herself back into her arms. "Yes. That would be amazing. Thank you!"

"Welcome to the team."

"Okay, okay," said the receptionist, Terri. "We all love each other. Now to the important part." She waved a giant knife around. "Cake!"

"Well, we'd best dig in," Dr. Fullerton said. "I think Terri might begin a murder spree if she doesn't get her sugar fix soon."

Piper certainly didn't need any more of that in her life at the moment. She gave Terri the nod and the receptionist began dishing out Black Forest cake to everyone.

"So when do we get to meet this handsome new beau of yours?" Dr. Fullerton asked.

"Today, actually," Piper said. "He's giving me a ride home. My car is temporarily indisposed." She thought it best not to go into detail about her messed-up life to her future employer and coworkers.

"Well, you'll have to bring him in and introduce us."

Piper grinned like a lovesick idiot at the thought of introducing Aiden. She was just about to dig into her piece of cake when her phone vibrated in her pocket. She pulled it out and checked the display. It said: *Inspector Samuels.*

"Oh, sorry," she said to Dr. Fullerton. "I've got to get this." She ducked out of the noisy room before hitting the accept button.

"Hello?"

"Hello, Piper Summers?"

"Inspector Samuels."

"Is this a good time?"

"Yeah. I have a moment." A roar of laughter erupted from the break room, so she shut the door and walked to the other side of the empty waiting room. "What's going on?"

"I wanted to let you know that I checked into that customer of yours. Barney Miller. Turns out his prints were all over your car last night."

"So he trashed my car? Are you sure it couldn't have been Laura from SFAAC? The spray-paint job is definitely her handiwork."

"Well, he claims he happened to be driving by and saw someone messing with your car. Supposedly, he went to check it out."

Feeling a chill slither through her, she wrapped the lab coat around her. "What was Barney doing there in the first place?"

"That's what we asked him. And that's when he lawyered up." She could hear the annoyance in the inspector's voice. "Since your car was parked around the back of the building, it was hit in between the officers' routine walk-arounds. Barney must have been watching nearby until they were clear. I suspect he's been keeping a close eye on you for a while now."

"You think he's been stalking me?"

"Well, his car was spotted roaming through the neighborhood around the rescue center the night of the fire. And he was spotted in the area over the next couple of days by our surveillance guys. It wasn't until we went to have a little chat with him that we saw the car and started putting the pieces together."

"You're kidding."

"We're still investigating as to whether he was involved with any of the other incidents."

Bracing herself against the windowsill, she stared sightlessly out to the street. She thought back to Friday night, to her tussle. The arsonist was a male. That much was clear at the time. She tried to picture Barney as her attacker, the height, the build. It was possible, but she couldn't be sure. Not a hundred percent. Could it have been him that night? But he'd practically left her for dead. Sure, he was a pervert, but was he capable of murder? And if so, had he been the one who tried to cream her with a car in the alley?

"And here I always thought he was harmless," she said. Sure, she and Sam's receptionist, Lindsey, had their text message precaution when Piper went to Barney's house, but she never thought he was truly capable of anything violent. How many times had she gone to that psychopath's house all alone?

"You can never be too careful," the inspector said. "Do you have someplace safe to stay for the next while?"

She bit her lip, wondering if she would have to ask someone for a place to crash. Addison or Zoe maybe. Was it too soon to ask Aiden? She didn't want to be the one to push their relationship beyond its limits. To push it too far too soon.

"Yeah, I do," she lied. Then she frowned. "Why do you ask? Should I be worried? Isn't Barney in custody?"

"Unfortunately, no. But don't worry. We're working on tracking him down. We've got our units on alert. We'll have enough evidence to hold him once he's here."

"That's good." Piper suddenly remembered her surprise visitor. She told Inspector Samuels about Laura showing up and what she said—not that it helped much since she didn't really give a whole lot of information.

He grew quiet and she got the impression there wasn't much more to say at the moment. It gave her a lot to think about, but despite this new information, she didn't feel as relieved as she thought she would. There was no way to know if Barney was behind everything or if she had others to worry about.

"Well, unless there's anything else you'd like to know, Miss Summers, that's about all I had to tell you. I'll keep you informed if anything new arises in the case. Just be careful for now."

"I will." She came back to reality and looked around her. Really looked around. That's when she noticed something strange, something oddly familiar, like she'd seen it a thousand times but never took note. And she'd been staring right at it for the last five minutes.

"Miss Summers? Are you still there?"

"What kind of car?" she asked.

"I'm sorry?"

"What kind of car does Barney drive?"

"A Buick."

"Is it a Buick LeSabre? Roughly nineties? Like a light, metallicy blue?"

"Yes," he replied hesitantly.

"With damage to the front end like someone had crashed into it in an alley?" Her date with Aiden flashed through her mind. The mystery car chasing them, the Buick, her leaping onto it. Had Barney been parked there watching her and Aiden? Following her? Had he still been in the car as she was nearly run over?

Inspector Samuels was quiet for a moment. "How did you know all that?"

Raising her phone to the window, she took a snapshot of the view outside and sent it to Inspector Samuels. She heard a chime on the other end, indicating he'd received it.

"Because I'm looking at it right now," she said.

"Where are you?"

She rattled off the address, and all she heard was mumbles as he spoke to someone on the other end. After a moment, he came back. "Stay where you are, Miss Summers. We've got someone on the way. I'll stay on the line with you until they get there. Avoid confrontation with him."

"Yeah, no problem." She ran to the double front doors to dead-bolt them. Heart pounding, she reached out, but before she could snap it home a dark shadow passed outside, behind the frosted glass. The handle squeaked and the door cracked open.

She cried out in fright and shoved her body against the door, battling the weight on the other side of it. But he was stronger than her. The same desperate fear she felt the night of the fire rushed through her veins, knowing he was stronger than her but also knowing her life depended on fighting him off.

Another wave of cheers and laughter filtered into the reception area from the staff room. She opened her mouth to scream for help, but then she heard the voice on the other side of the door.

"What's going on? Piper, is that you?"

It was Aiden. With a sob of relief, she wrenched open the door and dragged him in. When he was safely inside, she flicked the dead bolt closed. She'd barely had time to turn toward him before his arms were around her, crushing her.

"What's wrong?" he asked.

Inspector Samuels's voice blasted through her phone. "Hello? Piper? Answer me. Are you there? What's happened? The police are on their way."

She shoved the phone back to her ear. "I'm still here," she said. "I'm okay. I'm safe." She tilted her head to Aiden. A fearsome concern creased his handsome features, his strong arms locked around her like a protective cage, and she knew it was true.

"I'm safe."

But when she glanced out the front window again, the Buick was gone.

27

Barking Mad

The light turned green. Aiden's foot dropped until metal hit metal. The Jaguar's engine screamed between gear changes as he accelerated, whipping in and out of traffic.

Piper had never seen him so mad. There was no sign of that calm, rational CEO demeanor. She recalled his reaction at the hospital after she filled him in on the new suspect number one. If the cops hadn't arrived to chase down Barney Miller when they had, she thought Aiden might have done it himself—and in a less legal manner. But Barney was long gone.

The wheels chirped on the pavement as Aiden took the next turn. "I wish you would have told me about this guy sooner," he said.

It had been hours since it happened, but she was still shaken by the incident. Her response came out a little sharper than she intended. "Why? What would you have done?"

His jaw clenched and she thought better about the

direction she wanted to take the conversation in. He was concerned, that was all.

"Look," she said less defensively. "I thought he was harmless." Then she remembered the text message system she had prepared with Lindsey. "Mostly."

His hand wrapped around the gearshift and tightened until his knuckles turned white. "It's disgusting. Ordering you every week like you're some kind of stripper for hire."

Lately it had been more than once a week, but she didn't think that would help his mood, either. "I quit Barney's gigs a couple weeks ago. Besides, I'm used to it. People treat me that way all the time. Why do you think Sam wants us in such revealing costumes? He makes more money that way. Because it works."

He made a sound in the back of his throat, clearly repulsed.

As he slammed the shifter into another gear, she laid a comforting hand over his. "It worked on you, didn't it?"

He bit the inside of his cheek and glanced at her out of the corner of his eye. "That's not why I followed you out of the office that day." His grip relaxed and the speedometer dropped a little. "Not completely, anyway," he relented with a little dimple flash.

She smiled. "It doesn't matter now, anyway. I'll fill out a restraining order. They'll find him, and I'll never have to worry about him again."

"But that's just him. What about all the other disgusting pigs like him?"

"It's not like I can quit. I don't get to start at the vet hospital until I'm licensed. I still need the telegram job."

He pressed his lips together like he was struggling with whatever he wanted to say. Piper knew it was something along the lines of he could support her until then. Wisely, he chose to say, "Congratulations on the job offer, by the way."

"Thanks. I'm really excited. I feel like things are finally turning around. It's been hectic, what with the center and all."

"It has been rough, hasn't it?"

"Just another week in the life of Piper Summers." She laughed humorlessly. "Been like this ever since high school. Well, maybe not quite this bad," she admitted. "After this sneak peek, you sure you want to stick around?"

Placing her hand on the gearshift, he covered it with his own. "Definitely."

They pulled up to the next stoplight, and she could feel his gaze shift to her. She turned to him. He was considering her carefully, a little frown line forming between his brows. "What happened in high school?"

"What?" The question caught her off guard. "Oh." She stared down at her lap, jarred by the rapid emotional turns the conversation was taking. "That's when my dad died."

He nodded, his hand squeezing hers around the gearshift. The light turned green and they pulled away. "You never told me how he died."

"It was skin cancer," she said. "I guess all those years in the fields without sunscreen caught up to him. Now I cringe when I hear the term 'redneck.' Kind of has a new meaning, you know?" She laughed without really meaning to joke.

"My dad got too sick to work on the farm. My mom and I did what we could with the help of a hired hand. But all the spare money went straight to hospital bills. Eventually we ran out."

"What about your brother? Where was he during all of this?"

She made the same sound of disgust he made earlier. "Rising in the ranks of his law firm." She huffed, shaking her head. "You know, my parents put a second mortgage on their house to put him through college. Gave up a lot, struggled because of it. Yet as Dad was going in for his second bout of chemo and we had to sell the John Deere just to afford the treatment, my brother was buying his first BMW."

Bitterness crept into her voice as she spoke about it, even after all these years. At least he was looking out for their mom. Maybe he'd felt guilty afterward and that's why he asked them to move up to Washington years before. Maybe it was his way of trying to make amends. It might have been enough for her mom, but it wasn't enough for her.

Piper was still staring at her lap, but she could sense Aiden nod. "I see," he said as though a picture was beginning to form. "He did nothing to help your family, even though he could."

"After my dad died, my mom had to sell the farm to break even. She got a job here in town, and we moved into my aunt's old apartment because it was rent-controlled." She hated talking about it, hated the sadness that threatened to choke her every time, but she felt it was time she shared it with him.

"It was a while before my brother started sending a few sparse checks in the mail. And sometimes I think he wanted to show off rather than help us out. I told Mom not to take the handouts, that we would be fine. I guess I didn't want to give him the satisfaction, you know. I mean, where was he when we needed him?"

She peeked over at Aiden. He had his eyes on the road, but he was listening intently. She shook her head, like that would clear it of the memories and resentment that still lingered.

"Anyway," she continued. "When my mom decided to move closer to him, she wanted me to come, of course, like we could still be some big happy family. But I wanted nothing to do with him and his pathetic handouts. So I stayed here."

Aiden was quiet for a few minutes, and Piper watched the houses shrink in size as they neared her place, the apartment buildings draining of color, becoming dingier. Their dull facades blended into the night. Instead of the streetlights making her crummy neighborhood brighter and safer, they highlighted how poor it was.

At the next stop sign, Aiden checked the mirror, moved the shifter into neutral, and put the parking brake on. Reaching across the car, he laid a hand on her cheek so she was forced to look at him, to hold his intense gaze.

"Piper," he said. "I'm not your brother." He said it slowly, loading each word with importance.

"That's a relief. Because this"—she pointed between the two of them—"would be really awkward."

"I'm serious. I'm not trying to rub my money in your face. I just want you to be happy. Or at the very least, not in danger."

"I know."

"Do you?"

"I do. And I appreciate it." She tried her best to keep any hesitation from her voice, because it was true, even if she had a tough time saying it. She knew it was something she needed to work on, especially dating a rich CEO. Baby steps, she told herself. It wouldn't be easy, but she could do it.

"I don't like the idea of you spending the night in your apartment with this Barney guy still out there somewhere." He put the car in gear and continued driving. His brow creased, his eyes intense. "Would you consider sleeping at my place tonight? Please?"

How long had Piper dreamed to hear those words coming out of Aiden's mouth? And he was practically begging her.

Of course she wanted to say yes. Hell, she wanted to race back to his house and drag him to his room. Or the foyer, if they didn't make it that far. Okay, probably the driveway. If only it had been under normal circumstances. She didn't want them to spend their first night together because she needed to be bailed out once again. Aiden to the rescue.

"Thank you for worrying. But I'll be fine."

He flinched at her response and an unhappy grunt rumbled in his throat, but he said nothing more. His eyes, however, said it all. They were tight, narrowed, maybe at her refusal to let him help or maybe at the situation. She wasn't sure. Unblinking, he focused his gaze out the windshield.

Colin gaped up at Piper from his perch on her lap with a, *What the hell is wrong with you?* stare.

It had been a long time since she'd let a guy distract her—not that she would admit it out loud to anyone. Her education had been her priority for the past eight years, and her licensing exam was coming up. She wasn't about to lose focus now. A tiny little voice in the back of Piper's mind reminded her that there was something else still holding her back.

Aiden cared for her. That much was clear, but too many questions lingered between them, acting as a barrier. And all of it surrounded his work and his way-outdated business practices. His number one, black and white rule: *I don't like mixing business with pleasure.* Clearly he'd broken that rule with her, but he was obviously struggling with the new grey area their relationship had created. It's not like she'd ever been a CEO of a big, important company, so she knew it was more complicated than that. But how could she fully trust someone who didn't trust her enough to tell her . . . whatever he was keeping from her?

As they approached her apartment complex, Piper started giving Aiden instructions down winding roads and one-way streets. He turned at the right places, but she could tell he was distracted by whatever was going on beneath that bedhead hair of his.

"I just don't like it. What if this Barney guy isn't the one who started the fire? And obviously he wasn't the one who tried to hit us with a car in the alley. Someone else that's involved in this is still out there." The heated leather steering wheel squeaked as his grip tightened around it. "It might not even have anything to do with the center. They could be targeting you personally."

She rubbed her fingers over her temple where a headache was forming. She recalled what Inspector Samuels had said the night of the fire. What if they were targeting her simply because she fought so hard to keep the center afloat? "We don't know that for sure."

He snorted, like he didn't believe that. Hell, neither did she. It was wishful thinking.

"Please stay at my house."

"I'll be fine. Don't worry," she said, more to convince herself than him. She was twenty-six years old. She could sleep all by herself, no night-light or anything. Well, Mr. Wiggles, her ratty childhood teddy bear, might make an appearance, but no one but Colin had to know about that. To the rest of the world, she was just fine, fine, fine. She felt that uncertain question mark pop into her head again.

Piper pointed to the building ahead. "Here we are. Casa de Summers."

It was an old sixties cement block with tiny uniform windows covered in aluminum foil—the poor man's attempt at temperature control—and people's tighty-whities hanging above their balconies.

Aiden pulled into a guest parking space next to the broken-down Chevy truck that had been a permanent fixture since she'd moved in. He killed the engine, and in the silence that followed Piper laid her head back against the leather seat and took a deep breath.

She was exhausted. Between her practicum shifts at the hospital, preparing for her exam, pulling more time at the center, graduation, taking extra work with the telegram agency, and oh yeah, fighting for her life, the only thing that seemed safe, constant, was Aiden—despite all the uncertainties she'd yet to confront him about. When she was around him seemed like the only time she could relax.

Something touched Piper's cheek. She jolted in her seat, blinking rapidly at the digital clock on the dash. It told her it was eleven o'clock at night.

"You still with me?" Aiden asked, his voice hushed. "I thought you might be more comfortable sleeping in a bed rather than my cramped car."

"You haven't seen my apartment yet," she said sarcastically.

She cracked open the car door. The air rushed in, raising goose bumps, clearing the sleepy fog from her brain. Colin hopped down to the pavement, searching for a tire to pee on.

"Can I walk you to your apartment, at least?" Aiden asked.

She thought of the crumbling stucco ceiling in the foyer, the chipped paint on the peach walls, the stale smell of over fifty years of cigarette smoke marinated into the very bones of the building. She fidgeted with her purse. "I'm fine, really."

He flinched again, like an annoyed twitch.

"Besides, you might get the carpets clean with your shoes."

He exhaled in a resigned sort of way. "All right. Call me first thing in the morning?"

She leaned over and gave him a quick kiss. "Definitely."

"I'll wait until you get into the building."

Before she crawled out, she raised her eyes to the third floor of her building, wishing her home wasn't such an embarrassment, and that's when she noticed something off about it. She paused for a moment, counting a second time, just to be sure. The second apartment in, third from the bottom—yes, that was her apartment. The lights were on. She was positive she'd turned them off. Her insides melted as she began to dread what that meant.

Aiden must have seen the worry in her expression. "What's wrong?"

"I might not be spending the night alone, after all."

"What do you mean?"

"I think someone's in my apartment."

Grabbing her purse, Piper called for Colin and headed to the building's back door to unlock it. Aiden's Jaguar chirped as he set the alarm and followed her. When she whipped open the entrance door, she wrinkled her nose at the smell of boiled cabbage that permeated the stairwell.

"Home sweet home," she muttered under her breath.

Usually the smell felt familiar, comforting even, after the last eight years, but that night it seemed unusually pungent and palpable. Conscious of Aiden there, she noticed the mystery stain on the second-landing carpet for the first time.

It wasn't the mansion Aiden's home was, but she wasted no time worrying about what he thought. She took the stairs as fast as her legs would let her. She hoped, wished, that her apartment was still intact, wished for it over and over as if the power of it could make it true. Like any time she bought a lottery ticket.

But it had yet to work for the lottery, and as her apartment came into view she knew her wish didn't work that night, either.

28

Dog's Breakfast

Piper's apartment door was flung wide open. The wooden frame was cracked where the lock had been pried free. Scratches, maybe from a crowbar, marred the fake plastic coating. It looked so violent and wrong. Her life had been turned upside down that weekend, but this was different. This was her home, her place of solitude. It was supposed to feel safe. Now it felt violated.

Colin sensed something was amiss and struggled in her arms. Numbly, she set him down. She was also dimly aware that Aiden was on the phone with the cops, but her focus remained on the wreckage in front of her. She only had to take a couple of steps into the sixties apartment to see the kitchen and living room, or at least what once resembled them.

The mismatched Ikea table and chairs were overturned, and most of the legs had been busted off. Cupboard doors hung at angles from their hinges, dish fragments decorated the floor like mosaic artwork, and it looked like the fridge had vomited its contents on the kitchen floor—not that there'd been much more than condiments.

Piper's gaze moved across the room, taking in the things that were hers but now felt like a stranger's. She gaped at the living room. Stuffing spewed from several knife gashes in her secondhand floral sofa, the drapes had received a drastic trim, and an Ikea table leg had found its way through her small TV screen—not that it mattered since the cable company had probably canceled her service already. New mystery stains marred the dingy carpet, which wasn't much of a loss since it hadn't been great to begin with. There were shredded books, diced houseplants, and overturned furniture.

Piper turned away, unable to take stock anymore. It was pointless; nothing had gone untouched.

Aiden hung up the phone and reached out to place a comforting hand on the back of Piper's neck. But she didn't cry, she didn't gasp and swear, she just exhaled and leaned against the wall resigning to it, like "That just figures."

"The cops were already called," Aiden said. "They're almost here."

"Sorry the place is such a mess," she told him. "I gave the maid a day off." A bubble of laughter floated up to Piper's lips and she had to clamp them down to hold it back. She wondered if it was the stress combined with the lack of sleep. It could all be a big hallucination. Maybe she was losing her mind. One could only hope, right?

At least Aiden hadn't seen what her place was like before, she told herself. Maybe he'd assume it looked like crap because of the ransacking. But in reality, it was a dump either way. A giggle popped out before she could stop it. She ran a hand though her hair, feeling like she could laugh and cry at the same time.

They waited in the hall in silence until the cops arrived. She answered the usual questions, the who, what, where, when, and why. If only she knew who the "who" was. Another hour passed before their identification unit started poking around her stuff, observing the state of her junk, lifting things with pens, taking photos.

Oh God, she thought, her mind racing in wild, not completely rational directions. *They'll find my stash of vibrators.* But she figured they saw worse stuff than that. Besides, she had more important things to worry about besides her purple Rabbit.

"Why would someone do this?" she asked. "What would someone have to gain from ruining my cheap crap?" Crap it might have been, but it was *her* crap, selected and arranged specially to form a home, her home. And as cheap as it might have been, it's not like she had the money to replace it.

"It could be the same person that's targeting the rescue center. Or Barney Miller, if he's not one and the same."

"Or Laura." She glanced at him sidelong. "Or your PR, Tamara."

"Not that again. Tamara wouldn't, couldn't, do something like this."

"You just haven't seen the real her."

"Look, all I'm saying is that it has to be connected. It's not a coincidence."

"Either that or I'm the unluckiest person I know."

"I'm not kidding. I'm worried about you. Someone is out to get you." He gripped her by the shoulders. "This is serious."

"Do I look like I'm laughing?"

"You're staying with me tonight," he said firmly.

Despite the seriousness of the situation, her heart skipped a beat. That would be one way to get her mind off things.

"Oh, it's going to be much longer than just a night," a male voice said from the stairwell behind them.

Piper spun to find her landlord's round beer belly poking through the entry into the hallway, like he was going to give birth to a beach ball at any minute. He scowled at the state of her apartment.

"Steve. Don't worry," she said. "I'll get this cleaned up."

"You're damn right you will. And you've got three days to do it." He used the back of his hand to wipe the sweat off his face from climbing the stairs.

"Three days? Until what?"

"Until you're out on your ass." He jabbed a finger at her. "Consider this a notice of eviction."

She scowled at the short man. "Eviction? Steve, you can't mean it. This wasn't my fault."

Aiden straightened his tie, like a boxer would slip on his gloves, preparing for a fight. "You can't evict her because someone broke into her apartment. If anything, your building's poor security features led to the destruction of her property."

"Right," Piper said. "What he said."

Steve snorted. "You mean the destruction of *my* property."

"This is my home. My stuff. Or . . . it was," she amended lamely.

"It's only your home as long as you pay for it." Sighing, he pulled off his bifocals and cleaned them on his stained polo shirt. When he put them back on it was like he was able to see something other than red. "Piper," he said, a bit calmer. "You haven't paid up for the month. I can't let you live here for free."

Aiden's head swiveled to her and her cheeks flared hot, but she pretended like she hadn't noticed. "Look, I'm sorry. I was trying to scrape by until payday, and then I got really . . . busy." Which was a gross understatement.

She dug into her purse, fishing for the check Aiden wrote her on Friday for dog walking. Whipping it out, she waved it in the air. "Look. See? Here's my paycheck. I can sign it over to you right now."

Ducking into the kitchen, she rifled through the pile of clutter on the tiles from the overturned junk drawer. When she found a pen, she signed the check over to Steve on the back of a frying pan.

"Here." She slipped back into the hall and waved it in his face until he snatched it from her.

He glanced at the amount. "This isn't near enough. And it's two weeks late."

She bit the inside of her cheek, wishing Aiden weren't there to witness this. "Come on. I'm clean. I'm quiet. I'm a good neighbor. Just ask anyone."

"Good neighbor?" His eyebrows shot up. "Your neighbors say that you've been hooking."

She gasped in indignation. "Hooking?! I'm not hooking."

"They said they've seen you come and go at all hours of the day in . . . costumes."

She noticed one of the cops inside turn his head toward their conversation. "*I'm not hooking,*" she told him.

Steve studied Aiden, his tailored suit and Cartier watch. He leaned closer to Piper, whispering behind his hand, "That's not your john, is it?"

Piper swatted him away, mostly to waft the smell of Budweiser out of her face. "I'm not a hooker. I'm a telegram girl."

"If it's a matter of money . . ." Aiden reached for his back pocket.

Piper held up her hand. "I thank you," she said as sincerely as she could between clenched teeth, "but if you finish that sentence I'm going to hit you with this frying pan." Baby steps, she reminded herself. Death threats weren't a good start to making progress with accepting help. She tried to give him a tight smile to show that she was kidding . . . mostly. Okay, not really.

"Look, Piper," Steve began. "If it was a matter of a late rent, I'd let you stay. Despite the graffiti I had to clean off your window."

"Yeah, I'm sorry about that. It was harder to get off than I anticipated."

"You're a good kid. But you know the rules." He tilted his bald head toward the apartment.

Colin stood in the middle of the living room, his barrel chest swollen proudly as though he'd swallowed his own beach ball. His tail whipped back and forth. He scampered over and presented a gift to Piper clamped in his jaws: Mr. Wiggles.

"Oh," was all she could say in defense.

"Hey, get that dog out of the crime scene!" one of the cops yelled.

Colin threw his head back to get a better grip on her stuffed animal. He clamped down again, and the toy blew out a pathetic *sque-e-e-ea-a-a-ak*. But to Piper's ears it sounded more like *You're screeeeeeewed*.

Aiden cleared his throat. "That's my dog. Colin, here, boy." He bent down and Colin trotted over to show off his toy.

Steve held up a hand. "Save it. I can see the dog food spilling out of the pantry from here."

Aiden reached for his back pocket again, but Piper threw him a glare that stopped him dead. Groaning in frustration, he ran his hands through his hair until it looked like he'd just tumbled out of bed.

"But Steve, please. I'm begging you. I have my licensing exam next week. As in my *final* exam. Eight years of my life working toward this. I can't handle worrying about graduating and moving out."

"No buts, Piper. You're out. You have three days, as per your broken agreement."

The air whooshed from her lungs like he'd kicked her in the chest. She gripped the doorframe as though the floor had fallen out from under her feet. Forget all her broken crap; forget homicidal maniacs in cars; forget pyromaniacs who wanted to set her entire world on fire. *Now* she was freaking out. She had finally reached her limit.

"I'm sorry. Rules are rules." Steve raised his hands to show her there was nothing he could do. "And keep the dog under wraps," he said. "I don't want the other tenants finding out. Next thing you know I'll be running a zoo."

He gave her a look loaded with pity, and without meaning to, her back straightened and her chin rose. She knew she had problems if Steve pitied her.

The cop who interviewed her hovered at the threshold to her apartment. "Miss Summers?" she said. "Can you please explain this?"

Oh no, she thought. They'd found her vibrators. Was it the purple one? For the love of God, not the red one! How did she let Zoe convince her to purchase that monstrosity? That wonderfully effective monstrosity . . .

Piper swallowed hard, but when she looked at what the cop was holding she frowned at it for a moment. It was a piece of black lace hanging off the end of a pen.

The skin on her neck prickled, heat creeping up it, spreading over her cheeks. "Umm, that's my underwear."

Steve whistled. "That's not underwear. That's what I use to floss my teeth."

Piper juddered slightly as her skin crawled. She flashed him a dirty look. Aiden shifted, looming over him, his face darker than she thought possible for the self-controlled businessman. Steve wisely chose to look abashed and avert his gaze to the stained carpet.

The police officer took a second pen and slid it through the other leg hole until Piper could see right through, well . . . the most important part of the panties.

Piper gasped. "What happened to my crotch?"

"They all seem to be like that," the cop said.

"All of them?" Piper's voice rose an octave.

"Yeah. Looks like the intruder took a pair of scissors to the entire drawer. We, uhh . . ." Her face colored a little and she cleared her throat. "We can't find the other pieces. It looks like they took them home as a souvenir."

Piper closed her eyes, covering her mouth with her hand. "I think I'm going to be sick."

She felt more than saw Aiden stiffen, his jaw clenching as he forced an angry puff of air out of his nose. His self-control was certainly being tested that weekend.

The police officer recovered from her embarrassment. "Do you have any other thoughts about who would have broken into your apartment tonight and mutilated your underwear drawer?"

The skin crawling returned like she was covered in cockroaches, a feeling she experienced often. Once a week, in fact. Every time she went to see him: "Barney Miller."

"Is that a boyfriend of yours?"

Piper's gag reflex activated without warning, but she took a deep breath before she hurled. "No. Definitely not. He's a regular client of mine. Or was."

"A john?" asked Steve.

"I'm *not* a prostitute," she snapped. "He hired me to sing telegrams. We had a disagreement a couple of weeks ago and I quit on him. Apparently, he's been stalking me. A report was made earlier today." She didn't exactly feel like reliving it.

The thought of Barney's disgusting little hands riffling through her underwear drawer, fingering her panties while he cut out the crotches, made bile rise in her throat again.

She turned away from the thong and braced herself against the wall.

Aiden grabbed her chin and fixed her with a stare that said he meant business. "You're staying at my house tonight."

She wasn't sure if he said it because she had someone, or maybe several someones, after her or because her crotchless Victoria's Secret panties were still dangling off the end of a ballpoint pen. Either way, she wasn't about to argue.

29

Throw a Dog a Bone

Piper trudged into Aiden's house and dropped her overnight bag and backpack next to the side table. By now, the numbness that had taken over her body at her apartment had faded, replaced with raw sensations of fear, weariness, and, most frustratingly, helplessness. The door slammed behind her, making her jump. She turned around to find Aiden glowering at her. Sophie greeted them from the bottom of the steps, but he didn't seem to notice her.

"Why didn't you tell me?" Aiden demanded.

She flinched at the hostility in his voice, and so did Colin and Sophie. "About what?"

"About what? About everything. How about the creep who's been perving on you at work? Or let's start with the fact that you couldn't pay rent and now you're homeless."

Her back straightened at his tone. "Because, quite frankly, my finances are none of your business." And they weren't. He wasn't her boyfriend. He wasn't the boss of her. Okay, well, technically he was. But still . . . "This is my problem, not yours."

Colin and Sophie shared an uncomfortable look and decided to head into the other room to give them privacy.

"But it's such an easy problem for me to fix," Aiden said. "You know perfectly well that a month's rent isn't going to break the bank. Why didn't you just ask?"

She'd been zapped of energy, it had been another long day, she had a headache, and the last thing she wanted to do was fight. "What's done is done. It doesn't matter, anyway. I can't stay there now that Steve knows I have a dog."

Aiden sighed, loosening his tie like he wanted a truce as much as she did. "All right. We can deal with it tomorrow. I know of a good moving company. They can take care of everything in a single afternoon."

"Right"—she laughed dryly—"and move to where?"

He snorted. "I run a little company called Caldwell and Son Investments. I'm not sure if you've heard about us. We own a property or two."

"You think I can afford one of your luxury properties that have some pretentious name like the Nottingham Lakeview Estates? Even though it's not really an estate and it's nowhere near a lake," she babbled, flustered by the suggestion. "That comes with doormen, and elevators, and fancy swirly numbers on the doors, and probably not even a single cockroach?"

"Yeah, I'm pretty sure the owner won't mind if you stay for free."

"Forget it." She crossed her arms. "I'm not bumming off you."

He scowled. "You won't be *bumming* off me."

"Fine, then I'll be freeloading off your company dime."

"What does it matter?" He ran his hands through his hair again. It had only just fallen down since the last time. She wondered if he did it enough times if it would get stuck like that. He threw his hands up in the air, voice loud enough to carry throughout the house. "I'm trying to help you. Why won't you let me?"

"I'm *fine,*" she said, emphasis on the word "fine."

He laughed, a little crazed, she thought. "You're not fine. Stop saying you're fine. A single word has never irritated me so much in all my life."

"I don't need your help," she snapped. "I don't need your money. I can take care of myself."

"Clearly." He waved a hand to encompass everything that happened that night. Or maybe that week. Or maybe even in her life.

She thrust her fists onto her hips, and winced slightly as she hit her bruise. "And what's that supposed to mean?"

"I didn't mean . . ." He made a visible attempt at collecting himself and his thoughts. "It's just that everyone seems to need me for something. For money, or contacts, or leverage, but you–"

"Me what? The CEO doesn't have enough people under his thumb; he needs me under it too?"

"Under my thumb?" he repeated incredulously. "Where is this coming from?"

"Do you have some crazy desire to feel needed by everyone?"

"No!" he blurted. "Not by everyone. I just want to feel needed by you. Because . . ." The anger faded from his face, his tone softening, like the fight had fled his body. "Because *I* need *you.*"

And just like that, she'd been bucked from her high horse. A second before she had a response ready for almost anything he could say, but she hadn't been ready for that.

"But the one person that I want to help the most," he said, "doesn't want my help. Not even when she's about to become homeless, not even for the rescue center that she loves so much. Don't think I didn't notice you never cashed my check. And I practically threw a job at you and I still had to convince you to take it."

It was true. She couldn't deny it. "I told you," she muttered, "I don't like handouts."

"The money means nothing to me. It's nothing for me to give it to you. It's not a big deal."

"Well, it's a big deal to me."

"Why?" His voice was still thick with frustration, but he stared at her like he really wanted to know, to understand.

"Because I worked hard to get where I am. It may not be great, it may not be glamorous, but when you consider how far I've come it is. I did this." She spread her hands wishing she could display all her accomplishments before him. "On my own. And I didn't need anyone to do it."

"Dammit, Piper." He banged his fist against the wall, the sound echoing around the grand foyer. "I feel like an asshole standing by and watching your life fall apart when I can do something about it."

"My life isn't falling apart. This *is* my life." She laughed without humor, like it was ridiculous to think it could be anything but. "And it has been for the last eight years. It's called being a starving student. My life fell apart in high school and I've gotten by just fine on my own up until now. And I'll continue to get by. Life doesn't change because I'm dating Mr. Big-Shot CEO."

"Shouldn't it?" he asked, seeming to find the crux of his argument. "Shouldn't it get better? When you find someone and decide that you want to be with them, isn't it because they make your life better, not harder? I know you make my life better." He tried to reach out to her, but she pulled away.

"Right. I make life real easy. You know, between the evictions, the unemployment, losing cars, the hit-and-runs, and arson—"

"And the laughs," he interrupted, "and how easy it is to talk to you, and how, when I'm with you, I can be myself. I never feel pressured to be Mr. Big-Shot CEO, as you put it. I'm not a paparazzi target, or the front-page news of the society pages. I'm just Aiden. Cargo shorts, plaid-wearing, dog owner Aiden."

A chuckle rose to her throat, but she was too angry for it to reach her lips. "Don't forget the Hawaiian shirt."

Closing the distance between them, he reached out and held her face in both of his hands. "You may not think you make my life better, but you do. You make me better. I haven't felt like I could be myself since my father died and I had to step into his big shoes. I've needed you in my life for longer than I ever knew. To have someone that, when you're together, makes the weight of the world feel like a feather."

She stared back, trying to imagine it. If she could allow herself to lean on someone else a little, to share the weight she'd been carrying for so long, what would that feather feel like?

When she couldn't find an argument, he took her hand and drew her into the sitting room. They sat down on the leather club sofa and he turned to face her.

"Would you want to see Addison or Zoe thrown out on the street with nowhere to live?"

She rolled her eyes, but more at herself because she was beginning to see his point. Why did he have to make so much damned sense? And why was it so hard to admit it out loud? "No. I'd do everything I could for them."

"Well, it just so happens that I can do more than most. Are you going to hold that against me?" he asked. "You only have a week left until you graduate, until your exam. Are you going to throw it all away because you're living in a cardboard box? Because you're too proud to accept my help?"

"I suppose not. No."

"Besides"—he grinned—"if you want me to spend nights at your place, well, I find drain water disagrees with my complexion. And don't get me started on park benches. They play up my lower back."

She smiled despite herself. "Well, I was thinking of something more like a spot under a staircase. You know, nice and dry. Or maybe an underpass."

"Sounds lovely. We could put up some newspaper curtains, plant some flowers in the drainpipe."

"Whoa. Hold on a minute." She held up her hands. "You're already moving in? We're moving a little fast, aren't we?"

He grabbed her hands in both of his, kissing her knuckles before leveling her with a firm look. "You're strong, independent, resilient, and really, really persistent. I know that you will be just fine on your own. But I don't want you to be just *fine*." He squeezed her hands. "I want you to be amazing."

"But you said so yourself, nothing in life worth having comes easy." Even she could hear the lack of conviction in her voice. Her argument had lost its punch.

"So would an easy life with me not be worth having?" he asked seriously.

She bit her lip, wanting to scream, "Yes! It would be worth everything." If only it weren't for her damned stubborn pride. Not to mention those uncertainties and questions that were still rolling around inside her head, waiting to be answered. So instead, she looked him square in the eye and said, "I just don't want to be your charity case."

"I don't want you to be my charity case, either," he said. "I want you to be my girlfriend."

It was suddenly hard to breathe, like the air had thickened around them. Her eyes began to sting. She blinked to keep them from tearing up. She opened her mouth to speak, but her voice caught like she was drowning in all the words that bubbled up inside her, fighting to be the first ones out, like, "Eeek" and "Are you sure?" or "Hell, yes!"

But the first words to find their way out were, "I don't want a boyfriend."

His imploring grip around her hands slackened and he leaned against the tufted backrest.

She smiled, reaching for him. "I want a partner."

He leaned forward again like he wasn't sure if he heard right. "A partner?"

"Fifty-fifty." She pointed at him. "Those are my terms. Take 'em or leave 'em."

A grin spread across his face, his dimple finally making an appearance. "Fifty-fifty." He nodded. "Those sound like reasonable terms. I'll have my lawyer draw up the contract."

"Should we shake on it?" She held out a hand between them.

"No." He reached over and pulled her toward him. She slid across the hard leather until she was wrapped in his arms. "No more handshakes." And he sealed the deal with a kiss.

Eventually, he pulled away, but Piper grabbed him by the tie. "Oh no. We're not finished here."

"We're not? I thought we came to a pretty good resolution."

"That's just the start." Standing up, she pulled on his tie, forcing him to his feet. "I've got a whole list of demands for you."

"You know, you'd make a good lawyer."

"Is that so?" She tugged on his tie, leading him toward the stairs like she had him on a leash. "Well then. Come on, counsel."

"Where are we going?" His voice growled low and thick, stirring something inside her.

"To continue our negotiations in your chambers," she purred.

He followed her up the stairs and down the hall to his bedroom. The room was dark but for the streetlights glowing through the row of old multipaned Georgian windows. There was a scuttle of little footsteps that chased after them, nails clicking on the hardwood floor.

Aiden met the two dachshunds at the door. "Sorry, guys. This is human playtime only."

The second he closed the door, soft whining drifted from the other side.

"They'll get over it." Piper slipped her hand into his and led him farther into the room.

"I can be a pretty a hard negotiator, you know," Aiden said.

"So I noticed." Her eyes roamed over his suit pants that were growing tighter by the second. "Hard is good."

Wanting to finally see what that suit and tie had been hiding, Piper stopped in front of the windows where the slanted streetlight glowed against his white button-down shirt. Aiden bent his mouth to hers. She pulled at his tucked shirt and ran her hands across the firmness of his abs. Two, four, six, and yup, there were eight.

Desperate to see more, she tugged furiously at his buttons. His tongue slid in and out of her mouth, caressing hers, making buttons seem like brain surgery. With only two left to go, his muscular chest so close, she said, "Screw it," and yanked his shirt open. The buttons popped and flew across the dark room. Oh, well, she thought, he has two dozen more just like it.

As she pulled his shirt back, she wasn't disappointed. His gym membership was well worth the money. She'd have to remember to thank them. She may not have been a customer, but she was definitely satisfied.

He took more care with her clothes as he slid her jeans

off, making sure not to rub against the bruise on her hip. Her tank top, however, he tugged down beneath her breasts, and he popped the clasp on the front of her bra before she could even gasp. His mouth was moving across them in seconds, licking, suckling, like a starving man.

She moaned and arched against him, running her hands through his hair, pushing his face into them. "I take it you're the kind of man who devours his dessert rather than savors."

"Oh, I have savored you." He ran his tongue up her neck, sucking her earlobe. "Every time I've seen you in one of your little costumes, I've savored, I've studied, I've thought about it while I've pleasured myself."

Piper gasped at his husky voice. His words tickled her ear, a direct line to her hips, which automatically pressed against his. These words, his voice so full of craving and hunger, surprised her. They were not the words of her orderly, reserved CEO whom she dreamed of ravaging.

"I've had enough of looking at you," he said. Hooking his thumb under the lace of her thong—the only one left with a crotch—he dragged it down her body until it fell to her feet. Scooping her up, he tossed her lightly on his bed. "I'm ready for a taste."

And taste her he did. Every. Square. Inch.

He started with her toes, kissing each one. He nibbled his way up her calves, gliding his tongue along her thigh. She held her breath as his mouth worked its way up the inside of her leg until she could feel his hot breath tickling between her thighs. She watched his head bob up and down as he took his time exploring everywhere but the spot that called to him the most.

Unable to stand it anymore, she wove her fingers into his thick hair and drew his luscious mouth closer. At the last second, he turned his face away and kissed her hip. Her breath left her in a frustrated grunt and he chuckled in satisfaction. She felt the rumble in her belly, stirring something deep inside her that Zoe's vibrators could never reach.

Tucking his thumbs under the tank top around her waist, he slid it up over her breasts. He paused to admire. Tongue swirling in delicious circles, he toyed with each nipple in turn until they stuck out, as hard and aroused as the bulge rubbing eagerly between her legs.

"How have I pleaded my case so far?" he asked.

She pretended to think for a moment. "Not bad, but I think I'd like to reexamine your briefs." Piper reached down and unfastened his pants. She slid her hand along the waistband of his boxer briefs, teasing him like he was teasing her.

His breath hitched. "I think you'll like what you find."

Just as she drew the elastic down around his hips, he pulled away. "But not yet."

She pouted, narrowing her eyes playfully. "I object. You're out of order."

With a wicked grin, he knelt between her parted legs. In the dim light filtering into the room, she could see him half-peeking out of the top of his boxers—and half was more than enough already. But he was annoyingly just out of reach. She licked her lips at the thought of him inside of her.

"I told you I was a hard negotiator," he said. "You'll just have to wait."

"Is that up for debate?"

"If it's a debate you're looking for, then I'll give you a good tongue-lashing." The grin on his face carried a warm surge through her belly.

Aiden settled on his stomach, nestled between her legs. He took his time exploring every satiny smooth inch that her recent trip to the wax salon had exposed. Each kiss brought him closer to her sweet spot. When she could feel his hot breath tickling it, so very close, the air caught in her chest and fire ran through her nerves, building higher, hotter, almost painful until he pressed his lips against her. So light, so soft and sweet, but her sensitive nerves exploded with the relief.

Piper gasped with each soft peck he gave her until her hips were grinding closer, craving more. His tongue darted out over and over again, building her need until he finally dragged it all the way up, long and slow.

Her eyes rolled into the back of her head and she fell back against the pillow. All she could focus on was the swirling of his tongue, his lips closing around her, holding her there. Soon his fingers joined in and it all blended into one mind-blowing sensation that made her toes curl, her hips rock, her legs quiver. This was definitely better than her vibrator.

She'd lost complete control of her body. It bucked on its own, her back arching to the movement of his fingers. Her moans grew louder, building steadily. Then, with a curl of his finger, like he was motioning for her to come, he took her by surprise. She cried out and clenched the sheets beneath her as her body began to convulse with pleasure.

Long after her shudders subsided, the sensations continued to run through her veins like a drug. Aiden kissed his way up her body to end on her lips. She kissed him back hungrily, craving more than his tongue, his fingers. She wanted all of him.

Piper knew that whatever issues might lie between them still, it would never be enough to keep them apart. She trusted Aiden, wanted him, and at that moment she desperately needed him inside of her.

Rolling on his back, he reached into his bedside table. He'd barely finished rolling the condom down his exquisite length before she threw a leg over him. Unable to wait another second, she finally opened herself up to him, her heart, her soul, her body. Sliding down, she took him in all at once, his own moan of pleasure rivaling hers.

Piper felt a sudden onslaught of satisfaction and fulfillment after imagining that moment a hundred times since the day they met. She rocked her hips back and forth, feeling his girth slide in and out of her. He met her with thrusts of his own, matching her greed for more, to fill her, all of her—her longing, that need in her life, to escape from her worries and fears, from the stress and the loneliness. She didn't have to do it alone. They would do it together.

And together they did.

His hands came up to grip her hips, moving her faster and faster, matching the rhythm of her delighted pants until the world, everything going on in Piper's crazy life, melted away into oblivion. It was just her and Aiden.

When his final moan joined hers, their bodies shuddered and trembled together, and in that moment the weight of the world seemed as light as a feather.

30

In the Doghouse

When Piper rolled over in the California king bed Monday morning, she reached out, searching for Aiden, but her hand landed on empty Egyptian cotton sheets. He'd already gone to work. In his place, however, she found a little box of her favorite chocolates—and two big lazy balls of fur. It seemed Colin and Sophie had joined her in a snuggle session at some point that morning.

As tempted as she was to eat chocolate for breakfast, she thought a balanced meal would better prepare her for another full day at the center. It was Zoe's turn to open early—well, to show up, since no one was allowed inside the building yet. Piper had planned to arrive at the same time; however, she was currently transportationless. As it was, she didn't know how she was going to get to her telegram gig.

Aiden's collared shirt was still lying crumpled on the floor where she'd stripped it off him the night before. She slipped it on and headed for the kitchen. After pulling out some ingredients for an omelet, she headed to the sink. While she washed the vegetables she tried to organize her day, but her disloyal mind wouldn't cooperate. Instead, it wandered back to her night spent with Aiden.

Things couldn't have been more perfect. They were finally on the same page together. *Together.* The word instilled a calm in her, a fullness. Rather than feeling as though she'd given something up, had become dependent upon this other person, she felt stronger for it. It wasn't about being reliant or needing help. She was part of a team. They were definitely headed in the right direction.

As she stared out the window above the sink, something red caught her attention in the driveway. It was her VW Bug. Abandoning the vegetables, she ran upstairs to throw on some clothes—she remembered to make a mental note to pick up some more underwear that day—and headed outside.

The fresh new poppy red paint job sparkled in the late morning sun, hiding any evidence of Laura's love note. Piper rounded the car and noticed the passenger window had been fixed.

Grinning, she opened the VW's door to have a look, and a wave of pine freshness hit her. It had that new car smell to it. All the broken glass had been cleaned out, every nook and cranny. Her old VW Bug looked like new. Well, sort of.

She went back inside for her phone and texted Aiden while she continued to make breakfast.

You fixed my car!

A few minutes later her phone chimed. *I was able to get it into the shop early. Tamara drove it back this morning. Are you mad?*

Piper's mouth twisted at the mention of Tamara's name. For a brief second, she worried about sabotage. How hard would it be for the girl to cut her brakes? As she considered her response, she received another text.

I also had them address that check engine light.

But it's been there forever. It could have waited.

Until when? When you were on your way to your exam, or your first day at work, and it exploded?

It wasn't going to explode :P

Your car? Yes. It would have.

Ha-ha. Don't hate the car just because you're jealous.

She stared out the window at her perfect VW and knew she wasn't mad. It was actually a very thoughtful gesture. It also fixed her transportation issue.

Thank you. To show she was sincere, she added a *:)*.

You're welcome. X.

Relying on others wasn't really her thing. It didn't come naturally to her. She avoided being indebted to anyone—you know, except for the bank, the credit card company, and the taxman. But with Aiden she didn't feel indebted, at least not since they'd talked it over. It was about give-and-take, and she looked forward to doing nice things for him in return. She went to get ready for work, smiling as she imagined how she would pay him back when he got home that night.

That smile remained there as she crawled into her VW Bug with Colin and headed to her telegram gig—only after testing the brakes. It didn't even disappear when she noticed that, instead of the same Katy Perry CD that had been stuck in her ancient stereo deck for the last two years, she heard the radio tune in. Startled, she glanced down to see her old one had been replaced with a brand-new, very expensive-looking system. Even then, her smile didn't waiver . . . much.

They headed across town in her pine-fresh car to the UCSF campus to tell someone they did a "super" job that year. She'd considered bringing Sophie, but Colin was enough of a handful as it was. He didn't match her Supergirl costume, but she'd never had to explain his presence during the occasional performance in the past. Everyone would just call him adorable and want to pet him. He'd lap up the attention while Piper would rake in the tips, which were always better when he was with her—because apparently he was cuter than she was.

On her way to the rescue center, she began to think that life was starting to turn around. Sure, she'd been evicted, all her stuff was destroyed, and she was nearly killed a couple of times, but her contentment surrounding Aiden overshadowed all that. As though that giddy joy could get her through anything life could throw at her, even when she took on way too much.

Snorting, she shook her head at her pathetic self. She was starting to think like Addison. But maybe now she understood what her friend was talking about. All those sunshine and rainbow feelings when it came to love.

Love. There wasn't even a hint of sarcasm in her attitude as she thought of the word. Was it too soon? Was it possible? With Aiden, she felt anything was possible. With him, nothing was *too much.*

Of course, there were still those doubts, those questions plaguing Piper, about his work, about why he'd been so secretive, doing everything he could to keep her in the dark about the center. But every doubt she'd had so far always turned out to be something silly and insignificant, something that could be explained away. And this was probably the same. She determined that when Aiden got home that night from work she'd talk to him about everything that had been bothering her. There had to be a simple explanation for everything. Right?

But her life was never that simple, as it decided to remind her the moment she pulled into the rescue center parking lot that afternoon. The smile that had been lingering since she woke that morning melted from her face. Lording over the lot was a sign with the title in big, black glaring letters. *Rezoning Application.*

She parked the car and frowned at Colin. "Rezoning for what?"

Colin leaned against the passenger window, staring at the sign in the same confused way she was. He glanced over his shoulder and gave her what was most certainly a shrug. *"Beats me."*

Piper slipped on a light coat over her costume and grabbed her backpack with her change of clothes. They jumped out of her car, marching over to the ten-foot sign. Colin sniffed around the pinewood post before raising his leg and letting the sign know exactly what he thought about it.

Piper stared at the enlarged map at the top, at its lines and measurements, over and over, trying to understand what she was seeing. Or rather, trying to find some other explanation, some way to deny what it was telling her. With a shaking hand, she slid her sunglasses on top of her head as though that might make things clearer.

The plot of land in question encompassed not only the Dachshund Rescue Center but several of the surrounding properties as well. They wanted to change the classification from commercial to residential. She read the details of the proposal, thinking there must be some mistake, but it confirmed what the map told her. They wanted to build something where the rescue center was. Her beloved rescue center.

Holding out a steadying hand, she leaned against the sign, her breaths coming faster and faster. Right in front of her face, she found a note at the bottom of the sign that said: *Further information can be obtained from Caldwell and Son Investments Ltd.*

Of course, she thought, tears prickling her eyes. Because the only person who could apply for rezoning was the owner. Her boyfriend.

Hot on the Scent

Gravel crunched under Piper's tall, red Supergirl boots as she followed Colin, running around to the back courtyard. She unlatched the gate and barreled though, yelling, "Addy? Zoe? Have you seen that sign—"

A lens reared out of nowhere and into her face. She stumbled, catching herself on the tall wooden fence. She got a whiff of Chanel before she was eating a microphone.

"Piper Summers," Holly accused. Or at least it sounded like the annoying reporter, but Piper couldn't see anything but her distorted reflection in the camera lens. "What do you have to say for yourself?"

Dogs barked in the courtyard, Colin growled protectively around her ankles, and everywhere Piper turned the camera blocked her path. She shoved the lens away. "Get out of my face."

Holly snapped her fingers. "Hey, You. Back off. I can't interview her when you're two inches from her giant pores. How are the viewers going to see me?" *Achoo!* She rubbed her nose. "Damned allergies."

Hey, You scrambled back a couple of paces, giving Piper enough room to glare at the reporter, but she heard his lens zoom in on her shocked face. "What the hell is this?"

Her friends stood on the other side of the courtyard watching the interaction with dismay. Addison struggled to hold back Toby, who jerked against his leash, fixated on Holly's fuchsia pantsuit. Addison gave Piper a shrug, like she wasn't sure what Holly was talking about.

Zoe opened her mouth to say something, but Holly flew in Piper's face again, shaking her finger. "I'll tell you what this is. This is me busting out my investigative journalist skills. You think you can make a fool out of Holly Hart?" She planted a fist on her hip. "Let me tell you. I've worked too damn hard to get where I am to let someone like you discredit me."

"Discredit you?"

"And my getting this job had nothing to do with those rumors that I slept with the producer. Nothing! I deserve this. I'm a real journalist now." Drawing herself up, she smoothed the wrinkles in her pantsuit and prepared to take it from the top. She cleared her throat. "Piper Summers, is it true that Aiden Caldwell bought the Dachshund Rescue Center a month and a half ago?"

Piper's annoyance level spiked. "Are these the amazing investigative skills you're busting out?"

She ignored that. "And isn't it also true that ever since Aiden Caldwell bought the rescue center it has been plagued with misfortune?"

"Well, it has been a bit unfortunate—" Piper's anger flared as she realized where Holly was going with this line of questioning. "But—"

"I wouldn't call three separate attacks *unfortunate*."

"But he wasn't involved with any of them, if that's what you mean." She wanted to say more, to defend Aiden with what she knew, but Inspector Samuels said that the dirt they had on Barney Miller couldn't go public yet. They were still investigating him.

"Didn't Mr. Caldwell just happen to stop by the day of the vandalism?" Holly's cynicism oozed from each word.

"He came by to see me."

Holly made a point of scanning Piper from head to toe before widening her eyes at the camera. "Right. And he just happened to be in the neighborhood the night of the fire too, I suppose?"

"Yes. He came by to . . . to see me."

"Just in time to save the day? Only moments after your attacker escaped?" she asked sarcastically before wheeling in on Piper. "Giving him enough time to circle around the building and come back inside as the hero," she declared triumphantly. *Achoo!*

"That wasn't him. I know it wasn't. He'd never do anything to hurt me." And besides, since that night she'd become well acquainted with Aiden's body. His shape, his size, the weight of him on top of her. She knew for a fact that he wasn't the pyromaniac. But again, she couldn't exactly use that as an argument on Channel Five News. It was Barney. It must have been.

"Then maybe he had an accomplice," Holly insisted. "Someone else working with him. That way, he could get the job done while making himself out to be the hero."

"Excuse me?" Piper couldn't help but laugh at the ridiculousness of it. "That's a good imagination you have there. Maybe you should go back to the tabloids where you belong."

Colin gave a bark of agreement. Holly glared at him as though she didn't like the tone of his voice.

Waving Holly aside, Piper tried to open the courtyard gate so she could tell them just where they could go. Colin barked at their heels, nipping at the air threateningly.

Before she could unlatch the gate, Hey, You blocked her path and Holly jumped right back into the shot.

"Isn't it true that you're dating Mr. Caldwell?" She shoved the microphone back into Piper's face like a weapon.

Piper scowled. "I don't see what that has to do with anything."

"How do you respond to the allegations that you're in cahoots with him?"

"In cahoots? What does that even mean?" She threw up her arms in frustration. "Who's alleging that?"

"I can't reveal my sources."

"Your sources, meaning *you*."

"Why are you avoiding the issue, Miss Summers?" Holly huffed, flicking a stray hair out of her face. "You were always around for the incidents. All three of them, to be exact. And Mr. Caldwell and yourself were the only witnesses the night of the fire."

"What are you saying? That we had something to do with it?" Piper narrowed her eyes, hit with a sudden urge to wrap the microphone cord around the nosey reporter's neck. Her voice shook with emotion. Zoe must have heard it too, because she came over and wrapped an arm around Piper's shoulder in support, ready to jump in if she asked her to. Addison was still trying to soothe Toby with all the commotion.

Piper took a deep breath, trying to control her annoyance, which was in the yellow, bordering on red. She gripped her car keys in her hand until they bit into her skin. "What would I have to gain from burning down the rescue center?"

"I couldn't help but notice the new paint job on your car as you drove up," Holly commented innocently.

"My car?"

Hey, You shifted the camera to point out the gate door and into the parking lot for a shot of the VW Bug.

"Lovely," Holly said. "I bet the job was expensive. Was it a gift? Or was it a way to buy you off?" she finished with a snarl.

Oh, what bad timing. "Have you lost your mind? Aiden and I could have died in that fire."

Holly stomped her stiletto heel on the ground, her eyes round like that of a bull about to charge. "You used me for my fame to cover for your sick crimes, to get donations. Did you pocket the money?" She gasped a long-drawn-out breath. "Is that how you paid for the paint job? I bet it wasn't the only upgrade to your piece of crap. Was it? Let's have a look inside, shall we?" She reached down to rip the keys right out of Piper's hand.

Piper wanted to take her car and drive right over Holly. "Get away from me!" she yelled. "You're nuts."

Holly wrapped her fingers around Piper's forearm. Colin took ahold of Holly's pant leg and began tugging. Hey, You backed up to get a panorama of the fight.

"All right. That's enough." Zoe grabbed the reporter by the waist, trying to pry her off her friend. "Holly. You and your camera guy both need to leave. Now."

But Holly had a death grip on Piper. Her manicured fingers pried open Piper's hand and the keys dropped to the ground. Zoe held her back, but Holly scrambled to grab them, her bright pink butt wiggling in the air as she simultaneously fought Colin off. He was growling viciously, Holly was screeching, Piper and Zoe were threatening, Hey, You was laughing, and it was at that moment that Addison lost her grip on Toby.

Tongue lolling out of the side of his mouth, the dog leapt at Holly. The force of his lust drove her headfirst into the ground over, and over, and over again at the cameraman's feet.

Achoo! "Ouch!" *Achoo!* "Ouch!" *Achoo!* "Ouch!"

Hey, You backed up to get a wider shot with a look on

his face that said it was Christmas morning. Piper dove for the keys and shoved them into her pocket.

When Addison wrenched the German shepherd off—although she took a little longer than necessary—Holly scrambled to her feet. Her hair lay flipped to one side like an eighties hairstyle, her blazer collar stuck up like the Fonz, and there was a suspicious brown smudge on her knee.

"Tell the truth!" she screamed at Piper. "You got the old lady who runs the place out of the way so you could shut it down. No one would ever suspect you. It's the perfect crime. No cameras, no alarm system—"

"Because we couldn't afford one!"

"—and no witnesses, except for the poor dogs. And they can't testify against you, can they?" She shoved a shivering Chihuahua at Piper like the ultimate weapon of guilt to drag the confession out of her. *Achoo!*

Piper gripped her head, feeling like she was going insane. "Where did that come from? Why does she have a Chihuahua? That's not even one of ours!"

"That's it," Zoe said, yanking the microphone right out of Holly Hart's talons. "We're done here."

Holly's eyes were wild, the size of Denny's pancakes. She spun toward the tall Japanese girl, but Zoe stepped forward, towering over the reporter despite her stilettos.

"We're done," Zoe repeated, shoving the mic into Holly's chest.

Tugging down her blazer, Holly tossed her head and sniffed. "Don't worry. I have all the information I need to run the story, anyway." She began backing away to the gate, the camera still rolling. "Everything except motive."

Piper wrenched open the gate. To make sure they left, Addison let Toby's leash out, inch by inch, ushering them out with the threat of humping close at their heels.

"Motive, right." Piper slammed the gate shut in their faces and threw her body weight against it to keep them out. The red and yellow *S* on her blue spandex crop top peeked out from under her raincoat.

Zoe noticed it and raised an eyebrow in question. Piper shrugged.

"So what is it, Miss Summers?" Holly's disembodied voice called over the fence. "Insurance fraud? A marketing ploy? An excuse to close up shop so Caldwell and Son Investments can begin demolition?"

Piper paused, her hand reaching for the latch. "Demolition?"

Holly scoffed, "Don't pretend like you don't know."

Piper's breaths turned to short gasps. Her stomach dropped into her shiny red boots. Dizziness washed over her, and she slumped against the fence, looking from Addison to Zoe. "He's demolishing the rescue center? Is that what the rezoning application is for?"

Zoe bit her lip. "I'm sorry, Pipe. We just found out this morning."

"We wanted to call you." Addison hesitated. "But we were waiting to find out more before telling you."

Piper tried to speak, but her mouth had gone dry. She licked her lips. "Before telling me what?"

"Wait; what?" Holly's disembodied voice called over the fence.

There was grunting and muffled swearing above Piper. She jumped away from the eight-foot-tall fence to see Holly peeking over it. Her arms pinwheeled before she reached for a plank of wood to steady herself. Clearly she was sitting on her cameraman's shoulders.

"You mean you really don't know?" Holly's face filled with a joy Piper had only seen in cartoons, like when Scrooge McDuck swam in his enormous vault of gold coins. "Oh, now *that's* entertainment."

"Entertainment?" Zoe snapped back. "I thought you were supposed to be reporting the news."

But Holly's rapt attention was on Piper. She smiled deliciously, every bit the tabloid journalist. "Your new boy toy is tearing down your doggy digs in order to build high-rise condominiums."

"No." Piper's head shook back and forth. "No. Aiden wouldn't do that. I know he wouldn't."

"He would. I checked it out this morning." She let out a high-pitched scream as she dropped from view. There were a few seconds of scuffling and grunting before the gate opened and Holly and Hey, You burst back into the courtyard. She had regained some semblance of calm confidence. The expression on her face was luminous.

"The paperwork's already gone to the city," she said. "There's a lot of support for the project since affordable housing is badly needed in the city. Sorry, sweetheart." She smiled gleefully. "But your prized pooch Aiden is a dirty dog."

"I don't know," Zoe said, her mouth pursing. "There's got to be a procedure for this kind of thing. Shouldn't the renters of the property get some notice or something?"

"Consider this your notice, honey."

Addison threw Piper a worried look. "Are you okay?"

She wasn't ready to answer that question. She wasn't even sure what to believe since Holly wasn't exactly the most nonpartisan source of information when it came to Aiden. "Have either of you spoken to Marilyn?" she asked. "We have to call her. She must know something about this."

"We tried," Zoe said, "but we still can't get through, and she hasn't returned any of our calls. Her ship docks tomorrow morning. We probably won't hear from her until then."

Addison managed to get Toby into one of the doghouses and latched the little door to keep him at bay. "But what about the insurance? I thought Aiden was taking care of the renovations with the claims adjuster."

Piper thought back to Saturday. Aiden had been so busy with the insurance company and investigators. She'd assumed he was getting everything organized . . . then he handed everything over to Tamara. She frowned. Could Tamara have something to do with this? No. She was just his PA. He had the real power over the major decisions.

Piper ran her hands through her hair and gripped it like that might be the source of her pounding head. "I thought so too."

"Do you see any hot construction men strutting around here this morning?" Holly waved an arm around them. "You're not getting it. Think about it. Why would you fix up a building that you've been planning to tear down for weeks? Months, even."

"Months?" Piper repeated.

Of course. This had been in the works since long before she and Aiden ever met each other. She recalled when she'd asked about his mysterious advanced deadline. *You'll find out soon enough.* Those cryptic words, the look on his face. He was smug. He was pleased with himself.

If it was really true, if Aiden had been planning to tear down the center while romancing her all along, then he was laughing at her. She was a joke to him. And so was everything she cared about. A big joke.

She covered her face with her hands. She felt screwed over—in more ways than one.

"I'm going to kill him," she said, although the lack of enthusiasm in her voice made it sound more like "I want to die."

"Hey, You!" Holly snapped her fingers. "Are you getting this? Premeditated. Murder one kind of stuff. Zoom in."

Piper sank to the ground, not even noticing the camera frantically filming shots from every angle. Zoe reached out and hissed something in Hey, You's ear that made his face go slack and caused him to lower the camera.

"Why would he do this?" Piper asked. "Why would he keep this from me?"

Holly snorted. "Probably so he didn't have to see that look on your face. Not exactly a turn-on when he's trying to get you into bed. Am I right? Huh?" She began making suggestive sex faces. "A little carnal action? Did you give in to your animal instincts? Maybe even a little *doggy*-style?" She giggled like they were on a girls' night out, you know, except for Hey, You eyeing Zoe in the background and holding his camera protectively in front of his crotch.

Addison cringed. "Well, at least he didn't get the satisfaction." When Piper looked up guiltily, she covered her mouth. "Did he?"

Piper winced but didn't answer. "Look. There has to be some other explanation for this."

Holly attempted to fix her hair using a compact mirror. "Explanation or excuse? Ever wonder why a rich boy like him didn't whip out the old checkbook to help the center after the first two incidents? Help you buy a security system? Especially if he was trying to get in your pants?"

"He did." She avoided Addison's and Zoe's stares. "But I wouldn't accept it."

"Accept it?" Holly scoffed. "He owns the building. If he wanted to make improvements, he would have."

Piper had never thought much about it at the time because she'd been so determined to fix things on her own. But he owned the building, after all. Of course it would have made sense for him to upgrade the center and make repairs if needed. And it wasn't like he was a cheapskate or anything, Piper thought, thinking of the new upgrades to her car.

"Because he didn't want to mix business with pleasure?" It didn't even sound right to her own ears, but she didn't know what was right anymore.

"Oh, it was business all right. And sounds like he got the pleasure part too." Holly winked.

Piper banged her fist on the ground, ready to deny the reporter's accusations. But even as she wanted to stick up for him, negative thoughts started to creep into her brain. Like how stupid she'd been. A rich, hot CEO interested in her? A telegram singer? She thought back to his history, his life story as told by the tabloids, and developed even more doubts. It was too good to be true, and she'd even known it the day he offered her the job. She wished she'd applied at McDonald's, after all.

The last couple of weeks with him montaged through her mind, how he made her feel, his lips on hers, the way he held her when he thought she was in danger, and how he instinctually wanted to take care of her—as annoying as it was sometimes. She mentally slapped herself for even considering him guilty of anything. Her instincts told her this was all wrong. Aiden just couldn't . . . He wouldn't—

Jumping to her feet, she grabbed her backpack and headed for the gate. Colin trotted next to her and back to the parking lot like a faithful sidekick—well, she thought, she was probably more of the sidekick. But this time, she was the one who was going to kick some bad guy butt. Or maybe that was the Supergirl costume talking.

"Wait!" Holly stumbled after her, Hey, You following like her shadow. "Where are you going?"

"To talk to Aiden," she said. "It's the only way to get some real answers."

"Do you think that's safe?" Zoe asked.

This brought her up short. She stopped walking and spun around. "Safe? Why wouldn't it be?"

"Well, what if it's true?" Zoe gave a small cringe to apologize for being the devil's—aka Holly's—advocate. "What if Aiden is somehow involved in all this?"

Piper didn't want to think about it. She'd entertained Holly's conspiracy theories enough for one day. "I've heard enough. I'm going."

"Wait!" Addison cried, grabbing Zoe and locking the gate. "We're coming too."

Holly looked like she was about to have a fit from all the excitement. "Ooh, confrontation."

Zoe held up a hand. "Not you, Jerry Springer."

"We'll take my car!" Addison unlocked her MINI convertible with the remote.

The soft top was down, and Piper controlled the urge to Dukes of Hazzard it over the hood and flip herself into the car. Instead, she opened the passage door, threw her bag on the other seat, picked up Colin, and scrambled into the back. She wanted to get away from Holly and her badgering questions as soon as possible. Questions that made her uncomfortable. Yes, they might have sounded like conspiracy theories, but the worst part was they were starting to make sense.

She gripped her knees, digging her nails into her bare skin as Addison and Zoe got in and buckled up. Not soon enough, the little four-seater car pulled out of the parking space, kicking up gravel that ricocheted off the new sign. Piper's short red cape sticking out of her jacket caught the wind and flowed out behind them as they flew off.

The last thing she heard Holly yell as she ran after the car was, "I get the exclusive, right?"

Addison's blue eyes flicked to Piper's reflection in the rearview mirror. She gave her a confident we'll-get-you-to-the-ball-Cinderella look. "I'm sure this is all a misunderstanding."

Piper held Colin close, for her own comfort and his

protection as Addison took the next corner like they were in a high-speed chase. "I hope so."

Zoe remained silent, staring out the passenger window, but Piper could see her expression in the side mirror. It didn't look like she agreed with Addison's point of view, but she kept her mouth shut, throwing worried glances at Piper now and then.

Addison cranked the wheel, tires squealing. "He cares about you, Piper. Anyone can see that. He's your Noah."

"Her what?" Zoe asked. "Oh, I get it. As in Noah's Ark, right? A reference to their two dachshunds?"

"No. As in Noah from *The Notebook*. You guys are soul mates, Piper."

"I thought he was my Richard Gere."

"No, he's much more than that."

He was. At least, she thought he'd been. But Holly's words chased her all the way to the Financial District. No matter how fast the MINI went, the girls couldn't outrun them.

She didn't want to believe it. Aiden was no attempted murderer or cold-blooded businessman. But facts were facts; he was trying to destroy her beloved center, to take away the home of her friends.

Over her dead body, she thought. She just hoped that wasn't a real possibility.

32

Snoop Dog

The MINI convertible whipped into the underground parking beneath Aiden's office building. Piper's heart began leapfrogging in her chest. She wasn't sure how it could still beat so fast and break into a million pieces at the same time. Aiden knew what the rescue center meant to her, and yet he planned on taking it away from her.

No, she told herself. There had to be another explanation for it. Holly was trying to get a rise out of her again. Nothing more.

Addison pulled into a visitor-parking stall and killed the engine. She turned around and gave Piper a hopeful look. "Here we are."

"Thanks for the lift," Piper said. "I won't be long. I promise."

Zoe spun around in her seat. "Oh no. You're not going in without us."

"Yeah, we're your reinforcements," Addison said.

Piper couldn't help but smile, grateful for friends' support. "This is Aiden's office we're talking about. Not Fort Knox. I'll be fine." She rearranged her raincoat to make sure it hid her costume. Because while Supergirl would be formidable considering her powers, Piper had none to speak of, you know, besides the ability to make men's pants grow tighter.

Zoe gnawed at her lip. "Unless, of course, Aiden really is somehow involved in all this. And I'm not saying he is." She threw her hands up. "I'm just saying that this person, whoever it is, tried to kill you twice now. There's a connection. I'm trying to think logically. And I don't want to see anything happen to you."

"But to be fair. The car thing was more of a spur-of-the-moment maiming rather than a planned thing," Addison argued. "Maybe."

"Yeah, much better." Zoe hopped out of the front seat before Piper could protest.

Addison leapt out of the driver's seat. "This is like an action movie. Or maybe some spy operation. We're like Charlie's Angels."

"Who's Charlie in this instance?" Zoe asked.

"I guess that would be Marilyn."

Piper turned to Colin. She couldn't leave him behind. "Well, Colin. I guess that makes you Bosley. But you'll have to hide in here for now." Unzipping her backpack, she emptied the contents and tucked him inside, leaving an opening big enough for him to watch her back as they headed for the elevators.

Piper fidgeted all the way up to the fortieth floor. Addison used the mirrored doors to pretend she was a Charlie's Angel, pointing her fingers like a gun. Zoe remained silent, thoughtful.

The doors slid open to reveal Veronica arranged behind her glass desk. Piper wondered if she practiced poses and held them all day or if she waited for the elevator *ding* before positioning herself like she was in a game of musical chairs.

When she saw it was just Piper, she slumped back into her chair and threw her head back, cackling at something someone said into her Bluetooth.

"She did not. No way. No way! OhmyGod," she said like it was all one word.

Piper tried several times to get her attention, but Veronica spun her chair, angling away from them, as though if she didn't see the three girls she couldn't be accused of ignoring them. However, Piper lacked the patience for her today. Leaning over the desk, she plucked the Bluetooth from her ear and tossed it onto the desk.

She smiled sweetly at Veronica's Botox-petrified expression. "I need a word with your boss."

"He's in a meeting at the moment, and can't be interrupted."

"I'll wait."

"It's a long meet-ing." She enunciated each word like Piper didn't understand English.

Piper's eyes narrowed. "Then I guess he'll need a break," she shot right back.

"They ordered in for lunch."

But Piper wasn't about to back down. "I need to speak with him. So hit that little button of yours and let me through. I'm sure he'll understand. This is important."

Veronica's bleached smile didn't reach her eyes. "So is his meeting, and he doesn't need you coming in here at all times of the day interrupting him. Tamara's told me all about you."

She rolled her eyes at the mention of the PA. "I'm sure she has. Now let me through those doors." She reached around the desk to hit the release button, but Veronica slapped her hand away.

"This is not a dating service. This is his place of business." Veronica straightened in her chair and clipped the Bluetooth back to her orange ear.

What exactly did Tamara tell her? "Well, unfortunately, I've discovered that his recent business involves me." Piper grabbed the Bluetooth again and tossed it over her shoulder. She was done playing nice.

Veronica bolted upright. Her chair flung back, rolling away on the polished floor. She glared at Piper across the glass desk, her skin flushing until her orange tan appeared peach. "I don't understand why you should have any business at all talking with a sophisticated man like Mr. Caldwell, far less dating him. You're an uncouth, uneducated, and uncivilized . . ."—her eyes raked over Piper, pausing at her neckline—"prostitute."

Piper glanced down. The telltale *S* peeked out from beneath her coat. Grabbing her collar, she ripped her coat open further like it could transform her into the superhero. She was certainly mad enough to lift the desk up and throw it at the orange girl. "I'm not a prostitute," she said between clenched teeth. "I'm a telegram singer."

"And she's educated," Addison said. "She's going to be a veterinarian."

"Yes. A *doctor,*" Zoe added. "And she also happens to be your boss's girlfriend. So are you looking to get fired? Or are you just stupid?"

Colin chose that moment to poke his bony head out of Piper's backpack and give Veronica a growl of disapproval. Yeah, because toting around an oversized purse dog like the trailer park version of Paris Hilton helped Piper's argument. She tucked his head back in.

"Well, Supergirl. I'm the administrative assistant to the CEO of this company. And I say that unless Aiden has a sick cow in his office, you won't be seeing him today."

"We don't need to go into his office to see a cow," Zoe muttered. "We've got one right here."

"Excuse me?" Veronica leaned on her desk like she was ready to stab a pen into Zoe's eye.

For a skinny Japanese girl, Zoe was tall, with looks that could kill. In fact, she'd persuaded more than one cold-footed groom down the aisle with nothing more than an arch of her eyebrow. And right now she looked like she wanted to rip Veronica's hair extensions right out of her head.

Piper's focus was on the catfight in the making, so she didn't notice Addison sidle to the other end of the reception desk until she heard an innocent, "Whoops."

Then came the crash.

All three girls turned from the desk. Colin poked his head out in curiosity. Next to Addison's ballet flats sparkled the shattered remnants of the giant crystal vase and its scattered Casablanca lilies.

"It was an accident?" And it would have been believable if Addison weren't grinning mischievously.

Veronica stomped her heel. "All right. All of you need to leave before I call security."

"I can't," Addison said too cheerfully. "I'm afraid to move. What if I cut myself on all this glass?"

"It's not glass. It's Swarovski crystal. Or rather, it was. Now get out!"

Addison crossed her arms. "I could bleed to death. Lose a toe. How would your boss feel about an amputation in his office?"

Veronica huffed. "Don't move. I'll get a broom."

Heels clicking on the marble floor, she walked to the side of the room and slipped her hand into a notch in the wall. Like magic, a hidden door appeared to reveal a room Piper didn't know existed. Apparently, even the closets were modern. Veronica ducked inside, the wall sealing off again behind her.

"Now's your chance," Zoe hissed. "Hurry."

Piper glanced back at the wall. "Are you sure?"

"Yeah, we've got you covered," Addison said. "There's plenty of stuff to break in here." And by the look in her eye, Piper knew she'd do it.

"Okay, but don't hang around too long. I'll meet you down at the car."

Eyeballing the wall, Piper scurried past the invisible door and hit the button behind the desk. The lock on the door clicked open and she slipped through. She slowed her pace, strolling down the corridor of glass-walled offices. Nothing said "I don't belong here" like frantically bolting through a building.

Gaze forward, she strode to the end of the hall until she stood in front of Aiden's office. She couldn't see inside. The shutters were drawn shut, probably because he was in a meeting. Taking a deep breath, she tapped on the glass door, not wanting to alert anyone else in nearby offices.

There was no answer. Either he didn't want to be disturbed or his meeting was being held elsewhere. Piper glanced over her shoulder, shifting from foot to foot. Colin sensed her growing anxiety and he squirmed in her bag, digging his little paws into her back. The longer she stood out in the open, the more likely it was Veronica would come searching for her. Or worse. Security would.

A loud crash followed her up the hall from the reception area and Piper cringed. Addison sure made one hell of a distraction. A chair squeaked in an office nearby. Someone had stood up to go investigate the ruckus.

Body frozen in indecision, heart hammering, Piper finally tried the door. It was unlocked. She supposed it wasn't like anyone would dare break into the CEO's office. But, as he'd once pointed out, Piper wasn't one for rules.

She hurried inside and closed the door behind her. It latched shut only a second before footsteps thumped outside. Piper's muscles tensed and she held her breath until the sound receded down the hall, away from Aiden's office. She breathed a sigh of relief.

The office was empty. The lights were off, but she didn't dare turn them on in case someone noticed. The light filtering in through the tinted window overlooking Montgomery Street was bright enough to see by. Now that she looked around the room, at the fastidious arrangement of pens, notepad, and coffee cup, at his neatly hung jacket on the back of the door, the invasiveness hit her. She had no right to be here, in this world. Without him, it felt so foreign and wrong.

She considered escaping before anyone noticed, but then she heard another loud crash from up front and decided against it. Digging into her bag, past Colin's squirming body, she grabbed her phone and texted Addison.

I'm in. Get out. Will meet you guys at the car.

She hit *send,* hoping they wouldn't be leaving in handcuffs.

Feeling like an intruder, Piper took a seat across from Aiden's desk and let Colin out of her backpack. She wasn't doing anything wrong if she just sat there, right? Surely Aiden wouldn't mind if she waited for him in his office. At least . . . so long as he had nothing to hide. So long as he wasn't trying to kill or maim her, that is.

And if he was? Then what? She'd call the cops, of course. Testify against him in court. But that was the easy part. No big deal. It was the resulting misery that she pondered as she waited, dreading her heart being crushed like possum roadkill on the side of Highway Sixty-Six. Then there would be the accompanying emotional baggage that an African elephant couldn't lift. Not to mention, a very likely future filled with too many cats that would eat her face after she died alone in her apartment.

No biggie. She'd be fine. Fine. Fine. Fine . . . ?

Unable to suppress the growing anxiety, she took out her phone and texted Aiden four little words that no one liked to hear. But how else could she put it? There was nothing else to say.

We need to talk.

Hoping he would respond, she paced around the room, growing more uncertain of her plan by the moment. Maybe she was overreacting. Maybe she was taking things too far. She should force him to sit down and explain everything, business or not, like she should have done a long time ago. But she knew that wouldn't work. He'd been keeping secrets from her all this time, and not just because it was business. Why would he be honest with her now?

But why would he lie? This was Aiden, after all. *Aiden.* She hated to even think these things about him.

Colin sniffed about like Sherlock seeking clues, but after uncovering nothing more than a dust bunny under the desk, which he took a moment to chew on, he curled up next to the chair.

Piper wanted to take this to be a good sign, an undeniable affirmation of Aiden's innocence. Animals had a way of knowing these things, of sensing danger and evil. Right? Colin's danger radar was off the charts. And Colin had taken to Aiden right away. Whereas Holly Hart loved to stir up trouble. She was only toying with Piper's emotions again.

Feeling ridiculously gullible, Piper grabbed her bag and tried to coax Colin back inside.

He stared up at her like, *Do I look stupid to you?*

"Come on, we gotta go."

She reached out for him, but he took a couple of steps back, stubbornly digging his paws in. Pulling out a treat from the front pocket, she tossed it into the bottom of the backpack.

And with that, Colin leapt in without another complaint, munching away happily.

Plopping the bag on Aiden's desk to zip it up partway, she knocked a folder off. The papers scattered across the floor and under the desk.

"Crap. Way to go, Watson," she mumbled to herself.

Desperate to leave before anyone knew she was there, she scrambled to pick the papers up. She arranged them into some semblance of order, tapping them to align their edges, and slid them back into their file. Once the folder rested on his desk, lined back up with the corner, the label at the top caught her eye. It was an address. One that was all too familiar. The rescue center's address.

Her hand hovered over the paperwork for a second as she battled with her conscience. It was wrong to snoop. Piper knew that. Especially since it was important to Aiden to keep his business separate from his personal life. But hadn't she come there to find out the truth? And if Holly was telling the truth, Aiden might not be forthright about it.

She cared for Aiden, and wanted to trust him. But trust went both ways, and she found out that afternoon there were already things—major things—he'd kept from her. She'd vowed to protect the rescue dogs, she'd promised Marilyn, and that was what she was going to do.

Flipping the folder open, she riffled through the forms. There were property assessments, graphs, contracts from builders. Finally, she came across conceptual drawings. Condos. Multi-level, sky-rise condos right where the Dachshund Rescue Center was. Just like Holly said.

Piper's legs gave out and she fell into the desk chair. Her stomach shriveled up like a raisin and she wanted to throw up. She'd trusted Aiden. She'd put her faith in him, relied on him, opened up, and let him into her life, and he took advantage of her. She felt a complete fool for it.

That wasn't the worst of it. If that was all, she could walk away angry, swearing and calling him every name in the book. But it wouldn't be so easy, because deep down she knew how she really felt about him. To avoid the looks of pity in their eyes, she'd deny it to Addison, to Zoe, even to Colin, but every time she would call Aiden an asshole inside it would cut her, because underneath the nasty name-calling what she'd really mean was that she'd loved Aiden.

She paused on a concept sketch of the front entrance of this new grand dwelling. A designer sign above the entrance doors displayed the name of the apartment building. It stung like a final slap in the face. It was the fake name she made up when he'd tried to convince her to move to one of his properties. *Nottingham Lakeview Estates.*

She wanted to laugh. Or cry. But before she could make any sound, the rhythmic beat of footsteps sounded in the hall. Slow, purposeful, approaching.

33

Doxie Detective

Piper dropped the file onto the desk and stared at the office door, willing it to remain closed.

Don't come in here, she thought. *Don't come in here.*

Aiden's muffled voice filtered through the door and her heart lurched painfully in her chest.

Colin recognized it too, because his tail began to wag inside the backpack. Swiping her bag off the desk, she ran, but as she was trapped in an office, her journey took her in a full circle. She was a trapped rat. One way in, and one way out.

For a second, she lunged to hide under the desk, but all the sleek lines offered little cover. The same went for the rest of Aiden's office. Damned modern furniture, she cursed in her head. Her darting eyes fell on a tiny notch in the wall and she remembered the hidden closet in the reception area.

Aiden's voice drew closer. She dashed across the room, fiddling with the door latch until the door popped open. With shaking hands she pushed coats and spare suits aside and crammed herself into the space. Aiden's voice became clearer. He was inside the room.

Colin's tail still wagged frantically, swishing inside the canvas bag. His head snaked out of the opening in the zipper and he searched for Aiden. Piper lowered herself to the floor, shifting as far back as the tiny space would allow. She drew Colin close to her chest and placed a hand on his snout.

"Shh," she hushed next to his ear, hoping that despite his lack of training, or obedience, or any sort of judgment at all, this one time he might actually listen to her. What the hell had she been thinking? Hiding in Aiden's office? It was too late to leave now.

"—don't know what you're so worried about," Aiden was saying.

"I just wish you wouldn't run off and make your own plans without involving me." Piper recognized Larry Williams's voice, snide and condescending, even to the man who was supposed to be his boss.

"I wanted to keep the company out of it. This was a personal undertaking."

"Personal. Right. A little too personal, if you ask me. You've let your attachment to that telegram girl cloud your judgment."

"Keep Piper out of this. I feel bad enough hiding all this from her as it is."

At the mention of her name, Piper inched closer to the door. It occurred to her that if Holly was right, and Aiden's company was up to no good, they'd hidden it well up until now. She'd need proof of some sort. Taking out her cell phone again, she opened the old app she used for recording classes the year before and hit *start*. She placed it on the floor, sliding it closer to the crack beneath the door.

"The secretary says she's already come sniffing around,"

Larry said. "Hopefully they find her before she discovers anything she shouldn't."

"Look, I'm a good businessman," Aiden said. "I haven't lost sight of what's important."

Larry snorted. "You've completely lost your objectivity. What's important is getting rid of those damn dogs."

There was a bang, and Piper imagined Aiden bringing a fist down on his desk. "And I've done just that, haven't I? With them out of the way, we can move forward with the condos."

Piper jolted at that. What was he saying? He didn't mean . . . She wished she could see his face, his expression. He sounded angry at Larry, but did he look regretful? Was he admitting to the fire? To getting rid of them so he could tear down the center? Her arms slackened around Colin and he stretched his snout toward the door, his chest quivering as he sniffed in and out rapidly. She strained to listen, barely daring to breathe, sure that she must be hearing wrong.

"Yes, but if you'd just left it to me–"

"I'm perfectly capable of making decisions for my own company," Aiden said.

"But was it the right one?" Larry's voice was loud, like he was standing in front of the closet or pacing the room. "Without the right planning, the right countermeasures in place . . . Once the media gets wind of this, they'll start putting things together. All the evidence will point to us. Your timing couldn't be worse."

"They've got no proof," Aiden stated. Piper cringed at the lack of emotion in his voice.

"That doesn't matter. You know better than anyone the damage this could do to our reputation even if we somehow don't get indicted for the crimes. A bad rep equals a huge downturn in profits. Look at the year one of our contractors had that accident on Market Street. The newspapers had a heyday with that."

Aiden sighed. "You're right about that. Holly Hart has been breathing down my neck. We'll get PR involved. Head off any stories before they start."

"Yes, we need to make sure we look like the good guys. Twist it to work in our favor and decrease the risk of accusations coming our way. I wish you would have just let me take care of all this."

A chair squeaked and she imagined Aiden falling into his desk chair. "I can see the headlines now. They'll probably call it Puppygate."

God! He was joking about this. He was actually joking. Piper couldn't believe her ears, but everything they were saying . . . how could she deny it any longer?

Piper's fist clenched and she bit down on a finger to stop the angry sobs that were building in her chest. Colin leaned closer to the door, straining against Piper's hold on him, like he'd caught whiff of a badger. He pawed at the base of the door, and Piper had to grab him before he began to whine. Her own panicked and furious breaths were starting to match his rapid sniffing.

"I promised my father I would take care of this company," Aiden said. "And that is exactly what I've done. Let's just hope it works out for the best."

"Yes. For the best. It certainly seems to be so far. God works in mysterious ways." Larry chuckled. "And I've always been a godly man myself."

So they were both in on it. All along. She closed her eyes and tried to regain some measure of calm, but with Colin struggling against her like his life depended on it, Piper could barely hold on to him. In his efforts to get free, he scratched her leg and her forearms. She flinched and he squirmed away, flopping out of her arms and onto the floor. His head bonked against the door. Before Piper could react, it popped open.

Both men whipped around, Aiden practically jumped out of his seat. Piper swore. Colin barreled into the room all barks, and teeth, and snarls. She'd never seen the doxie so wild before. Sausage legs moving in a blur, he charged at Old Spice.

The old man leapt from his chair in surprise, but not quick enough. Colin latched onto the hem of his pants, tugging and snarling. Backpedaling, Larry tried to clamber onto Aiden's desk.

Piper grabbed her phone, still recording audio, and crawled out from her hiding place. She did nothing to stop Colin's attack. She was too shocked, too humiliated, too furious. It was all she could do to not launch herself at one of the men and start tearing him apart herself.

Aiden's eyes were wide with surprise at her jack-in-the-box arrival. She glared back at him, panting as though she'd completed a marathon, hands on her hips. He glanced down, and she followed his gaze to see her coat had been flung open, revealing her Supergirl costume. She refastened the belt, waiting for some explanation from him, some excuse that didn't mean her life had turned into an episode of *Days of Our Lives*.

Old Spice flopped back onto the desk to safety with Colin dangling from his pant leg. The doxie gave one good final tug. The hem gave way. The fabric ripped up the seam of the pants. Spitting the piece of fabric out, Colin barked and growled from the floor, hopping at the base of the desk like he'd discovered a badger burrow. And when Piper stared at the man crawling on the desk, she realized why.

Larry's ankle was exposed where his pants had torn away. From beneath his argyle sock bulged a thick white bandage.

For the first time, Piper noticed the flat wool cap on his head. Fists clenched at her sides, she stormed over and ripped it off. And there was all the proof she needed. Beneath a poor attempt at a comb-over bulged a purple goose egg in the exact spot where she'd whacked the arsonist over the head.

Instead of looking guilty or caught in the act, Larry appeared indignant, even cowering on top of the desk. "This is no place for animals. That little monster attacked me. I could call Animal Control, you know. I could have him put down for that."

Piper's muscles tensed with all the ways she wanted to make Larry pay. "I should have you put down!"

"Now, look here, young lady–"

"No, you look." She threw the hat on the floor where Colin pounced on it, hungry for any piece of him. "I could have died in that fire. You could have killed all of those dogs."

"What? Piper," Aiden began, reaching a hand out to her. When she wheeled her furious expression around to him, he snatched it back.

"And you," she said. "You knew. You were in on it. Did you order him to do it?"

He flinched like she'd slapped him. "No, I . . . What are you—"

"I trusted you. I cared for you. I . . . I lov—" The word stuck in her throat because that emotional baggage was getting heavier by the moment. How could he still pretend he was innocent when Larry's wounds were like physical confessions of the dirty act? But she hadn't told Aiden about the wounds she inflicted on the arsonist the night of the fire. He still thought he could get away with it.

Aiden held a hand to his chest. "I swear, I don't know what you're talking about."

"Save it," she snapped.

"Look, little girl," Larry said. "I don't know what you think you heard—"

"Oh, but I'm sure the cops could help a little girl like me figure it all out. Because I've recorded your entire conversation." She waved the phone in his face before tucking it into her bra for safekeeping.

Aiden still seemed dazed. He shook his head back and forth, like he couldn't believe he'd been caught, Piper thought. "Let's just talk about this."

"Oh, I will." Scooping up a growling Colin, she yanked open the door. "To the cops."

Those eyes, that look of hurt, of innocence. Even now Aiden had power over her. His expression tugged something inside her, like he'd tied a string around her heart and trained it like a dog on a leash. How blind she'd been. How stupid.

"Piper. I love you."

And her breath whooshed out of her in a grunt, like he'd taken that string and ripped her heart right out of her chest. Her nose tickled and her eyes stung with impending tears. She scowled, trying to clear them.

Larry gripped her arm, fingers digging into the muscle. He was stronger than he looked—she found that out the night of the fire. "You're jumping to conclusions. You don't have enough proof," he hissed, his voice low now that the door was open.

"I don't need any more proof." Piper wrenched out of his grip and began to back out of the office. "Animals just have a way of knowing."

Colin growled at Larry, lips curling over his bared teeth.

She spun on her heel, thinking, hoping, it was all over. That she could raise her chin and march right out the building to call the cops. But she realized they weren't going to let her get away that easily when Larry grabbed her backpack from behind. Aiden ordered him to stop, but he kept tugging violently.

Piper plopped Colin on the floor and slipped her arms out of the straps, struggling against the jerking. Unfortunately, she also lost her jacket in the process.

Abandoning her school bag, she plucked Colin up and dashed down the hall toward the elevators. Old Spice called out behind her.

"Security!"

34

Wonder Wiener

One by one, heads poked out of their glass offices to swivel down the long hall in search of the commotion. It didn't take them long to see that it was a bird. No, it was a plane. No, it was Supergirl—err, well, it was Piper charging down the hall with a black wiener tucked under her arm.

Piper faltered at the line of people between her and the exit. She considered barreling past them all to make it to the elevators, but then Veronica pounced to block the other end, her orange skin flushed vivid coral. Her arm whipped up and she pointed Piper out to two burly guards. They began charging at her. Piper didn't like her chances. Because she wasn't, in fact, *super* in any way.

An exit sign buzzed in an alcove to her right. She heard Old Spice grunt behind her and felt another tug, this time on her red cape. She wrenched out of his grasp and darted toward the emergency exit.

The sounds of heavy footfalls and shouting followed her. Mostly "Stop, you little bitch!" from Larry Williams. But others had joined the chase too, all babbling curiously.

"What's going on?"

"Get that Supergirl!"

Aiden chased after her too. "Piper, wait. Please just listen. Everyone, stop!" he yelled, but his voice was drowned out in the commotion.

She burst through the exit and stumbled into the stairwell. His voice drifted after her, pleading with her that it must be a misunderstanding. Claims of innocence echoed down forty flights, following her down, down, down. Her feet flew over steps; her lungs gasped for air; her legs shook from fright. But it was her heart that hurt the worst. It ached. Only it wasn't from the panic.

The stairwell spiraled on forever and it soon felt like Colin was the size of a Saint Bernard. Piper wished she did have Supergirl's powers of strength. Even flight would help, or that handy laser eye thing.

People yelled above her; doors slammed; shoes clacked on steps, dress shoes, rubber-soled shoes. The noise bounced off the close walls, reverberating in the space and inside Piper's head.

At each new floor's landing, she expected the door to fly open and reveal security. Then it would all be over. Although just what that meant she didn't want to dwell on. She already knew what the company was willing to do to protect their assets. She didn't want to find out how far their limits went.

But no doors flew open; no one caught up to her; no one tackled her from behind. It wasn't like this was Alcatraz, but the panic coursing through her veins could have fooled her.

Piper wasn't sure why she was running. *She* hadn't done anything wrong. She wasn't sure what she expected them to do when they caught up to her. It wasn't like they were going to off her. But when she snuck into Aiden's office, she hadn't expected to discover the hideous truth, or to be chased through the building by half the office, either.

So it was the unknown that kept her moving on sheer animal instinct, the instinct to survive. The only thoughts that raced through her brain were of Larry's threats and those frantic footfalls behind her. She just needed to get out, to clear her mind, to figure this all out. But first, she had to get away. She focused on the rhythm of her legs, of increasing her speed. One, two, one, two.

Finally, she reached the door labeled *P2* in big bold letters. Holding Colin in one arm, she turned the handle and thrust her body against the metal door. She stumbled into the parking garage. It only took her a moment to scan the level for a Caribbean Aqua–colored convertible before she realized Addison's car wasn't there. Had they left? Did she get out on the wrong floor?

Behind her, muffled sounds of the angry mob thundered down the stairwell. She could either follow the slope up or the slope down, farther underground. Trying to remember how many levels they drove down when they arrived, she settled on up. If she didn't find the car, at least she would have a chance of reaching street level.

She urged her legs forward. The muscles tightened in protest, aching from the long descent, and her shiny Supergirl boots—which were *not* meant for a quick getaway—pinched her feet. She stumbled halfway up to the next level and saw the blue uniforms of two security guards jogging around the bend.

"Down here!" one called. "She's here."

The other ducked his head toward the microphone clipped to his shoulder. "She's on level P Two."

Shifting her weight, Piper ran back the way she came and slipped past the stairwell door. From the corner of her eye, she saw it crack open. An arm reached out as she whipped past. It clamped down on her cape, dragging her back, choking her. She caught a glimpse over her shoulder, of dark hair, wild eyes, hissing close to her ears.

Tamara.

Colin shifted in Piper's arms. Snarling, he snapped at the hand that held her. There was a yelp of pain and Piper was released. She lurched forward, not daring to spare a second to look back. The quick, sharp clicking noises behind her told Piper that Tamara was in hot pursuit—no surprise there—but her high heels were slowing her down.

"Thanks," Piper said to Colin, and he nestled back into her arms.

Sprinting past Land Rovers never taken out of the city and sports cars used to drive to Starbucks, she followed the slope down and around and around until she ran out of parking garage to run through. There was no more down to go. No doors, no hiding spots, no exits.

Her head whipped back and forth, breaths coming in panicked gasps. Footsteps approached, pounding on the pavement, closing in on her. Backing toward the farthest, darkest corner, she did the only thing she could do and hid. She inched back until she hit the wall and squeezed in front of a car bumper.

Remembering the phone in her bra, she pulled it out to call the cops or, just as effective, Addison and Zoe. But there was no reception; she was too far underground. She held it in the air, angling it this way and that, but it was no good. Sighing, she tucked it back into her bra.

She closed her eyes, willing her heartbeat to slow. It sounded thunderous in her ears, banging like a drum, and she wondered if her pursuers could hear it too. Exhausted, her head fell against the wall with a thump. She waited, unable to do anything but cower there until they found her. Some Supergirl she was.

Colin remained quiet and cooperative in her arms, for once, like he understood the urgency of the situation, could sense the anxiety leaking from Piper. He gave her an encouraging lick on her hand as they waited in silence. She scratched him behind the ears, needing the comfort and contact. They were in this together.

Voices were getting closer, clearer. The hollow responses chiming in on the two-way radios echoed off cement walls. She opened her eyes, preparing herself for flight or fight, and stared at the car in front of her. Dents and scratches marred the bumper, one headlight blown out. She frowned at it. It was a Prius.

For some reason, the information nudged her brain with a mental foot, trying to wake it up. Her poor, frightened brain struggled to put the pieces together. She wanted to smack her head against the pavement to see if it would help.

The Dog and Bone came rushing back to her, when she'd been inches away from kissing the grill of a car. An electric car, she realized, remembering the high-pitched whine of the engine as it sped toward her. A Prius was a hybrid.

She scrambled away from the car, as though it would come to life all on its own and squish her against the cement wall. Tamara showed up at the center in Aiden's BMW that weekend. He'd said that he loaned it to her because her car needed to go into the shop. She drove a Prius. This was her car.

Officer Tucker said Tamara was held up at work the night of their date. That must have meant Aiden helped her cover it all up. But why? And did he know she was crazy? Maybe he was just as crazy as her.

She hit the ground with her fist, pebbles biting into her hand. Was the whole damned company out to get her?

The mob closed in on Piper. She peeked over the dented hood of the car and saw blue guard uniforms approach, followed by a lot of white dress shirts and ties. She shrunk behind the car cradling Colin close, thinking this was what badgers felt like when hunted by dachshunds in their holes.

Somewhere nearby, tires squealed, the echo carrying down through the parking garage. An engine revved angrily, growling like a lion inside a cave.

"Stop!" someone yelled.

But the engine grew louder. There was yelling and more tire screeching.

Piper dared to crawl around the side of the car and peer out. Addison's convertible came power sliding around the tight bend. The suits and security guards dove out of the way, rolling toward the safety of parked cars on either side. That's when Addison saw the dead end ahead.

Her eyes widened. "Crap!"

"Look out!" Zoe screamed.

Addison slammed on the brakes, tires skidding. She looked back over her shoulder and threw the car in reverse, pulling into a space to turn it around.

Scrambling to her feet, Piper popped out and chased after her friends. Zoe noticed her first and told Addison to stop.

"Get in!" she yelled.

Piper plunked Colin onto the backseat. This time, she did pull a Dukes of Hazzard and threw herself into the back of the car in a way that would make Supergirl proud. The moment Piper's butt hit the leather, Addison hit the gas, peeling out of the space.

By this time, the security guards had collected themselves and were converging. They leapt out of the way again as the three girls went round and round the parking garage, climbing each level, closer to safety.

Around the next bend, they passed Tamara. She hissed and dove for the car, like she was going to jump in the backseat. Addison swerved. The PA's hand grazed the door handle, but her nails scraped along the paint, unable to find a grip. There was an *oof* as she landed hard on the pavement behind them.

When they reached the ground floor, the exit came into view. A plastic arm blocked their way out. Addison let off the gas. The attendant stepped out of his booth, looking curiously at the three of them, pausing on Piper's Supergirl costume.

"Do you think they'll validate our parking?" Zoe asked dryly.

"I bet Charlie's Angels never had to pay for parking." Addison said.

Piper heard the click of oxfords on cement behind the car. She turned to find Aiden closing in on them.

"Piper!" Aiden called between pants. "Please, can't we just talk about this?"

At the sound of his voice, Colin jumped up and leaned his front paws against the backrest to say hello. For once his danger radar was way off. How could he not realize that Aiden was the biggest monster of them all?

"Why?" Piper said. "So you can pay me off? Shut me up? Maybe try to run me over with another car?" She heard her voice crack, and she clenched her teeth against the tears threatening to spill down her face.

"What are you talking about?"

"Save it. I've already seen Tamara's car."

He honestly looked confused, but there was too much evidence stacked against him. She wasn't about to hear his bullshit excuses.

Addison argued with the parking attendant to let them through, throwing him every coin she had jingling in the bottom of her purse, but he kept insisting she return to a pay station.

Finally catching up to them, Aiden moved around the side of the car. "Piper, please . . ."

She threw him a look that stopped him dead. "Why did

you start dating me? How did that fit into your master plans? Or was I the spoils of your hostile takeover?"

"Piper. I–"

"Don't. Just don't."

Addison slammed a hand down on the wheel, fed up with the guard. "Ah, screw it."

Throwing the car into gear, she crushed the gas pedal and blew through the security arm. With a crack, it busted in half. Piper ducked as it flew over their heads. She looked back to watch it land at Aiden's feet. The guard started to yell after them, but Aiden held up a hand to stop him.

He didn't look angry, or thwarted like a proper villain should. He looked mystified. Like that lost little puppy Piper first fell for. Her stomach tightened at the sight and she finally let the tears spill over. In reality, he'd never been a puppy. He'd been a wolf right from the start.

The anguish on his face was the last thing she saw before they turned the next corner. Wiping away her tears, she pulled out her cell phone and dialed Inspector Samuels.

Lie with Dogs, Wake Up with Fleas

"I'm a good businessman. I haven't lost sight of what's important."

"You've completely lost your objectivity. What's important is getting rid of those damn dogs."

"And I've done just that, haven't I?"

Aiden's admission stung just as badly hearing it the second time around. Piper cringed at his words, like a dagger being slid farther into her back, tearing muscle fibers and nerves as it dug deep enough to pierce her heart.

Inspector Samuels took notes while he listened to the playback on her phone. His face remained placid, any thoughts or feelings kept in check. She gripped her Styrofoam cup full of lukewarm coffee heating her shaking fingers and eyeballed the one-way mirror and the camera blinking in the corner by the ceiling. She wondered if Aiden and Old Spice were being interrogated in a similar room, or if the police were making them sit and stew until they heard Piper's version of the story. The real one. She wondered if Aiden and Old Spice would try to deny it, like some big corporate cover-up.

When he'd heard enough, the inspector stopped the recording and grunted. "Quick thinking recording that conversation. It will come in handy during prosecution."

"Good," Piper said with a conviction she didn't really feel.

"You don't mind if we keep this in evidence for a few days, do you?"

At the thought of losing her phone, her only connection to the outside world, she clutched it to her chest. "You can't just keep a copy of the recording?"

"Considering your relationship with the suspect, we'll also need to review your call history, text messages, any photos of the two of you, that sort of thing. You never know what can help build a case, time lines, that sort of thing. He might have made slipups during previous discussions."

Reluctantly, Piper handed it over, glad the most embarrassing thing on her phone was the insane amount of photos of Colin. She would have to call Lindsey at Sam's office and let her know she wouldn't be taking any telegram gigs for a few days—not that she had the time, anyway, what with having to move and her life falling apart and everything.

It suddenly occurred to her that she was back down to one job. She'd been relying on the dog-walking paychecks to pay the next month's bills and to save up a damage deposit for when she found a new place—since she obviously wasn't going to get hers back from Steve. She guessed that was out now.

Inspector Samuels stood up from the metal table and Piper somehow found the strength to do the same. She gave her short red skirt a tug to cover her butt. Arriving at the police station in her Supergirl costume raised a few eyebrows, but she was sure they'd seen stranger things. At least Addison had a spare sweatshirt in the trunk of her car to lend her.

"Well, Miss Summers," he said. "I'm glad that you're all right. You've been through a hell of an ordeal."

"I'm just glad it's all over."

But it didn't feel *over.* It felt like a giant, open, festering wound. One that wasn't going to close anytime soon.

He walked her to the door and out into the bustling hallway.

"Do you think this was his plan all along?" she asked. "Right from the start?"

"There's no way of knowing. It's too soon in the investigation." He gave her an apologetic look, like he wished he had something more comforting to say than that. So did she.

She'd been such a fool. Inspector Samuels's words from the night of the fire came rushing back to her. *Arsonists have a habit of coming back to see the results of their work.* Aiden had been there after or during all the incidents at the rescue center and the near hit-and-run. He managed to witness the aftermath each time, reveling in the destruction of his own creation.

They arrived at the front stairs leading down to the lobby. She reached out and shook the inspector's hand. "I'm glad you responded as quickly as you did today. Thank you."

"Of course," he said. "But I was already on my way when you called."

Pausing at the top of the stairs, she spun to face him. "You were?"

"You weren't the first nine-one-one call we received."

"Who was the first?"

"Aiden Caldwell."

She nearly lost her footing on the stairs and tumbled to

the bottom. She gripped the rail and her jaw tightened. "A PR move, no doubt." In his office, he'd talked about involving them, to head off any stories before they started. Maybe this was their suggestion, to make the first move. Maybe they thought it would make them seem less guilty, more cooperative.

The inspector's face gave nothing away. "Perhaps." But something in his voice made her wonder if that was a "perhaps yes" or a "perhaps no."

Not that she cared. She knew enough. She wasn't going to ponder everything that happened, everything Aiden said and did over the last few weeks, over, and over, and over again. And that "perhaps" certainly wasn't going to keep her up half the night, wondering, remembering, daydreaming, and, most of all, most definitely not, hoping.

Nope. Not at all.

Piper trudged down the stairs and into the lobby. She was so lost in thought that she barely saw Addison and Zoe until she was smothered in hugs. Addison handed Colin to her, who attacked her neck and face with kisses, both excited and relieved, but probably not aware of why.

"Are you okay?" Addison asked. She and Zoe were staring at her like she was an abused pup that came into the center.

"Peachy," she said in her most chipper telegram girl voice. "My boyfriend's a megalomaniac who tried to have me killed. But no relationship is without its problems. You gotta work these things out, right?"

"I don't think he's like Richard Gere anymore. He's like Cruella de Vil. But with dachshunds instead of Dalmatians."

"At least you don't need to worry about getting murdered anymore." Zoe patted her back in a "go get 'em, Tiger" kind of way. "Or about the center, since, you know, everyone's in jail."

"Oh God. The center." All the worries that she'd put aside over the last several hours came crashing back, making her knees buckle with the weight of them. What was she going to tell Marilyn when she got back the next day?

She noticed a guy in the waiting area listening in on their conversation. His shirt was ripped, his eye black, and he was handcuffed to a bench. She found herself wanting to know his story, like hearing someone else's misery could lessen her own. But despite the fact that he was in rough shape and waiting to be processed, she worried her story might still trump his. You know you got it bad when—

Putting that depressing thought aside, she turned back to her friends. "What's going to happen? Will the center get repaired now that the man who owns it is, well, you know?"

"Evil?" Addison offered.

"There's so much to do. And Marilyn gets back to town tomorrow. And then there's my eviction. I have to be out in less than two days. Maybe I should reschedule my exam. I should call my mom too." She groaned. "Oh yeah, they took my phone . . . ," she petered off. The guy in handcuffs gave her a pitying look. Maybe her life really was that bad.

"Whoa, hold on there," Zoe said. "One catastrophe at a time. The center will work itself out. There's nothing we can do until we talk to Marilyn. That worry will have to wait until tomorrow."

"And as for moving out," Addison said, "we'll be there to help you."

"But—"

"But nothing," Zoe said. "You have enough to worry about with your licensing exam next week and moving out. Addy and I are here for you. In the morning, one of us will look after the place and fill Marilyn in, and the other will help you move all your crap out and into my guest room."

She could almost see the mental to-do list Zoe was writing in her head.

"Your guest room?"

"That's right, Roomie. Unless you have a better option than yours truly." She nudged Piper with an elbow. "Come on. Let us help you."

Maybe her time with Aiden hadn't been a complete loss. If Piper had learned anything by being with him, she'd learned that it was okay to rely on others—maybe not *him* specifically, but she knew she could depend on Addison and Zoe. Her shoulders, which had been creeping their way upward from stress, deflated, resuming their normal position. She closed her eyes and took a cleansing breath, thankful to have her friends in her life.

"Thanks, guys."

"Oh, here. I forgot this." Zoe handed over a fresh cup of Starbucks chai tea. "We weren't sure what you'd want for comfort food."

"So we bought it all." Addison waved a box of chocolates in the air.

"Don't worry," Zoe said. "There's wine waiting in the car."

Overwhelmed by their support, she pulled them in for another hug. "Thanks, but I think I just want to be alone tonight." Then she remembered the state of her apartment. Oh, well, she thought, she could flip the mattress onto the floor.

"Are you sure?" Addison asked. "I have like five flavors of ice cream in my freezer right now."

"Why so many?" Zoe asked.

"For emergencies. A different flavor for every kind of situation. Like last month. You remember that guy I'd met at the bookstore? And how his 'roommate' turned out to be his wife. That was a vanilla blackberry jube jube kind of situation."

"Do you have a flavor for my boyfriend tried to have me killed in a hostile corporate takeover?" Piper asked. "Because I'd like to try some of that."

"Hmm. No. But I have triple chocolate caramel fudge brownie."

She knew that if she gave in to that pain, the sucking chest wound where Aiden had ripped out her heart, it would lead to lots of tears and chick flicks on Addison's couch and she might never be able to pull herself out of it, or that tub of ice cream. Taking a deep breath, she put one shiny red boot in front of the other and headed to the front doors.

"I'll be okay," she said, holding the door open for her friends. "I just need to get home and get a good sleep. I'll start packing first thing in the morning."

They exited the police station. The cool evening air swirled around Piper's legs, raising goose bumps. She folded her arms across her chest, thankful for Addison's sweatshirt that covered her bare stomach. It appeared as though the entire day had slipped by while she recounted the horrors of the last twenty-four hours to Inspector Samuels.

At the time, they'd felt like some of the best hours of her life—the ones spent in Aiden's bed, not running away from him. The memory of his arms around her burned, making her wince each time his face unwillingly popped into her head.

Zoe caught one of those winces. "Are you sure you don't want to hang tonight?"

Piper shrugged. "Apparently, the rest of the world, including my landlord, Steve, doesn't care about my personal crisis. Besides, Aiden Caldwell has gotten in my future's way for long enough. I don't want to spend any more time on him, especially to mope."

Who was she kidding? She might have been dressed

like the girl of steel, but she wasn't actually made of steel. There would be moping. So much moping, in fact, that it would deserve a name, like Mopefest, or Mopalooza. But not until she was alone, and her only witnesses were Colin and Mr. Wiggles.

"Well, it looks like he's not out of the way yet." Zoe pointed to the bottom of the precinct's cement steps where a crowd had formed.

Colin's tail began to wag, smacking Piper's chest, so she knew Aiden was near before she saw him. He wasn't hard to spot. He was the one surrounded by all the cameras flashing like starbursts, and the microphones, and waving hands vying for attention like eager students. A grim-looking woman in her mid-forties hovered next to him. Between each question from the press, she whispered something in his ear before hunching over her tablet again, typing furiously on the pad. Piper assumed she was some kind of PR person sent for damage control.

His suit looked crisp and recently pressed, definitely not the one he chased her through his office building in earlier that day. The PR woman probably brought it for him so he could appear presentable for the press. Maybe only bad guys had wrinkled suits.

He looked good. Too good, she thought. This surprised her, as though once he'd revealed his true self some kind of spell should have been broken, transforming him into some creature with warts, or horns, or scales, or something. It was only fair. After everything that had happened, the very sight of him shouldn't have continued to stir something inside her.

But it wasn't her fault, not really. It was the pheromones, the laws of nature. What were humans but evolved animals, still subject to nature's bizarre reproductive whims? She had no more control over her desires than Toby could help humping everything that moved. But she was more evolved than that. She had this big brain that told her what was right and what was wrong. And Aiden was *wrong*.

No one had noticed Piper standing there with Addison and Zoe. Their focus was purely on the man of the hour, shouting questions and hanging on his every word, treating him as though he were the victim.

Aiden pointed to one hand waving in the back. "Yes, next question."

"Mr. Williams has been with Caldwell and Son Investments for forty years. What will happen to him now?"

"His actions put lives in danger and he will have to answer in court for that," Aiden said in a practiced tone, his face blank. "But as far as the company is concerned, he is no longer employed with us."

So that was it. He'd washed his hands clean, using Old Spice as a scapegoat. Guess it was good business to have a token fall guy.

One of the girls tugged on her sleeve to go, but Piper ignored it. Slowly, so he wouldn't notice her, she descended the stairs so she could hear the press conference better, watch his expressions from a better angle.

Aiden pointed to another hand.

"What was your reaction when you first heard the news?" Although the speaker was half-hidden among the tense horde, Piper recognized Holly Hart's high-pitched, eager voice right away.

"I was shocked and disappointed. Mr. Williams was a representative of Caldwell and Son Investments, and he acted in the company's best interest before that of the community that we serve. We work hard to support the people through our fund-raising and volunteer efforts. His actions opposed the very core values of the company, and his shortsighted behavior also seriously jeopardized my own plans for the much-loved local rescue center."

At that moment, his gaze roamed over the press, past

the blinding lights. As they landed on Piper, he did a double take, squinting past the camera flashes.

Their eyes locked, and a jolt ran through Piper's body, but she kept herself steady. She met his stare square on. He blanched at the sight of her, his confident, corporate certainty replaced with a sort of pitiful helplessness.

Waving a dismissive hand, Aiden said, "That will be all for questions."

Not moving his eyes away from Piper's, he began to descend the stairs. She took an automatic step back. Not because she was afraid of him, not outside the cop shop, standing there with all those witnesses, with Colin and her two girls at her back. She was afraid of herself, of that scolded puppy look in his eyes, of hearing a single word of his bullshit in case it confused her more. He'd worked out a cover story to protect himself and his company. He no doubt had polished up a little speech for her too.

But when he moved, the crowd of cameras and reporters moved with him, jostling microphones knocking him on the head and camera lights blinding him. He stumbled, nearly falling down the steps. During the shuffle, Holly took the opportunity to squeeze her way to the front, until she was practically pressing up against his body, berating him with more questions.

Piper had never been happier to see her.

Zoe looped an arm through Piper's, dragging her attention away from the scene. "Let's get out of here."

Addison popped open the box of chocolates and offered an emergency hit of delicious comfort. Colin licked Piper's cheek in support. She felt much loved.

They turned to head for her MINI in the parking lot, but Piper couldn't help but glance back. Aiden watched her go and looked like he might follow her, but the grim PR woman yanked on his jacket sleeve and hissed something into his ear.

His jaw clenched while he listened. He gave a brief nod. With one last lingering look at Piper, he turned back to the press, and she turned to look ahead, to graduation on the weekend, to her exam, to her upcoming job at the veterinary hospital, to her future. A future without Aiden.

"You know what?" she told the girls. "I think I could use some of that ice cream now."

Call Off the Dogs

Piper crammed the last box of belongings into the trunk of her car and rubbed her aching back. Colin supervised while she jimmied items into place so she could close the door. It was like putting together a puzzle, but once she'd figured out which pieces fit where she managed to slam the trunk closed. Mr. Wiggles' face was squished up against the back window, but it worked.

The fact that everything she owned in the whole world fit into the back of a VW Bug screamed pathetic, but after she and Addison had spent the morning picking through the wreckage of her apartment it was all that they could salvage. The rest ended up in the Dumpster—which was fitting since that's where most of her life belonged.

But she was getting things back on track. School had finished. All she had to do was show up for commencement and take her licensing exam. She'd worked out a plan with Zoe to stay at her place until she got her first official paycheck from the hospital.

Her life was moving forward into a new chapter. And it

felt good. Except for that one spot . . . that spot in the middle and a little to the left. The place where it ached like someone had taken a scalpel and excised a vital piece of her. But it was okay because it only hurt when she was alone, and it was quiet, or she thought about the dog rescue center. Or breathed. But that was hardly ever, right?

Colin sat by her side and stared at the pathetic collection of belongings. His barrel chest seemed deflated. He swung his head toward her as if asking, *Can't we go back to Sophie and Aiden's house? I liked it there.*

"No. Sorry, buddy. We're going to live with Aunt Zoe."

He rubbed a paw over his face. *But I miss them.*

"I know." She sighed. "So do I."

And out of some sick, masochistic urge, she went to the passenger side of the car and dug through her purse to see if Aiden had texted or called to beg for forgiveness. But then she remembered that the cops had kept it as evidence. Which was just as well, because she didn't care if he called, or texted, or if he fell off the face of the earth altogether.

Addison slammed the lid closed on the Dumpster and headed over, staring at her hands in dismay. Piper pulled out some hand sanitizer and gave her a squirt.

"Well, looks like that's the last of it," she said.

"Thanks for your help today, Addy. I really appreciate it. I couldn't have done it without you." It was getting easier, the admitting she needed help thing. She didn't always have to be *fine.*

"No problem. It was either that or spend the morning getting humped by Toby. But Zoe drew the short stick, so here I am." She spread her arms to indicate her thereness. "Do you think Marilyn's been to the center yet?"

Piper frowned, imagining Marilyn's reaction to seeing her beloved rescue center. "I don't know. I haven't heard from her since she left on her cruise. I don't get it." Or maybe Zoe had filled her in already and she never wanted to speak to Piper again.

Piper had wanted to be at the center first thing that morning when Marilyn arrived to, well, she didn't know what. Explain? Beg for forgiveness? But she didn't put it past Steve to call the cops if she didn't move out by her three-day deadline. And as sorry as she felt, Marilyn took a backseat to jail time.

Addison's phone chimed and she pulled it out of her pocket. She glanced at the screen, her nose wrinkling in confusion.

"What is it?" Piper asked.

"An address." She typed a response and hit *send*. "It's from Zoe. She wants us to meet her there."

"What for?"

Addison's phone chimed again. She shook her head. "She says it's a surprise. And to hurry the hell up."

"I think I've had enough surprises for one week."

"Well, let's hope it's a good one."

Piper read the address. "I've delivered pizzas around there. I know where that is. You can follow me."

With one last glance at her old apartment building, she loaded Colin up and pulled out of the parking lot to head across town. When she got closer to the address, she began checking street numbers. It was a quiet neighborhood. A mix of business and residential. She slowed as she approached a large property surrounded by a cute white picket fence. The lot itself was obscured by a row of thick acacia trees. She checked the swirly numbers on the fence—this was the place.

Two ornate metal gates were swung wide, allowing Piper to pull onto a newly paved driveway, the scent of asphalt still fresh in the air. Addison followed behind in her MINI, winding up the long driveway beneath the tendrils of pepper trees lining either side.

Piper's Bug broke through the trees, and a lovely two-story Victorian house came into view. While it was clearly old, it had been updated and renovated with add-ons to the back of the building from what she could see. Painted a soft pineapple yellow with white trim, it sat gracefully in front of half an acre of land, prime real estate in a city like San Francisco.

It wasn't until she pulled into the large parking lot in front of the house and crawled out of the car that she saw the sign. She read it three times before she finally believed her eyes, and even then she thought it must be some joke.

San Francisco Dachshund Rescue Center.

Addison pulled in next to her, staring out her windshield in awe. "As in *our* Dachshund Rescue Center? But how?"

Piper didn't answer. She was too busy rereading the sign.

A moment later, Zoe appeared on the wide, wraparound porch, waving them inside. "Come see!" she called, laughter in her voice.

Piper frowned at the house, trying to figure out what the hell was going on. Although when that painful ache, that hole in her chest, started to throb again, she had a sneaking suspicion. And she hadn't had nearly enough of Addison's ice cream to deal with it.

With a disbelieving laugh, Addison grabbed her by the hand. She half-dragged her up the stone stairs set into the gentle slope, past the beds of lavender, aloe, and poppies. Colin raced them up to the entrance, nails clicking on the steps, tongue lolling out of his mouth.

Daffodils and dahlias lit up the base of the house, the inviting smells welcoming Piper onto the covered porch. Hanging baskets dangled overhead at intervals, bursting with pansies. She climbed the wooden stairs and noticed the distinct lack of squeaks and groans. Instead, firm oak clacked beneath her shoes, smelling of freshly cut wood and stain.

"Isn't it amazing?" Zoe asked.

"It's incredible," Addison said. "I can't believe it."

"Believe it," she said. "Come on inside. There's so much I have to show you."

Zoe and Addison rushed through the double front doors, disappearing into the depths of the house. Piper lingered behind, hesitating, as though it were some kind of trap. Colin didn't seem to have the same misgivings. He trotted inside, sniffing out the new territory. Following him, she drifted through the set of French doors and into an open-concept reception room. Although, since it was larger than her old apartment, she wondered if they'd be receiving the queen.

High-quality laminate flooring stretched out underfoot, the perfect effect, grain, and color of rich hardwood but hardier against sharp little dog nails. Rockwork decorated the reception desk, matching the fireplace dominating one wall of the room. Plush chairs and an antique-looking sofa gathered around the hearth, making it seem homey, rather than a place of business.

A glint of metal caught her eye and she glanced overhead. A little brass bell dangled above the entrance—no, not just any brass bell, but their old one. It was a little dented but had been bent back into shape and buffed to a shine, the clacker reattached.

Reaching up, she tapped it with a finger, relishing the happy jingle that called her home once again.

The pleasant sound filled the room, and as though by magic, Marilyn appeared, reminding Piper of the day she first walked into the center eight years ago.

"Marilyn!" Piper cried. "You're a sight for sore eyes." The saying suddenly made so much sense, since her eyeballs ached with so many unshed tears that had been building up for days.

"Piper!" Marilyn hurried across the room to wrap her arms around Piper.

She sank into the woman's arms. Everything would be okay. Marilyn was finally home, and she could fix everything Piper had messed up since she left.

"I'm so sorry, dear," she said to Piper. "This is all my fault."

Or apparently not.

Piper pulled away to stare at Marilyn and saw a man enter the room behind her.

"Inspector Samuels!" Piper said. "What are you doing here?"

"He's come for a visit," Marilyn said. "For tea." She gestured to the tea on the coffee table by the hearth as though she needed evidence. "It's not unusual. I offer tea to all our guests."

Piper could have sworn the Englishwoman was blushing.

"Hello, Piper." Inspector Samuels chuckled. "Zoe said I could find you here today. I came to give you your phone back." Pulling it out of his pocket, he handed it to her. "We didn't find much else but an insane amount of photos of your dog." He smirked.

"I'm so glad you're here," Marilyn's forehead creased with concern and she began to wring her hands. "The girls and the inspector filled me in on everything that happened while I was away. What a mess I've caused."

"You caused? Marilyn, what on Earth is happening? What is all this?" She gestured with her arms to the house in general.

"It's a gift," Marilyn said. "From Mr. Caldwell."

She stared at Marilyn, uncomprehending. The seconds ticked by, and Piper wondered how long her brain could go without oxygen. She took a deep, shaky breath. That ache in her chest. Oh, the pain. Maybe it was a heart attack.

Her brain scrambled for an answer. "You mean Aiden built it after what happened with the fire? Was it some kind of plea bargain?" But that didn't make sense, either. The house couldn't have been renovated in a matter of days.

"Certainly not," Marilyn said. "It's been under construction for months."

Piper's mouth fell open. "Months? No, that can't be right."

"Maybe I can clear a few things up," Inspector Samuels said in his no-nonsense way.

Piper turned to him. Facts. Yes, she could handle straight facts. Facts made sense in their factliness, she reasoned numbly.

"Mr. Caldwell made a deal with Marilyn right after his company bought the property. If she agreed to move so he could build his apartment complex on the property, he'd build her a new state-of-the-art dog rescue center in return."

Her forehead creased like she was doing a complicated math equation. "That doesn't seem like a fair trade."

"It wasn't," he said, an amused smirk under his mustache. "That's why it's called charity."

"It was more of a blessing," Marilyn said. "He used all his own money. Nothing to do with his company." Her cheer faded. "I saw Zoe at the old center this morning. She explained everything that had happened." She began wringing her hands again. "And, oh, I just felt so terrible for keeping you girls in the dark about my deal with Mr. Caldwell. It's just . . . I thought it would be a nice surprise, you see. I never imagined how turned around things could get. And of course there was the poor timing of my vacation, and it all went a bit pear-shaped. . . ."

Pieces were beginning to fit together in Piper's brain,

calming the chaos erupting inside. "No, Marilyn. You can't blame yourself. It was just a misunderstanding. You didn't do anything wrong."

Piper coaxed her into one of the plush chairs, hoping some tea would calm her nerves, but mostly because she needed to sit herself. Her legs felt like two elastic bands at the moment. Colin whined, curiosity nagging at him to explore this new place further. But he sensed that Piper needed his emotional support more. With an impatient huff, he spun in two circles and settled onto the rug next to her chair.

Piper ran her fingers through his fur distractedly. "I tried to get ahold of you so many times," she told Marilyn. "I left a hundred messages on your voice mail and with the cruise ship too. Did you not get them?"

"Not until we docked in Los Angeles late last night. I was terribly ill the entire time I was away, you see. I'd swear it was food poisoning, and of course the seasickness didn't help. I spent the entire cruise locked in my room or in the infirmary."

"Oh no. I'm sorry to hear that, Marilyn."

"The second I heard all of your messages, I tried to call you right away."

"Inspector Samuels had my phone for evidence." She turned to him. Her brain had finally kicked in, questions coursing through her. "But Aiden . . . He might have built us this new center, but he still . . . I mean, the vandalism, and the fire, and the hit-and-run, and . . ."

Inspector Samuels sat down across from her. He was already shaking his head before she finished. "It seems he had no part in any of it."

"But the recording. He said–"

"Yes, it sounded that way at first, but it all comes down to perspective. You see, he'd been planning to build this place all along, only he neglected to let his Chief Operations Officer in on his plans." He turned his hands over like "What do you do?" "Since he was building the new center as a personal charity, he had Larry Williams do the bargaining on behalf of the company. Said he didn't want to mix business with pleasure."

Piper snorted but let him continue his explanation.

Inspector Samuels took a long sip of his black coffee. "Aiden told Larry to give Marilyn an offer she couldn't refuse."

Piper tucked her phone away. "I guess he didn't think of offering money," she said sarcastically.

Marilyn picked up her teaspoon and began to fidget with it. "Well, he did. He offered me a hefty sum. But it didn't feel right, what with Mr. Caldwell already building us this new place. So I turned him down."

"Aiden felt that if Larry knew about his plans for the new center he would try to lowball Marilyn," Inspector Samuels said. "So you see where the miscommunication happened."

"Of course," Piper said. "When Marilyn refused the money, Larry assumed that meant she was refusing to leave."

"Larry Williams then took matters into his own hands. It probably isn't the first time he's done business this way. I'm sure he has a few skeletons hidden in the company closet. We're digging into it. Years' worth of deals and community complaints. It will be a headache, but Mr. Caldwell has offered to assist us in undoing any misdeeds done on behalf of the company."

"So Aiden had nothing to do with the attacks on the center?"

"No," he said. "Up until your visit to his office yesterday, Aiden had been clueless."

She recalled part of the conversation she overheard from Aiden's closet. *What's important is getting rid of those damn dogs,* Larry had said.

And I've done just that, haven't I?

At the time, Piper had thought that meant Aiden was responsible for the fire, for forcing the dogs out. She thought she'd caught him red-handed. But he'd gotten rid of the dogs by building them a new home. She'd gotten it all wrong. She'd been so blinded by her anger and humiliation, the fear of betrayal. Guilt tore through her like a Tasmanian devil on a rampage.

"And what about the other stuff?" she asked him.

"You were right about the graffiti on your car and apartment window. Laura from the SFAAC was responsible. She confessed to it right away when we told her about everything else that she could be implicated for. But she didn't break your car window. That was Barney." His voice changed when he said the postal worker's name, like he was picking gum off the bottom of his shoe. "He'd been stalking you for some time, so he knew where you worked and where you volunteered, but he had yet to learn where you lived."

"I'm unlisted," she said. "I'm subletting from my aunt. Or, at least, I *was*. So he broke into my car to get my address. I take it he vandalized my apartment then?"

"That's right."

An image of her underwear dangling from a pen popped into her disorganized brain and she cringed. So far her instincts about those involved had been right, more or less. Only she hadn't expected the guilty party to be, well, all of them.

"And the attempted hit-and-run? That was obviously Tamara." When she saw the Prius at Aiden's office, she thought that he'd tried to help cover it up by lending her his own car. "Officer Tucker said that she had an alibi. That she was tied up at work."

"Ah yes, her alibi." His mustache turned down. "That was corroborated by Larry Williams."

Piper's eyes widened. It was starting to sound more and more like the conspiracy theory she'd first suspected. "They were working together?"

"No, but protecting Tamara worked in Larry's interest. It kept any investigators clear of Caldwell and Son Investments and from focusing on Aiden. He hadn't been wiped off our persons of interest list."

She straightened in her seat at the news. She'd had no idea they were investigating him. Then again, why would they share that with her? She was too close to be objective. Thinking of all the things she'd gotten wrong along the way, they were right not to tell her. Hell, they'd probably been investigating her too.

Colin grumbled next to her ankle until she scratched his belly. "I had no idea."

The inspector took a sip of coffee before continuing. "Apparently, Tamara had been following you during your date with Aiden. When she saw the two of you together, it seems something just"—he spread his hands—"snapped."

"Oh, it snapped a long time before that."

His eyebrows twitched up like he agreed with Piper's statement but was too professional to voice it. "She'll be going under a psychiatric evaluation. I don't think you'll have to worry about her for quite a while."

"Well, that's good." She'd thought that once somebody finally believed how crazy Tamara was she'd feel vindicated. But she only felt pity for the girl. "I hope she gets the help she needs." Piper stared at her hands. "So, you're saying . . . Aiden didn't actually do anything wrong?"

"I know it's a lot to take in after everything that happened yesterday."

Marilyn set her teacup down on the table, watching Piper. "He's here now, you know. Aiden."

Piper's heart skittered in her chest, proving that it was still working. "He is?"

"He's out back being interviewed by Holly Hart. *The* Holly Hart. Can you believe it?"

"I can't believe it," she replied flatly.

"Are you going to be okay?" Marilyn asked.

Yes and no, Piper thought. She wasn't sure what to think anymore. "Yeah. I just . . . I just need a minute, I guess."

"Of course." Marilyn cleared her throat and stood up. "Inspector Samuels, may I show you around the grounds awhile?"

"I'd like that. And please, call me Bob."

"Oh, all right."

Piper wasn't too distracted to miss Marilyn's expression. This time, Piper was certain that was a blush lighting up Marilyn's face.

Before she left the room, she gripped Piper's shoulder. "I'm so sorry, Piper."

She patted her hand. "It's not your fault."

Piper smiled as the two of them left the room, but she didn't exactly feel relieved. She was confused. Since the day before, she'd become used to feeling mad, to the anger that was justified by Aiden's heinous actions. But now that those actions had been nullified, where did that leave her anger?

It turned out, the only one to blame was her, for jumping to conclusions, for not talking to Aiden about them first. After everything that had happened, could it be so simple as to chalk it up to a misunderstanding? Could they move forward after this?

"Well, Colin?" she asked. "What do you think?"

But for once, he kept his opinion to himself. This was something she would have to figure out for herself. Well, she supposed there was only one way to find out.

Gathering her strength, she drew a deep breath and headed for the door Zoe and Addison had disappeared through. As she passed the reception desk, she noticed the wall behind it. Well, not so much a wall as the largest fish tank she'd ever seen in place of an actual wall. The fish swam by, glaring at her like she'd accidentally wandered into their home. There were so many that Piper could only name half of them off the top of her head.

She could hear Zoe and Addison giggling somewhere deeper inside the house. She followed the sound of their excited chatter, through a room with wall-to-wall shelves holding every kind of dog toy, treat, and accessory that Piper could imagine. It was like walking into doggy heaven. Colin paused in front of them, taking mental stock of all the items he would deem *his*.

At the other end of the house, a door opened onto the back porch, where the afternoon sun outlined the girls' silhouettes. She stepped outside to join them and saw the expansion that she'd noticed when she first drove up. A long, narrow building, the same style and color as the house stood at a right angle to it. It reminded her of a stable, but instead of horses, dogs wandered in and out of private doggy doors to play in an enclosure that took up practically the entire property. A chain-link fence wrapped around the clearing to where the privacy trees began.

Zoe laughed at Toby, who was running off some of his pent-up energy. "Isn't it amazing?" she asked Piper.

"It is," Piper agreed, her voice hushed.

Grass swished rhythmically as someone wandered next to the house. Muffled voices grew closer.

"—get you out here, in front of the grand opening banner. Just stand over there so we can get a clear view of the house and play area." Piper recognized Holly Hart's voice as she rounded the corner, ordering around her cameraman with nothing more than a snap of her fingers.

And then Piper heard *his* voice. "Over here?"

The hole inside Piper ripped wide open until it felt like a gaping chest wound. She found it hard to breathe and clutched at her chest. The pain, the panic on hearing his voice, of being so close. What was she going to say to him? What would he say in response?

A million possible scenarios flooded her mind, threatening to drown her. Her whole body shook with the instinct to run, and that hole throbbed worse than ever. She held a hand to her chest, half-expecting to find it had eaten right through her flesh. But despite the fear and uncertainty, without conscious thought her legs carried her closer to his voice.

Aiden had his back to the house. He positioned himself in front of the camera, Sophie rolling in the grass at his feet. He picked her up, brushing out her long hair with his fingers, picking out pieces of grass.

He wore a pair of khaki shorts and, was that . . . ? Yes, it was. A Hawaiian shirt. Piper would have laughed if she'd had the breath to spare. Colin padded out onto the porch to join her. She reached down and plucked him up into her arms and held him tight, breathing in his familiar, comforting scent.

Holly positioned herself a little too close to Aiden so that she brushed up against his shoulder. Hey, You counted down with his fingers and Holly brought the mic to her lips.

"This is Holly Hart for Channel Five News here at the brand-new San Francisco Dachshund Rescue Center to give this *tale* a happy ending." She laughed at her own joke. "I'm standing here with Aiden Caldwell, CEO of

Caldwell and Son Investments, and he's really got something to howl about. Aiden, can you tell us more?"

Piper's eyes locked on to Aiden, unable to notice anything else but him, that is, until he shifted and she could see Sophie in his arms. Colin noticed her too. Every muscle in his body tensed. He let out a querying bark, almost deafening Piper's right ear.

Sophie?

Sophie responded immediately, *Colin? Is that you?*

It must have been the answer he was looking for, because he launched himself out of Piper's arms. He dashed down the porch steps and around the corner, stubby legs surging him forward as fast as they could.

The second Sophie saw him, she squirmed in Aiden's arms until he put her down. Colin's tongue lolling out of his mouth, Sophie's luxurious copper locks flowing in the wind, they raced into each other's paws like a slow-motion scene from a cheesy romance movie.

Aiden spotted Colin and spun around, his eyes scanning the house, the windows, the porch. His eyes finally rested on Piper, and she found herself unprepared for what she saw.

The expression on his face was so pained, so tortured, that he might have been in true physical pain, so much like her own. And she realized it was because of her. She'd caused his beautiful face to look like that.

Her own features contorted in response. The rest of the yard grew still, expectant, and Piper was conscious of the audience. The camera still rolled and Holly was holding her breath expectantly.

Knowing whatever they had to say needed to be off the record, Piper tilted her head toward the house. Aiden understood and began to move her way.

Drawn to the drama, Holly began to follow them into

the center, but Zoe and Addison blocked her path. Piper couldn't help but notice the "We've got your back" look on Zoe's face. And next to her, Addison's face lit up with a "dreams do come true" expression.

Piper waited until Aiden was inside before closing the door for privacy.

"Aiden," she began; she had to swallow the lump in her throat. "I . . . I shouldn't have doubted you. I should have known you better than that. It's just . . . it looked . . ."

"Bad," he said, his voice breaking with emotion. "I know. I don't blame you."

"And well, Holly . . ."

"Yes. Holly." He laughed. Not in a ha-ha kind of way, but the kind of laugh that makes you think you might be able to laugh at it one day. Like maybe fifty years later. "I'll give her this, though. She had her facts straight. It was her drawn conclusions that needed a bit of editing." Any humor vanished from his expression; those dark green eyes grew darker by the second. "But with what information you had, and then what you heard in my office . . ."

She shook her head, laughing humorlessly herself. "Oh God. Your office. I shouldn't have been there. I don't know what I was thinking."

"During my interrogation," he said, "the inspector played your recording for me. I listened to it, trying to imagine what you must have been thinking. And, well, it was bad. Piper, I don't blame you for thinking that I had something to do with it."

"But I should have talked to you first," she said. "I'm sorry."

"You have nothing to be sorry for." He took a shy step toward her, causing her heart to leap in her chest. "Besides, you thought I was trying to kill you at the time. Not exactly the best conditions to sit down and have a chat." He stared down at his hands. "I'm sorry for not telling you about my plans for the center sooner."

"No." She shook her head. "Marilyn explained everything to me. How she asked you not to say anything."

"I kept trying to contact her, to get her permission to tell you about the plans once things started to get out of hand, but I couldn't reach her. It wasn't the way I was used to doing business. And then we started dating, and it all got so complicated. You know me, I hate mixing—"

"Business with pleasure," she finished for him. "I know. But you were right. That was your business and not mine. I had no right to know those things."

"That's where I was wrong." He took another step. Another leap of her heart. "When I asked you to be my girlfriend, you asked me to be a partner instead. And I didn't treat you like one. What I did wasn't fifty-fifty. I shouldn't have let anything, business or otherwise, come between us. Nothing is worth losing you over."

His hand rose, as though he wanted to reach out and touch her cheek, but then he thought better of it and reached for his tie. Discovering the lack of tie and a lot of Hawaiian, he ran a hand through his hair, making it stick up.

"There are some things money can't buy."

She took a deep breath, her numb mind flipping through the events of that morning, trying to find a path, a tangent that had yet to be explored. Could it be that simple?

"So, that's it?" she asked hesitantly. "Neither of us did anything wrong? It was all a big misunderstanding?"

Had it been such a small error, a little mix-up, that had torn Piper's life apart, created such a huge hole in her chest? That's when Piper realized just what Aiden truly meant to her. That his mere absence in her life, if only for a day, could obliterate it, could leave a hole in her chest big enough to swallow her.

But now she was frightened to reach out across that

hole, to fill it again with their love. Such a tiny misunderstanding, but such a wide gulf.

Humans thought of themselves as more evolved, with their opposable thumbs and their fancy brains. When she'd watched Colin and Sophie frantically greet each other like two loved ones reunited, running off to play without another thought, Piper figured it was because they couldn't comprehend the reality of it. But now she wondered if animals didn't have it right. Animals listened to their instincts. Maybe it was the brains that always got in the way.

Aiden reached out first. He held out a hand, palm upturned, his expression hopeful, pleading. And like it was instinct, her hand moved automatically to meet him halfway. Fifty-fifty.

"Can I show you something?" he asked.

She nodded, and he led her across the toy room, to a door marked with a nameplate etched in swirling letters. She paused to read it on their way in and her mouth fell open. It said: *Dr. Piper Summers.*

Piper's legs forgot how to move and Aiden had to steer her through the door. Once inside, she froze at the sight. It was a fully equipped veterinary clinic. No. Not just a clinic, she thought, scanning the pieces of diagnostic and surgical equipment, but a minihospital. It had everything a veterinarian could ask for. She could even perform emergency surgery if necessary.

"Aiden," she breathed. "This is . . ." Her words tapered off.

"Do you like it?"

"Like it? Aiden." Turning toward him, she flung her arms around his neck. "It's perfect."

"I may have been planning the new rescue center all along, but all this"—he waved a hand at the clinic—"I built this entirely for you."

"For me?"

"It was an addition that I added on after we met. You'll have everything you need to help the animals that come in now."

He'd been planning this all along. Every time he kept his "business" to himself, tried to hide phone calls and meetings from her, every time she wondered about his advanced deadline—which was no doubt due to the fire—he'd been working on the center, the new home for her friends. And this gift to her.

Guilt took another nip at her, and she knew of only one way to pacify it. Rising on her toes, she leaned into Aiden's embrace and pressed her lips against his, slowly, firmly, longingly.

He drew back just enough so that he could look into her eyes. "In case it wasn't obvious by now," he said. "I love you."

The morpho butterflies were back, filling every last square inch of that gaping hole, banishing the angry Tasmanian devil. Ever since her father died, Piper never needed or wanted to rely on anyone, but before Aiden came along she never thought it could feel so good.

"I love you too."

He pulled her in for another kiss, his face, once again, beautiful and worry-free. She reached up to his collar and one by one began to undo the buttons on his Hawaiian shirt.

"What do you say, Mr. Caldwell? Can we mix business with pleasure one last time?"

He pulled back, his expression scandalized. "Miss Summers. Are you suggesting what I think you're suggesting?"

"Please, Mr. Caldwell," she purred in his ear. "I've seen you eyeing me. I know you've wanted me since you hired me." She removed her sweatshirt to give him a shot of cleavage and pressed up against him.

"This is highly inappropriate." Keeping a straight face,

he reached up and straightened his shirt, playing along. "What would Human Resources say?"

Reaching down, she worked his belt, then his button, his zipper. "No one has to know. It will be our little secret."

"This is sexual harassment in the workplace," he said, looking around like someone might see, but not exactly fighting her off. She reached her hand down his pants, searching.

"It's only harassment if you don't want it. Don't you want it?" She found what she was looking for and grasped it.

It took him a moment to answer, and when he did it was a breathless moan. "Oh yes."

"You're not going to take me to HR, are you?"

Grunting, he gripped her by the hips and lifted her onto the stainless-steel metal exam table, spreading her legs open with his hips. "No. I have a better idea."

She ran her hands across the back of his shorts that were halfway falling down, enjoying the feel and curve of his butt. She pushed his shorts down the rest of the way. "And what's that?"

He grinned against her mouth. "You're fired."

Her groping hands froze with surprise and she laughed. "That's okay," she said. "I still have my telegram job. Come to think of it, I've got a few costumes packed up in the car. Maybe we could play cops and robbers."

He hooked a thumb under the hem of her tank top and lifted it, exposing her bra. "I think I've had just about enough of cops."

She leaned back on her elbows. He drew his mouth across her stomach, from her bra to her low-riding jeans. Her hips moved on their own, encouraging him to keep going. She sucked in a breath of air as he undid her pants.

"How about a sexy Swiss yodeler?"

His hand froze at the top of her jeans. "You yodel?"

"I've been known to yodel."

"Give me a minute and I'll make you yodel without the costume." His hand slid into her pants and she gripped the edge of the metal table beneath her.

A soft moan escaped her lips. "Marilyn Monroe, then?"

Aiden hesitated for a second, then shook his head. "No."

"Who do you want then?" she panted. "Tell me."

He hopped onto the table, his half-naked body hovering over hers. Lowering himself, he kissed her deeply. "I want you. Just you." He swept a stray hair off her cheek. "My Piper."

And once he pulled the privacy curtain closed around the exam table, he got exactly what he wanted. From that day onwards.

Which volunteer at the Dachshund Rescue Center will get her own romance story? Find out in . . .

Beauty and the Wiener

The second book in the Rescue Dog Romance series

To be unleashed Winter 2017